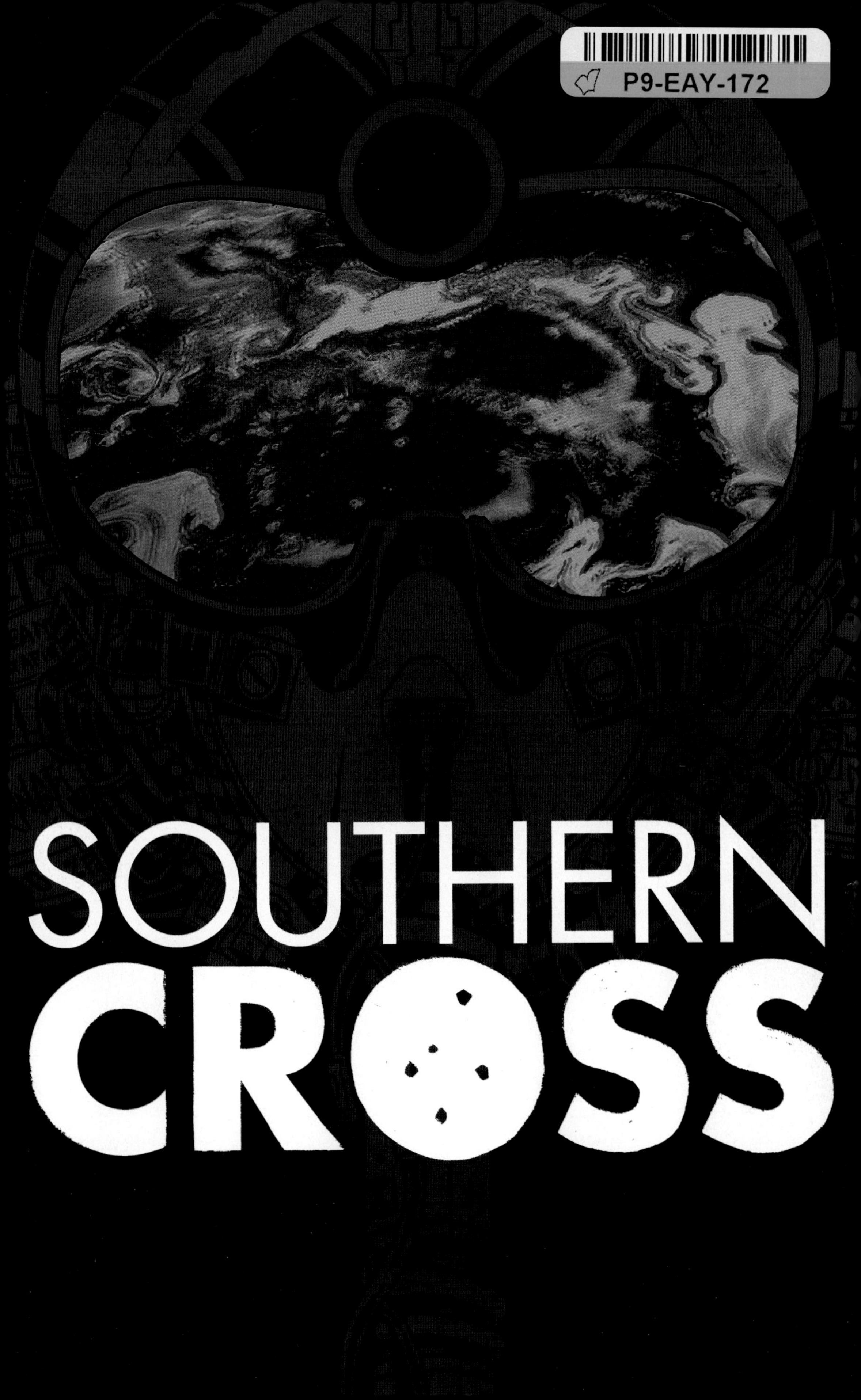

SOUTHERN CROSS

BECKY CLOONAN
STORY/COVERS

ANDY BELANGER
ART

Trade cover
issue #3 regular
series cover

LEE LOUGHRIDGE
COLOURS

SERGE LaPOINTE
LETTERS

SOUTHERN CROSS™, VOLUME 1
First Printing. January 2016. Copyright © 2016 Becky Cloonan & Andy Bélanger. All rights reserved. Published by Image Comics, Inc. Office of publication: 2001 Center Street, 6th Floor, Berkeley, CA, 94704. Contains material originally published as Southern Cross #1-6. SOUTHERN CROSS™ (including all prominent characters featured herein), its logo and all characters likenesses are trademarks of Becky Cloonan & Andy Bélanger, unless otherwise noted. Image Comics® and its logos are registered trademarks and copyrights of Image Comics, Inc. All rights reserved. No part of this publication may be reproduced or transmitted, in any form or by any means (except for short excerpts for journalistic or review purposes) without the express written permission of Becky Cloonan, Andy Bélanger or Image Comics, Inc. All names, characters, events and locales in this publication are entirely fictional. Any resemblance to actual persons (living or dead), events or places, without satiric intent, is coincidental. Printed in the United States.

For information regarding the CPSIA on this printed material call: 203-595-3636 and provide reference # RICH - 659476

For international rights inquiries, contact: foreignlicensing@imagecomics.com

ISBN: 978-1-63215-559-7

image

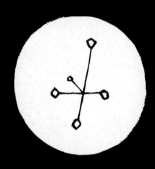

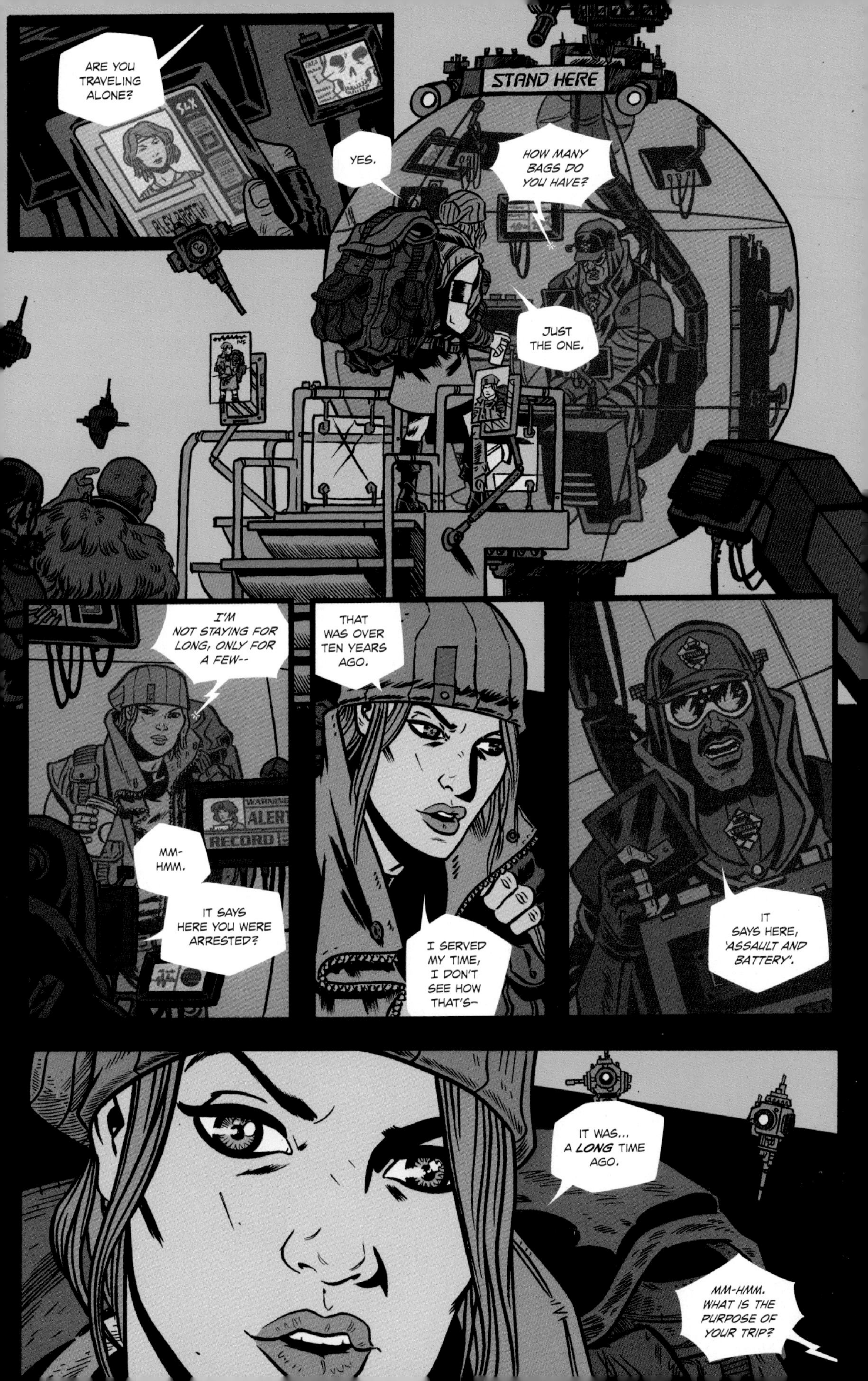
ARE YOU TRAVELING ALONE?
SLX
ALEX BERTH
STAND HERE
YES.
HOW MANY BAGS DO YOU HAVE?
JUST THE ONE.
I'M NOT STAYING FOR LONG, ONLY FOR A FEW--
WARNING
ALERT
RECORD
MM-HMM.
IT SAYS HERE YOU WERE ARRESTED?
THAT WAS OVER TEN YEARS AGO.
I SERVED MY TIME, I DON'T SEE HOW THAT'S-
IT SAYS HERE, 'ASSAULT AND BATTERY'.
IT WAS... A LONG TIME AGO.
MM-HMM. WHAT IS THE PURPOSE OF YOUR TRIP?

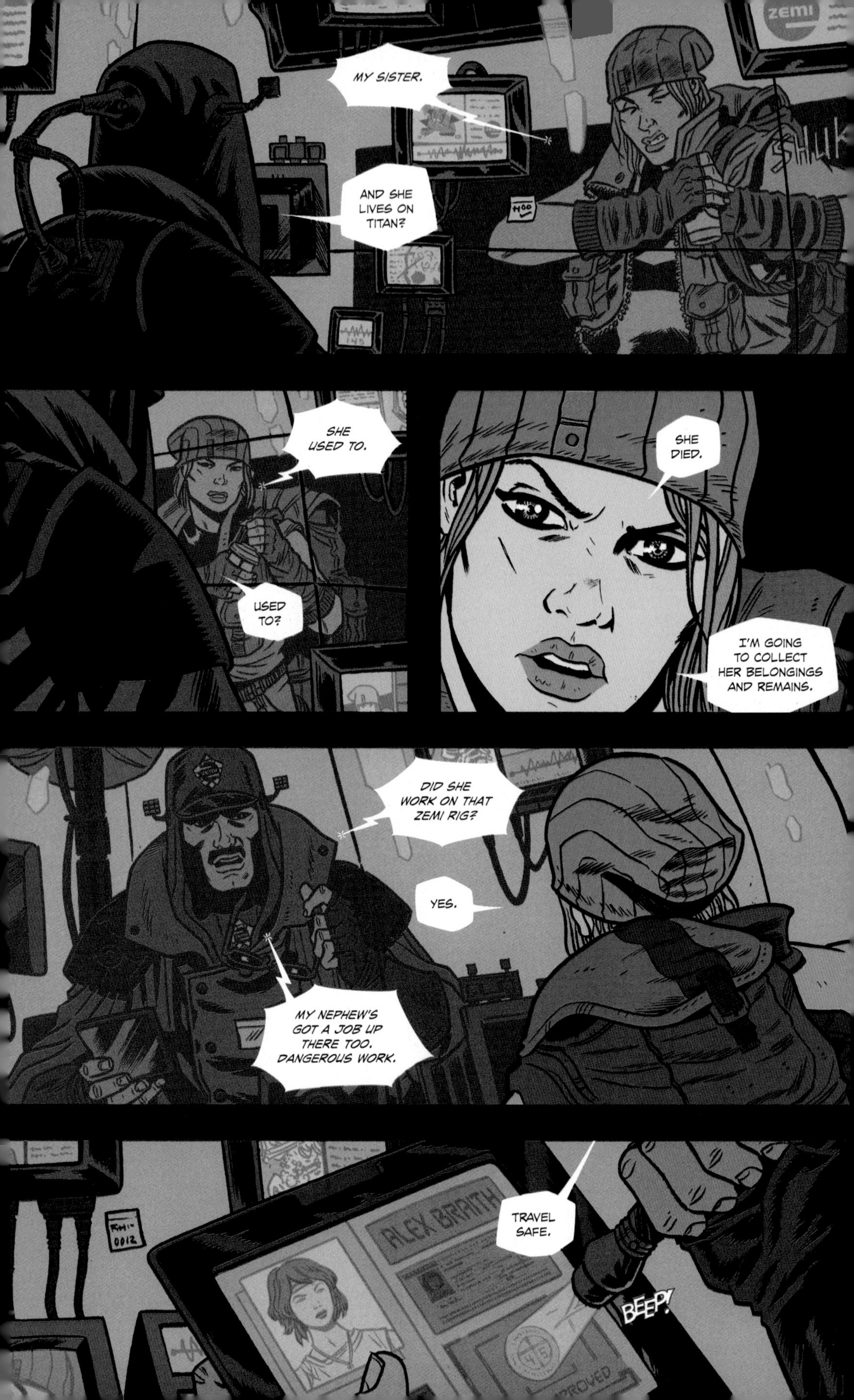
ZEMI
MY SISTER.
AND SHE LIVES ON TITAN?
SHE USED TO.
USED TO?
SHE DIED.
I'M GOING TO COLLECT HER BELONGINGS AND REMAINS.
DID SHE WORK ON THAT ZEMI RIG?
YES.
MY NEPHEW'S GOT A JOB UP THERE TOO. DANGEROUS WORK.
ALEX BRAITH
TRAVEL SAFE.
BEEP!

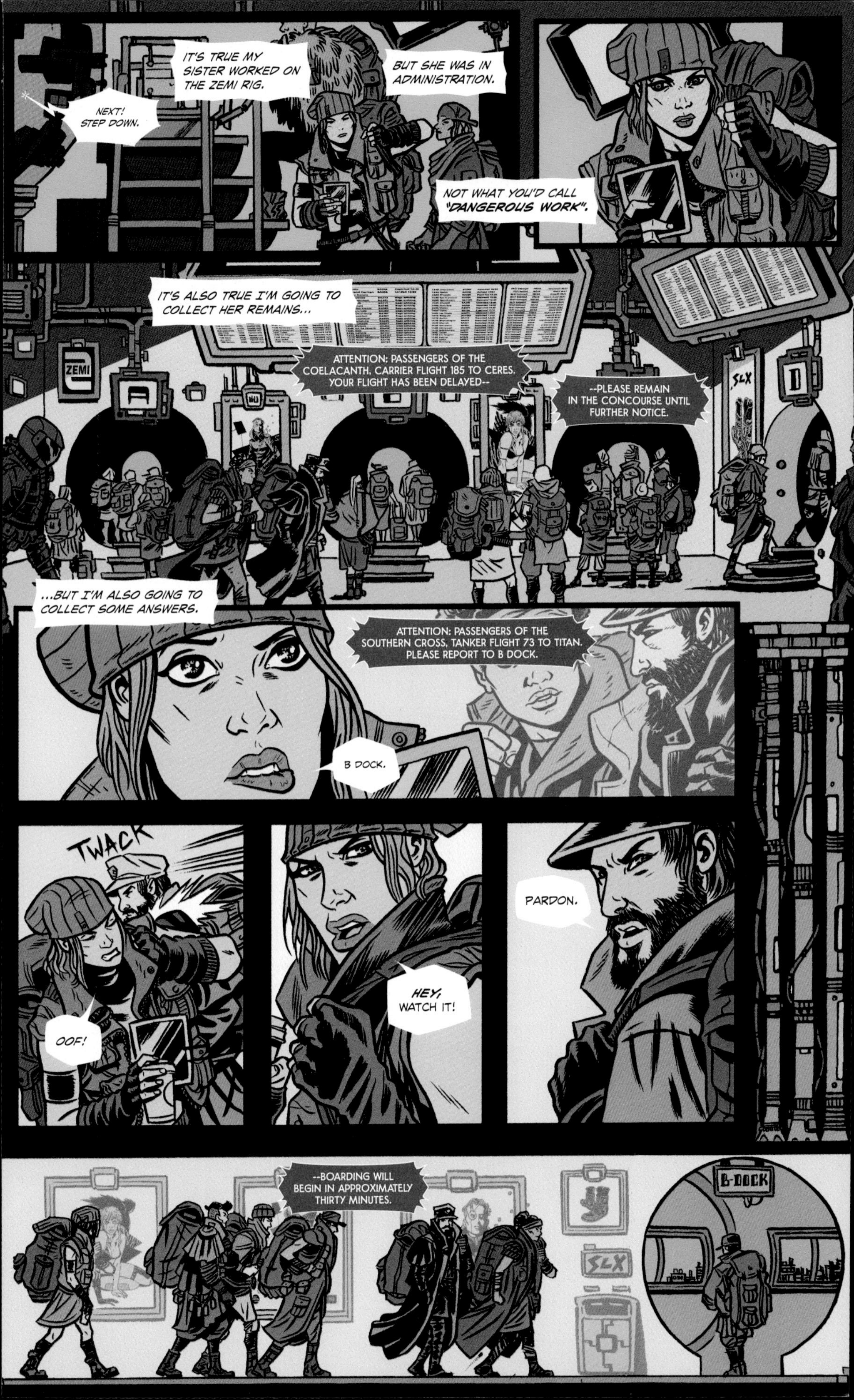
IT'S TRUE MY SISTER WORKED ON THE ZEMI RIG.
NEXT! STEP DOWN.
BUT SHE WAS IN ADMINISTRATION.
NOT WHAT YOU'D CALL "DANGEROUS WORK".
IT'S ALSO TRUE I'M GOING TO COLLECT HER REMAINS...
ZEMI
ATTENTION: PASSENGERS OF THE COELACANTH, CARRIER FLIGHT 185 TO CERES. YOUR FLIGHT HAS BEEN DELAYED--
--PLEASE REMAIN IN THE CONCOURSE UNTIL FURTHER NOTICE.
SLX
D
...BUT I'M ALSO GOING TO COLLECT SOME ANSWERS.
ATTENTION: PASSENGERS OF THE SOUTHERN CROSS, TANKER FLIGHT 73 TO TITAN. PLEASE REPORT TO B DOCK.
B DOCK.
TWACK
OOF!
HEY, WATCH IT!
PARDON.
--BOARDING WILL BEGIN IN APPROXIMATELY THIRTY MINUTES.
SLX
B-DOCK

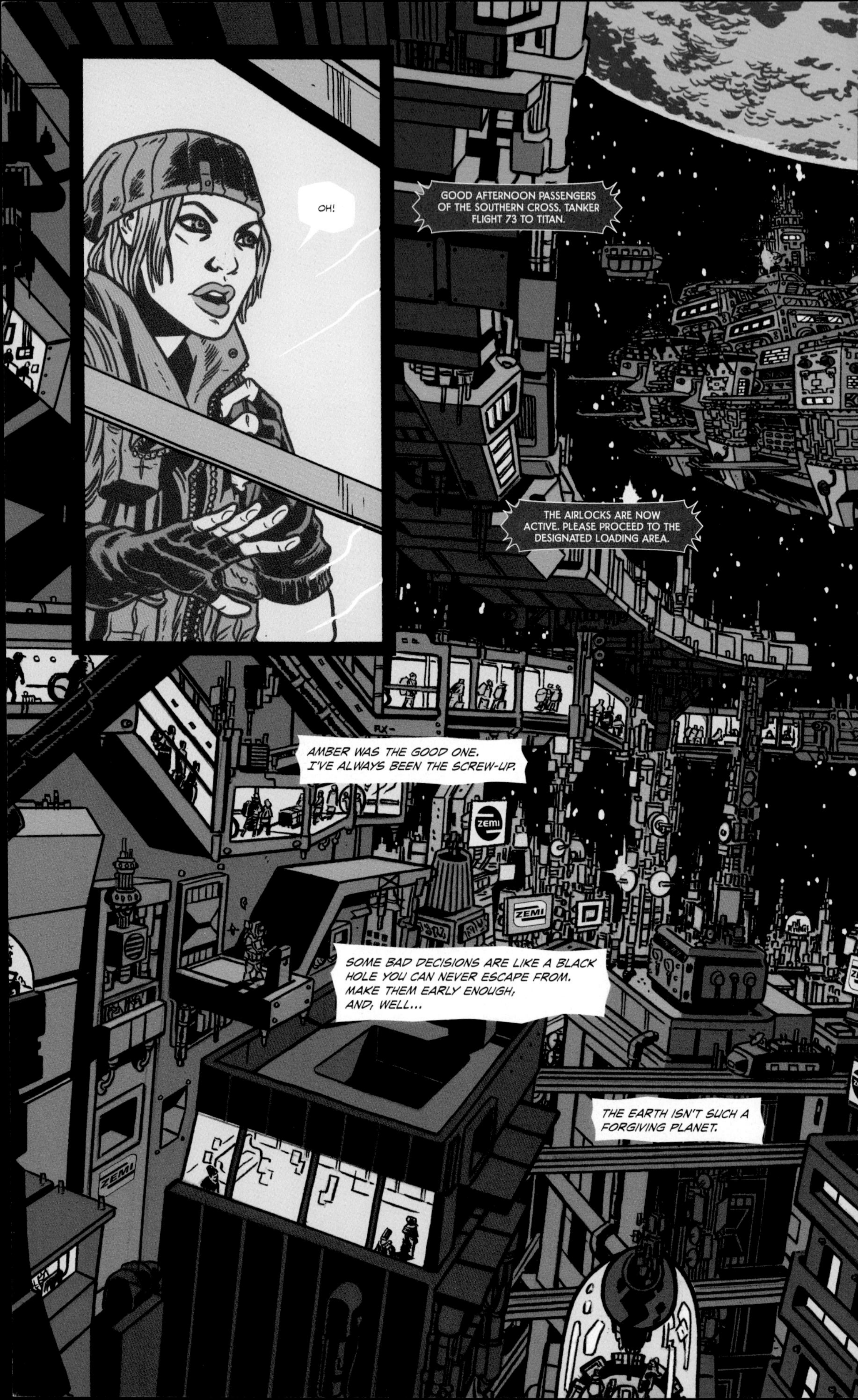
OH!
GOOD AFTERNOON PASSENGERS OF THE SOUTHERN CROSS, TANKER FLIGHT 73 TO TITAN.
THE AIRLOCKS ARE NOW ACTIVE. PLEASE PROCEED TO THE DESIGNATED LOADING AREA.
AMBER WAS THE GOOD ONE. I'VE ALWAYS BEEN THE SCREW-UP.
ZEMI
SOME BAD DECISIONS ARE LIKE A BLACK HOLE YOU CAN NEVER ESCAPE FROM. MAKE THEM EARLY ENOUGH, AND, WELL...
THE EARTH ISN'T SUCH A FORGIVING PLANET.

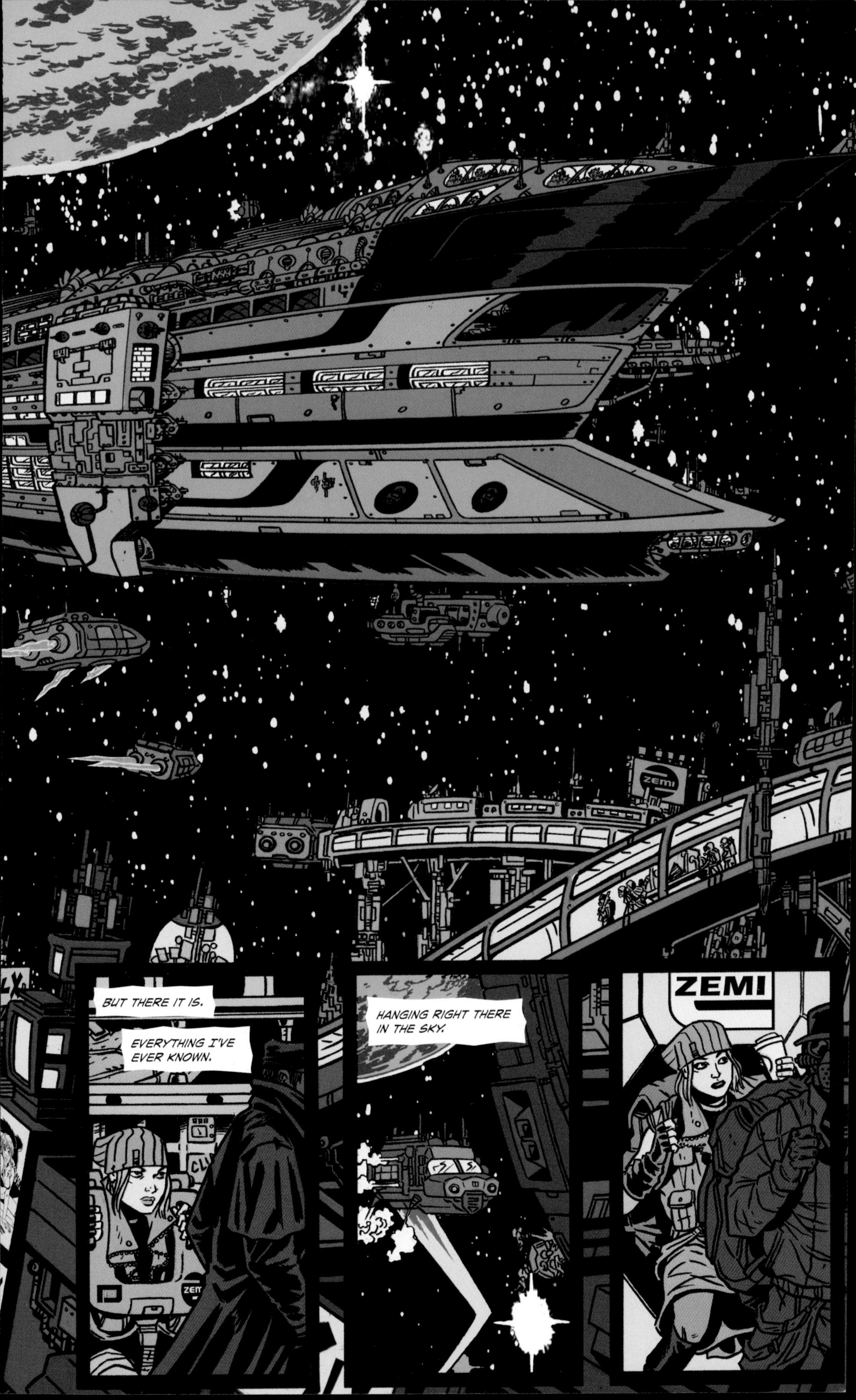
ZEMI
BUT THERE IT IS.
EVERYTHING I'VE EVER KNOWN.
HANGING RIGHT THERE IN THE SKY.
ZEMI

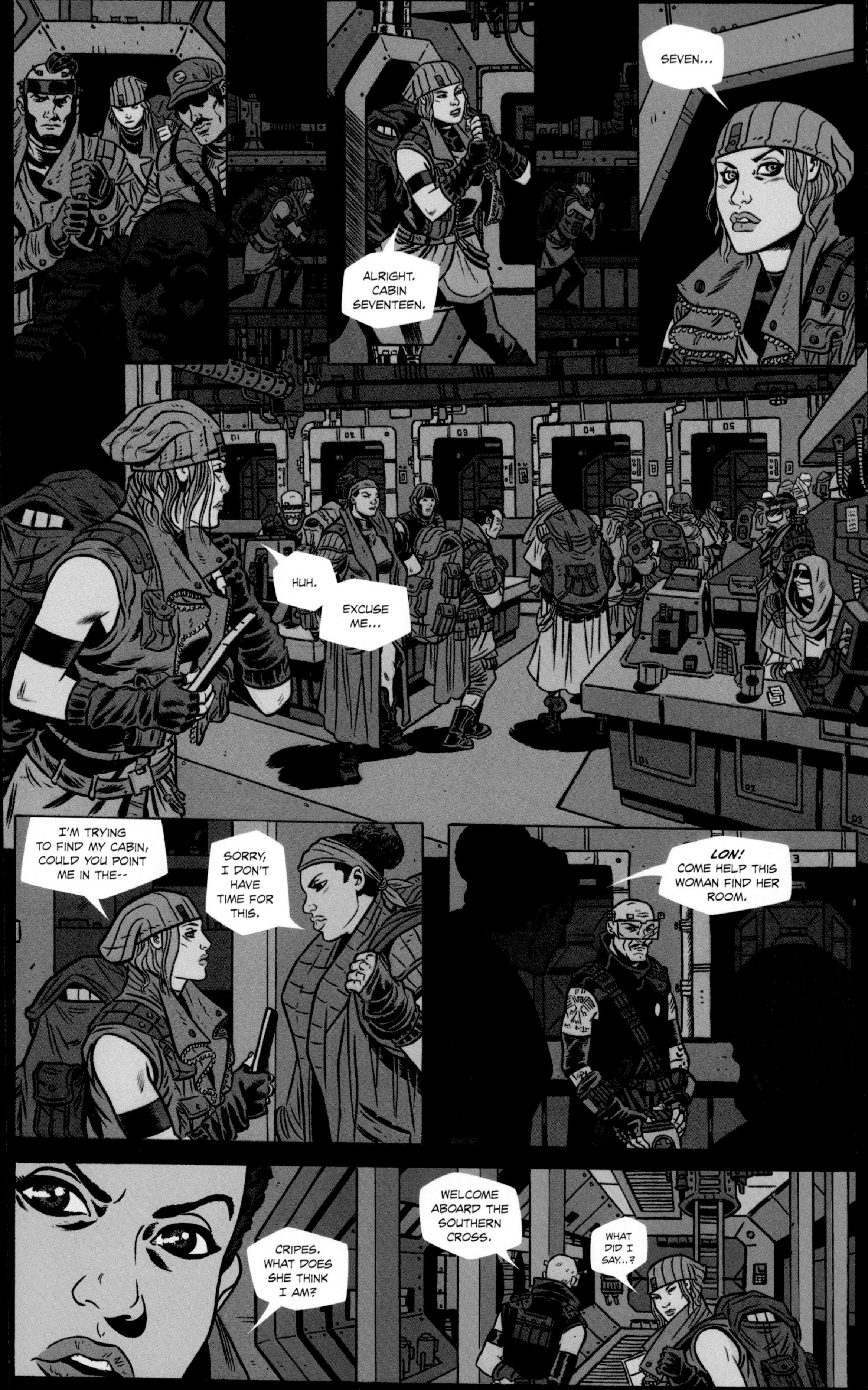
ALRIGHT. CABIN SEVENTEEN.
SEVEN...
HUH.
EXCUSE ME...
I'M TRYING TO FIND MY CABIN, COULD YOU POINT ME IN THE--
SORRY, I DON'T HAVE TIME FOR THIS.
LON! COME HELP THIS WOMAN FIND HER ROOM.
CRIPES. WHAT DOES SHE THINK I AM?
WELCOME ABOARD THE SOUTHERN CROSS.
WHAT DID I SAY...?

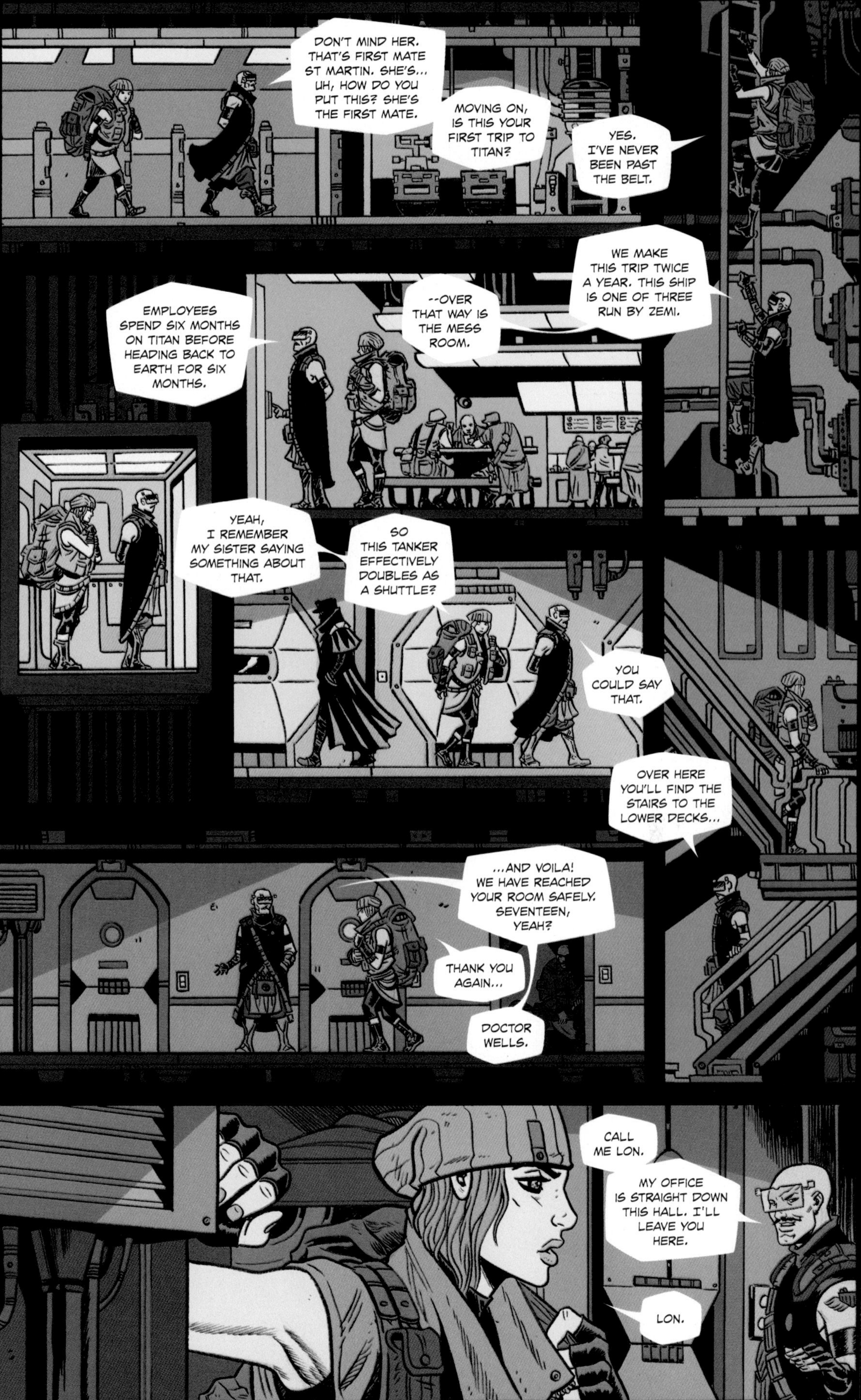
DON'T MIND HER. THAT'S FIRST MATE ST MARTIN. SHE'S... UH, HOW DO YOU PUT THIS? SHE'S THE FIRST MATE.
MOVING ON, IS THIS YOUR FIRST TRIP TO TITAN?
YES. I'VE NEVER BEEN PAST THE BELT.
WE MAKE THIS TRIP TWICE A YEAR. THIS SHIP IS ONE OF THREE RUN BY ZEMI.
--OVER THAT WAY IS THE MESS ROOM.
EMPLOYEES SPEND SIX MONTHS ON TITAN BEFORE HEADING BACK TO EARTH FOR SIX MONTHS.
YEAH, I REMEMBER MY SISTER SAYING SOMETHING ABOUT THAT.
SO THIS TANKER EFFECTIVELY DOUBLES AS A SHUTTLE?
YOU COULD SAY THAT.
OVER HERE YOU'LL FIND THE STAIRS TO THE LOWER DECKS...
...AND VOILA! WE HAVE REACHED YOUR ROOM SAFELY. SEVENTEEN, YEAH?
THANK YOU AGAIN...
DOCTOR WELLS.
CALL ME LON.
MY OFFICE IS STRAIGHT DOWN THIS HALL. I'LL LEAVE YOU HERE.
LON.

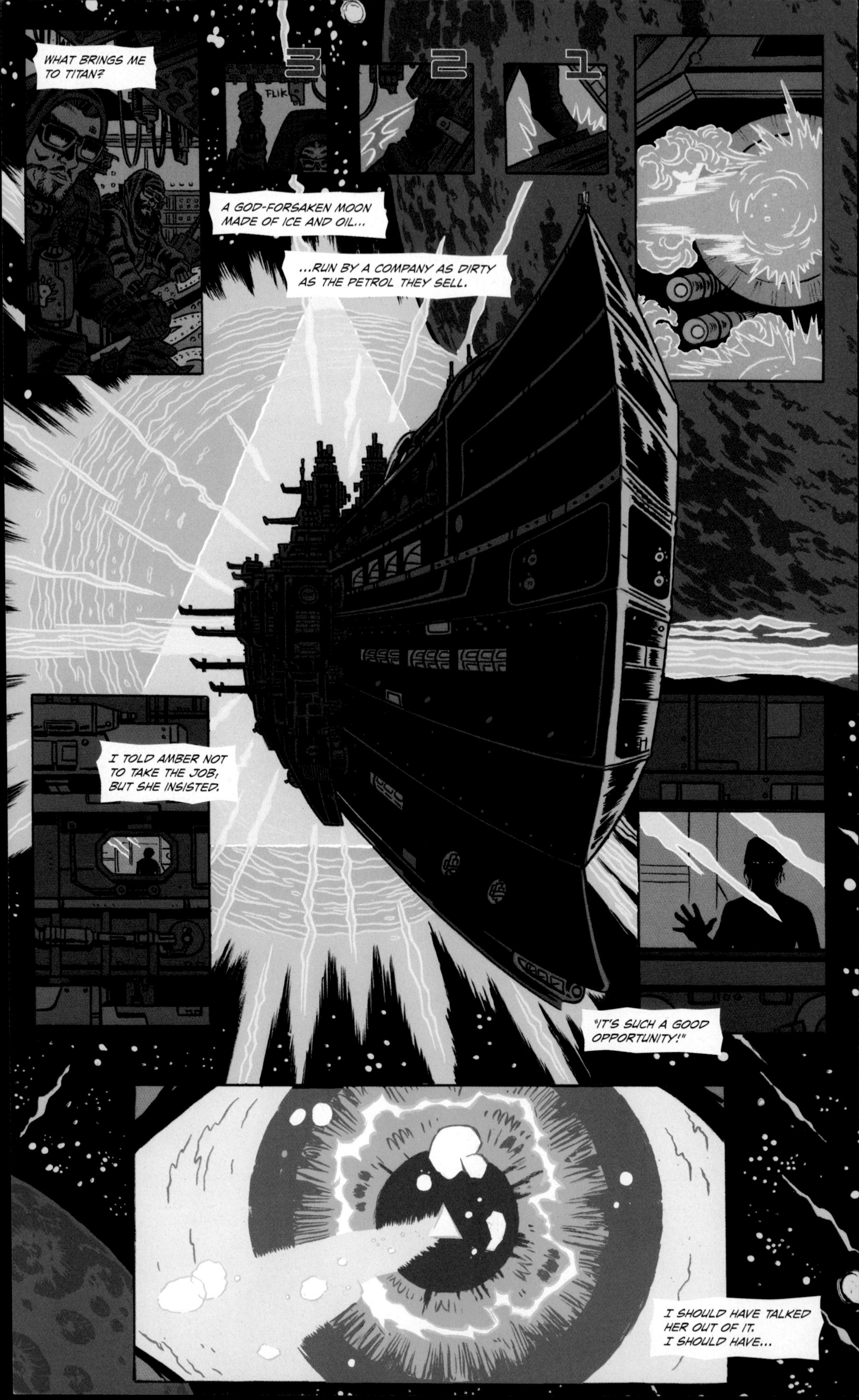
WHAT BRINGS ME TO TITAN?
3
FLIK
2
1
A GOD-FORSAKEN MOON MADE OF ICE AND OIL...
...RUN BY A COMPANY AS DIRTY AS THE PETROL THEY SELL.
I TOLD AMBER NOT TO TAKE THE JOB, BUT SHE INSISTED.
"IT'S SUCH A GOOD OPPORTUNITY!"
I SHOULD HAVE TALKED HER OUT OF IT. I SHOULD HAVE...

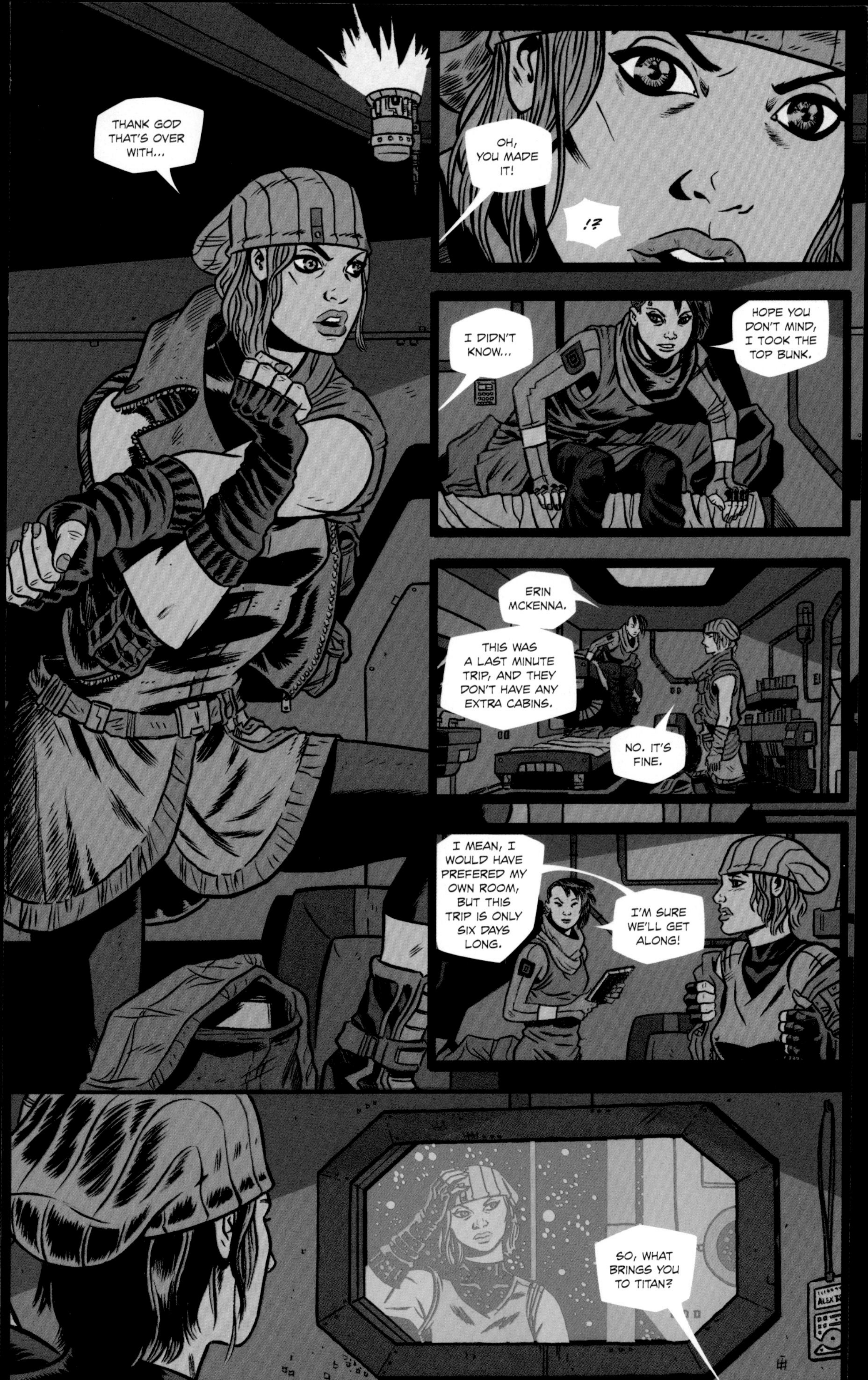
THANK GOD THAT'S OVER WITH...
OH, YOU MADE IT!
!?
I DIDN'T KNOW...
HOPE YOU DON'T MIND, I TOOK THE TOP BUNK.
ERIN MCKENNA.
THIS WAS A LAST MINUTE TRIP, AND THEY DON'T HAVE ANY EXTRA CABINS.
NO. IT'S FINE.
I MEAN, I WOULD HAVE PREFERED MY OWN ROOM, BUT THIS TRIP IS ONLY SIX DAYS LONG.
I'M SURE WE'LL GET ALONG!
SO, WHAT BRINGS YOU TO TITAN?

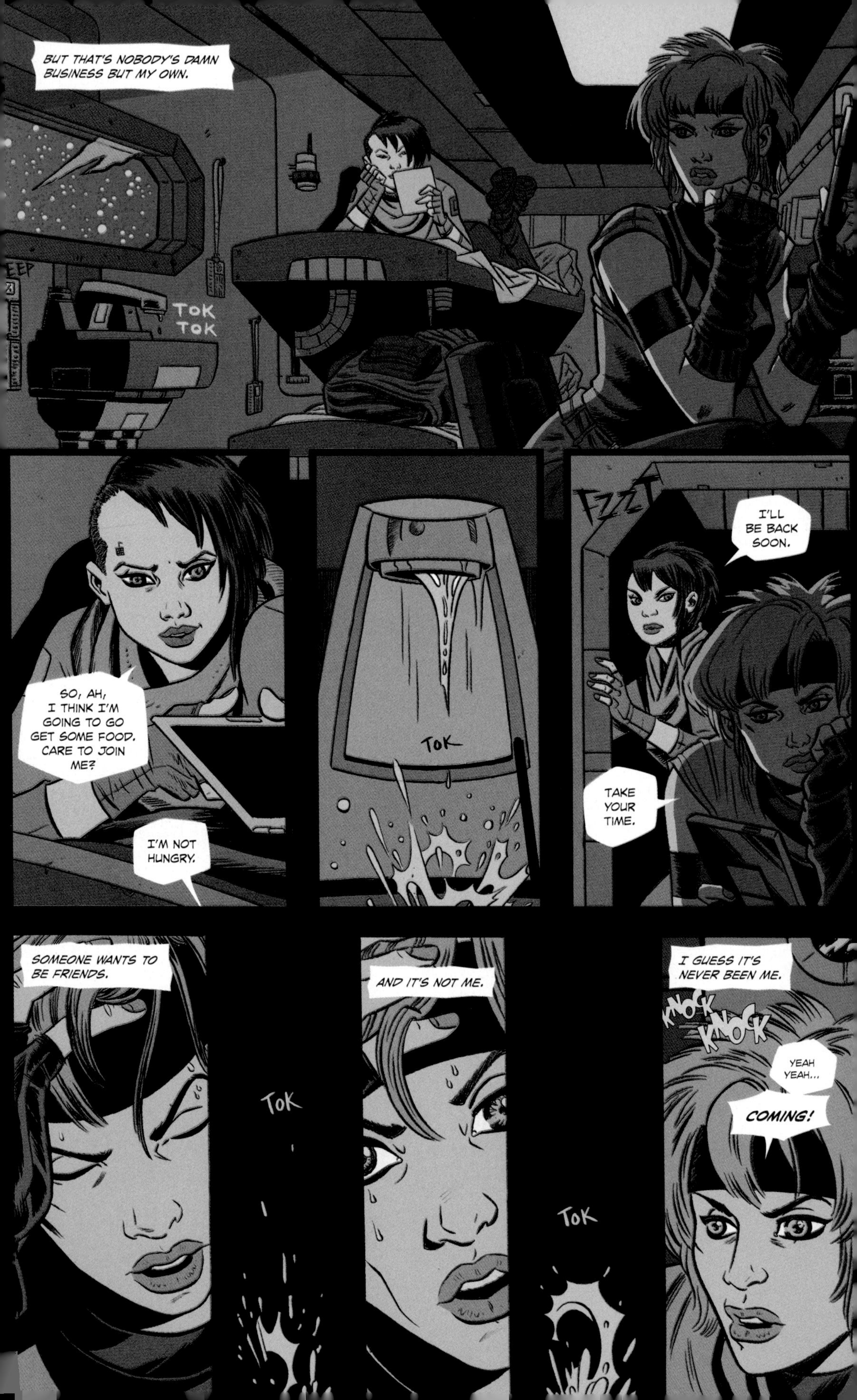

BUT THAT'S NOBODY'S DAMN BUSINESS BUT MY OWN.
TOK TOK
SO, AH, I THINK I'M GOING TO GO GET SOME FOOD. CARE TO JOIN ME?
I'M NOT HUNGRY.
TOK
FZZT
I'LL BE BACK SOON.
TAKE YOUR TIME.
SOMEONE WANTS TO BE FRIENDS.
TOK
AND IT'S NOT ME.
TOK
I GUESS IT'S NEVER BEEN ME.
KNOCK KNOCK
YEAH YEAH...
COMING!

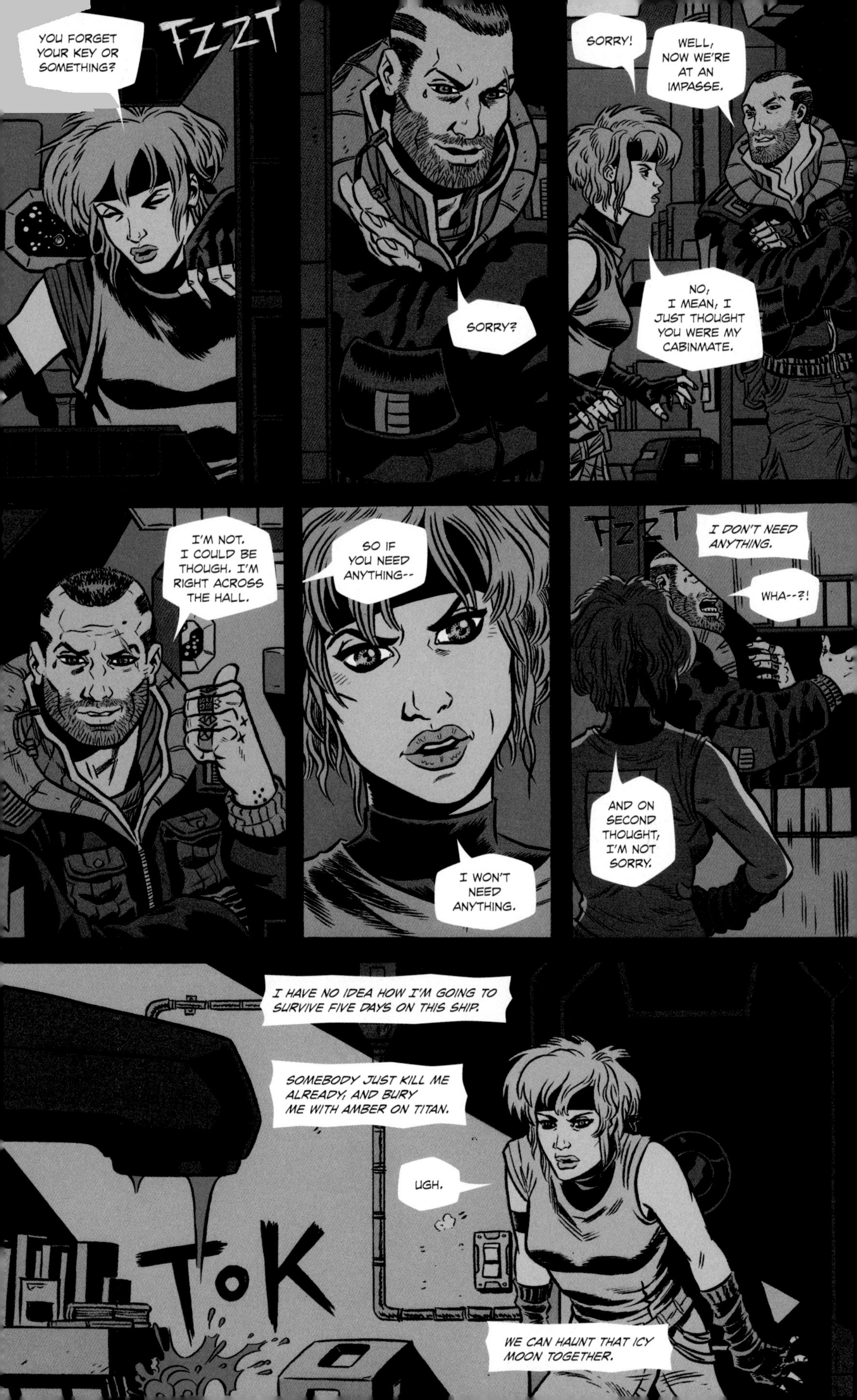
YOU FORGET YOUR KEY OR SOMETHING?
FZZT
SORRY?
SORRY!
WELL, NOW WE'RE AT AN IMPASSE.
NO, I MEAN, I JUST THOUGHT YOU WERE MY CABINMATE.
I'M NOT. I COULD BE THOUGH. I'M RIGHT ACROSS THE HALL.
SO IF YOU NEED ANYTHING--
I WON'T NEED ANYTHING.
FZZT
I DON'T NEED ANYTHING.
WHA--?!
AND ON SECOND THOUGHT, I'M NOT SORRY.
I HAVE NO IDEA HOW I'M GOING TO SURVIVE FIVE DAYS ON THIS SHIP.
SOMEBODY JUST KILL ME ALREADY, AND BURY ME WITH AMBER ON TITAN.
UGH.
TOK
WE CAN HAUNT THAT ICY MOON TOGETHER.

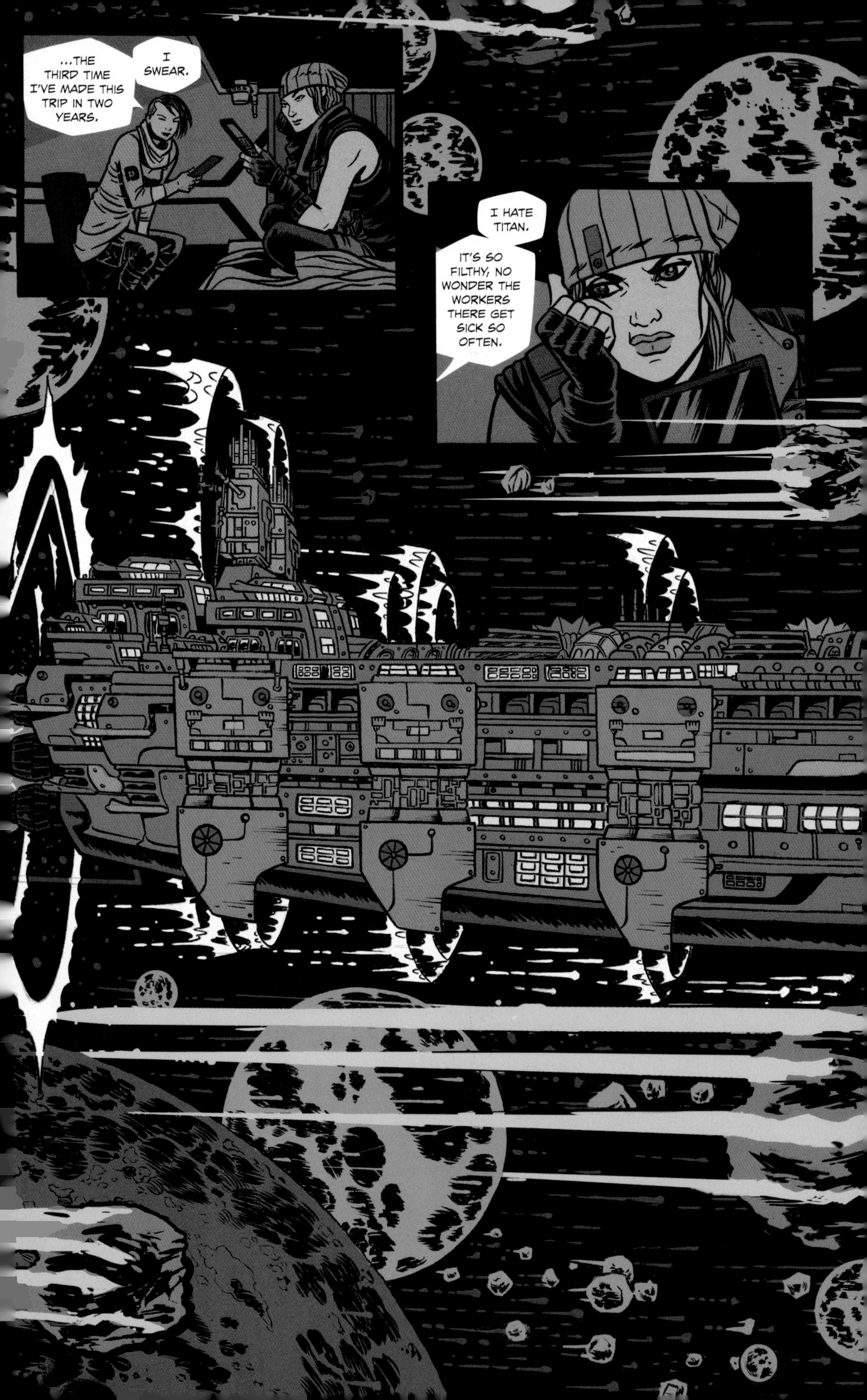

...THE THIRD TIME I'VE MADE THIS TRIP IN TWO YEARS.
I SWEAR.
I HATE TITAN.
IT'S SO FILTHY; NO WONDER THE WORKERS THERE GET SICK SO OFTEN.

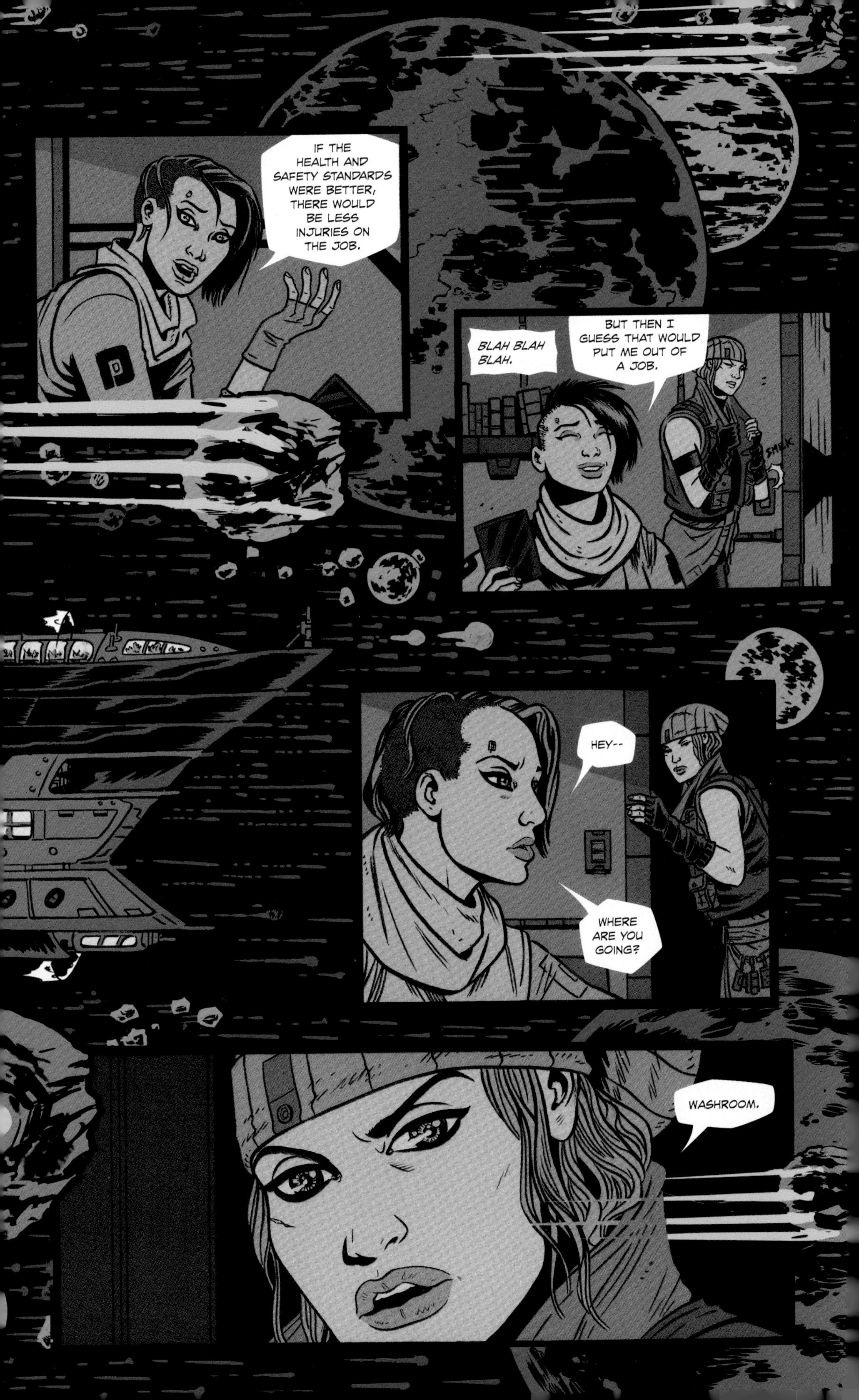
IF THE HEALTH AND SAFETY STANDARDS WERE BETTER, THERE WOULD BE LESS INJURIES ON THE JOB.
BLAH BLAH BLAH.
BUT THEN I GUESS THAT WOULD PUT ME OUT OF A JOB.
SHEK
HEY--
WHERE ARE YOU GOING?
WASHROOM.

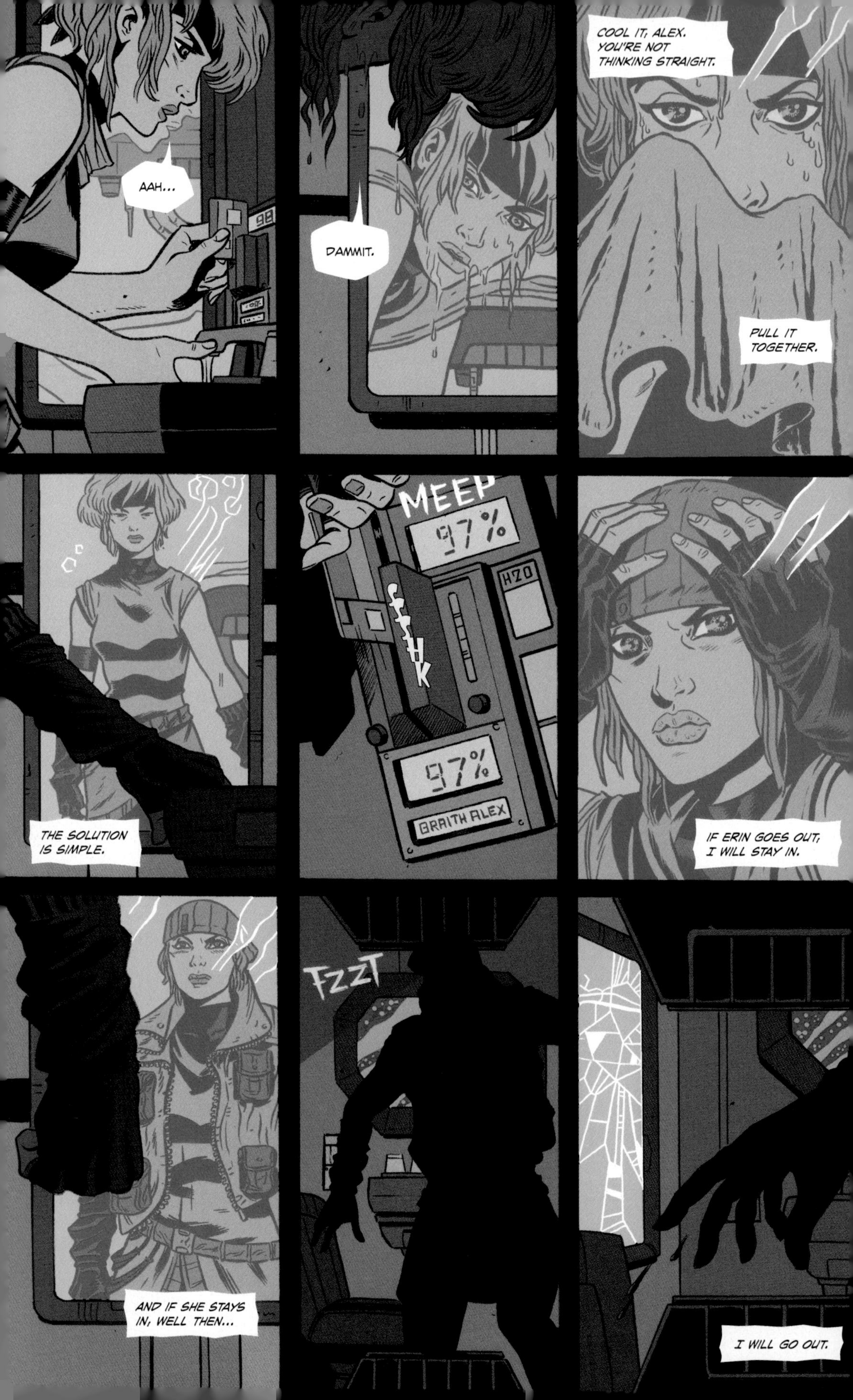
AAH...
DAMMIT.
COOL IT, ALEX. YOU'RE NOT THINKING STRAIGHT.
PULL IT TOGETHER.
THE SOLUTION IS SIMPLE.
MEEP
97%
H2O
SSHK
97%
BRAITH ALEX
IF ERIN GOES OUT, I WILL STAY IN.
AND IF SHE STAYS IN, WELL THEN...
FZZT
I WILL GO OUT.

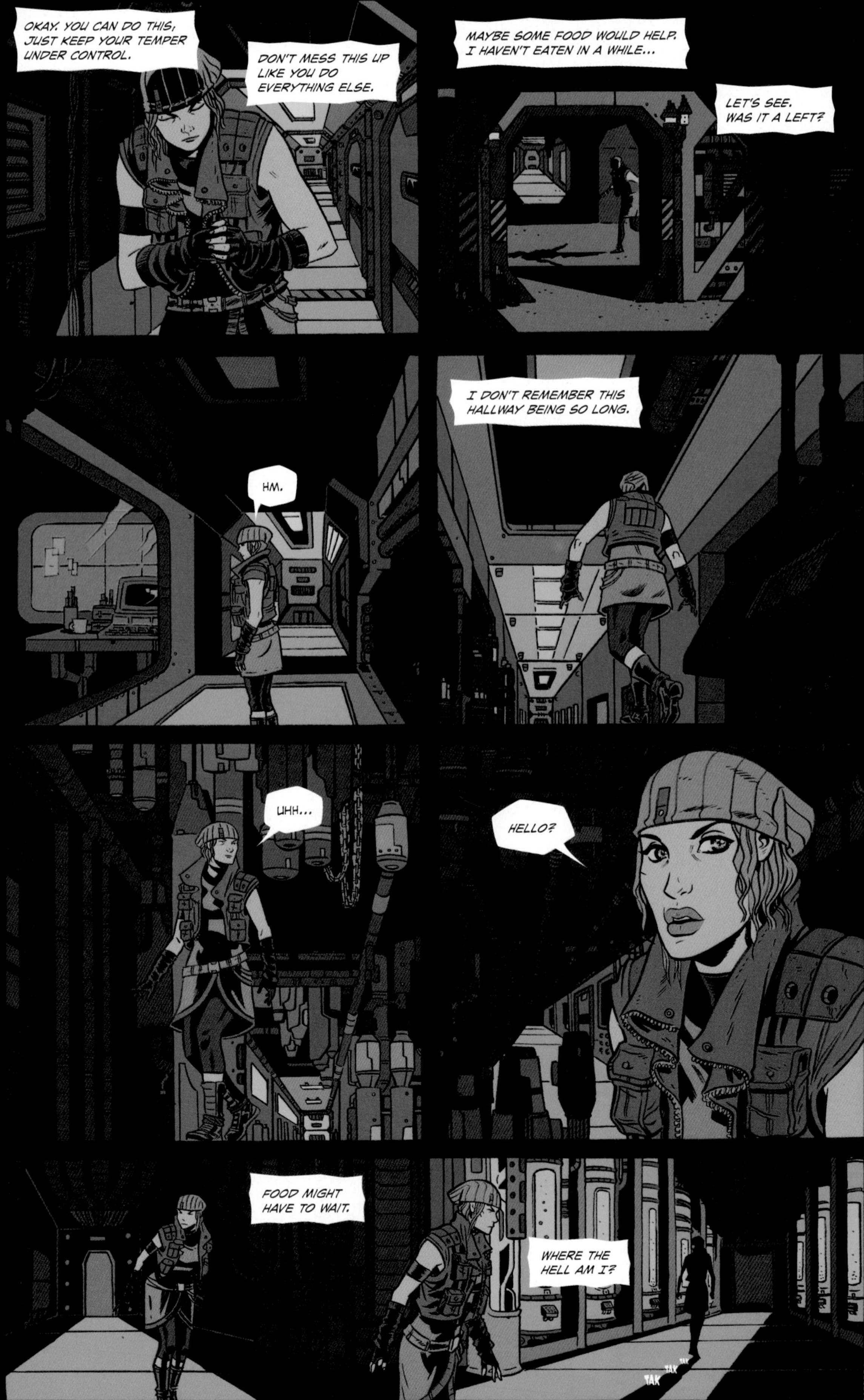
OKAY. YOU CAN DO THIS, JUST KEEP YOUR TEMPER UNDER CONTROL.
DON'T MESS THIS UP LIKE YOU DO EVERYTHING ELSE.
MAYBE SOME FOOD WOULD HELP. I HAVEN'T EATEN IN A WHILE...
LET'S SEE. WAS IT A LEFT?
HM.
I DON'T REMEMBER THIS HALLWAY BEING SO LONG.
UHH...
HELLO?
FOOD MIGHT HAVE TO WAIT.
WHERE THE HELL AM I?
TAK TAK TAK

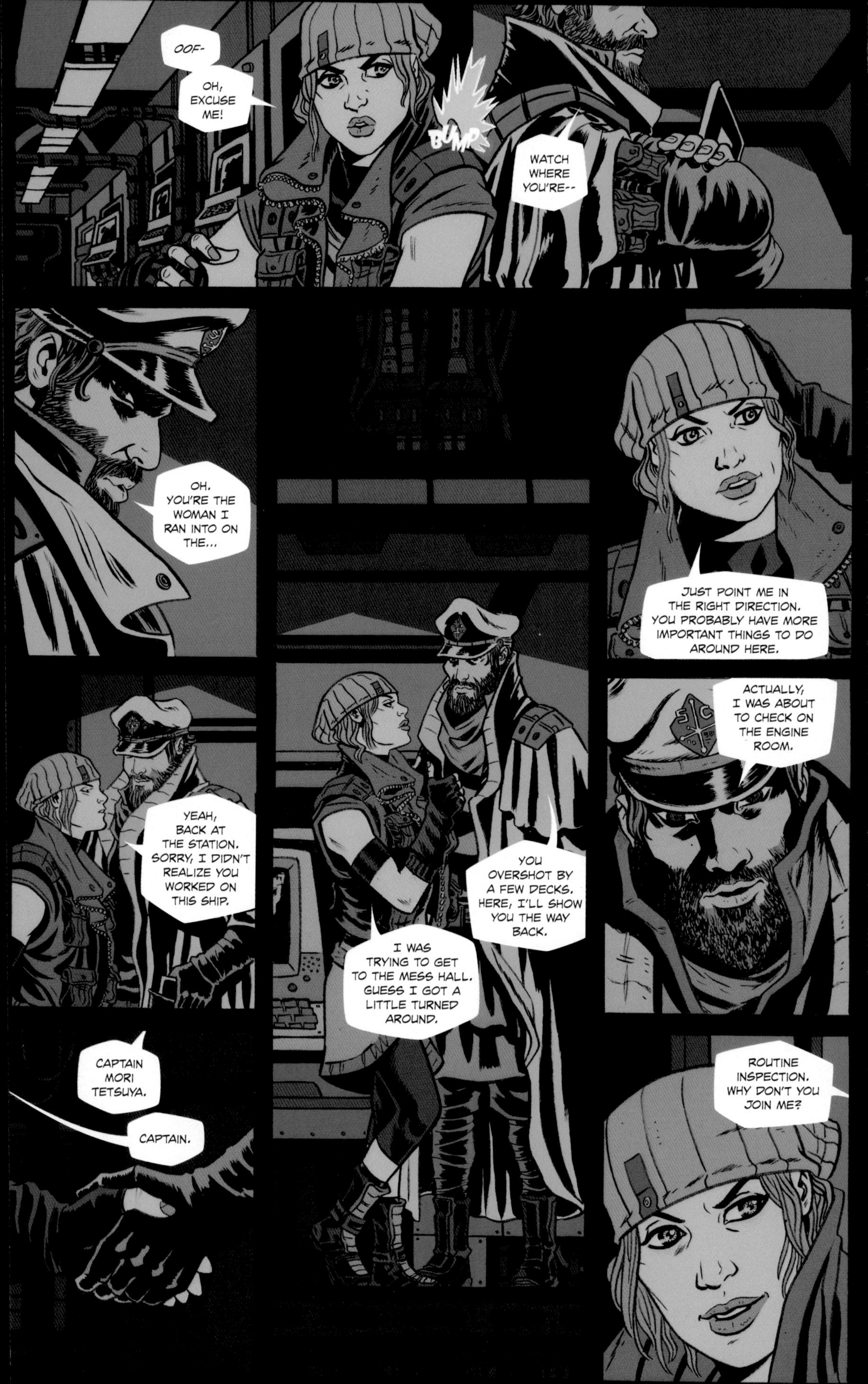
OOF-
OH, EXCUSE ME!
BUMP
WATCH WHERE YOU'RE--
OH. YOU'RE THE WOMAN I RAN INTO ON THE...
YEAH, BACK AT THE STATION. SORRY, I DIDN'T REALIZE YOU WORKED ON THIS SHIP.
CAPTAIN MORI TETSUYA.
CAPTAIN.
I WAS TRYING TO GET TO THE MESS HALL. GUESS I GOT A LITTLE TURNED AROUND.
YOU OVERSHOT BY A FEW DECKS. HERE, I'LL SHOW YOU THE WAY BACK.
JUST POINT ME IN THE RIGHT DIRECTION. YOU PROBABLY HAVE MORE IMPORTANT THINGS TO DO AROUND HERE.
ACTUALLY, I WAS ABOUT TO CHECK ON THE ENGINE ROOM.
ROUTINE INSPECTION. WHY DON'T YOU JOIN ME?

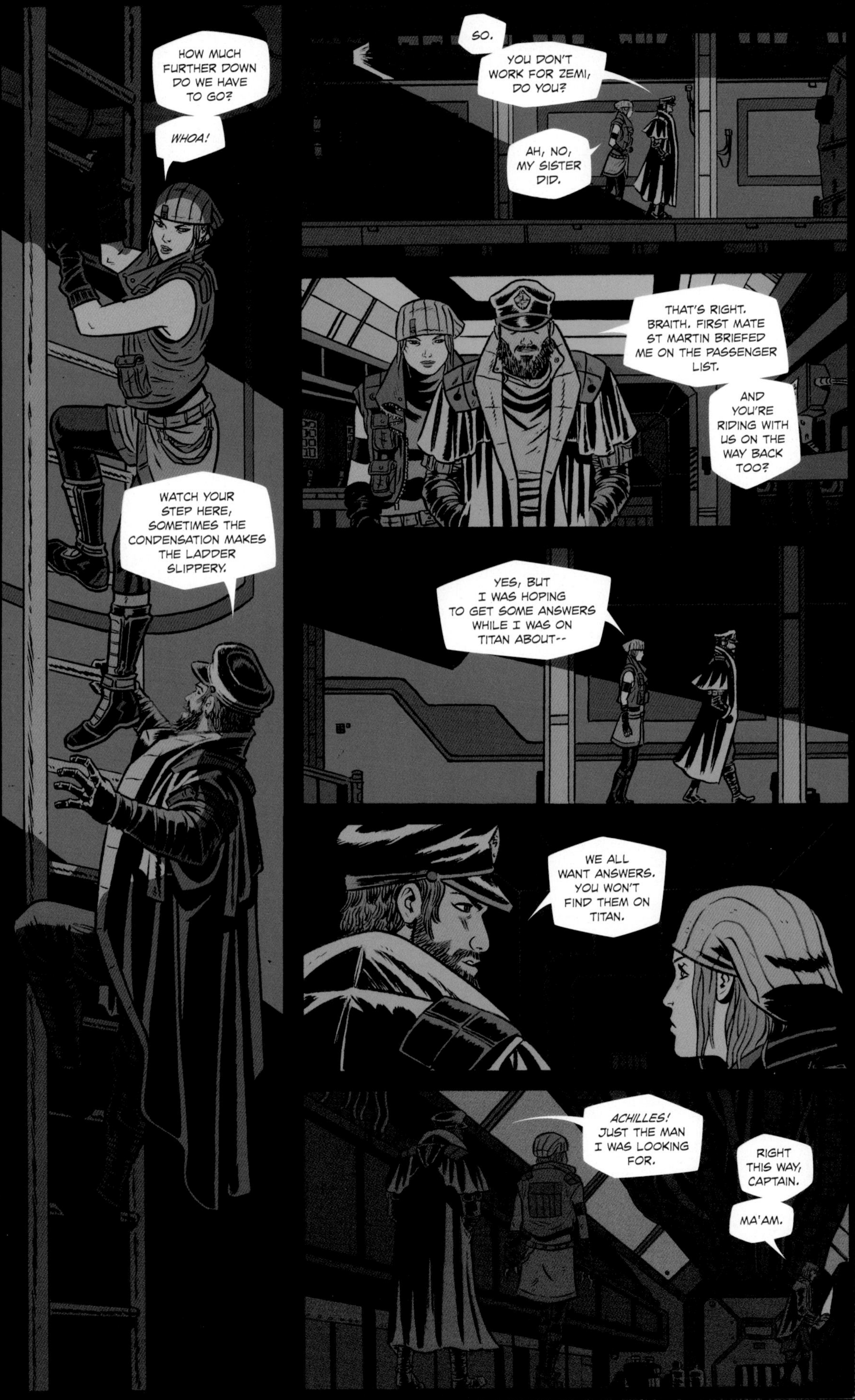
HOW MUCH FURTHER DOWN DO WE HAVE TO GO?
WHOA!
WATCH YOUR STEP HERE, SOMETIMES THE CONDENSATION MAKES THE LADDER SLIPPERY.
SO.
YOU DON'T WORK FOR ZEMI, DO YOU?
AH, NO, MY SISTER DID.
THAT'S RIGHT. BRAITH. FIRST MATE ST MARTIN BRIEFED ME ON THE PASSENGER LIST.
AND YOU'RE RIDING WITH US ON THE WAY BACK TOO?
YES, BUT I WAS HOPING TO GET SOME ANSWERS WHILE I WAS ON TITAN ABOUT--
WE ALL WANT ANSWERS. YOU WON'T FIND THEM ON TITAN.
ACHILLES! JUST THE MAN I WAS LOOKING FOR.
RIGHT THIS WAY, CAPTAIN.
MA'AM.

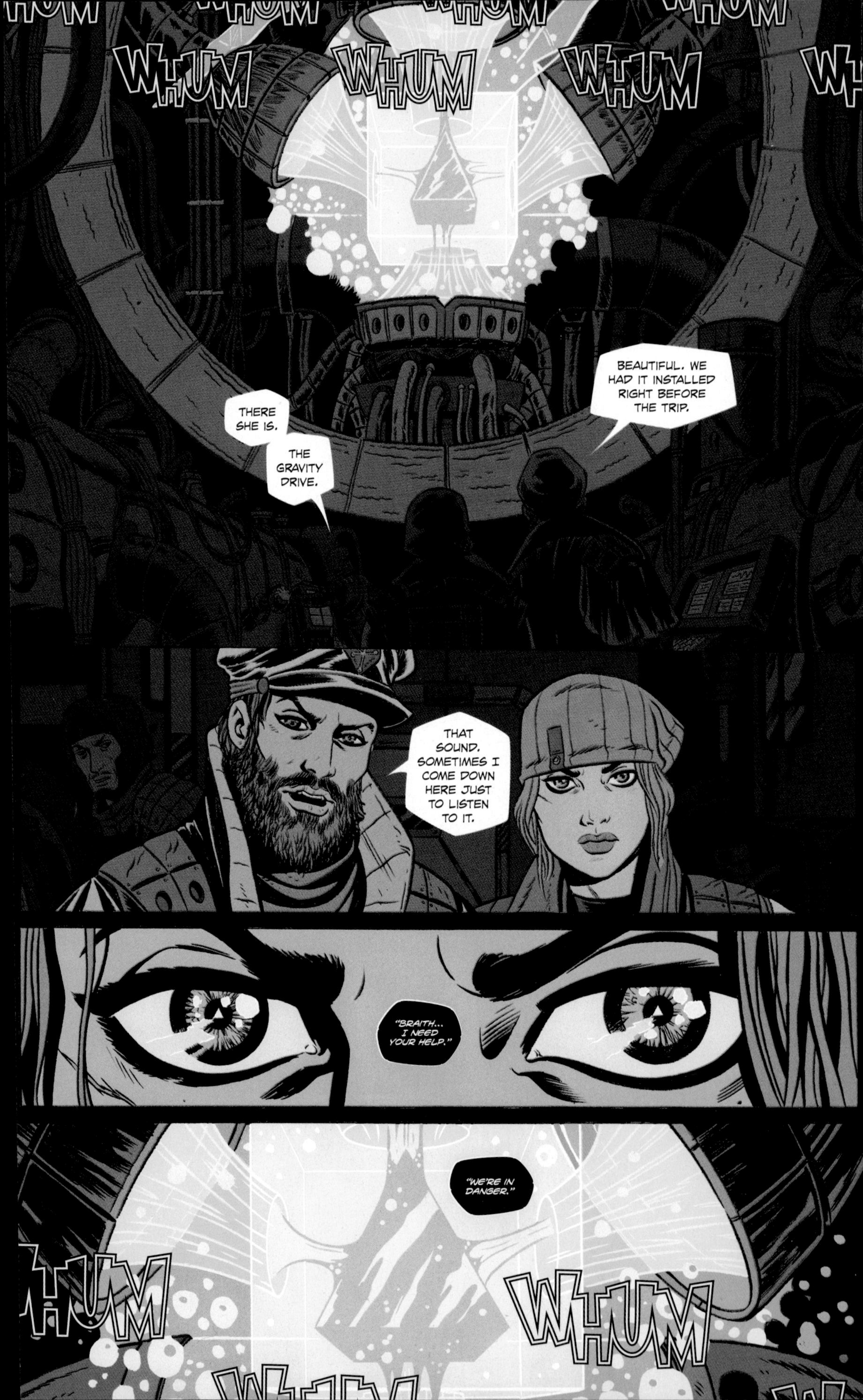
WHUM WHUM WHUM WHUM
THERE SHE IS.
THE GRAVITY DRIVE.
BEAUTIFUL. WE HAD IT INSTALLED RIGHT BEFORE THE TRIP.
THAT SOUND. SOMETIMES I COME DOWN HERE JUST TO LISTEN TO IT.
"BRAITH... I NEED YOUR HELP."
"WE'RE IN DANGER."
WHUM WHUM

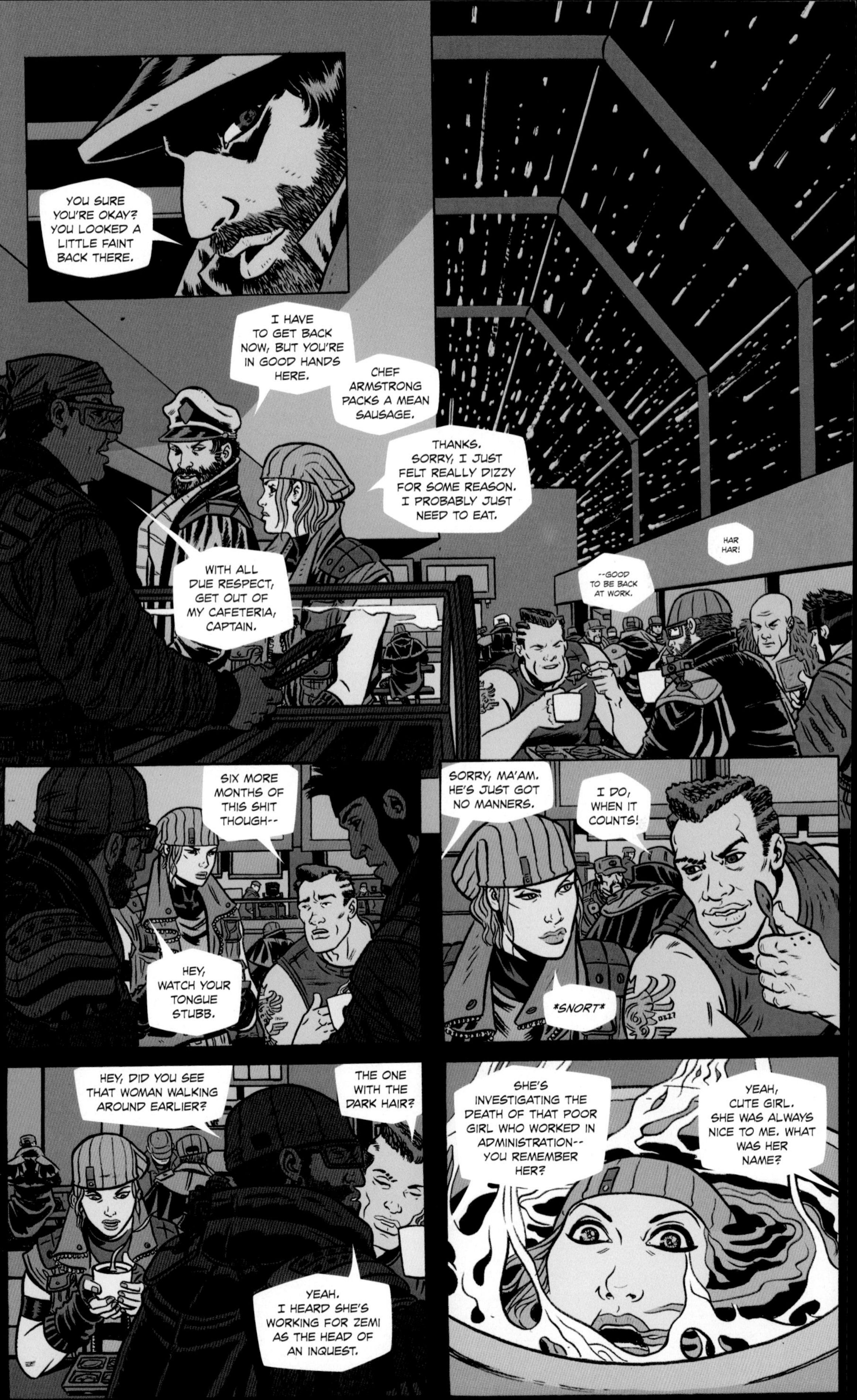
YOU SURE YOU'RE OKAY? YOU LOOKED A LITTLE FAINT BACK THERE.
I HAVE TO GET BACK NOW, BUT YOU'RE IN GOOD HANDS HERE.
CHEF ARMSTRONG PACKS A MEAN SAUSAGE.
THANKS. SORRY; I JUST FELT REALLY DIZZY FOR SOME REASON. I PROBABLY JUST NEED TO EAT.
WITH ALL DUE RESPECT, GET OUT OF MY CAFETERIA, CAPTAIN.
--GOOD TO BE BACK AT WORK.
HAR HAR!
SIX MORE MONTHS OF THIS SHIT THOUGH--
HEY, WATCH YOUR TONGUE STUBB.
SORRY, MA'AM. HE'S JUST GOT NO MANNERS.
I DO, WHEN IT COUNTS!
SNORT
HEY, DID YOU SEE THAT WOMAN WALKING AROUND EARLIER?
THE ONE WITH THE DARK HAIR?
YEAH. I HEARD SHE'S WORKING FOR ZEMI AS THE HEAD OF AN INQUEST.
SHE'S INVESTIGATING THE DEATH OF THAT POOR GIRL WHO WORKED IN ADMINISTRATION-- YOU REMEMBER HER?
YEAH, CUTE GIRL. SHE WAS ALWAYS NICE TO ME. WHAT WAS HER NAME?

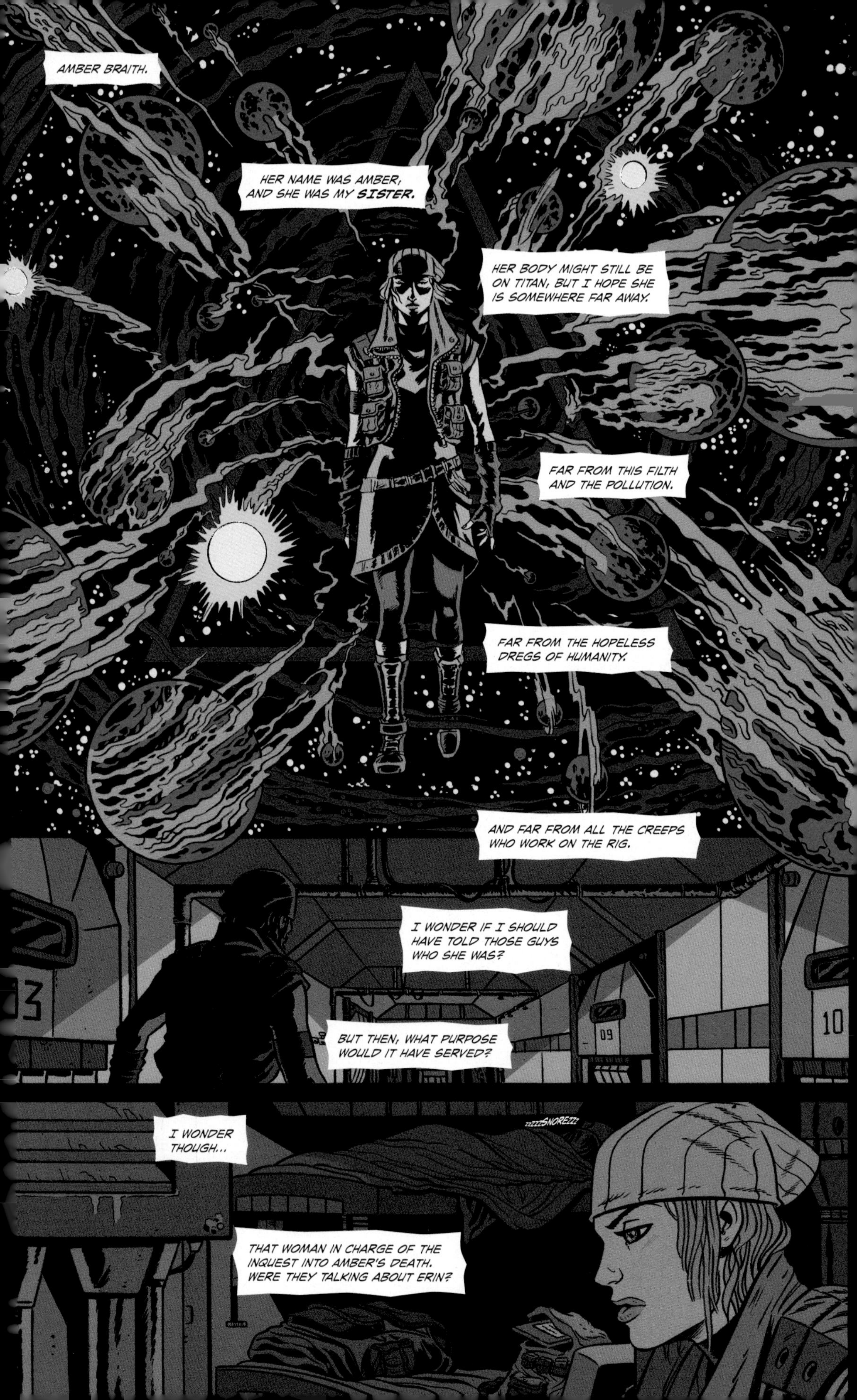
AMBER BRAITH.
HER NAME WAS AMBER, AND SHE WAS MY SISTER.
HER BODY MIGHT STILL BE ON TITAN, BUT I HOPE SHE IS SOMEWHERE FAR AWAY.
FAR FROM THIS FILTH AND THE POLLUTION.
FAR FROM THE HOPELESS DREGS OF HUMANITY.
AND FAR FROM ALL THE CREEPS WHO WORK ON THE RIG.
I WONDER IF I SHOULD HAVE TOLD THOSE GUYS WHO SHE WAS?
03
09
10
BUT THEN, WHAT PURPOSE WOULD IT HAVE SERVED?
I WONDER THOUGH...
zzzzzSNOREzzz
THAT WOMAN IN CHARGE OF THE INQUEST INTO AMBER'S DEATH. WERE THEY TALKING ABOUT ERIN?

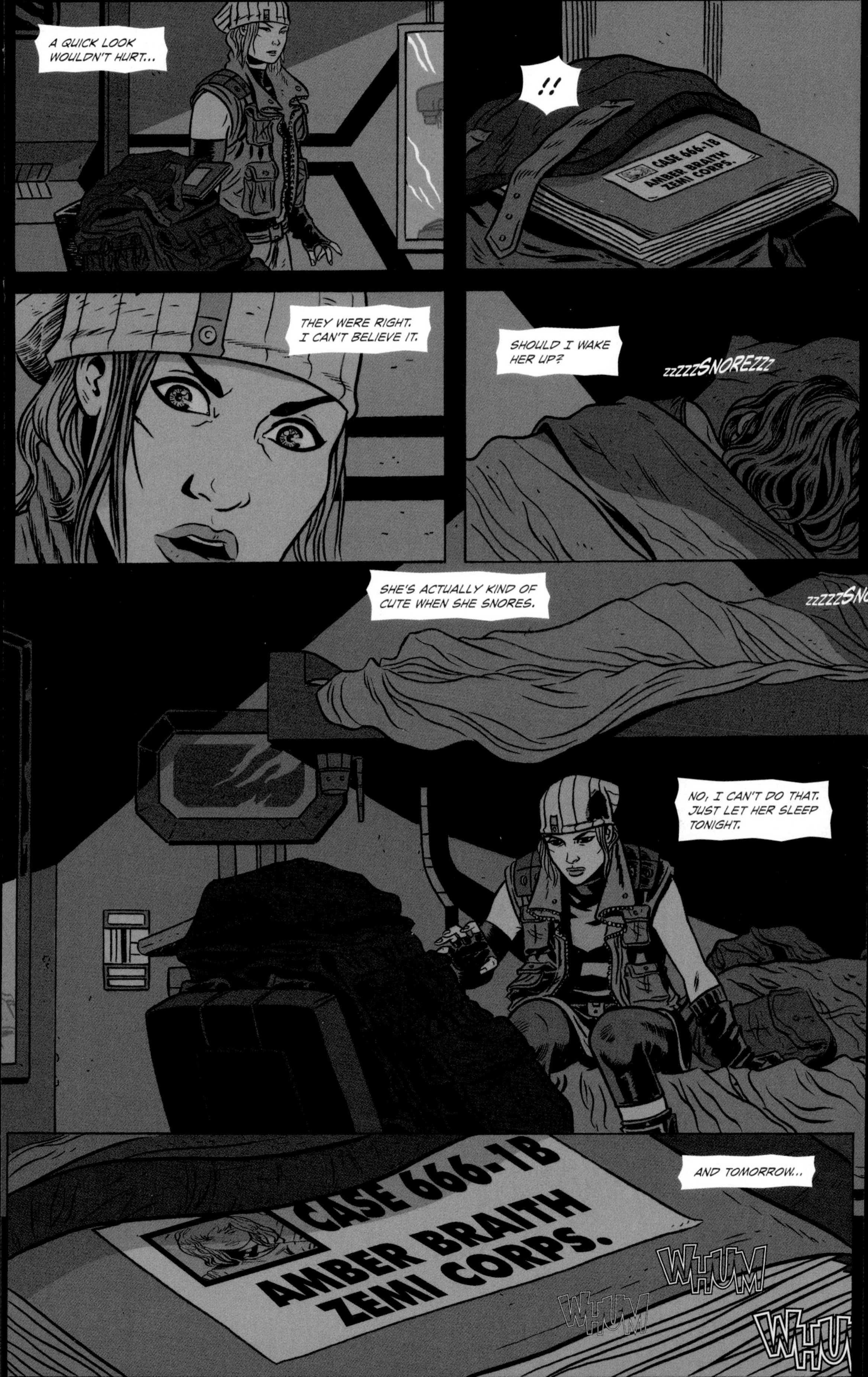
A QUICK LOOK WOULDN'T HURT...
!!
CASE 666-1B
AMBER BRAITH
ZEMI CORPS.
THEY WERE RIGHT. I CAN'T BELIEVE IT.
SHOULD I WAKE HER UP?
zzzzzSNOREzzzz
SHE'S ACTUALLY KIND OF CUTE WHEN SHE SNORES.
NO, I CAN'T DO THAT. JUST LET HER SLEEP TONIGHT.
CASE 666-1B
AMBER BRAITH
ZEMI CORPS.
AND TOMORROW...
WHUM
WHUM

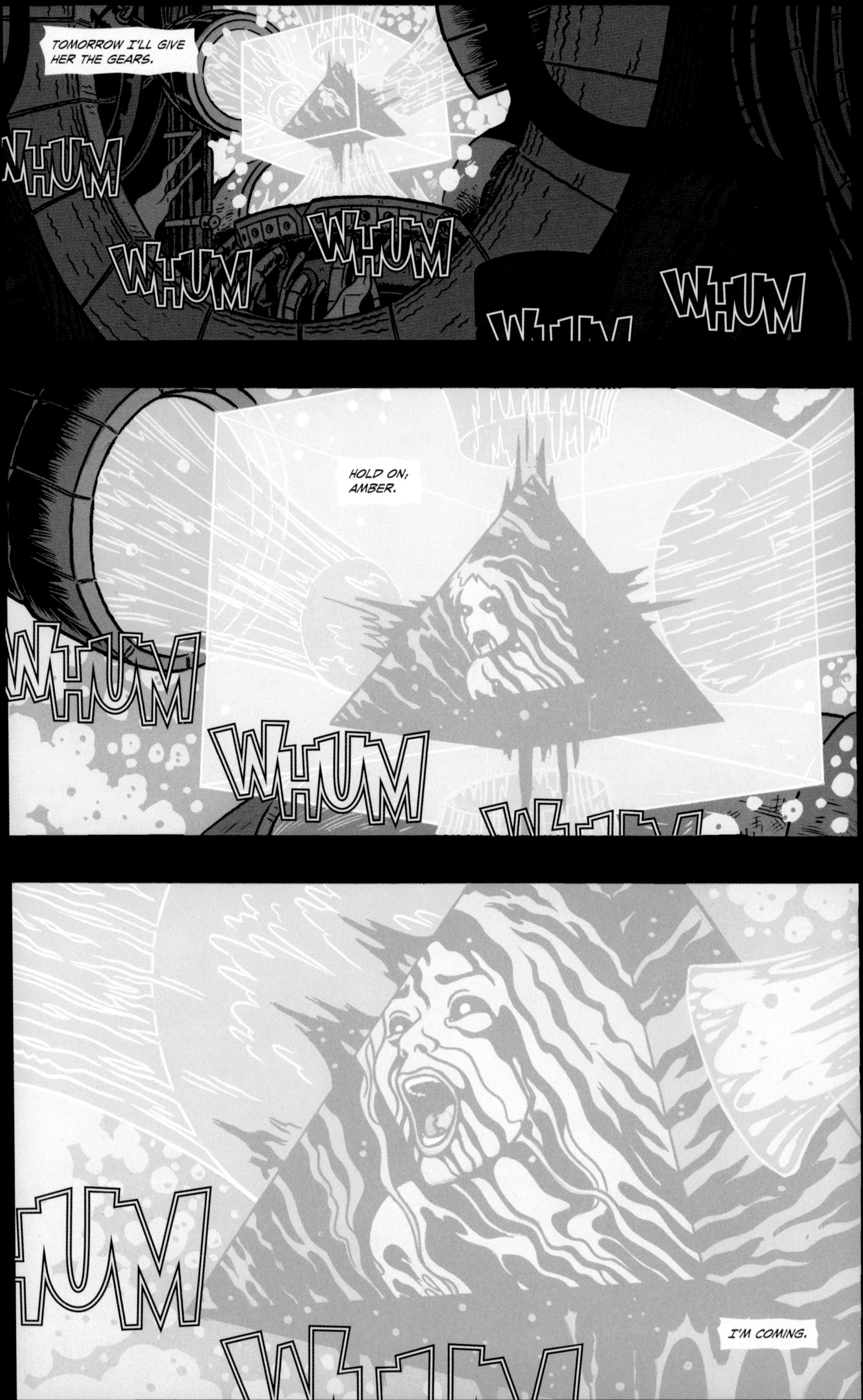
TOMORROW I'LL GIVE HER THE GEARS.
WHUM
WHUM
WHUM
WHUM
WHUM
HOLD ON, AMBER.
WHUM
WHUM
I'M COMING.

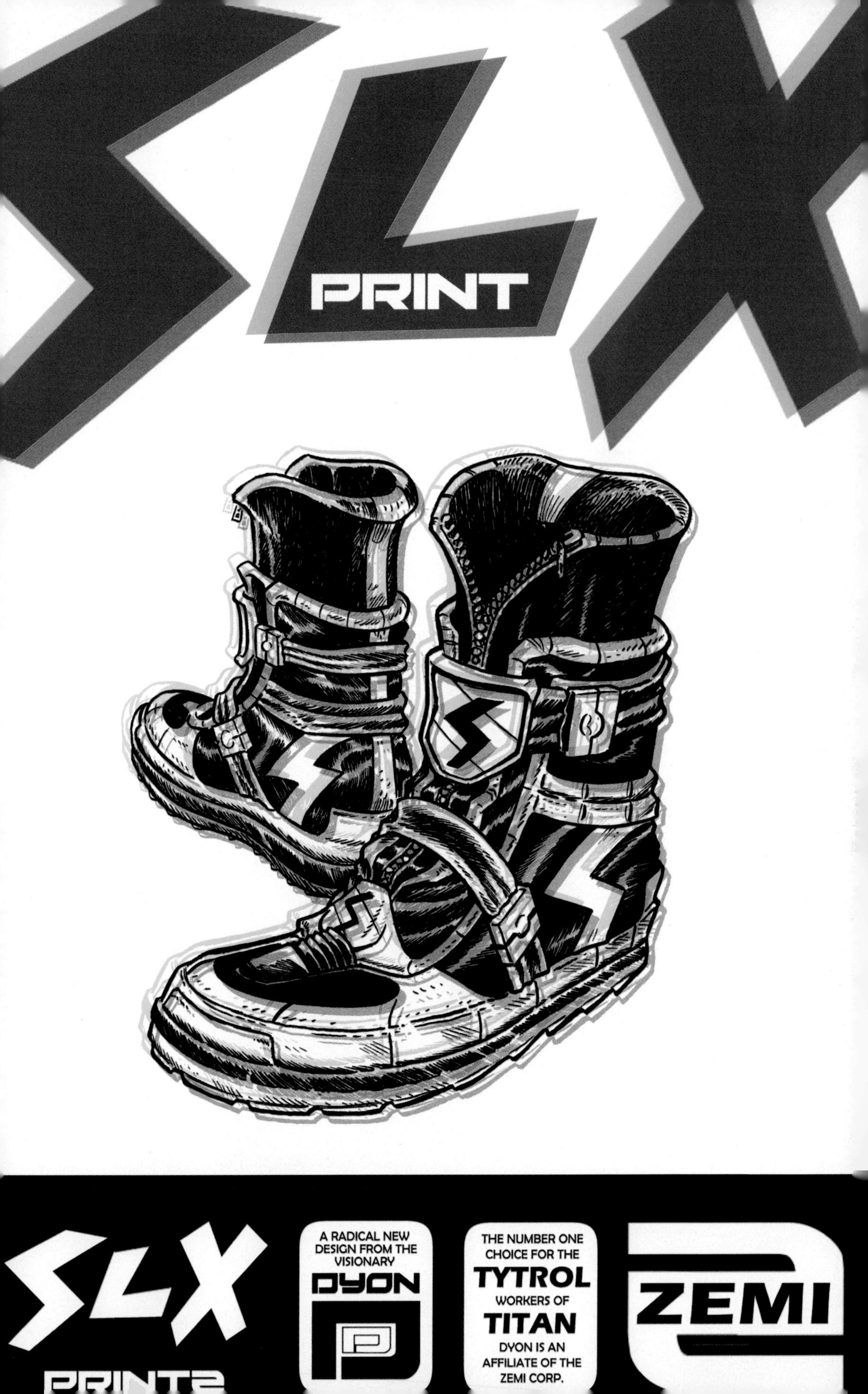
SLX
PRINT
SLX
A RADICAL NEW DESIGN FROM THE VISIONARY
DYON
THE NUMBER ONE CHOICE FOR THE
TYTROL
WORKERS OF
TITAN
DYON IS AN AFFILIATE OF THE ZEMI CORP.
ZEMI

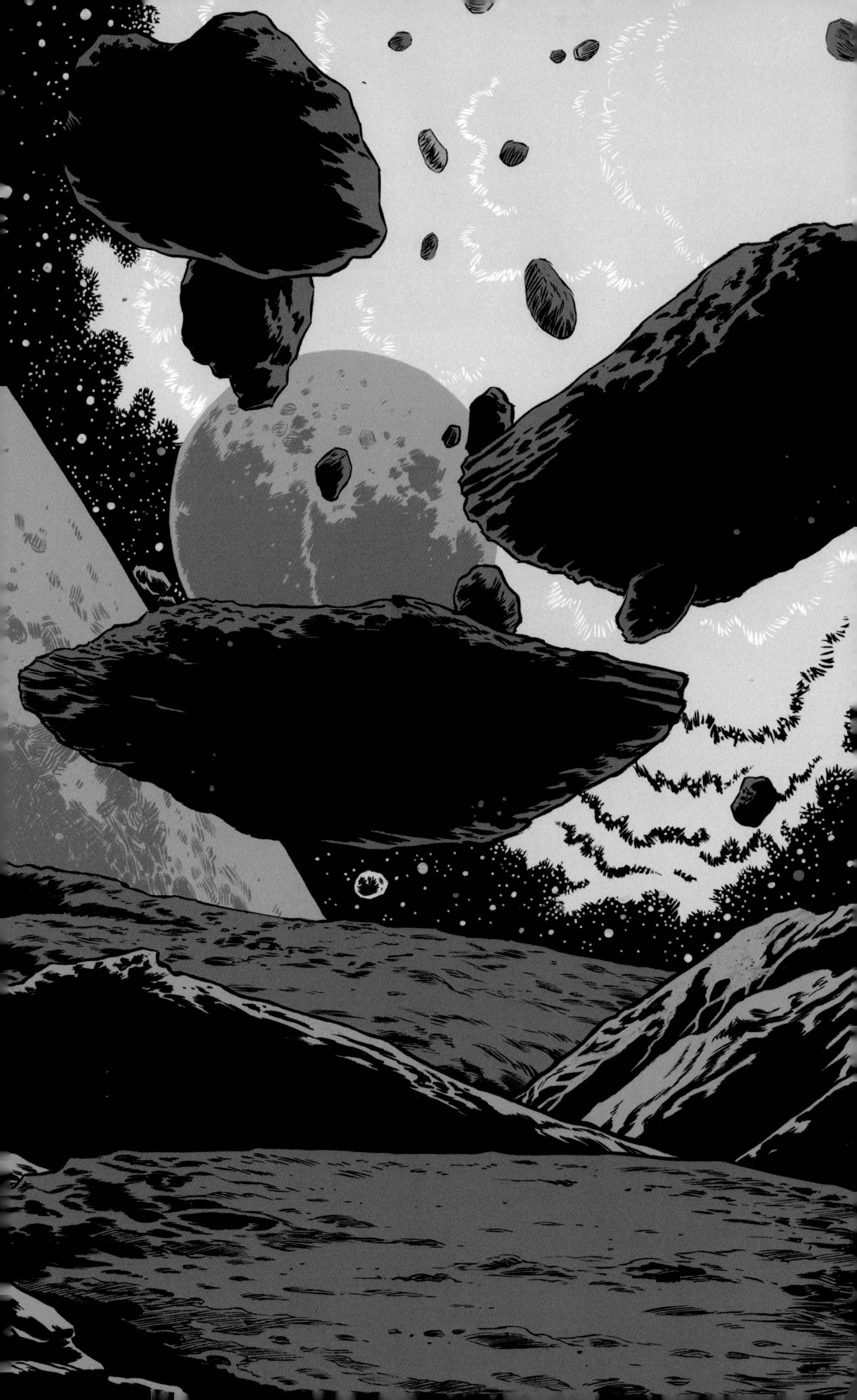

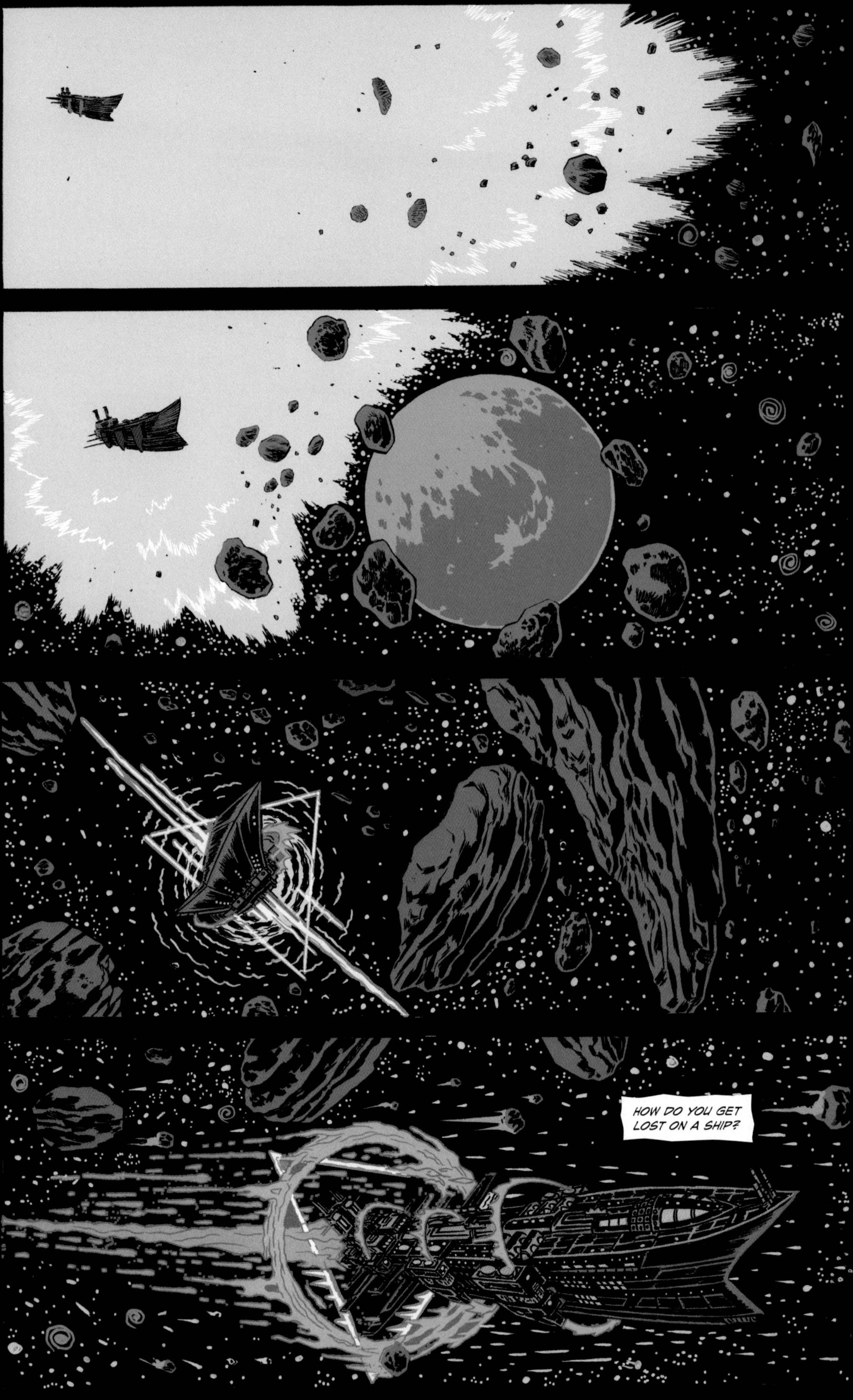
HOW DO YOU GET LOST ON A SHIP?

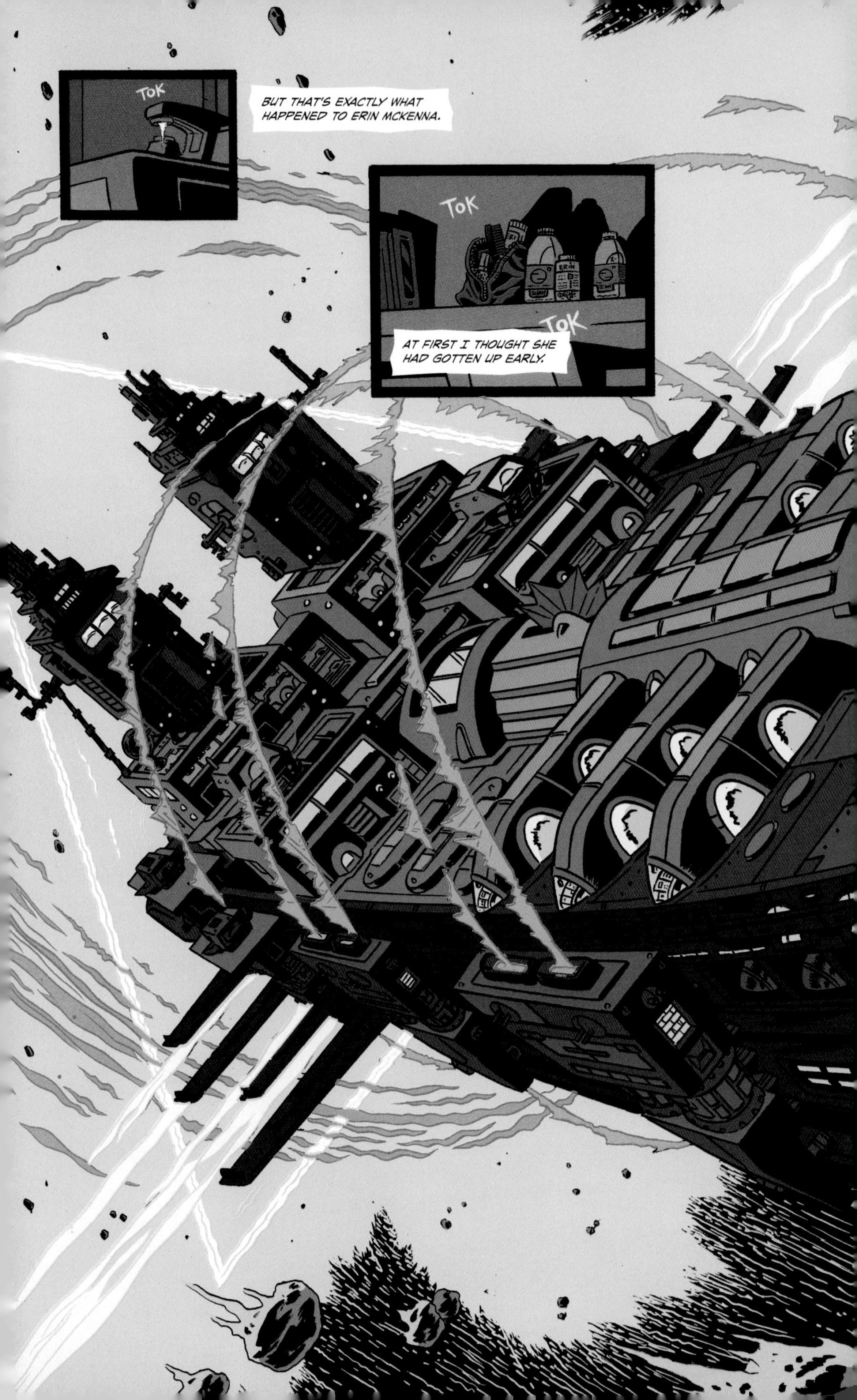
TOK
BUT THAT'S EXACTLY WHAT HAPPENED TO ERIN MCKENNA.
TOK
TOK
AT FIRST I THOUGHT SHE HAD GOTTEN UP EARLY.

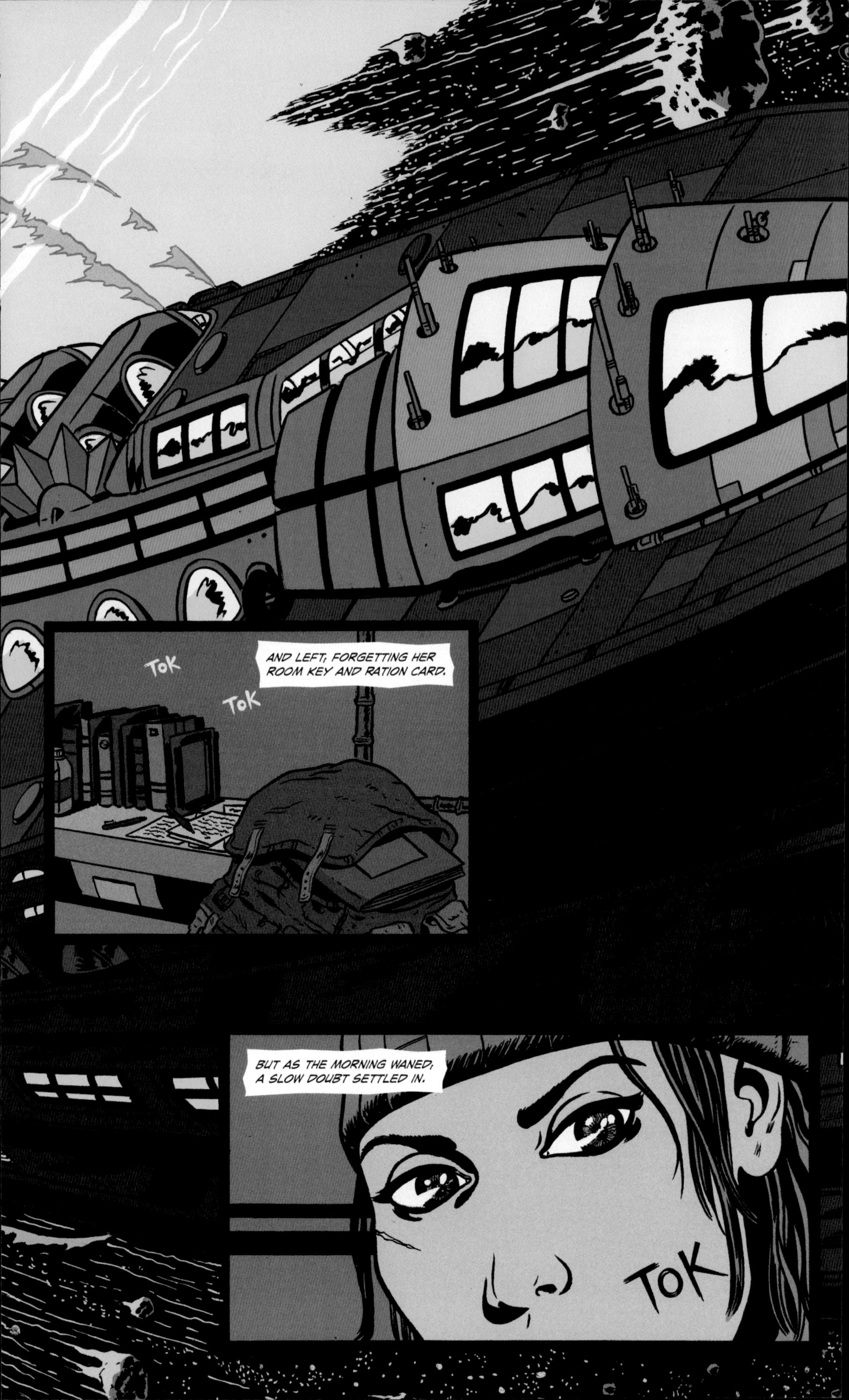
AND LEFT, FORGETTING HER ROOM KEY AND RATION CARD.
TOK
TOK
BUT AS THE MORNING WANED, A SLOW DOUBT SETTLED IN.
TOK

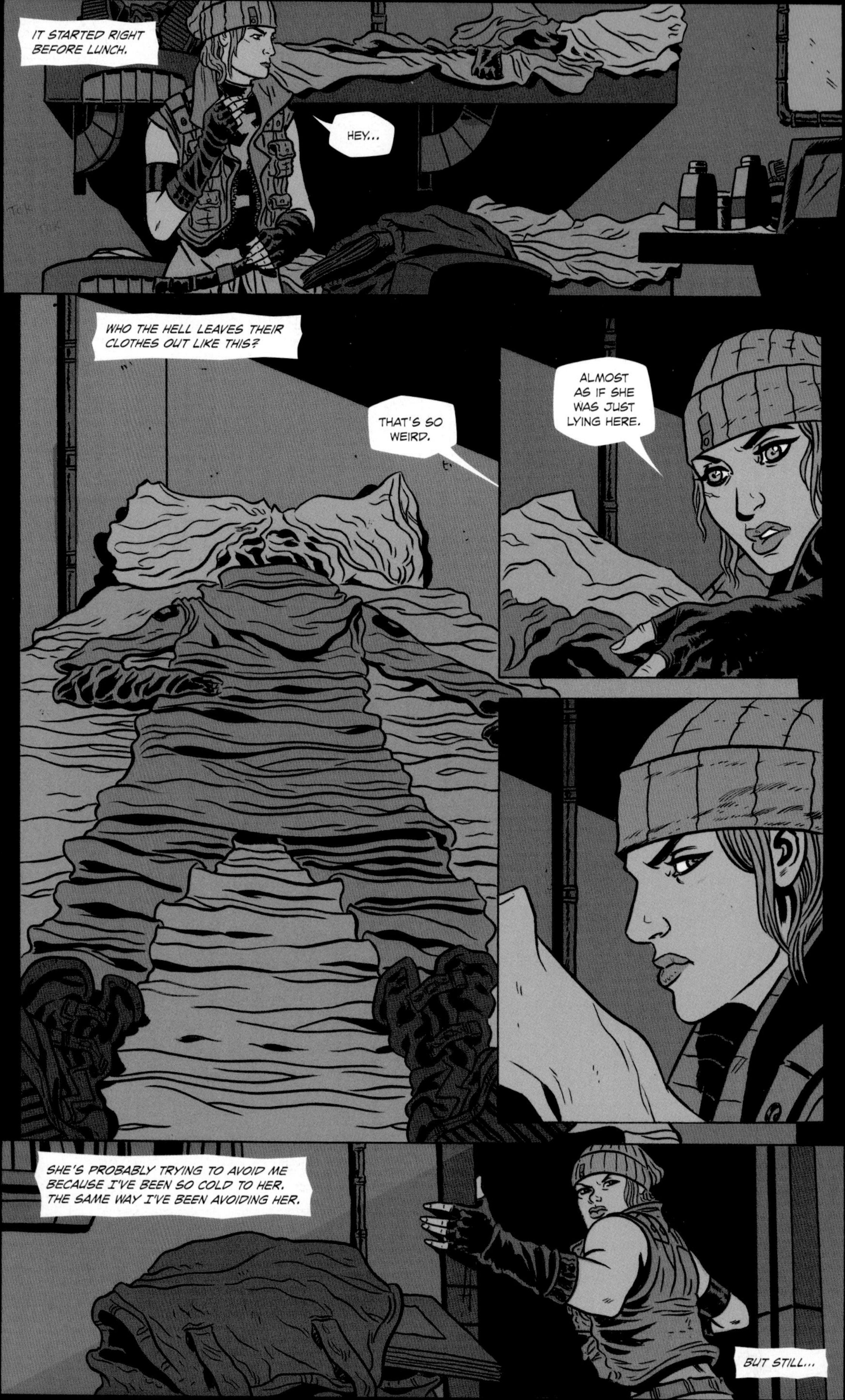
IT STARTED RIGHT BEFORE LUNCH.
HEY...
WHO THE HELL LEAVES THEIR CLOTHES OUT LIKE THIS?
THAT'S SO WEIRD.
ALMOST AS IF SHE WAS JUST LYING HERE.
SHE'S PROBABLY TRYING TO AVOID ME BECAUSE I'VE BEEN SO COLD TO HER. THE SAME WAY I'VE BEEN AVOIDING HER.
BUT STILL...

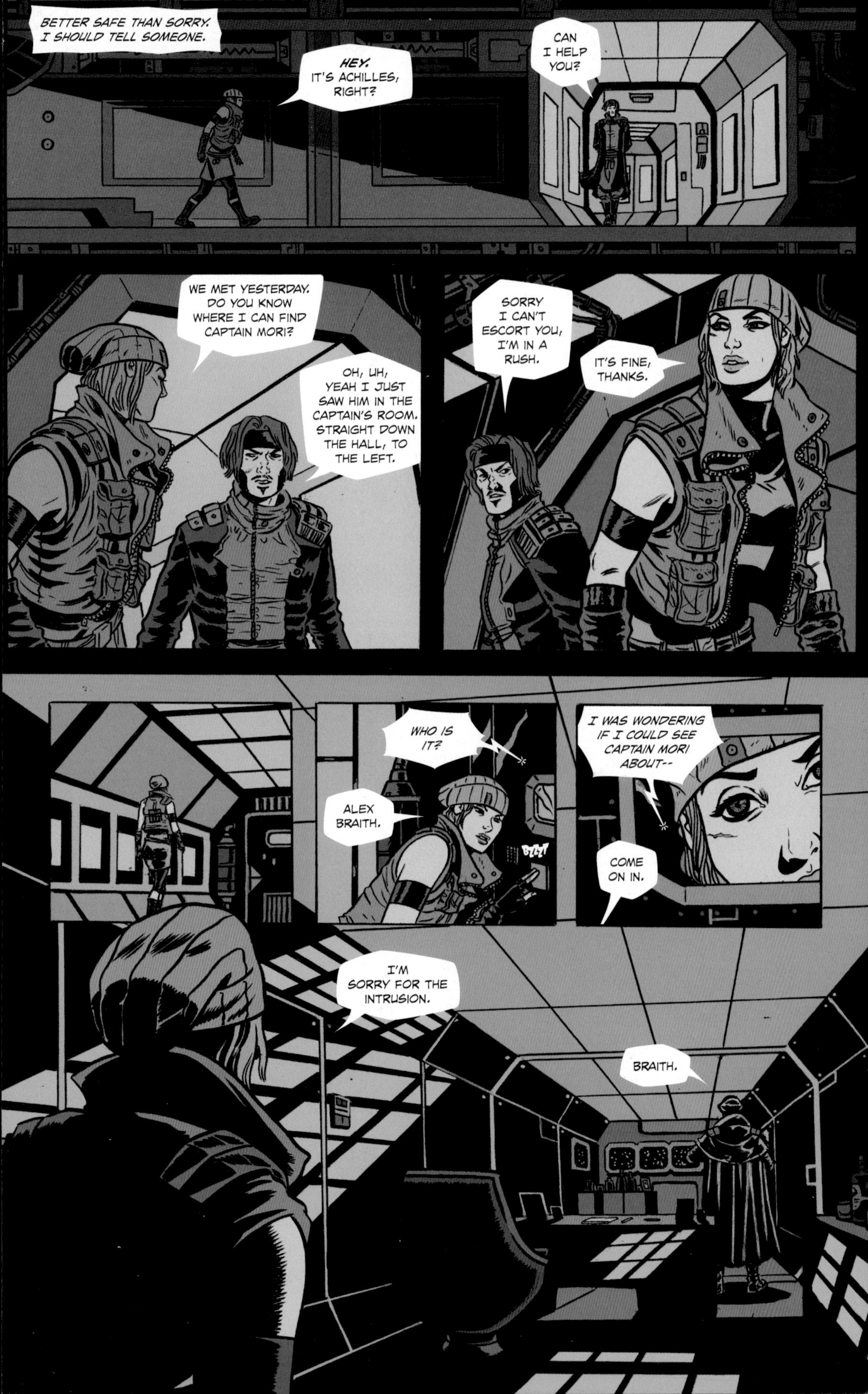
BETTER SAFE THAN SORRY. I SHOULD TELL SOMEONE.
HEY. IT'S ACHILLES, RIGHT?
CAN I HELP YOU?
WE MET YESTERDAY. DO YOU KNOW WHERE I CAN FIND CAPTAIN MORI?
OH, UH, YEAH I JUST SAW HIM IN THE CAPTAIN'S ROOM. STRAIGHT DOWN THE HALL, TO THE LEFT.
SORRY I CAN'T ESCORT YOU, I'M IN A RUSH.
IT'S FINE, THANKS.
WHO IS IT?
ALEX BRAITH.
BZZZT
I WAS WONDERING IF I COULD SEE CAPTAIN MORI ABOUT--
COME ON IN.
I'M SORRY FOR THE INTRUSION.
BRAITH.

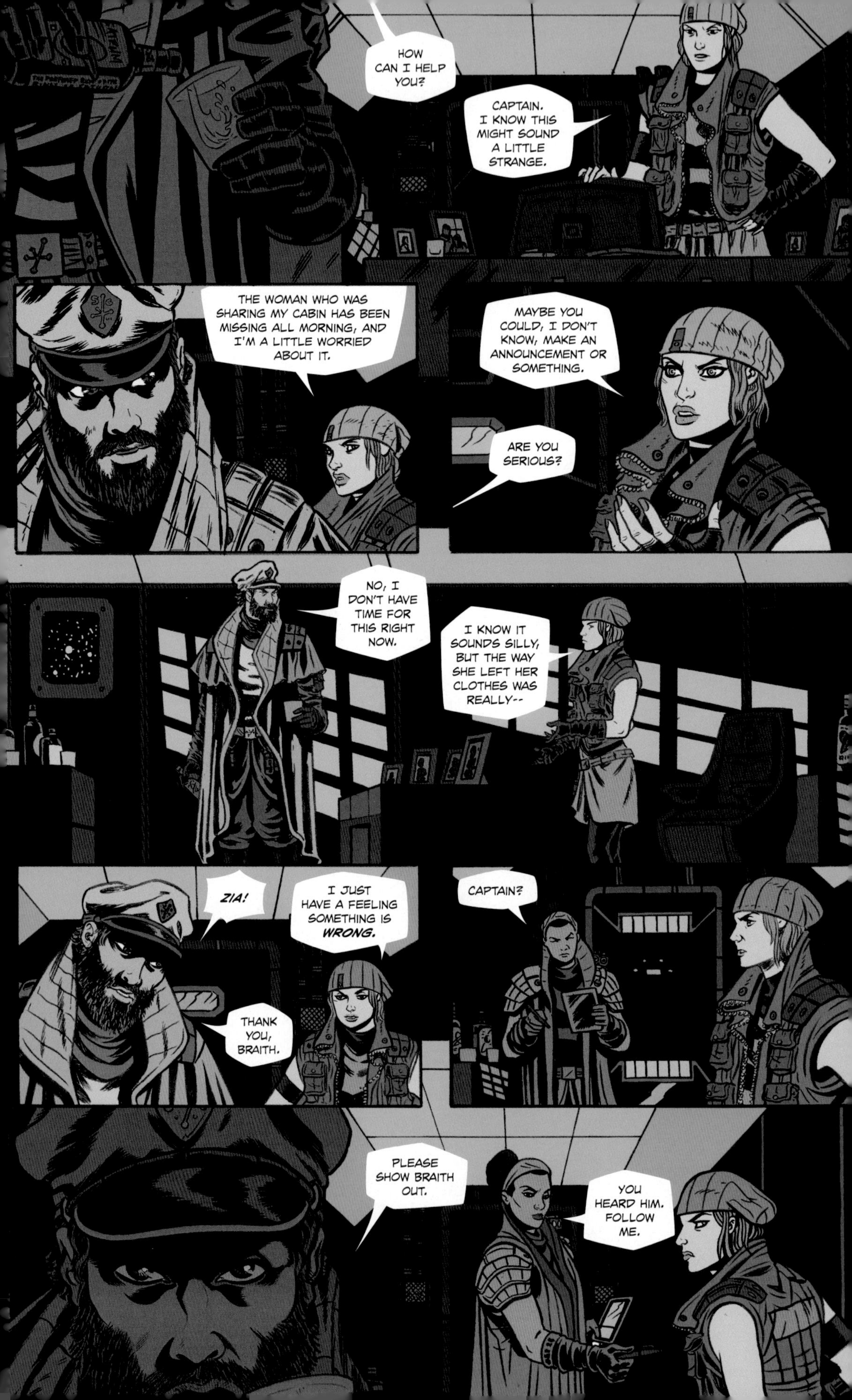
HOW CAN I HELP YOU?
CAPTAIN. I KNOW THIS MIGHT SOUND A LITTLE STRANGE.
THE WOMAN WHO WAS SHARING MY CABIN HAS BEEN MISSING ALL MORNING, AND I'M A LITTLE WORRIED ABOUT IT.
MAYBE YOU COULD, I DON'T KNOW, MAKE AN ANNOUNCEMENT OR SOMETHING.
ARE YOU SERIOUS?
NO, I DON'T HAVE TIME FOR THIS RIGHT NOW.
I KNOW IT SOUNDS SILLY, BUT THE WAY SHE LEFT HER CLOTHES WAS REALLY--
ZIA!
I JUST HAVE A FEELING SOMETHING IS *WRONG.*
THANK YOU, BRAITH.
CAPTAIN?
PLEASE SHOW BRAITH OUT.
YOU HEARD HIM. FOLLOW ME.

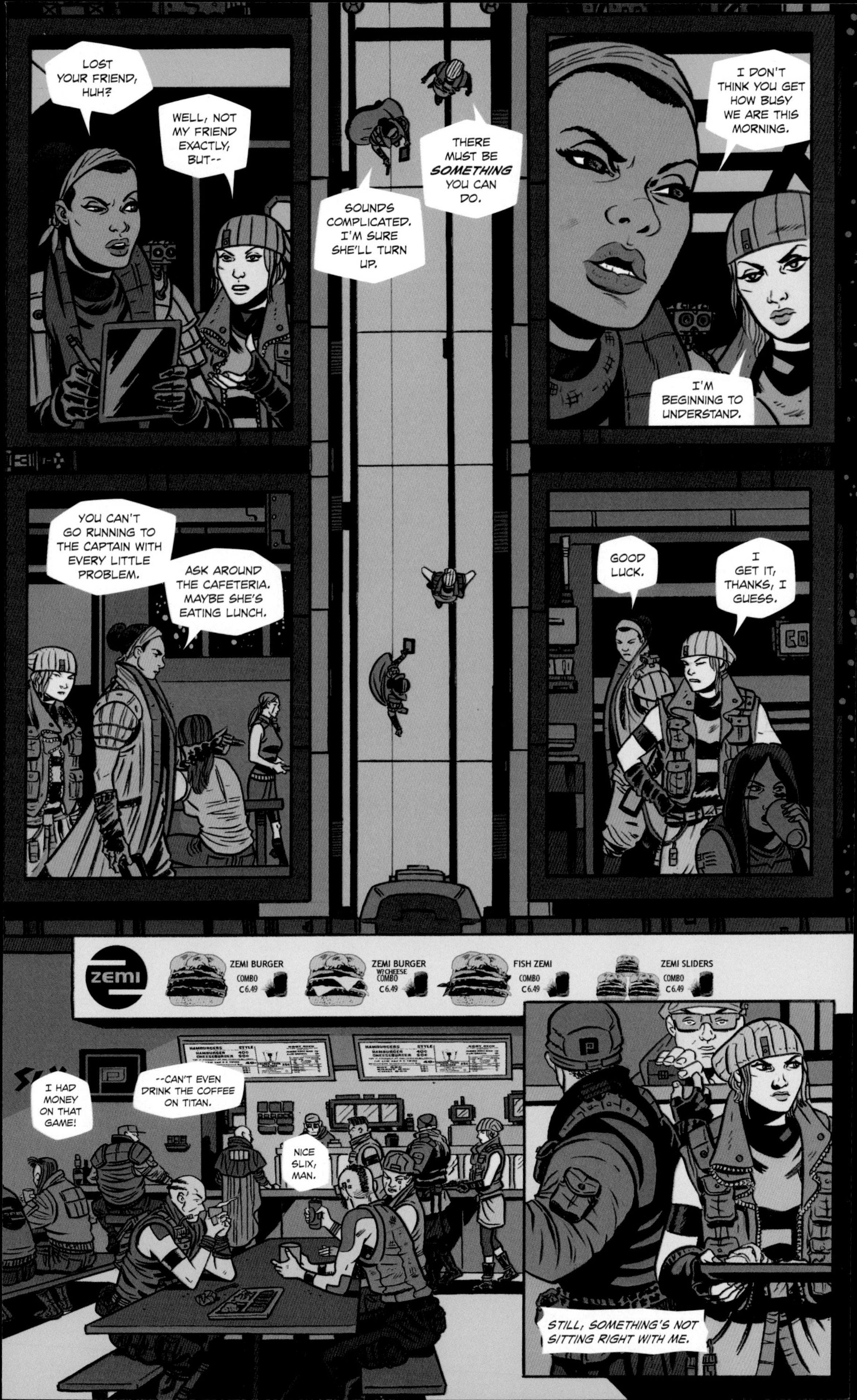
LOST YOUR FRIEND, HUH?
WELL, NOT MY FRIEND EXACTLY, BUT--
SOUNDS COMPLICATED. I'M SURE SHE'LL TURN UP.
THERE MUST BE ***SOMETHING*** YOU CAN DO.
I DON'T THINK YOU GET HOW BUSY WE ARE THIS MORNING.
I'M BEGINNING TO UNDERSTAND.
YOU CAN'T GO RUNNING TO THE CAPTAIN WITH EVERY LITTLE PROBLEM.
ASK AROUND THE CAFETERIA. MAYBE SHE'S EATING LUNCH.
GOOD LUCK.
I GET IT, THANKS, I GUESS.
ZEMI
ZEMI BURGER
COMBO
C6.49
ZEMI BURGER
W/ CHEESE
COMBO
C6.49
FISH ZEMI
COMBO
C6.49
ZEMI SLIDERS
COMBO
C6.49
I HAD MONEY ON THAT GAME!
--CAN'T EVEN DRINK THE COFFEE ON TITAN.
NICE SLIX, MAN.
STILL, SOMETHING'S NOT SITTING RIGHT WITH ME.

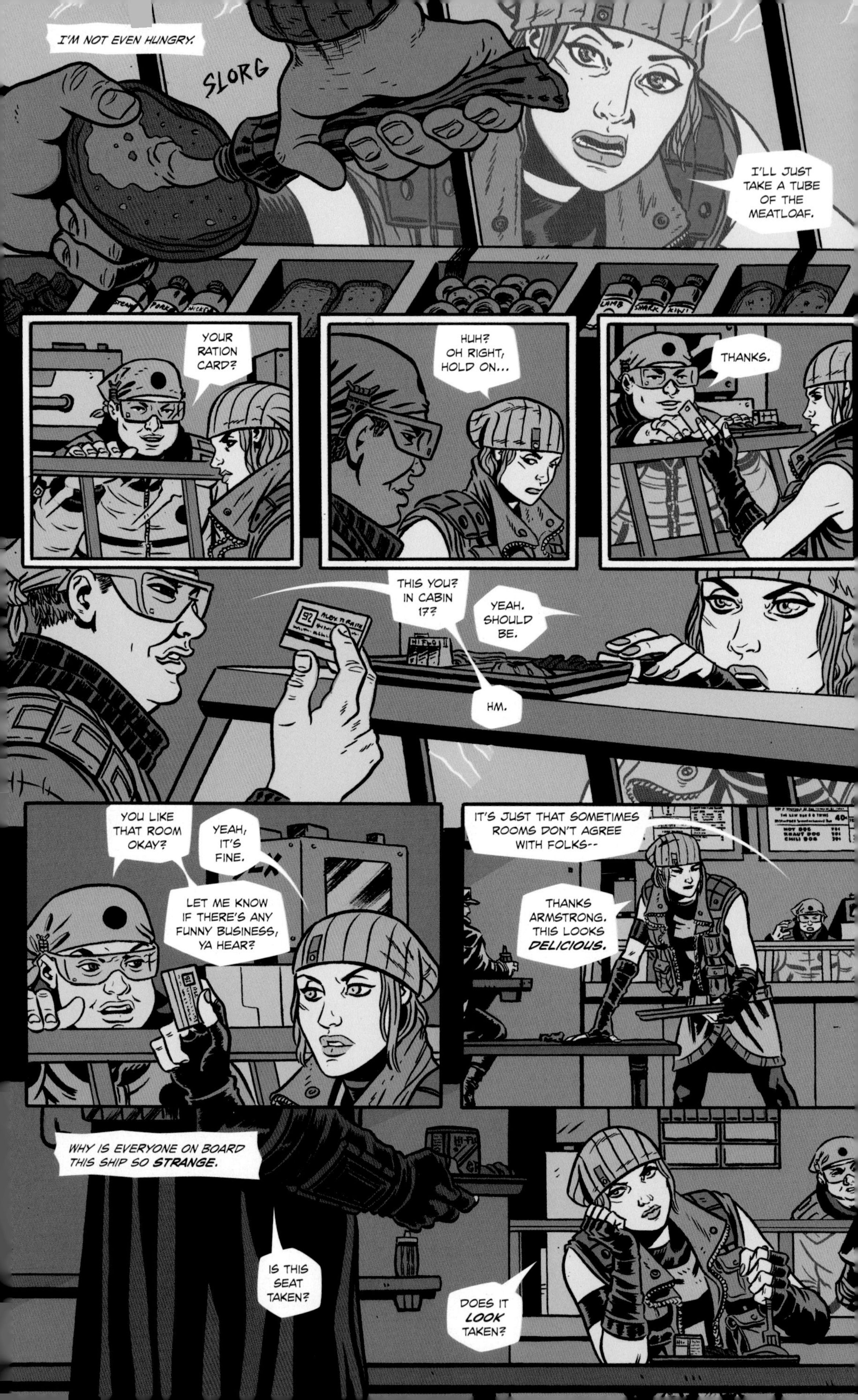

I'M NOT EVEN HUNGRY.
SLORG
I'LL JUST TAKE A TUBE OF THE MEATLOAF.
YOUR RATION CARD?
HUH? OH RIGHT, HOLD ON...
THANKS.
THIS YOU? IN CABIN 17?
YEAH. SHOULD BE.
HM.
YOU LIKE THAT ROOM OKAY?
YEAH, IT'S FINE.
LET ME KNOW IF THERE'S ANY FUNNY BUSINESS, YA HEAR?
IT'S JUST THAT SOMETIMES ROOMS DON'T AGREE WITH FOLKS--
THANKS ARMSTRONG. THIS LOOKS ***DELICIOUS.***
WHY IS EVERYONE ON BOARD THIS SHIP SO **STRANGE.**
IS THIS SEAT TAKEN?
DOES IT ***LOOK*** TAKEN?

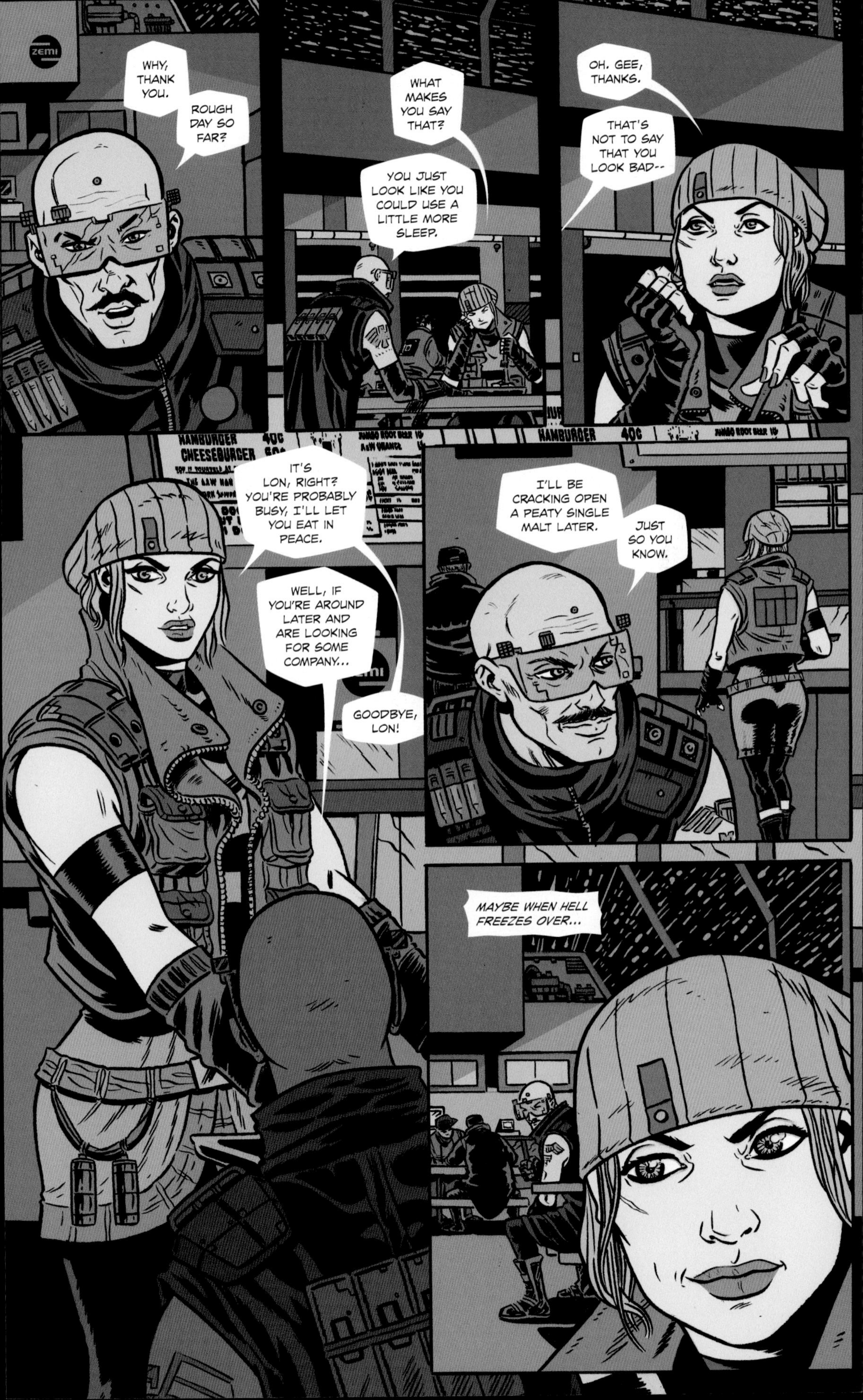
ZEMI
WHY, THANK YOU.
ROUGH DAY SO FAR?
WHAT MAKES YOU SAY THAT?
YOU JUST LOOK LIKE YOU COULD USE A LITTLE MORE SLEEP.
OH. GEE, THANKS.
THAT'S NOT TO SAY THAT YOU LOOK BAD--
HAMBURGER 40¢
CHEESEBURGER
IT'S LON, RIGHT? YOU'RE PROBABLY BUSY, I'LL LET YOU EAT IN PEACE.
WELL, IF YOU'RE AROUND LATER AND ARE LOOKING FOR SOME COMPANY...
GOODBYE, LON!
I'LL BE CRACKING OPEN A PEATY SINGLE MALT LATER.
JUST SO YOU KNOW.
MAYBE WHEN HELL FREEZES OVER...

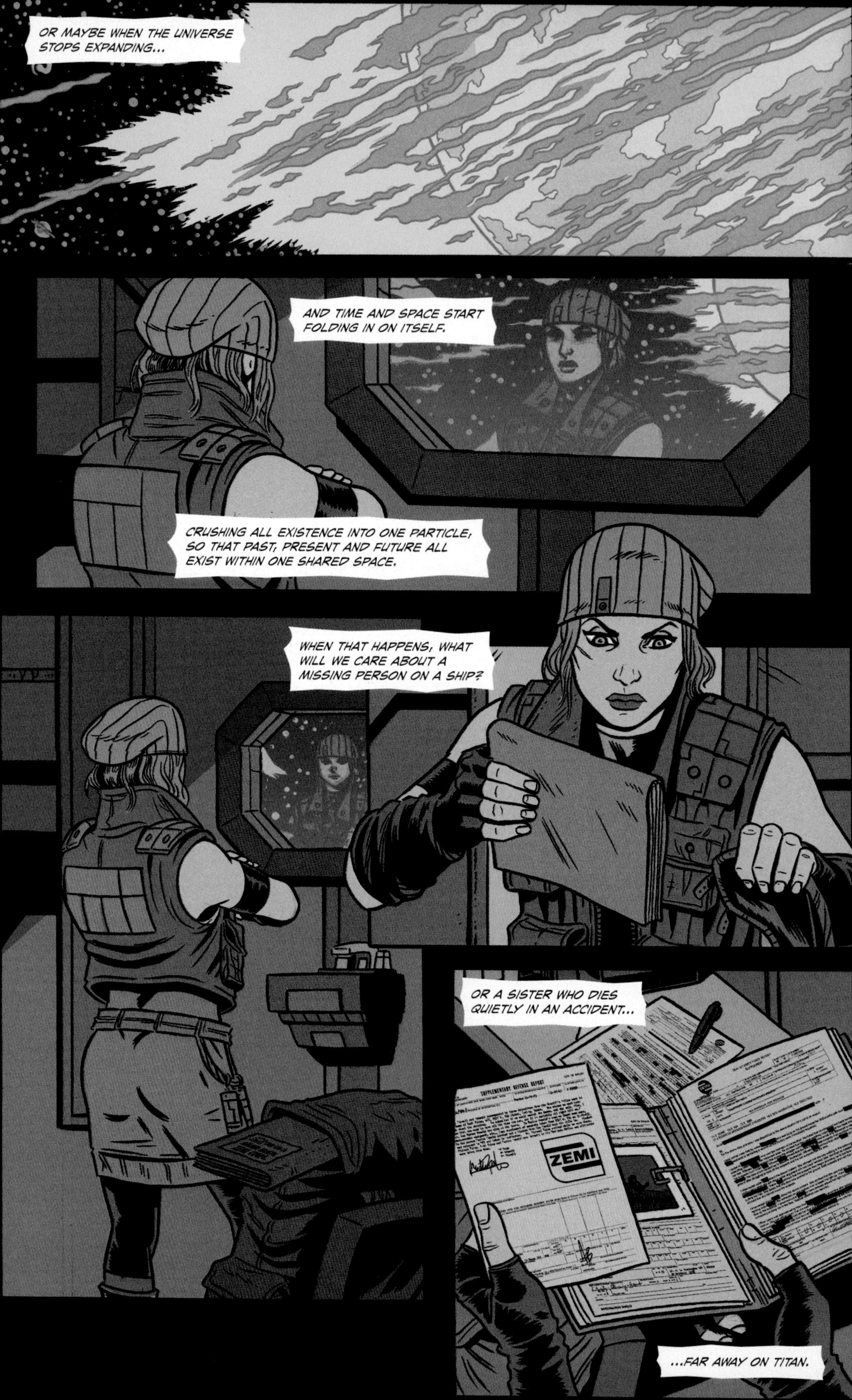
OR MAYBE WHEN THE UNIVERSE STOPS EXPANDING...
AND TIME AND SPACE START FOLDING IN ON ITSELF.
CRUSHING ALL EXISTENCE INTO ONE PARTICLE, SO THAT PAST, PRESENT AND FUTURE ALL EXIST WITHIN ONE SHARED SPACE.
WHEN THAT HAPPENS, WHAT WILL WE CARE ABOUT A MISSING PERSON ON A SHIP?
OR A SISTER WHO DIES QUIETLY IN AN ACCIDENT...
ZEMI
...FAR AWAY ON TITAN.

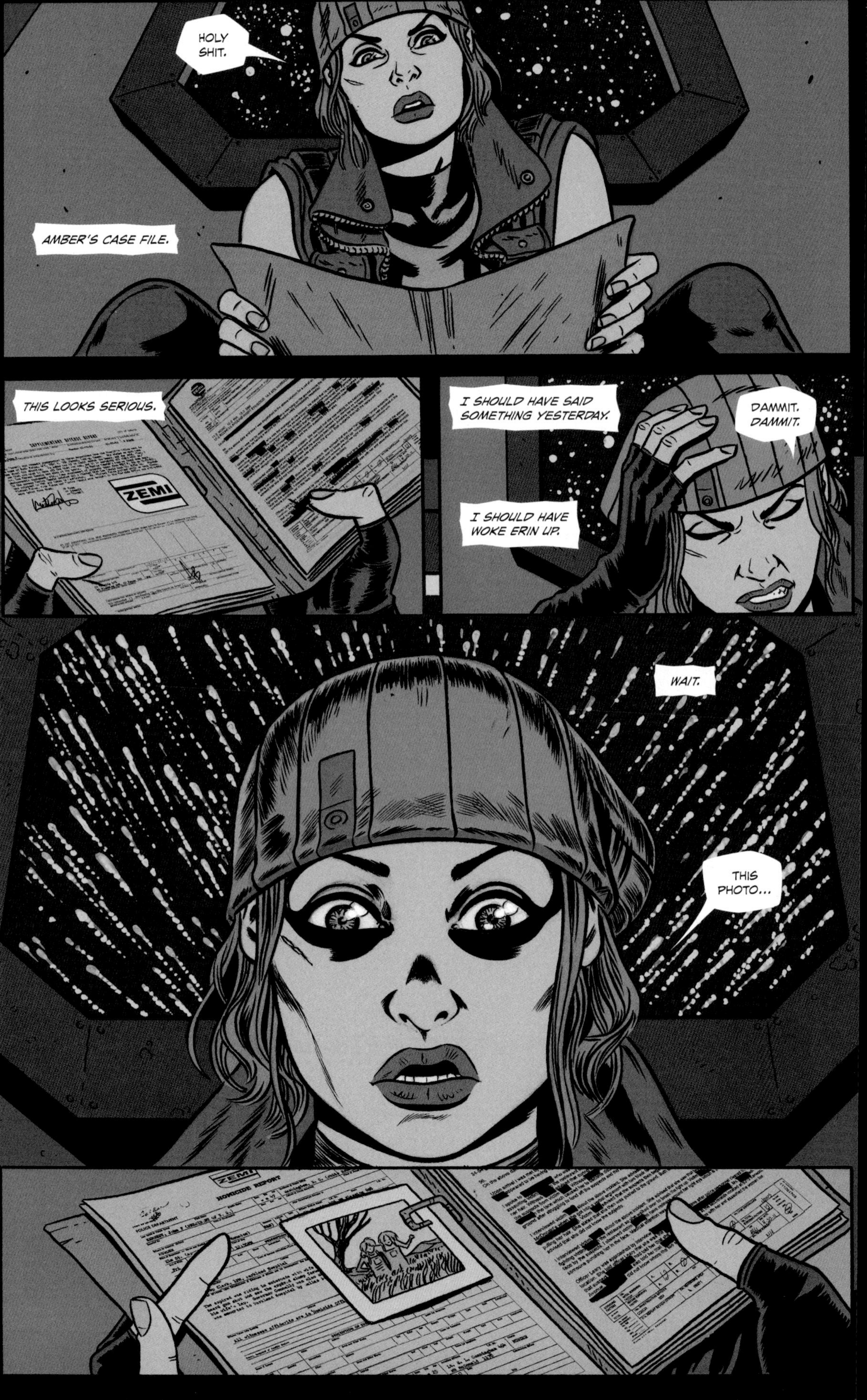
HOLY SHIT.
AMBER'S CASE FILE.
THIS LOOKS SERIOUS.
ZEMI
I SHOULD HAVE SAID SOMETHING YESTERDAY.
DAMMIT. DAMMIT.
I SHOULD HAVE WOKE ERIN UP.
WAIT.
THIS PHOTO...

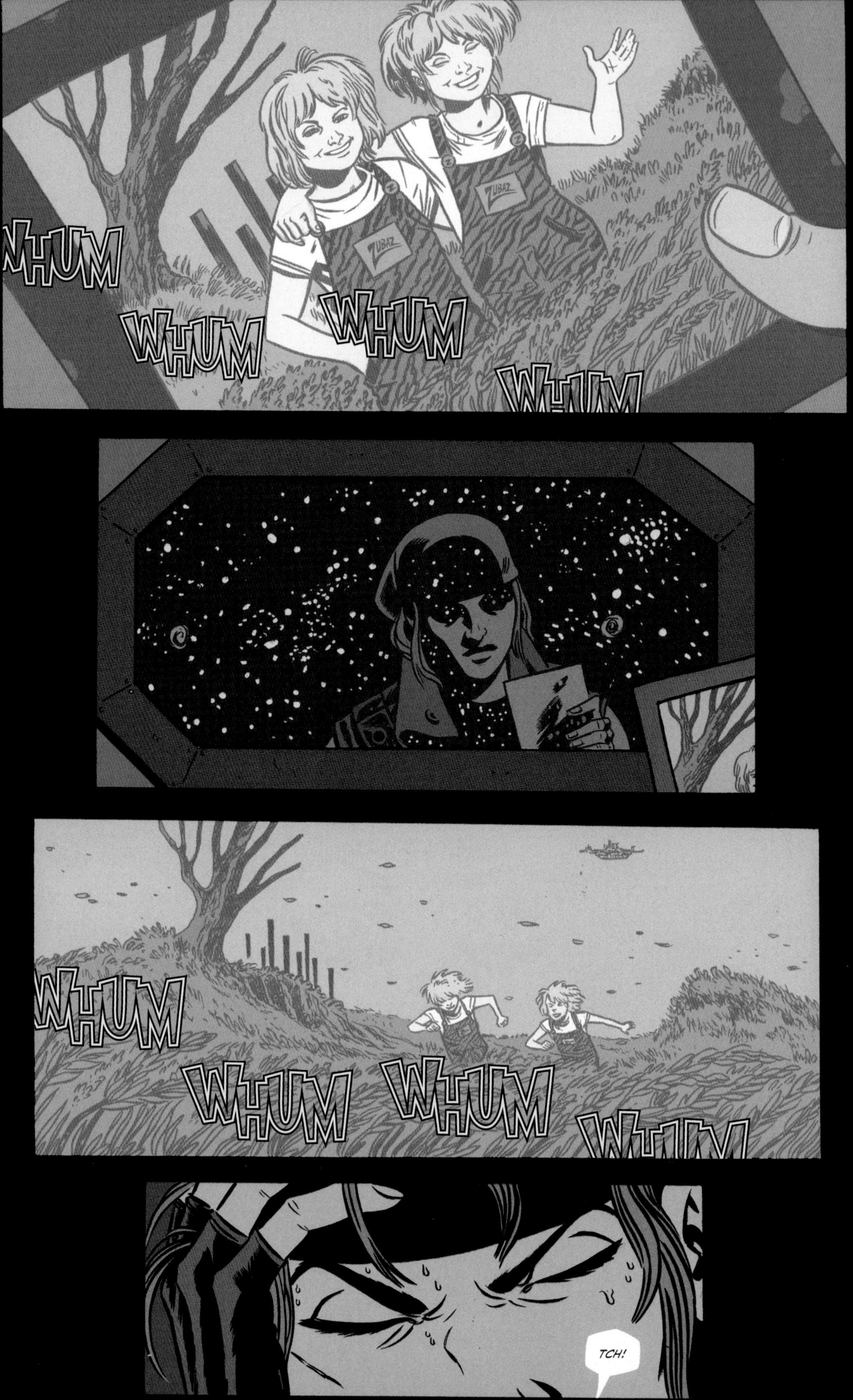
WHUM
WHUM
WHUM
WHUM
WHUM
WHUM
WHUM
TCH!

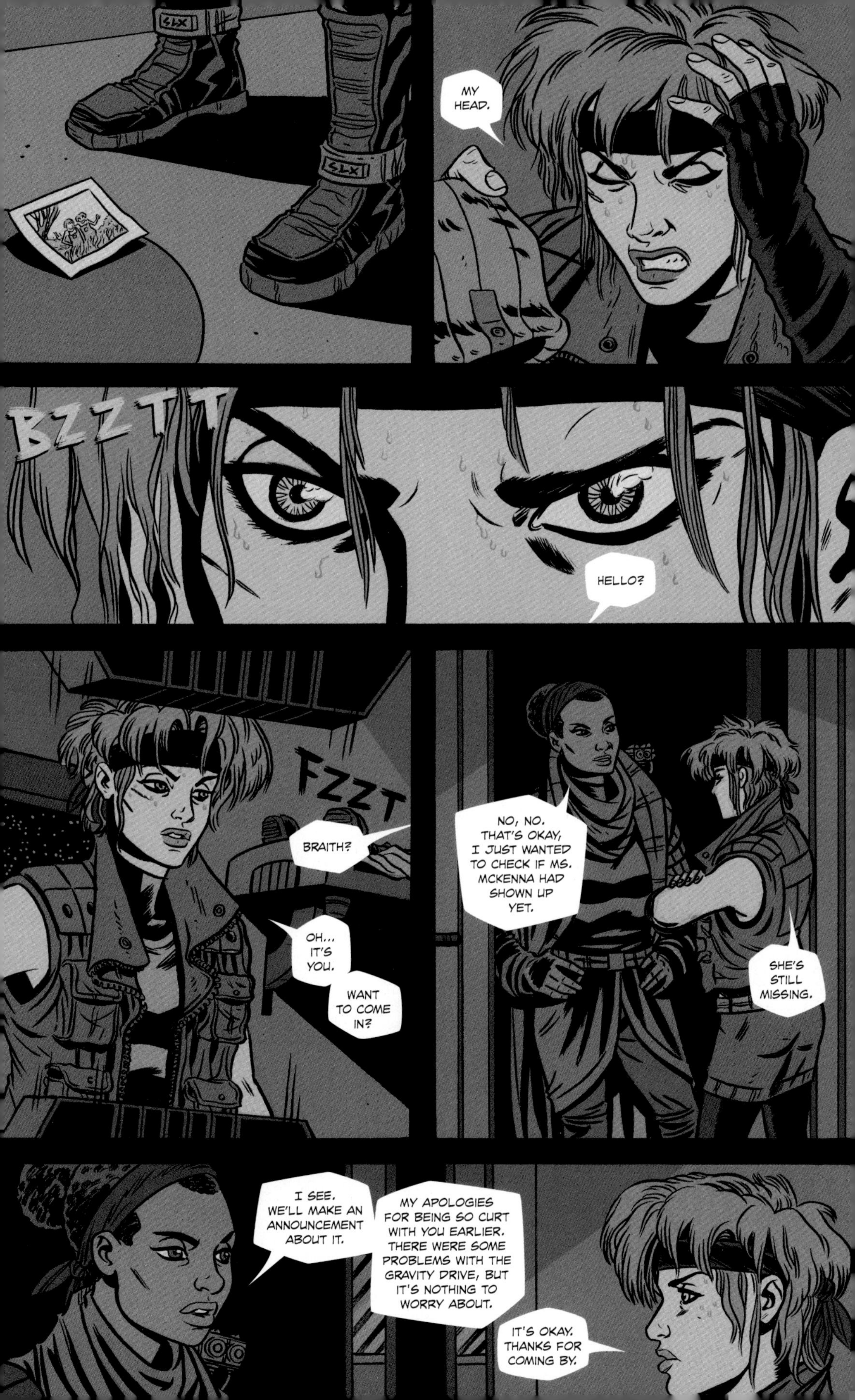
SLX
SLX
MY HEAD.
BZZTT
HELLO?
FZZT
BRAITH?
OH... IT'S YOU.
WANT TO COME IN?
NO, NO. THAT'S OKAY, I JUST WANTED TO CHECK IF MS. MCKENNA HAD SHOWN UP YET.
SHE'S STILL MISSING.
I SEE. WE'LL MAKE AN ANNOUNCEMENT ABOUT IT.
MY APOLOGIES FOR BEING SO CURT WITH YOU EARLIER. THERE WERE SOME PROBLEMS WITH THE GRAVITY DRIVE, BUT IT'S NOTHING TO WORRY ABOUT.
IT'S OKAY. THANKS FOR COMING BY.

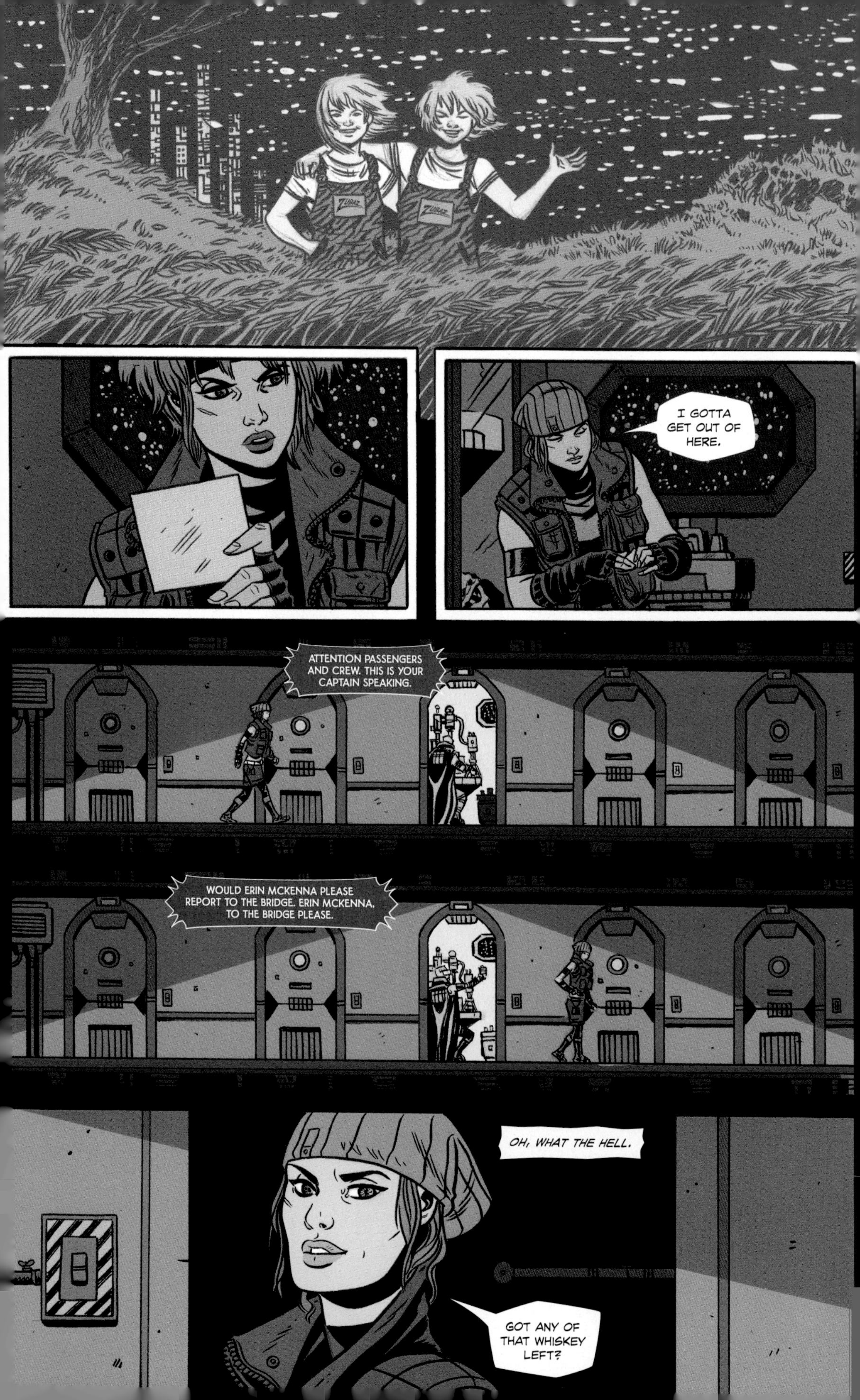
I GOTTA GET OUT OF HERE.
ATTENTION PASSENGERS AND CREW. THIS IS YOUR CAPTAIN SPEAKING.
WOULD ERIN MCKENNA PLEASE REPORT TO THE BRIDGE. ERIN MCKENNA, TO THE BRIDGE PLEASE.
OH, WHAT THE HELL.
GOT ANY OF THAT WHISKEY LEFT?

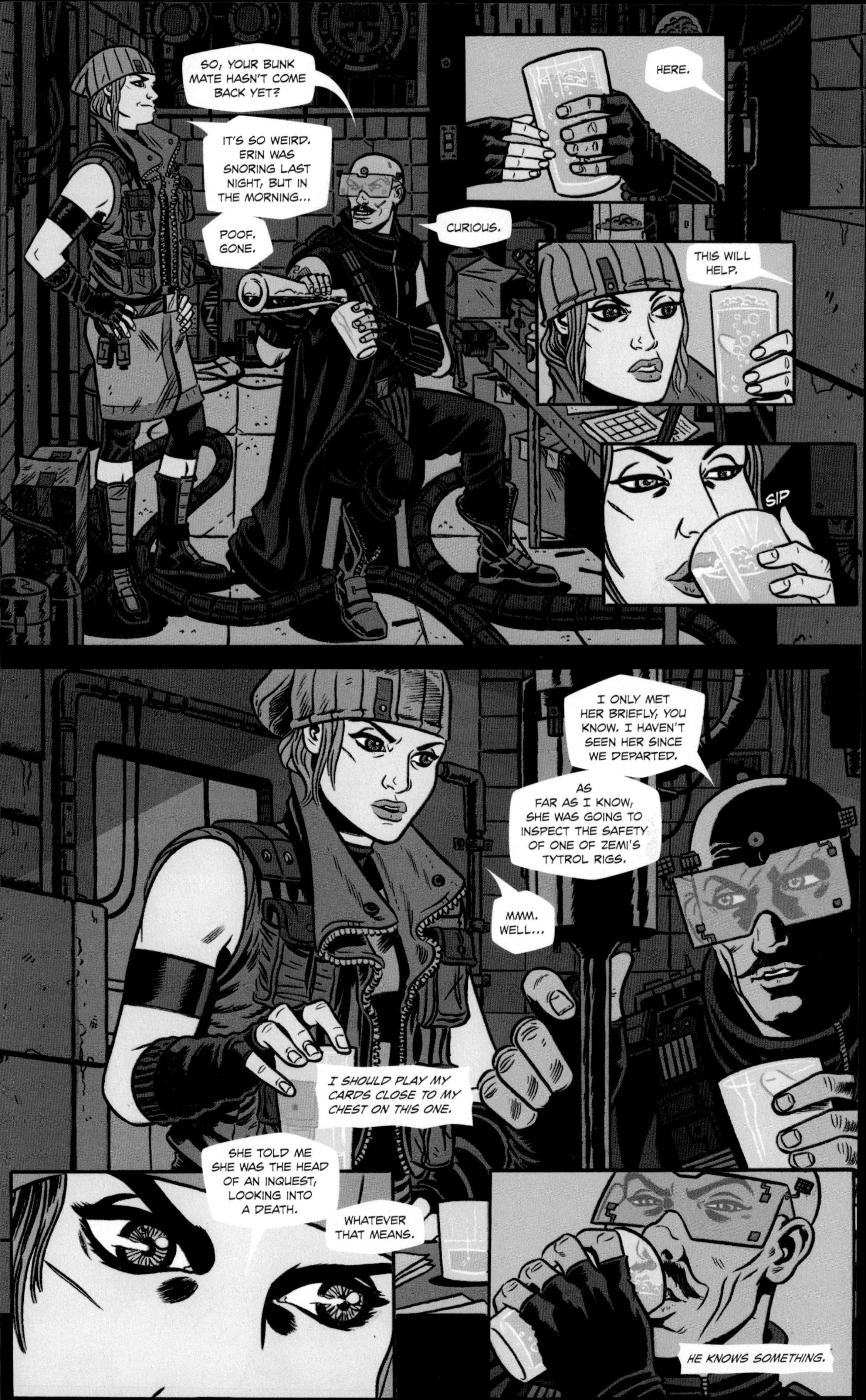
SO, YOUR BUNK MATE HASN'T COME BACK YET?
IT'S SO WEIRD. ERIN WAS SNORING LAST NIGHT, BUT IN THE MORNING...
POOF. GONE.
CURIOUS.
HERE.
THIS WILL HELP.
SIP
I ONLY MET HER BRIEFLY, YOU KNOW. I HAVEN'T SEEN HER SINCE WE DEPARTED.
AS FAR AS I KNOW, SHE WAS GOING TO INSPECT THE SAFETY OF ONE OF ZEMI'S TYTROL RIGS.
MMM. WELL...
I SHOULD PLAY MY CARDS CLOSE TO MY CHEST ON THIS ONE.
SHE TOLD ME SHE WAS THE HEAD OF AN INQUEST, LOOKING INTO A DEATH.
WHATEVER THAT MEANS.
HE KNOWS SOMETHING.

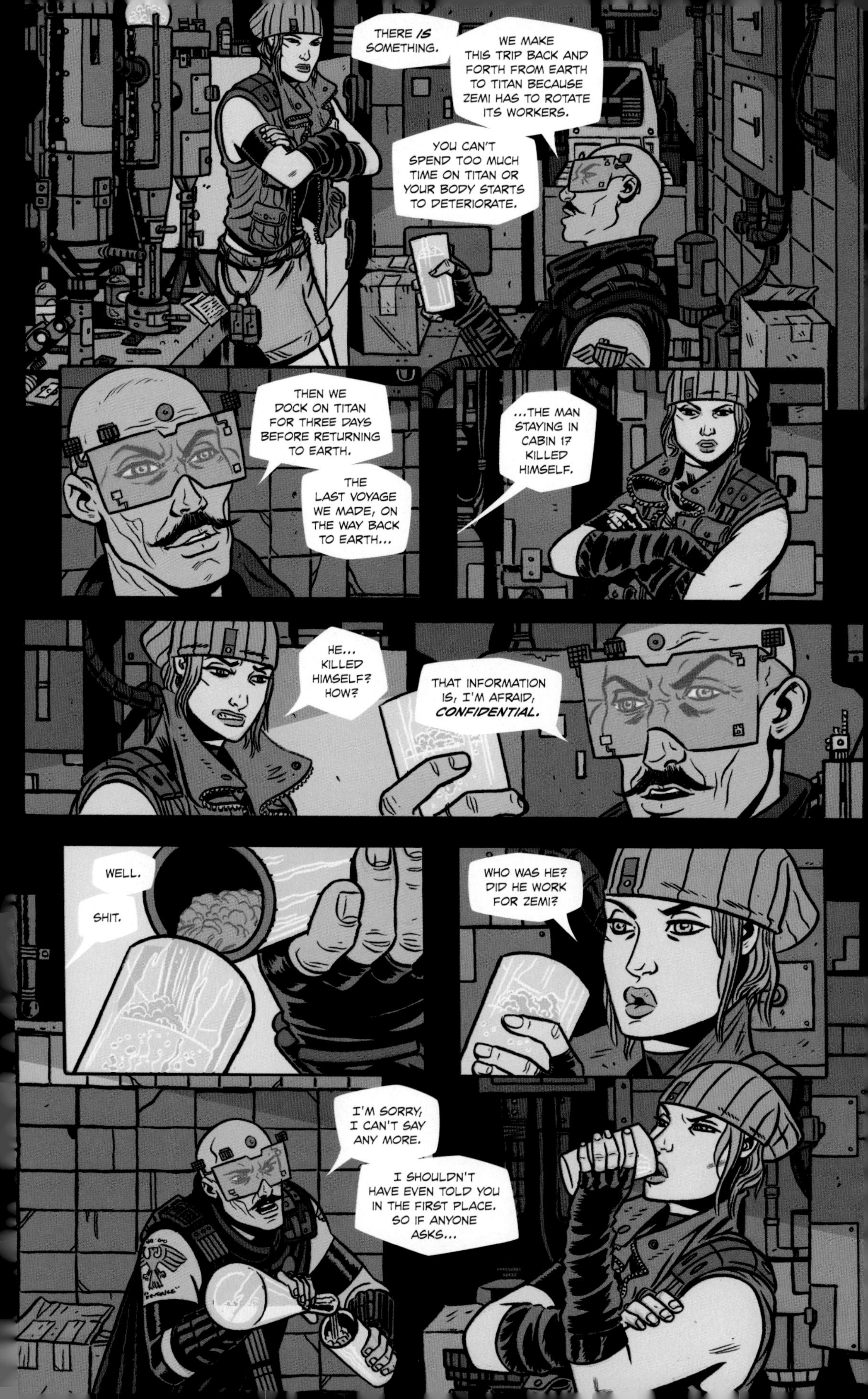
THERE *IS* SOMETHING.
WE MAKE THIS TRIP BACK AND FORTH FROM EARTH TO TITAN BECAUSE ZEMI HAS TO ROTATE ITS WORKERS.
YOU CAN'T SPEND TOO MUCH TIME ON TITAN OR YOUR BODY STARTS TO DETERIORATE.
THEN WE DOCK ON TITAN FOR THREE DAYS BEFORE RETURNING TO EARTH.
THE LAST VOYAGE WE MADE, ON THE WAY BACK TO EARTH...
...THE MAN STAYING IN CABIN 17 KILLED HIMSELF.
HE... KILLED HIMSELF? HOW?
THAT INFORMATION IS, I'M AFRAID, ***CONFIDENTIAL.***
WELL.
SHIT.
WHO WAS HE? DID HE WORK FOR ZEMI?
I'M SORRY, I CAN'T SAY ANY MORE.
I SHOULDN'T HAVE EVEN TOLD YOU IN THE FIRST PLACE. SO IF ANYONE ASKS...

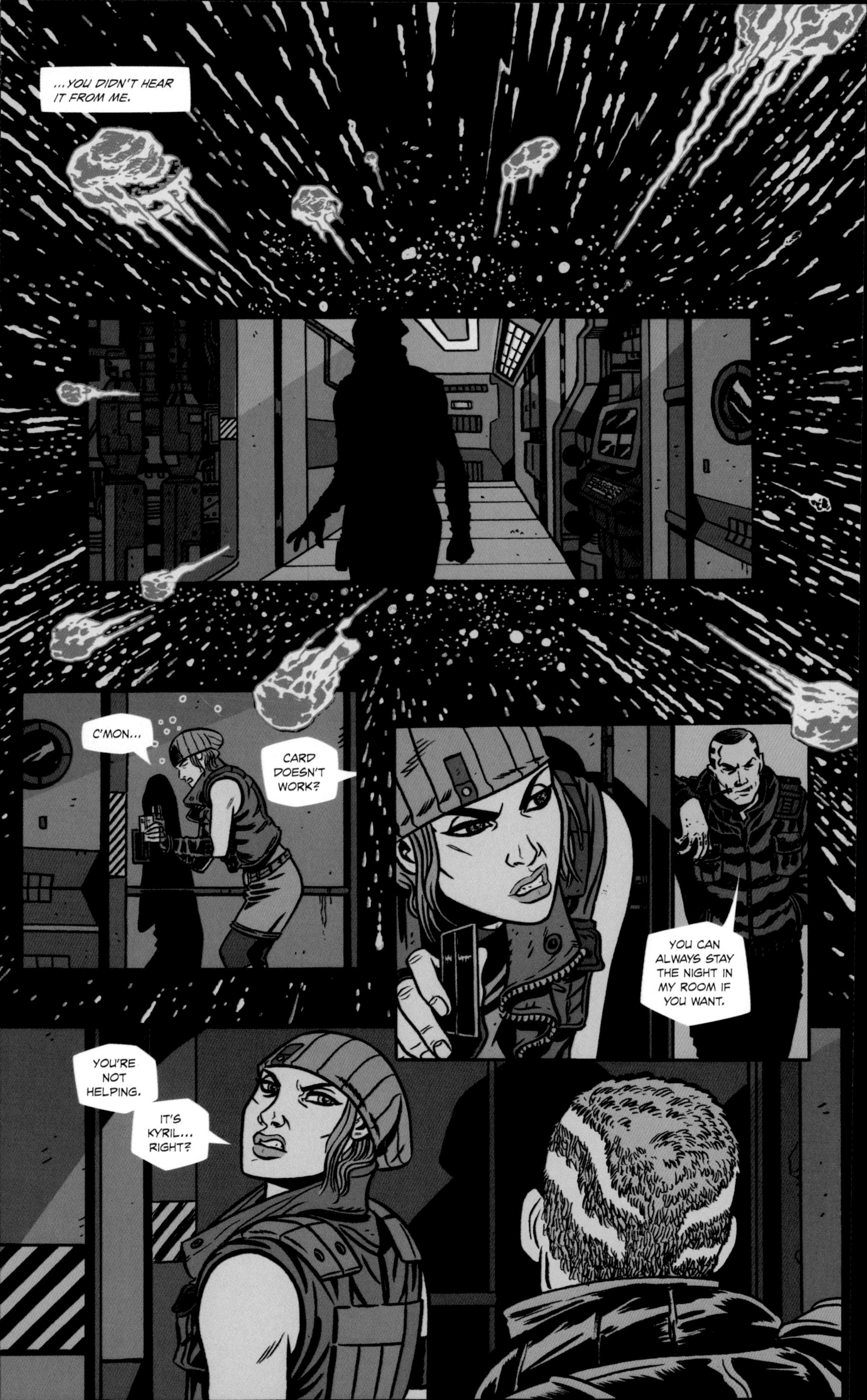
...YOU DIDN'T HEAR IT FROM ME.
C'MON...
CARD DOESN'T WORK?
YOU CAN ALWAYS STAY THE NIGHT IN MY ROOM IF YOU WANT.
YOU'RE NOT HELPING.
IT'S KYRIL... RIGHT?

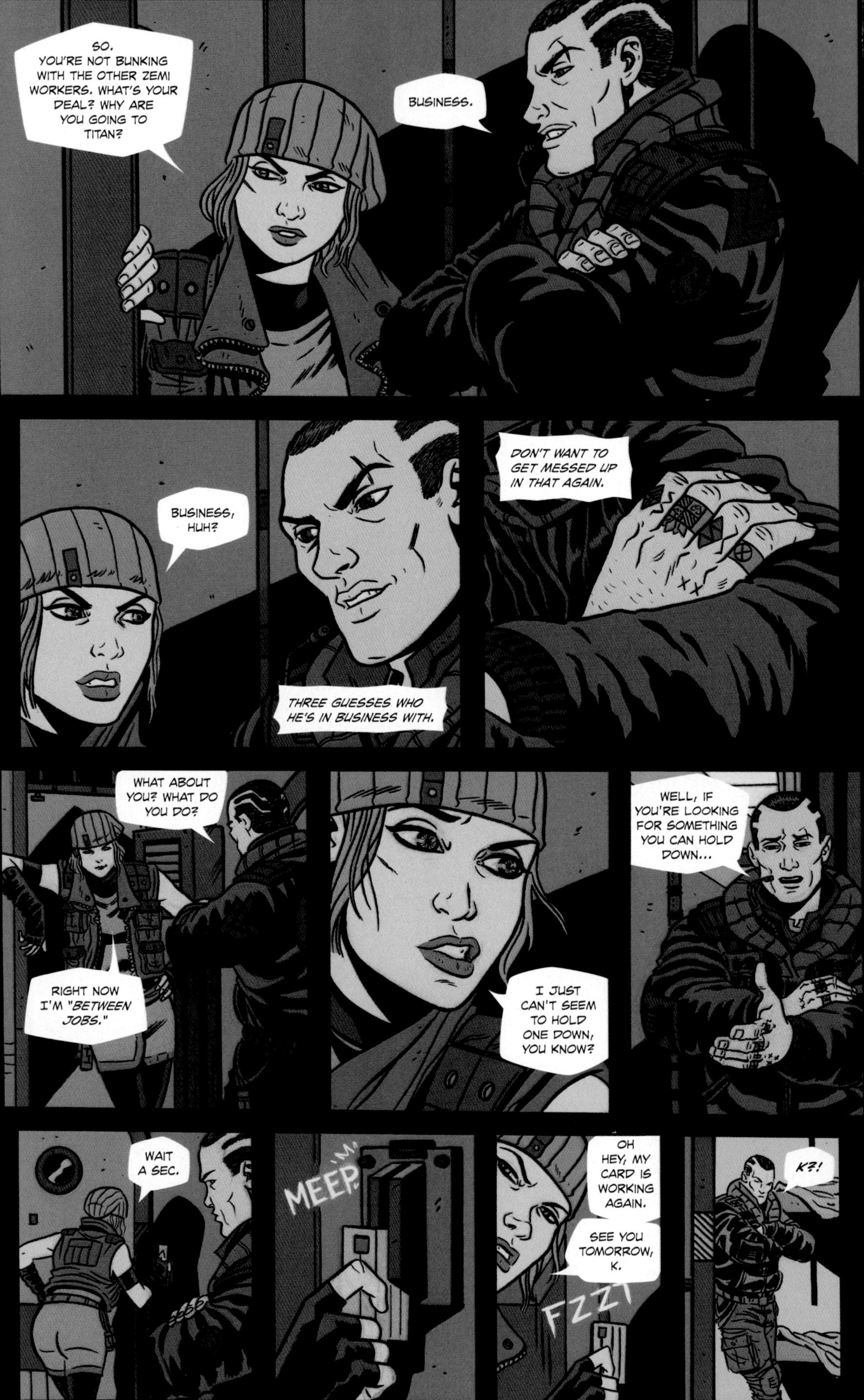
SO. YOU'RE NOT BUNKING WITH THE OTHER ZEMI WORKERS. WHAT'S YOUR DEAL? WHY ARE YOU GOING TO TITAN?
BUSINESS.
BUSINESS, HUH?
THREE GUESSES WHO HE'S IN BUSINESS WITH.
DON'T WANT TO GET MESSED UP IN THAT AGAIN.
WHAT ABOUT YOU? WHAT DO YOU DO?
RIGHT NOW I'M "BETWEEN JOBS."
I JUST CAN'T SEEM TO HOLD ONE DOWN, YOU KNOW?
WELL, IF YOU'RE LOOKING FOR SOMETHING YOU CAN HOLD DOWN...
WAIT A SEC.
MEEP
OH HEY, MY CARD IS WORKING AGAIN.
SEE YOU TOMORROW, K.
FZZT
K?!

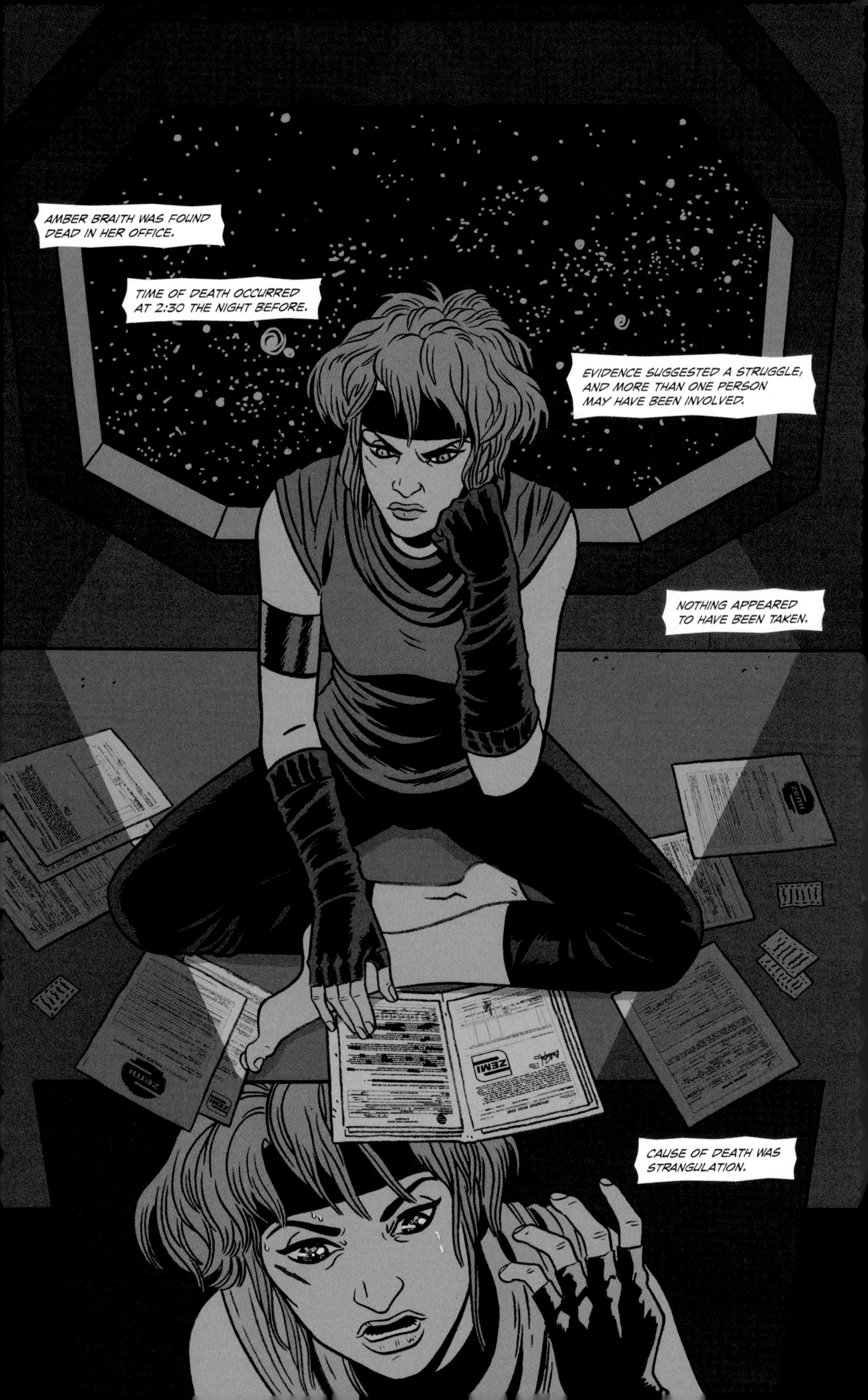
AMBER BRAITH WAS FOUND DEAD IN HER OFFICE.
TIME OF DEATH OCCURRED AT 2:30 THE NIGHT BEFORE.
EVIDENCE SUGGESTED A STRUGGLE, AND MORE THAN ONE PERSON MAY HAVE BEEN INVOLVED.
NOTHING APPEARED TO HAVE BEEN TAKEN.
CAUSE OF DEATH WAS STRANGULATION.

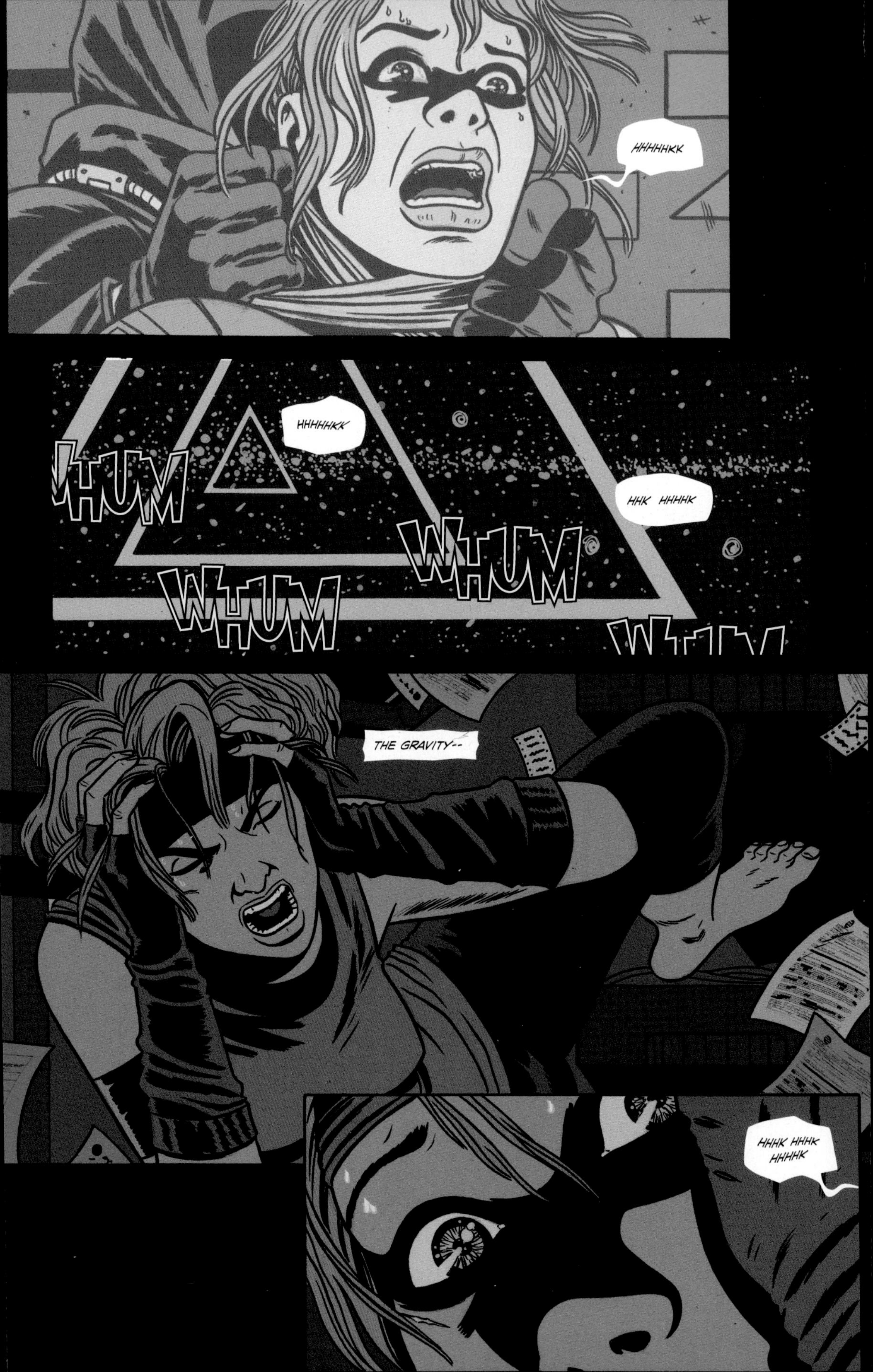
HHHHHKK
HHHHHKK
WHUM
HHK HHHHK
WHUM
WHUM
THE GRAVITY--
HHHK HHHK
HHHHK

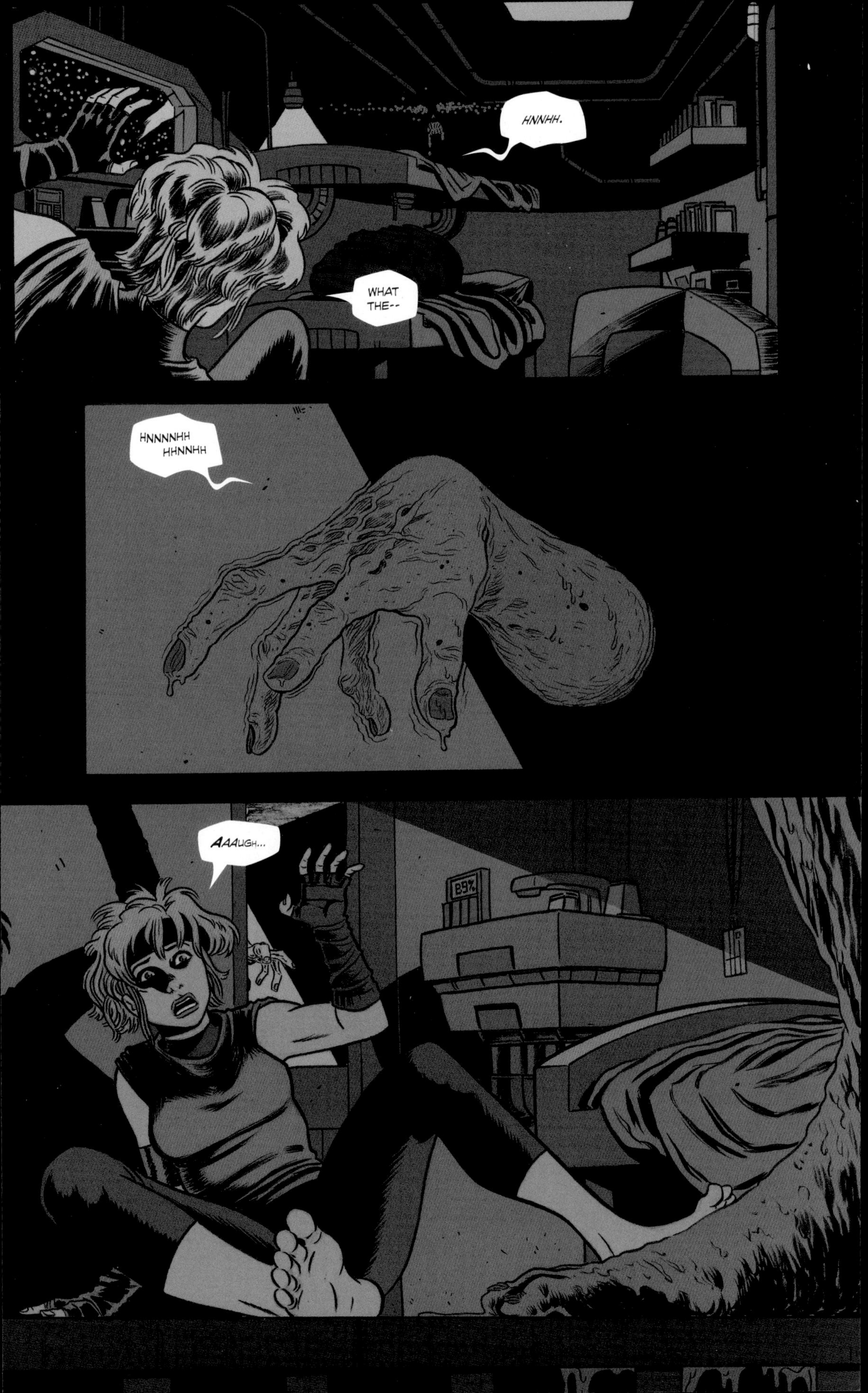

HNNHH.
WHAT THE--
HNNNNHH HHNNHH
AAAUGH...
89%

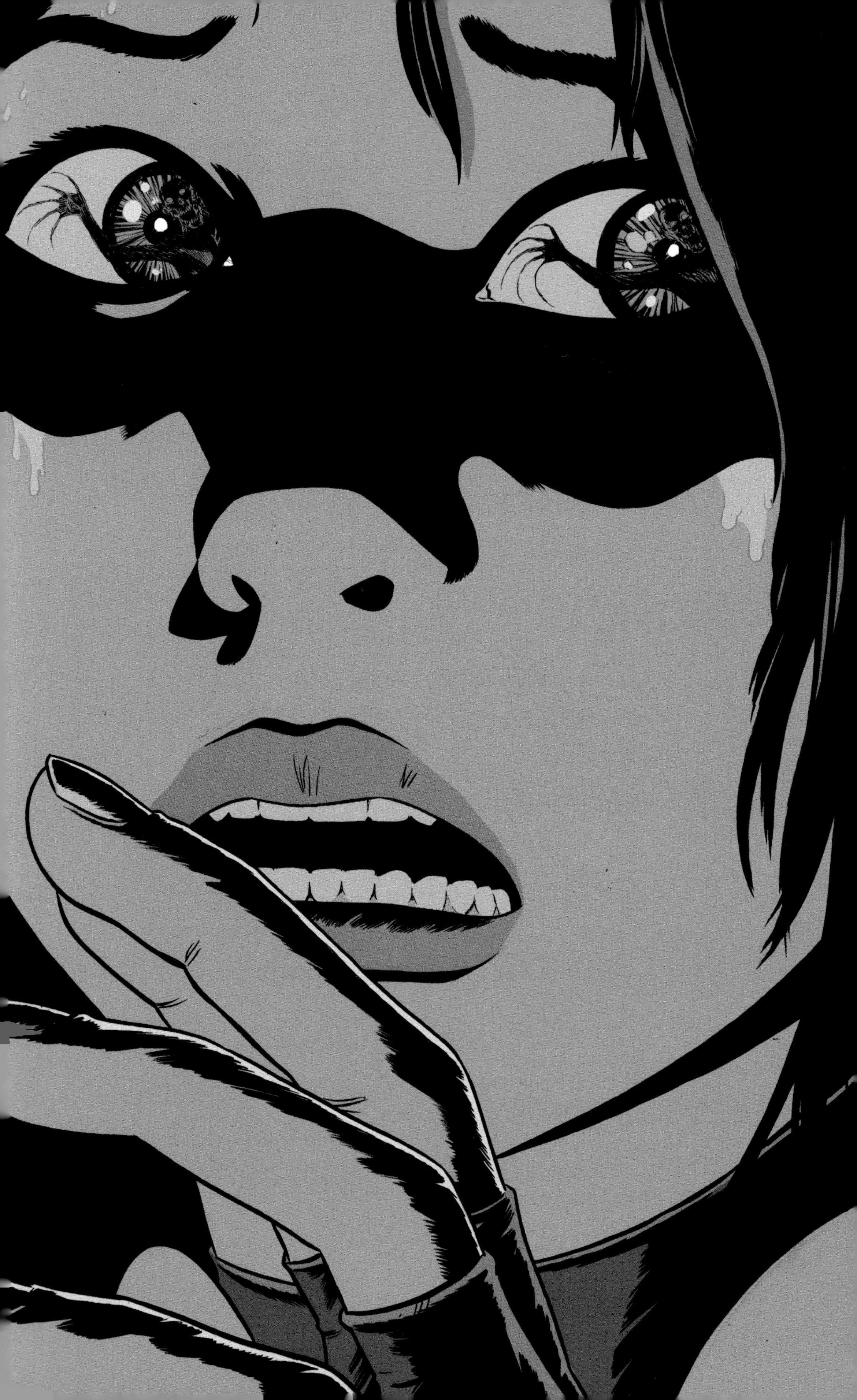

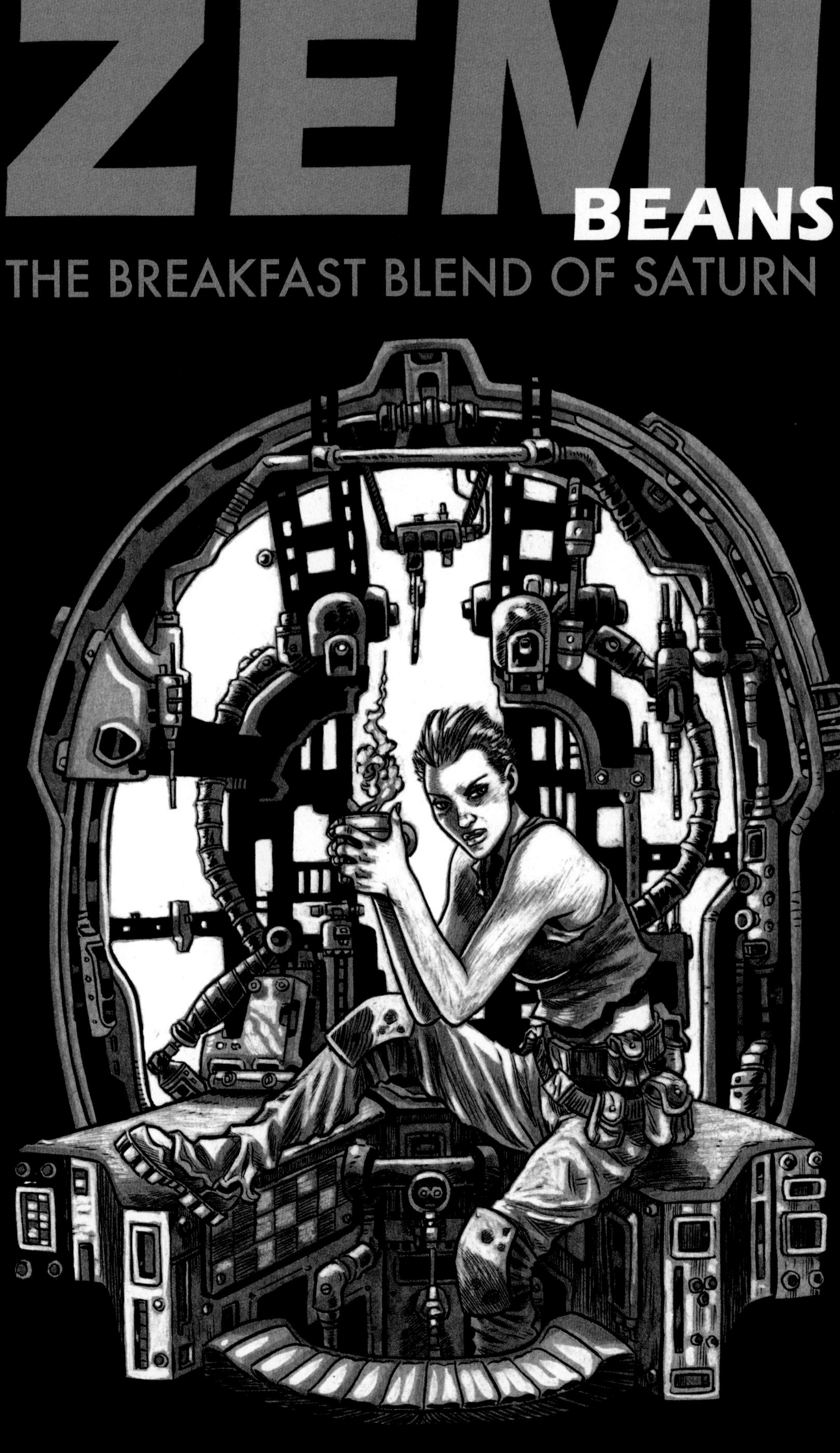
ZEMI
BEANS
THE BREAKFAST BLEND OF SATURN

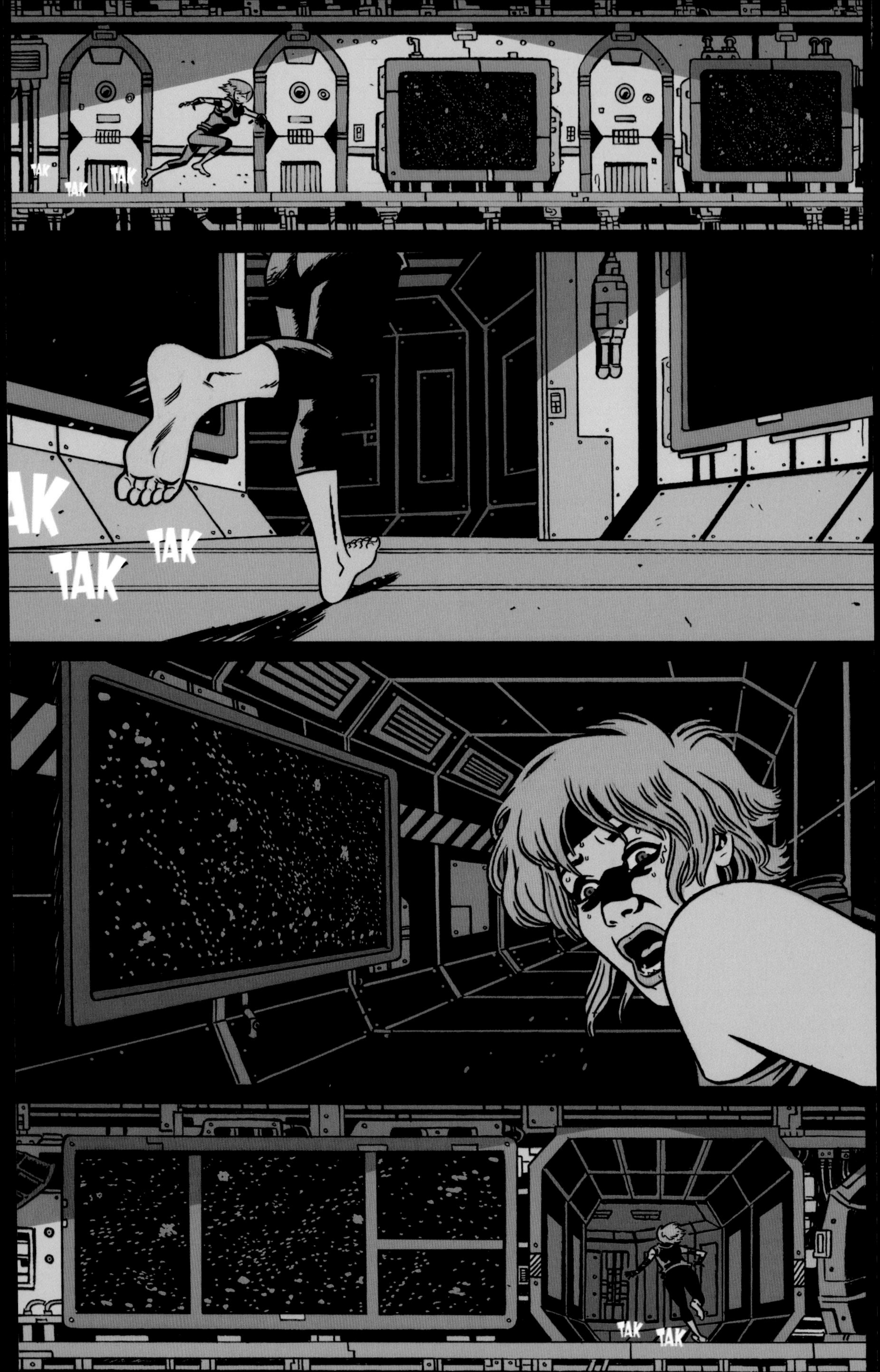

TAK
TAK
TAK
TAK
TAK
TAK
TAK
TAK

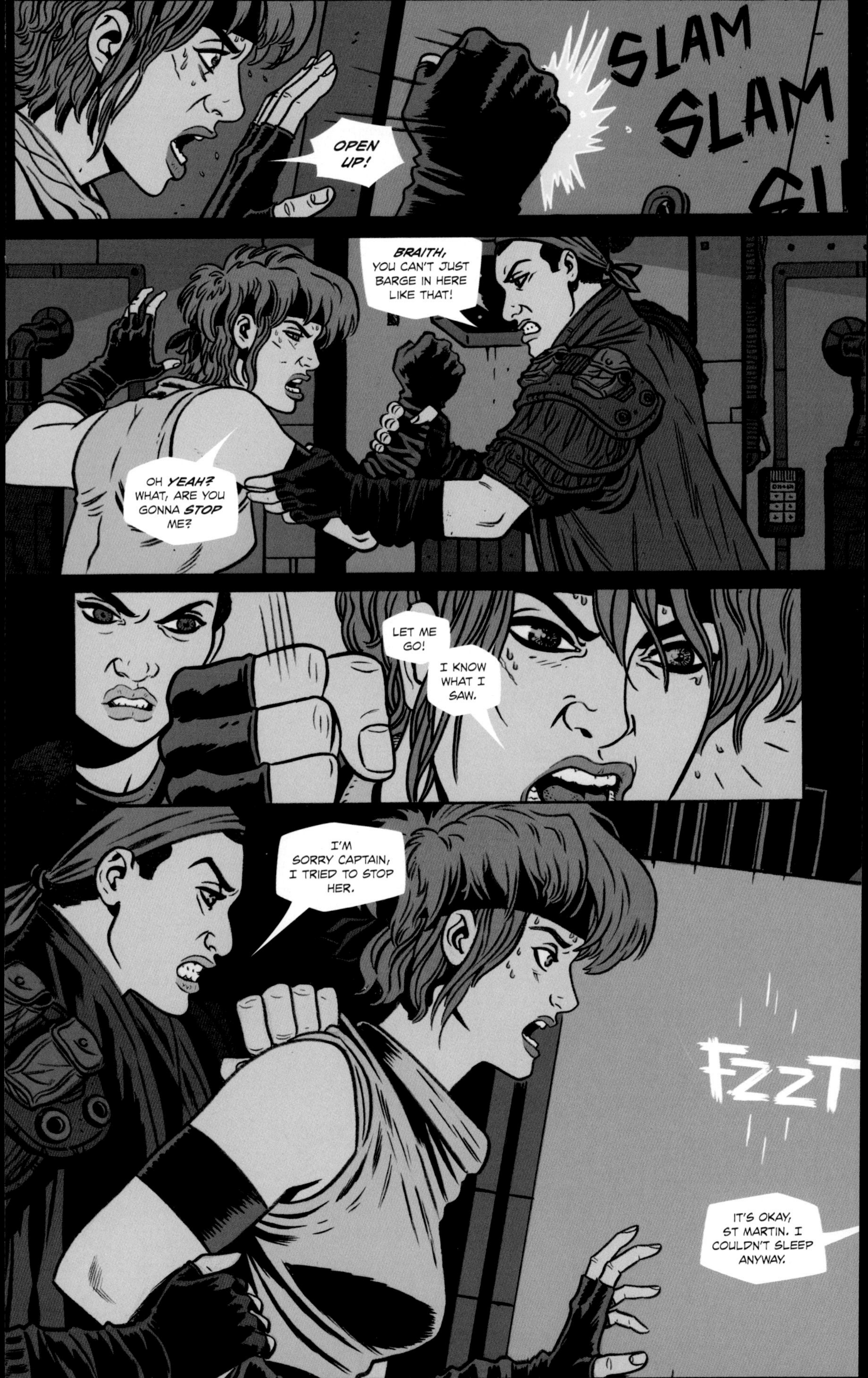
SLAM
SLAM
OPEN UP!
BRAITH, YOU CAN'T JUST BARGE IN HERE LIKE THAT!
OH YEAH? WHAT, ARE YOU GONNA STOP ME?
LET ME GO!
I KNOW WHAT I SAW.
I'M SORRY CAPTAIN, I TRIED TO STOP HER.
FZZT
IT'S OKAY, ST MARTIN. I COULDN'T SLEEP ANYWAY.

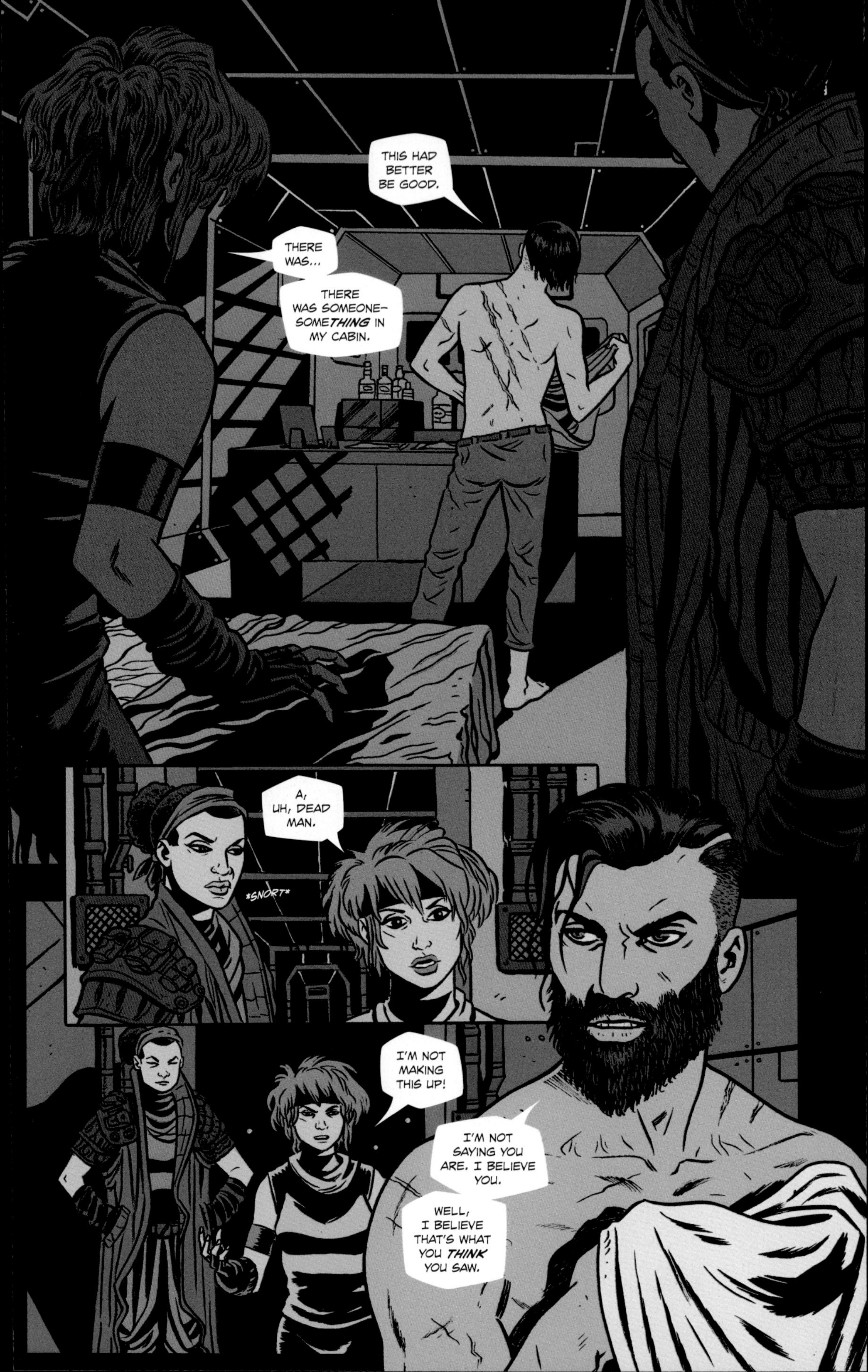
THIS HAD BETTER BE GOOD.
THERE WAS...
THERE WAS SOMEONE-SOME*THING* IN MY CABIN.
A, UH, DEAD MAN.
SNORT
I'M NOT MAKING THIS UP!
I'M NOT SAYING YOU ARE. I BELIEVE YOU.
WELL, I BELIEVE THAT'S WHAT YOU *THINK* YOU SAW.

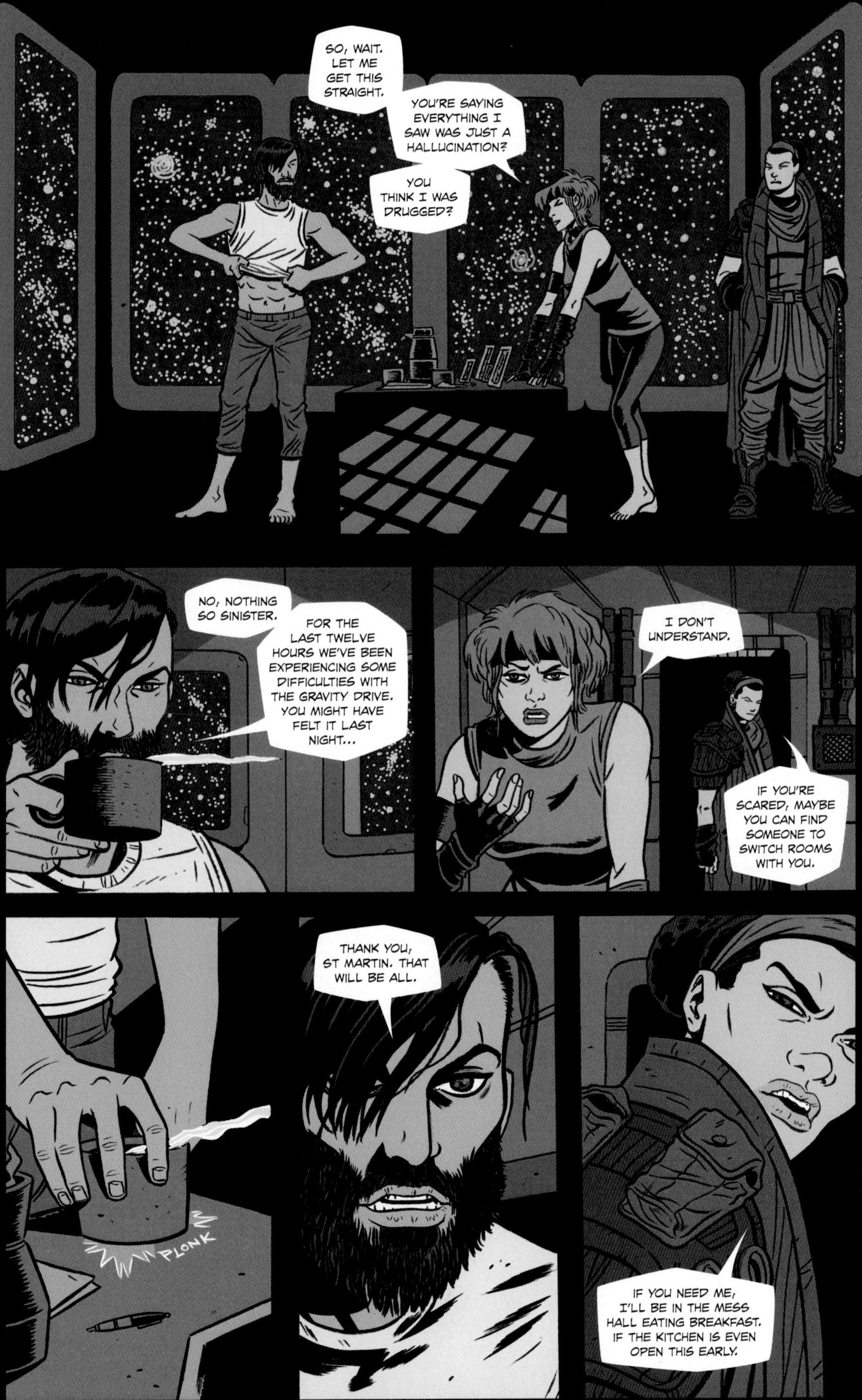
SO, WAIT. LET ME GET THIS STRAIGHT.
YOU'RE SAYING EVERYTHING I SAW WAS JUST A HALLUCINATION?
YOU THINK I WAS DRUGGED?
NO, NOTHING SO SINISTER.
FOR THE LAST TWELVE HOURS WE'VE BEEN EXPERIENCING SOME DIFFICULTIES WITH THE GRAVITY DRIVE. YOU MIGHT HAVE FELT IT LAST NIGHT...
I DON'T UNDERSTAND.
IF YOU'RE SCARED, MAYBE YOU CAN FIND SOMEONE TO SWITCH ROOMS WITH YOU.
PLONK
THANK YOU, ST MARTIN. THAT WILL BE ALL.
IF YOU NEED ME, I'LL BE IN THE MESS HALL EATING BREAKFAST. IF THE KITCHEN IS EVEN OPEN THIS EARLY.

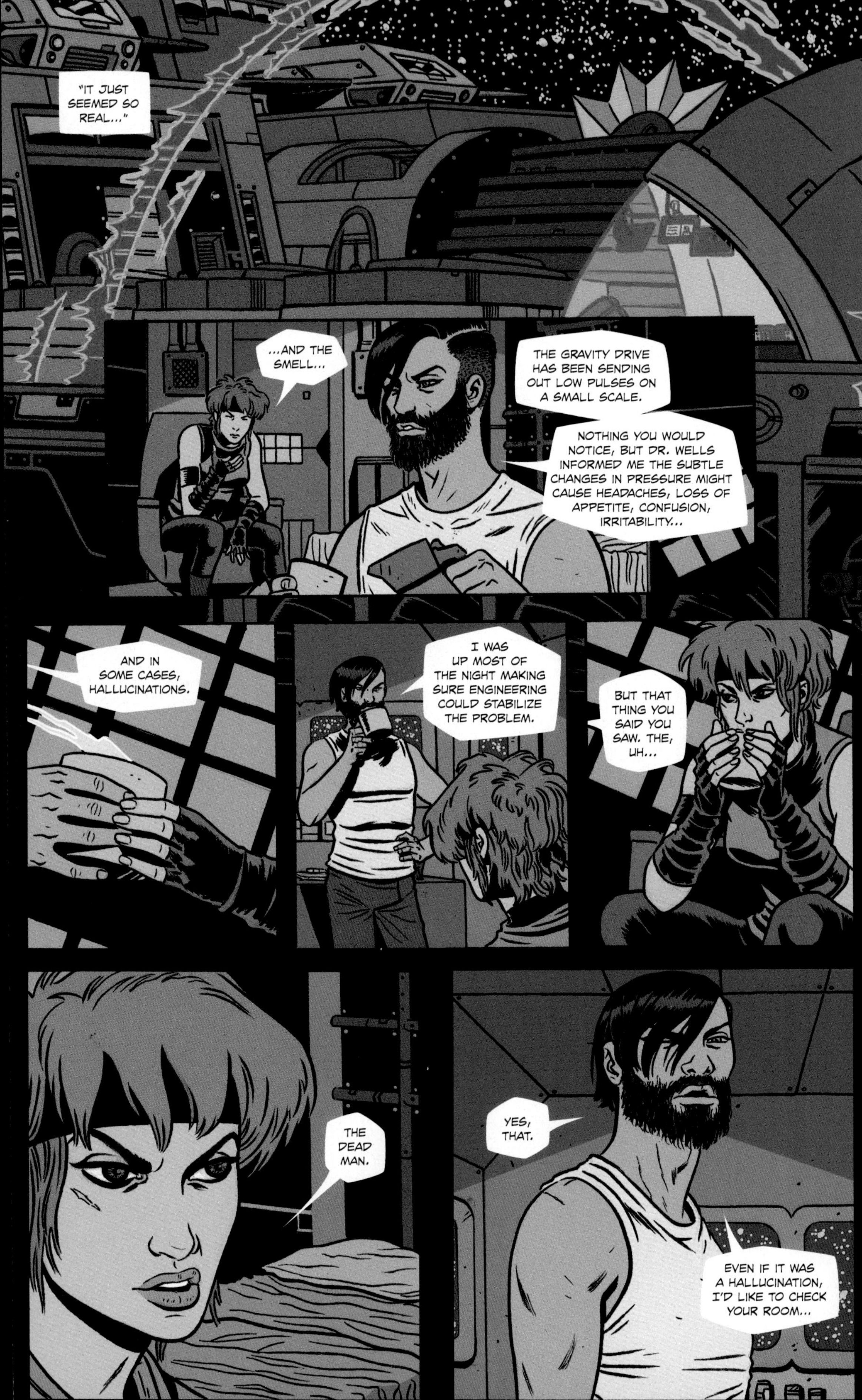
"IT JUST SEEMED SO REAL..."
...AND THE SMELL...
THE GRAVITY DRIVE HAS BEEN SENDING OUT LOW PULSES ON A SMALL SCALE.
NOTHING YOU WOULD NOTICE, BUT DR. WELLS INFORMED ME THE SUBTLE CHANGES IN PRESSURE MIGHT CAUSE HEADACHES, LOSS OF APPETITE, CONFUSION, IRRITABILITY...
AND IN SOME CASES, HALLUCINATIONS.
I WAS UP MOST OF THE NIGHT MAKING SURE ENGINEERING COULD STABILIZE THE PROBLEM.
BUT THAT THING YOU SAID YOU SAW. THE, UH...
THE DEAD MAN.
YES, THAT.
EVEN IF IT WAS A HALLUCINATION, I'D LIKE TO CHECK YOUR ROOM...

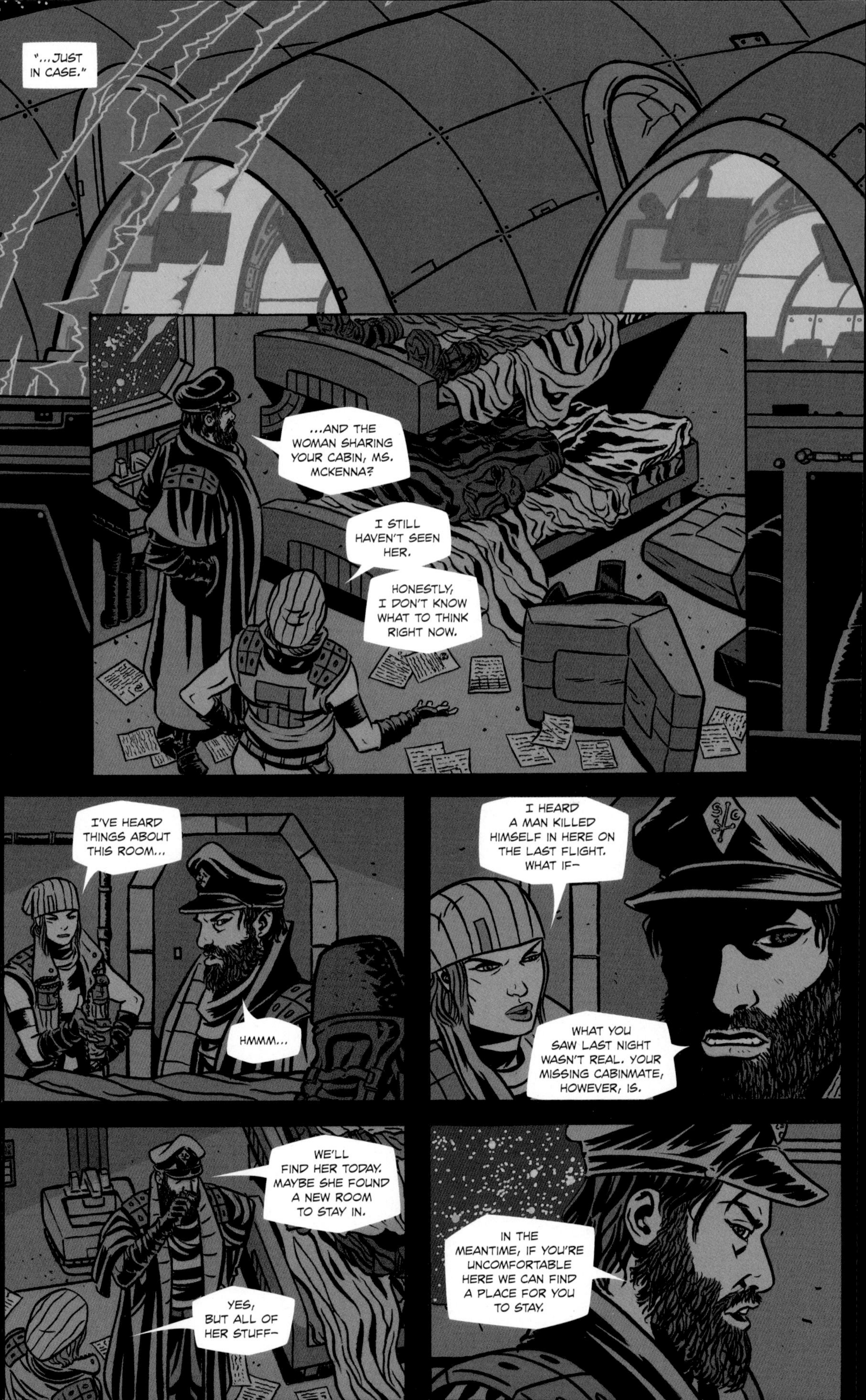
"...JUST IN CASE."
...AND THE WOMAN SHARING YOUR CABIN, MS. MCKENNA?
I STILL HAVEN'T SEEN HER.
HONESTLY, I DON'T KNOW WHAT TO THINK RIGHT NOW.
I'VE HEARD THINGS ABOUT THIS ROOM...
HMMM...
I HEARD A MAN KILLED HIMSELF IN HERE ON THE LAST FLIGHT. WHAT IF—
WHAT YOU SAW LAST NIGHT WASN'T REAL. YOUR MISSING CABINMATE, HOWEVER, IS.
WE'LL FIND HER TODAY. MAYBE SHE FOUND A NEW ROOM TO STAY IN.
YES, BUT ALL OF HER STUFF—
IN THE MEANTIME, IF YOU'RE UNCOMFORTABLE HERE WE CAN FIND A PLACE FOR YOU TO STAY.

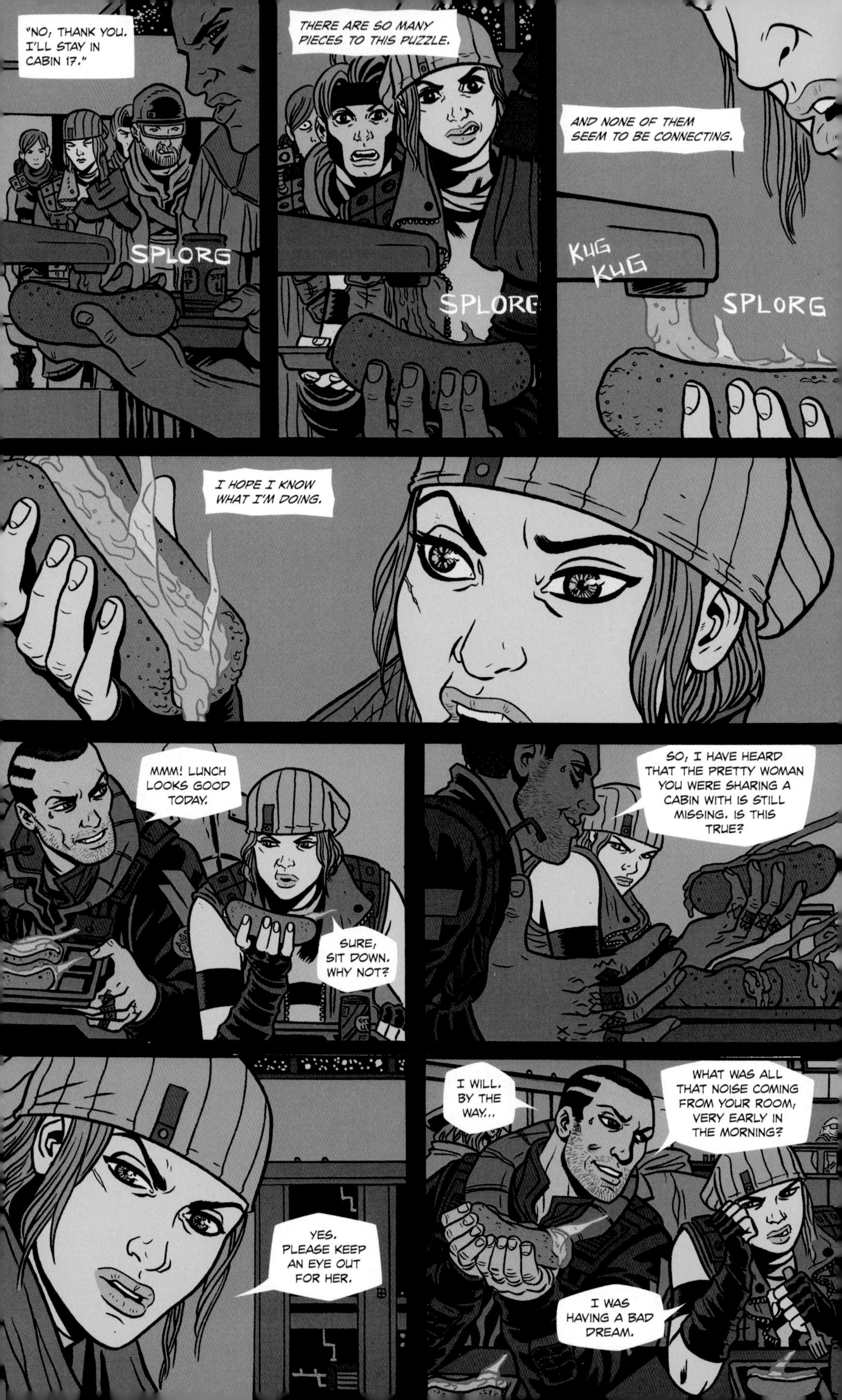
"NO, THANK YOU. I'LL STAY IN CABIN 17."
SPLORG
THERE ARE SO MANY PIECES TO THIS PUZZLE.
SPLORG
AND NONE OF THEM SEEM TO BE CONNECTING.
KUG KUG
SPLORG
I HOPE I KNOW WHAT I'M DOING.
MMM! LUNCH LOOKS GOOD TODAY.
SURE, SIT DOWN. WHY NOT?
SO, I HAVE HEARD THAT THE PRETTY WOMAN YOU WERE SHARING A CABIN WITH IS STILL MISSING. IS THIS TRUE?
YES. PLEASE KEEP AN EYE OUT FOR HER.
I WILL. BY THE WAY...
WHAT WAS ALL THAT NOISE COMING FROM YOUR ROOM, VERY EARLY IN THE MORNING?
I WAS HAVING A BAD DREAM.

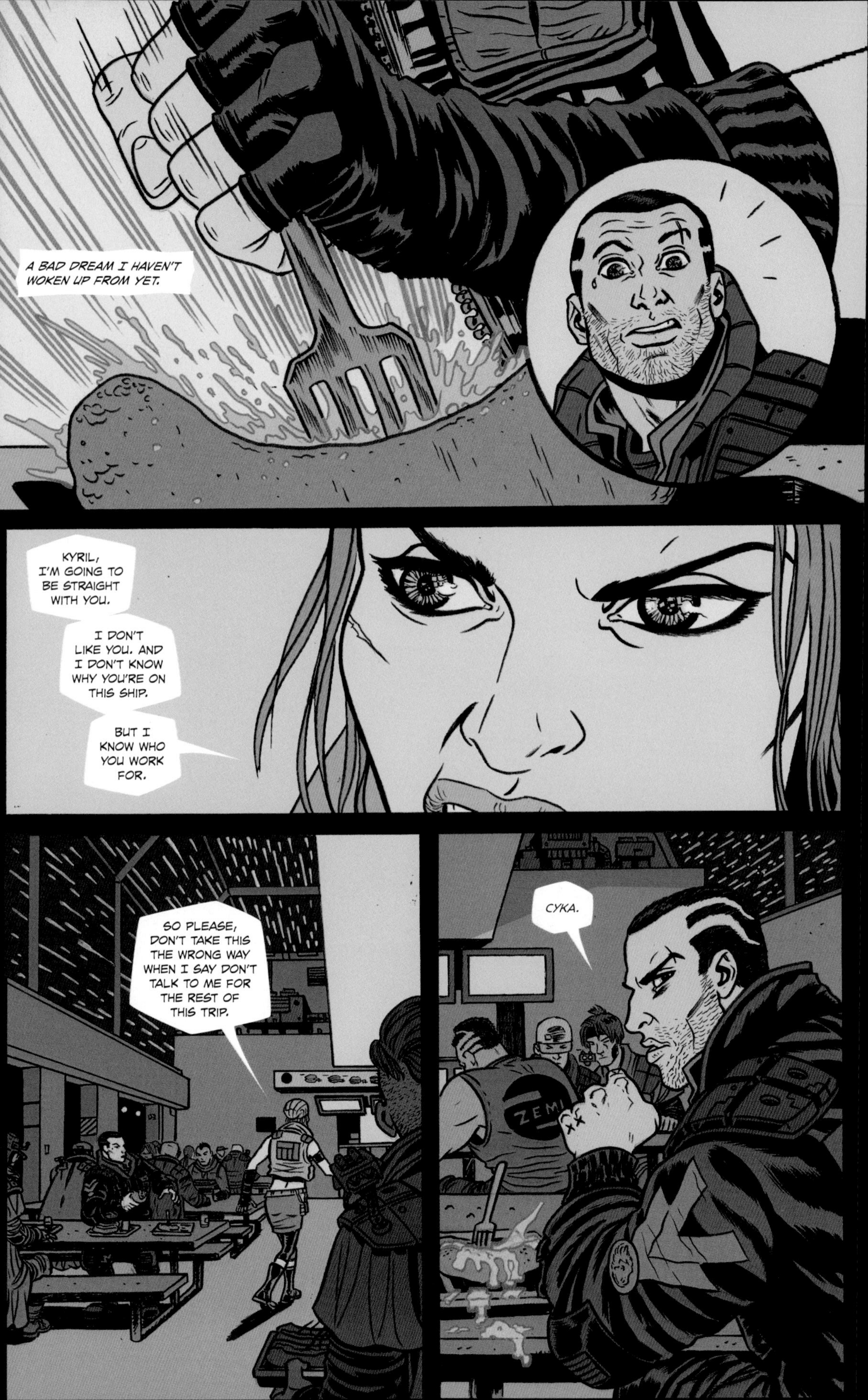
A BAD DREAM I HAVEN'T WOKEN UP FROM YET.
KYRIL, I'M GOING TO BE STRAIGHT WITH YOU.
I DON'T LIKE YOU. AND I DON'T KNOW WHY YOU'RE ON THIS SHIP.
BUT I KNOW WHO YOU WORK FOR.
SO PLEASE, DON'T TAKE THIS THE WRONG WAY WHEN I SAY DON'T TALK TO ME FOR THE REST OF THIS TRIP.
CYKA.
ZEM

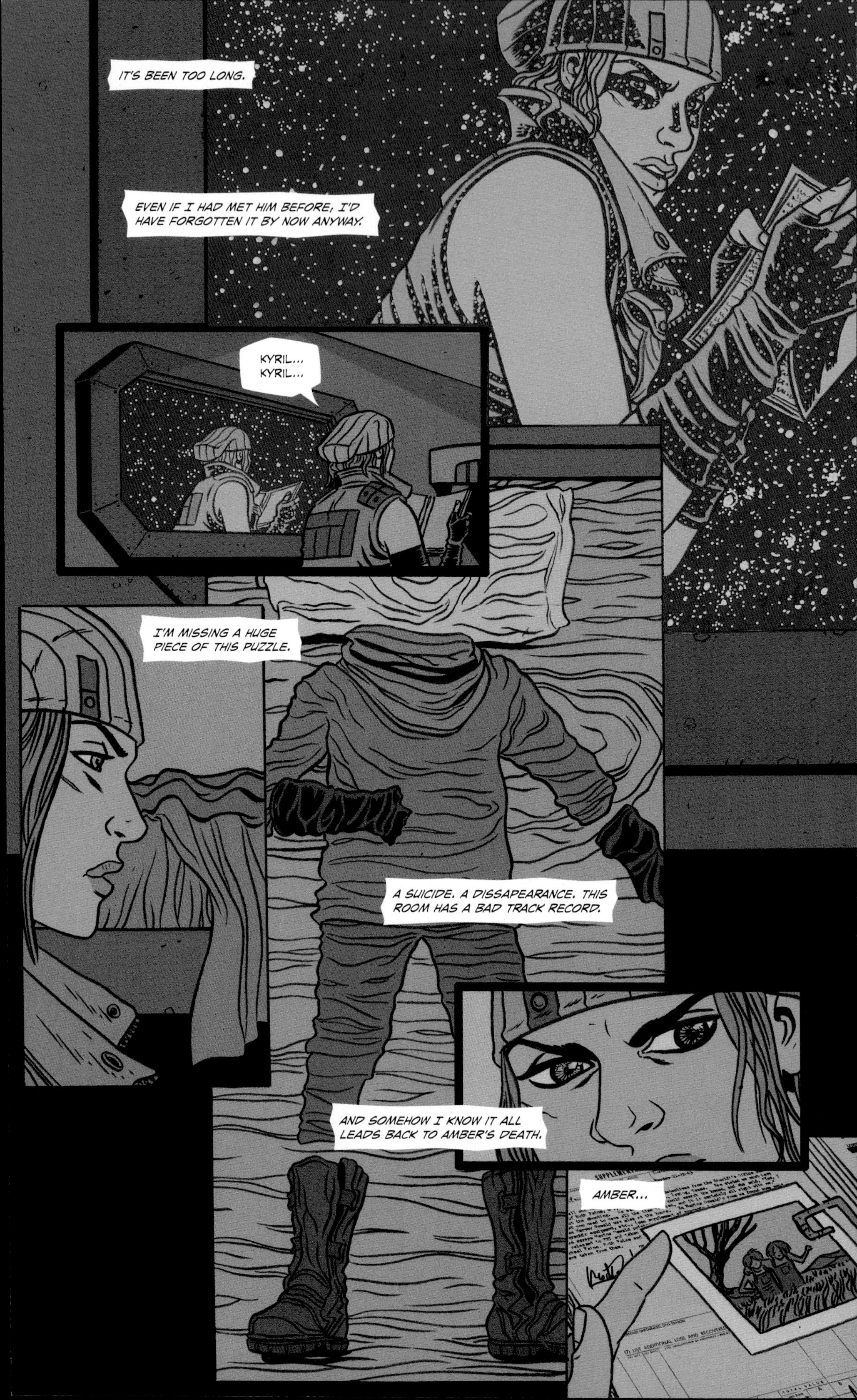
IT'S BEEN TOO LONG.
EVEN IF I HAD MET HIM BEFORE, I'D HAVE FORGOTTEN IT BY NOW ANYWAY.
KYRIL... KYRIL...
I'M MISSING A HUGE PIECE OF THIS PUZZLE.
A SUICIDE. A DISSAPEARANCE. THIS ROOM HAS A BAD TRACK RECORD.
AND SOMEHOW I KNOW IT ALL LEADS BACK TO AMBER'S DEATH.
AMBER...

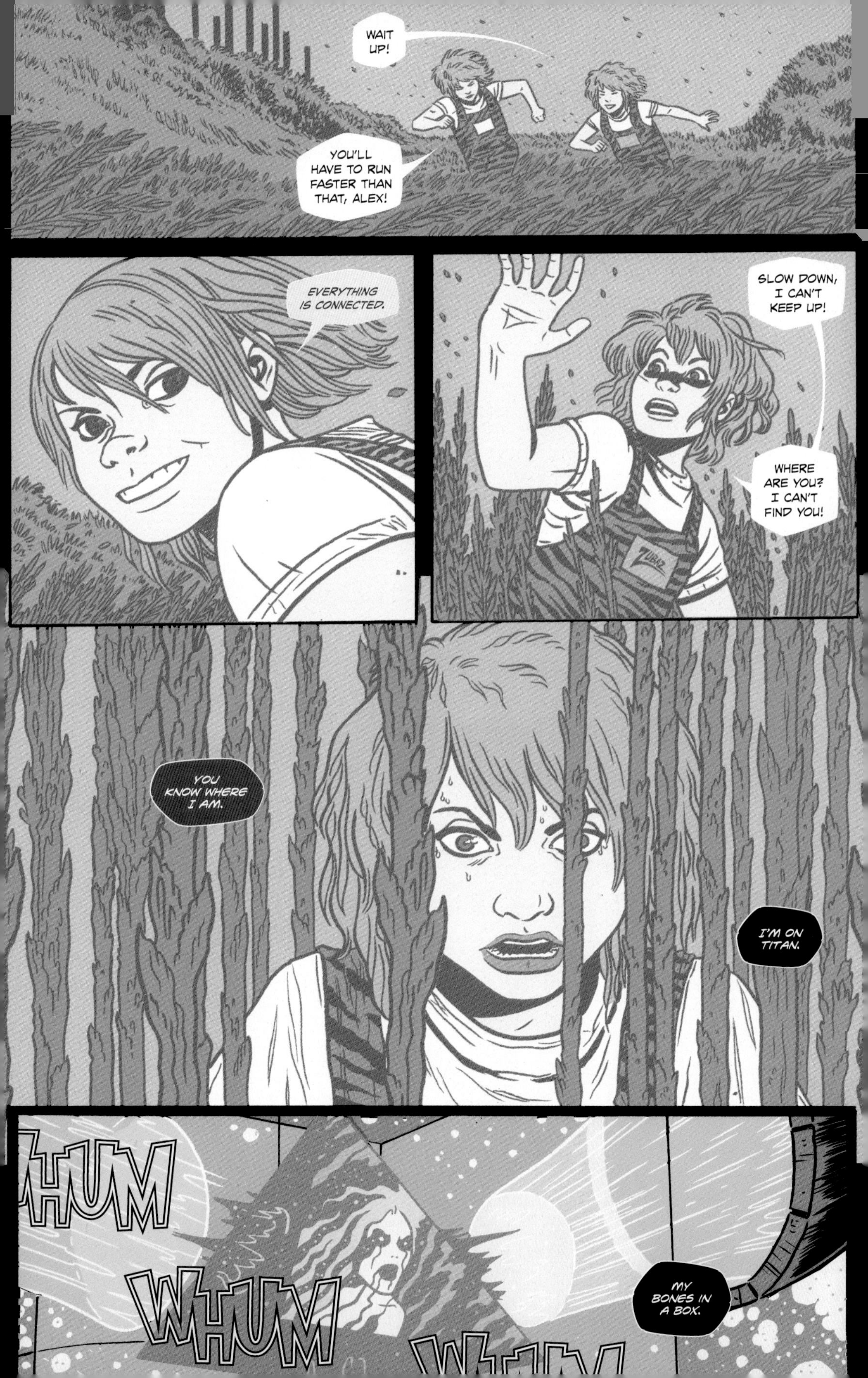

WAIT UP!
YOU'LL HAVE TO RUN FASTER THAN THAT, ALEX!
EVERYTHING IS CONNECTED.
SLOW DOWN, I CAN'T KEEP UP!
WHERE ARE YOU? I CAN'T FIND YOU!
ZUBAZ
YOU KNOW WHERE I AM.
I'M ON TITAN.
WHUM
WHUM
MY BONES IN A BOX.

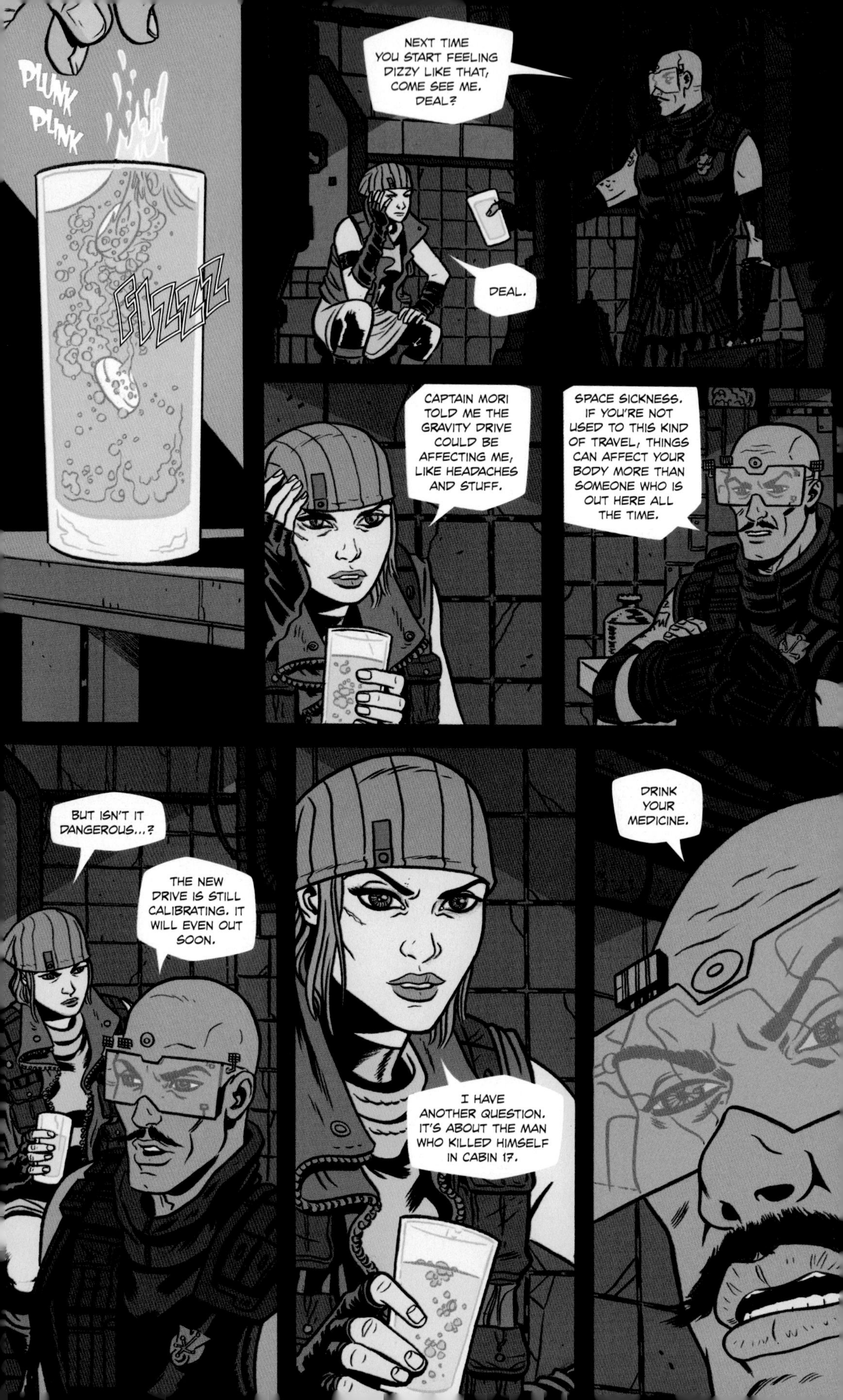
PLUNK
PLUNK
FIZZZZ
NEXT TIME YOU START FEELING DIZZY LIKE THAT, COME SEE ME. DEAL?
DEAL.
CAPTAIN MORI TOLD ME THE GRAVITY DRIVE COULD BE AFFECTING ME, LIKE HEADACHES AND STUFF.
SPACE SICKNESS. IF YOU'RE NOT USED TO THIS KIND OF TRAVEL, THINGS CAN AFFECT YOUR BODY MORE THAN SOMEONE WHO IS OUT HERE ALL THE TIME.
BUT ISN'T IT DANGEROUS...?
THE NEW DRIVE IS STILL CALIBRATING. IT WILL EVEN OUT SOON.
I HAVE ANOTHER QUESTION. IT'S ABOUT THE MAN WHO KILLED HIMSELF IN CABIN 17.
DRINK YOUR MEDICINE.

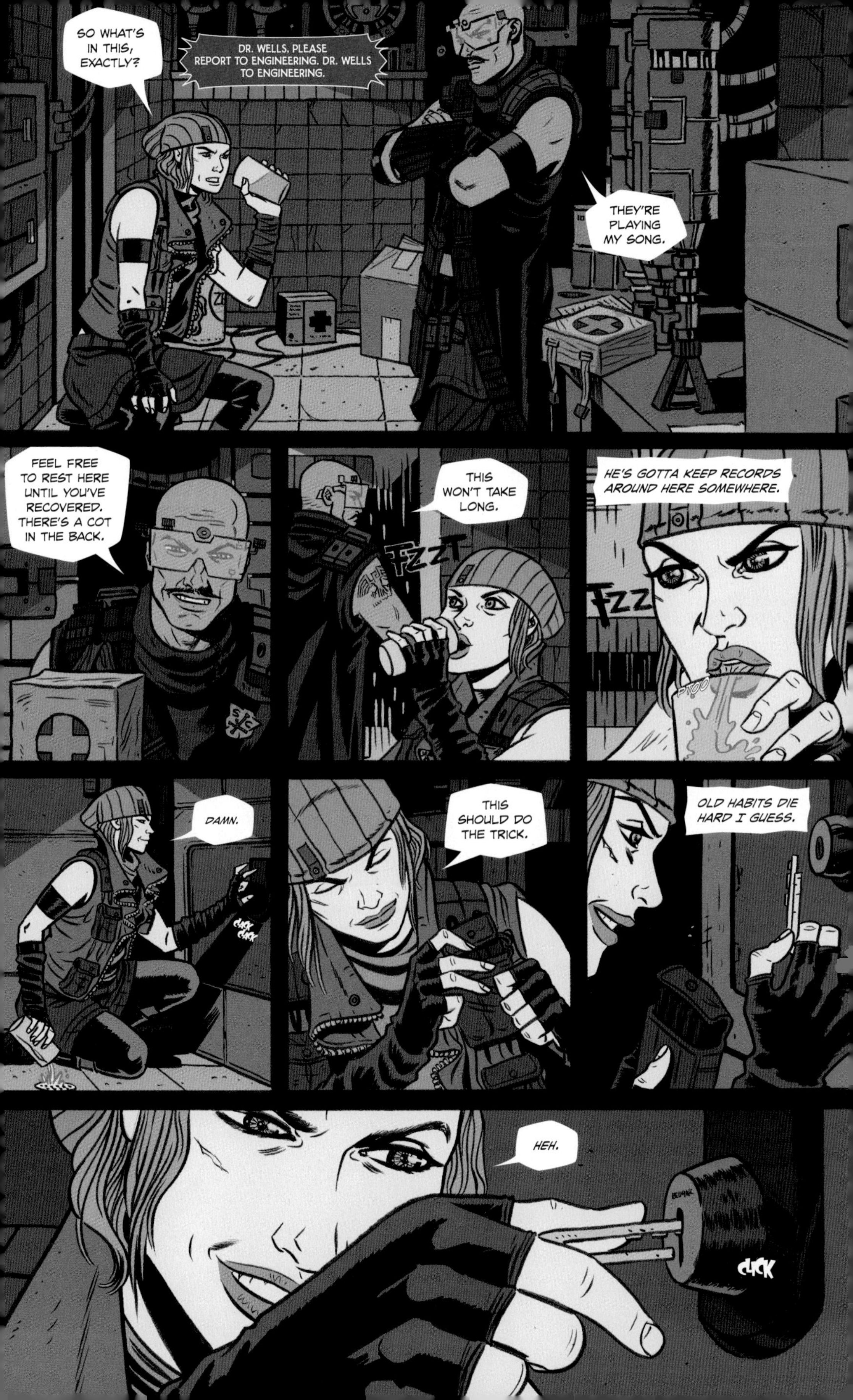

SO WHAT'S IN THIS, EXACTLY?
DR. WELLS, PLEASE REPORT TO ENGINEERING. DR. WELLS TO ENGINEERING.
THEY'RE PLAYING MY SONG.
FEEL FREE TO REST HERE UNTIL YOU'VE RECOVERED. THERE'S A COT IN THE BACK.
THIS WON'T TAKE LONG.
FZZT
HE'S GOTTA KEEP RECORDS AROUND HERE SOMEWHERE.
FZZ
PTOO
DAMN.
CLICK CLICK
THIS SHOULD DO THE TRICK.
OLD HABITS DIE HARD I GUESS.
HEH.
CLICK

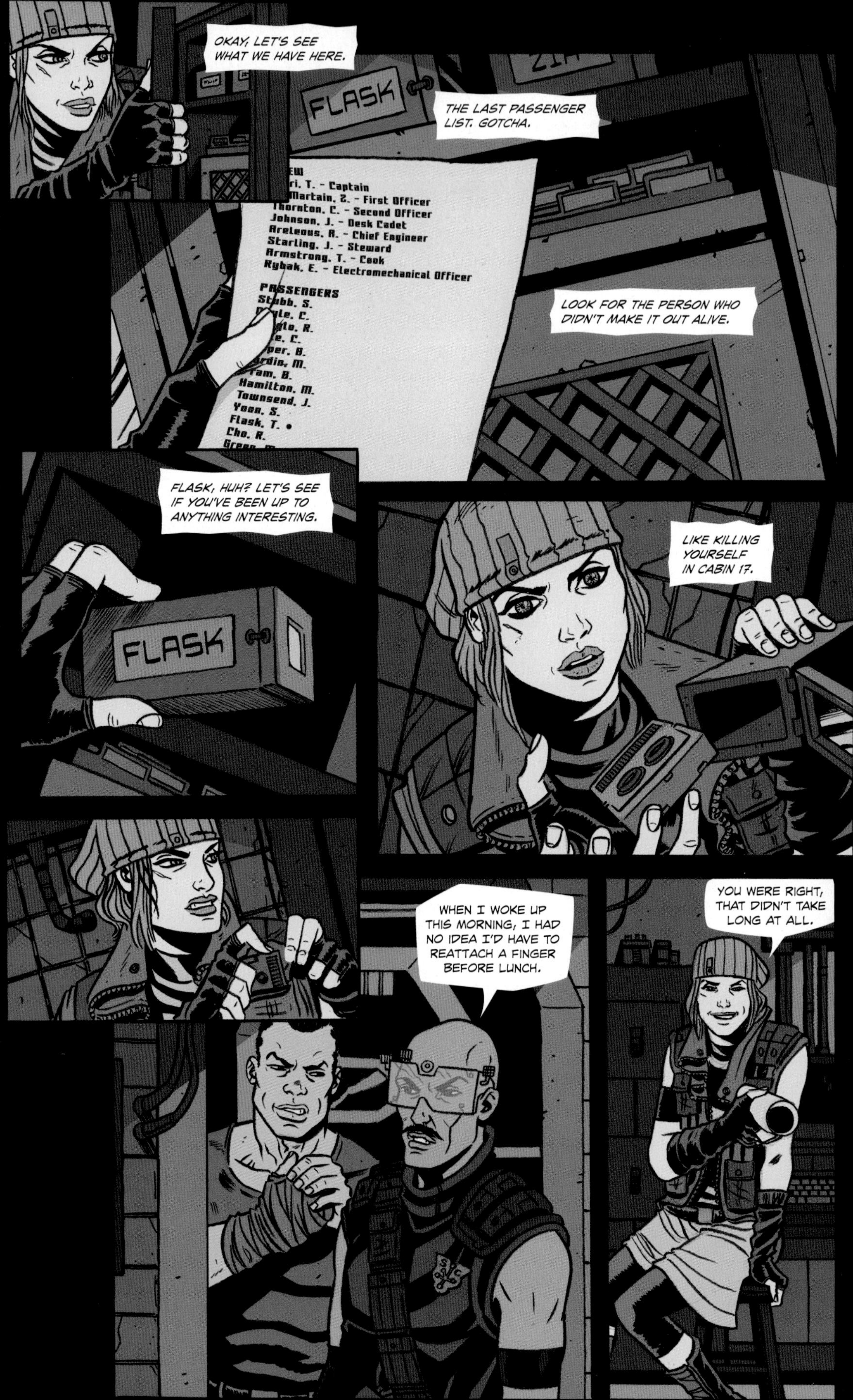

OKAY, LET'S SEE WHAT WE HAVE HERE.
FLASK
THE LAST PASSENGER LIST. GOTCHA.
Thornton, C. - Second Officer
Johnson, J. - Desk Cadet
Areleous, A. - Chief Engineer
Starling, J. - Steward
Armstrong, T. - Cook
Rybak, E. - Electromechanical Officer
PASSENGERS
Stubb, S.
Hamilton, M.
Townsend, J.
Yoon, S.
Flask, T.
Cho, R.
LOOK FOR THE PERSON WHO DIDN'T MAKE IT OUT ALIVE.
FLASK, HUH? LET'S SEE IF YOU'VE BEEN UP TO ANYTHING INTERESTING.
FLASK
LIKE KILLING YOURSELF IN CABIN 17.
WHEN I WOKE UP THIS MORNING, I HAD NO IDEA I'D HAVE TO REATTACH A FINGER BEFORE LUNCH.
YOU WERE RIGHT, THAT DIDN'T TAKE LONG AT ALL.

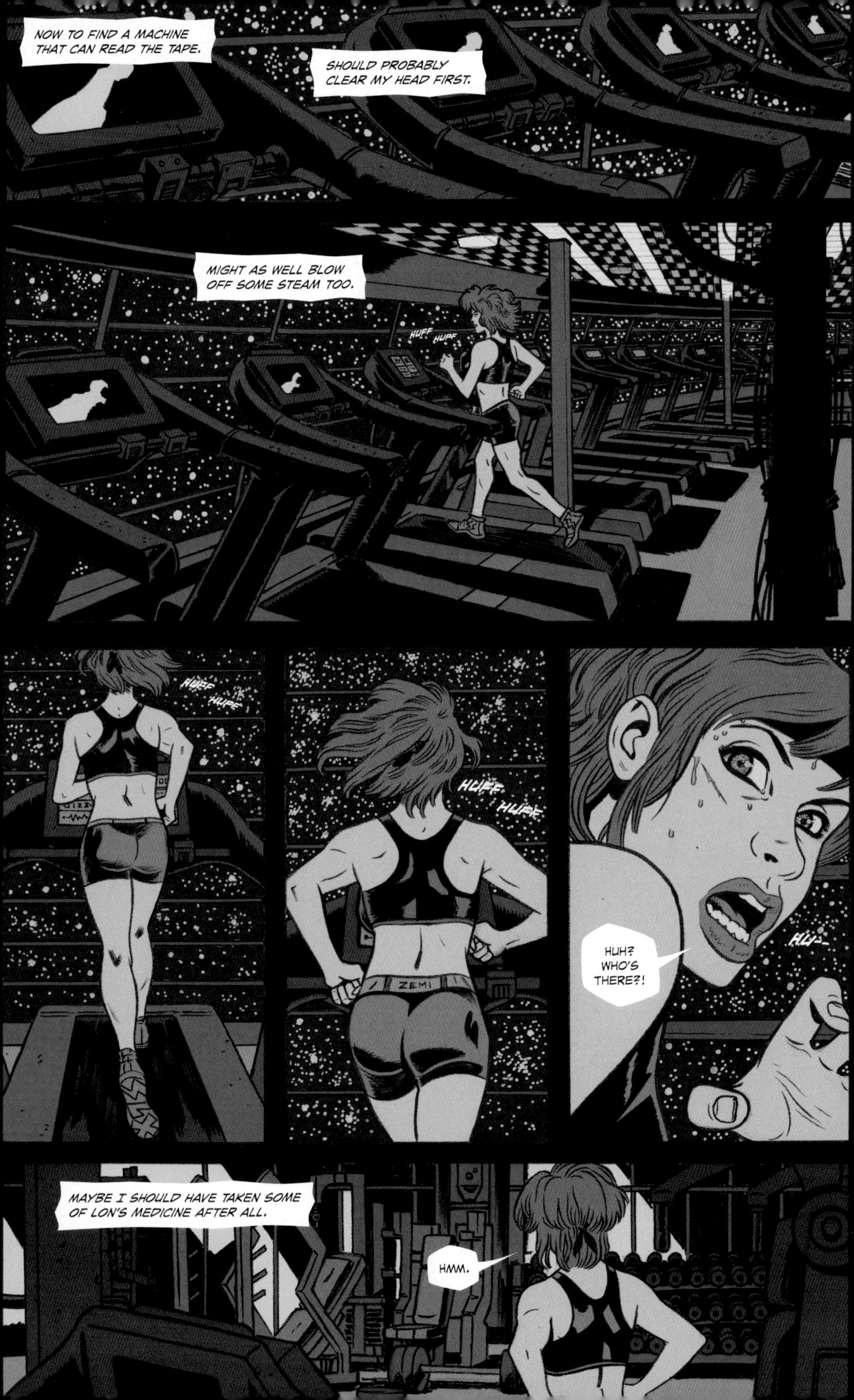

NOW TO FIND A MACHINE THAT CAN READ THE TAPE.
SHOULD PROBABLY CLEAR MY HEAD FIRST.
MIGHT AS WELL BLOW OFF SOME STEAM TOO.
HUFF HUFF
HUFF HUFF
HUFF HUFF
HUH? WHO'S THERE?!
MAYBE I SHOULD HAVE TAKEN SOME OF LON'S MEDICINE AFTER ALL.
HMM.

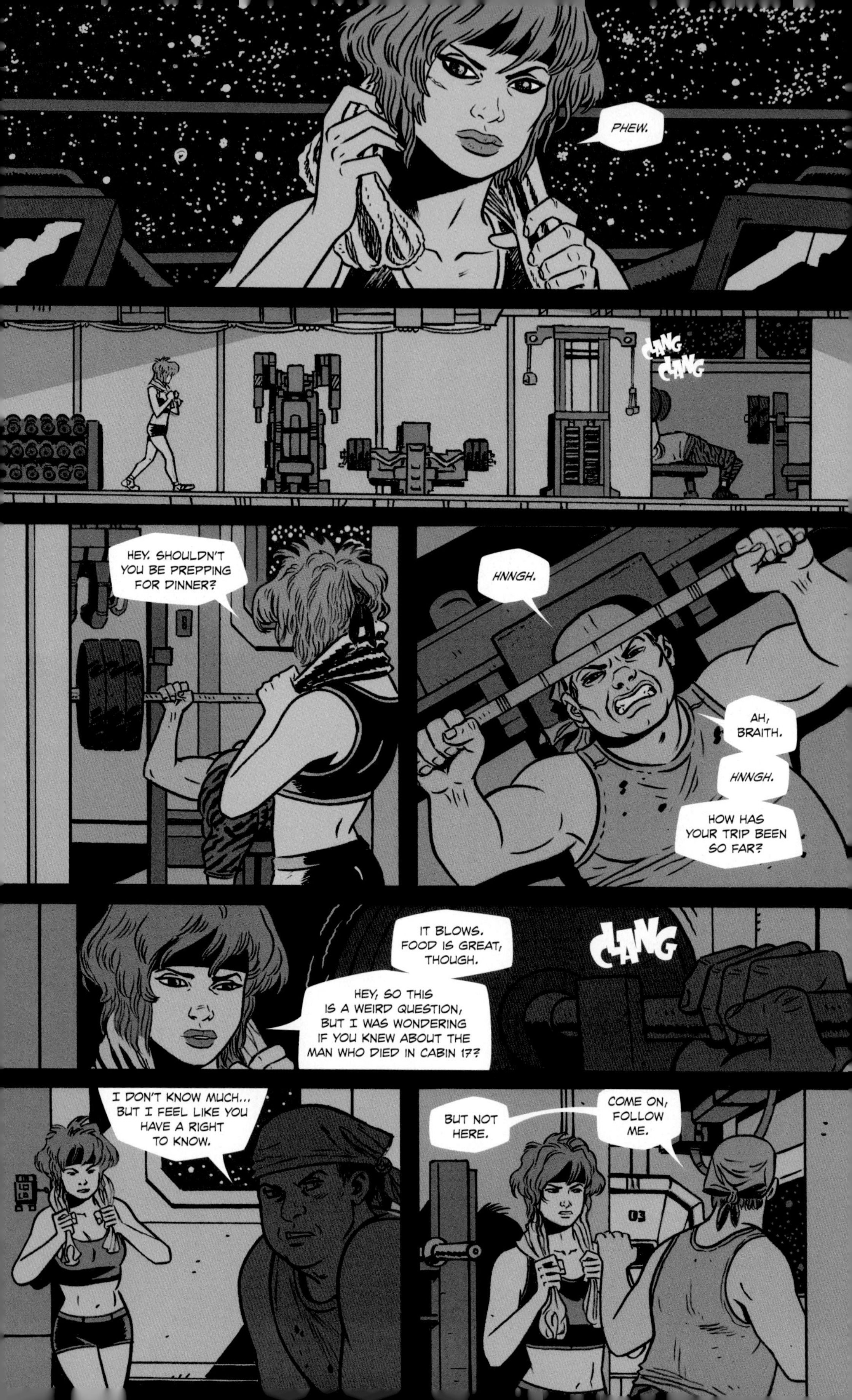
PHEW.
CLANG
CLANG
HEY. SHOULDN'T YOU BE PREPPING FOR DINNER?
HNNGH.
AH, BRAITH.
HNNGH.
HOW HAS YOUR TRIP BEEN SO FAR?
IT BLOWS. FOOD IS GREAT, THOUGH.
CLANG
HEY, SO THIS IS A WEIRD QUESTION, BUT I WAS WONDERING IF YOU KNEW ABOUT THE MAN WHO DIED IN CABIN 17?
I DON'T KNOW MUCH... BUT I FEEL LIKE YOU HAVE A RIGHT TO KNOW.
BUT NOT HERE.
COME ON, FOLLOW ME.
03

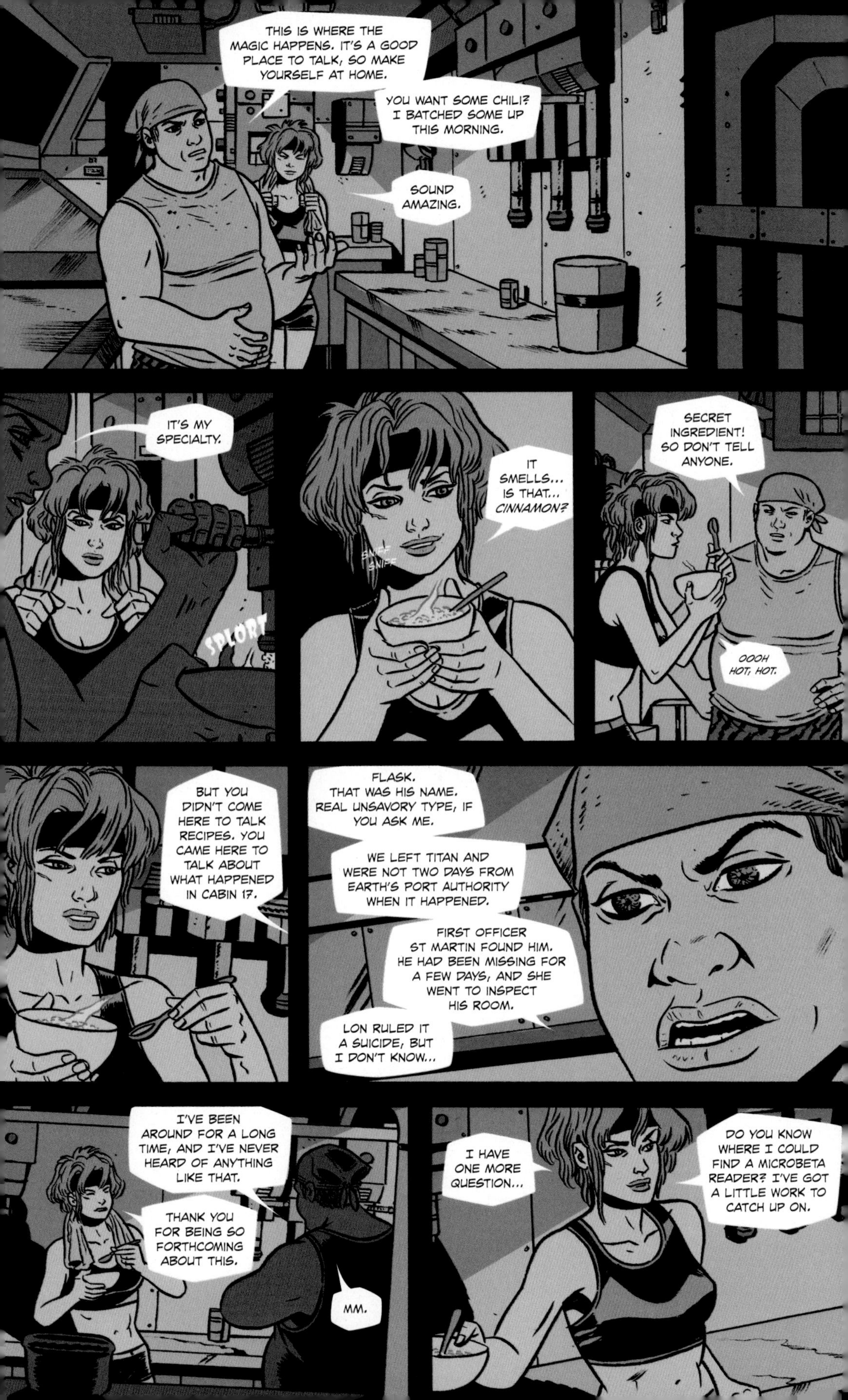
THIS IS WHERE THE MAGIC HAPPENS. IT'S A GOOD PLACE TO TALK, SO MAKE YOURSELF AT HOME.
YOU WANT SOME CHILI? I BATCHED SOME UP THIS MORNING.
SOUND AMAZING.
IT'S MY SPECIALTY.
SPLORT
IT SMELLS... IS THAT... CINNAMON?
SNIFF SNIFF
SECRET INGREDIENT! SO DON'T TELL ANYONE.
OOOH HOT, HOT.
BUT YOU DIDN'T COME HERE TO TALK RECIPES. YOU CAME HERE TO TALK ABOUT WHAT HAPPENED IN CABIN 17.
FLASK. THAT WAS HIS NAME. REAL UNSAVORY TYPE, IF YOU ASK ME.
WE LEFT TITAN AND WERE NOT TWO DAYS FROM EARTH'S PORT AUTHORITY WHEN IT HAPPENED.
FIRST OFFICER ST MARTIN FOUND HIM. HE HAD BEEN MISSING FOR A FEW DAYS, AND SHE WENT TO INSPECT HIS ROOM.
LON RULED IT A SUICIDE, BUT I DON'T KNOW...
I'VE BEEN AROUND FOR A LONG TIME, AND I'VE NEVER HEARD OF ANYTHING LIKE THAT.
THANK YOU FOR BEING SO FORTHCOMING ABOUT THIS.
MM.
I HAVE ONE MORE QUESTION...
DO YOU KNOW WHERE I COULD FIND A MICROBETA READER? I'VE GOT A LITTLE WORK TO CATCH UP ON.

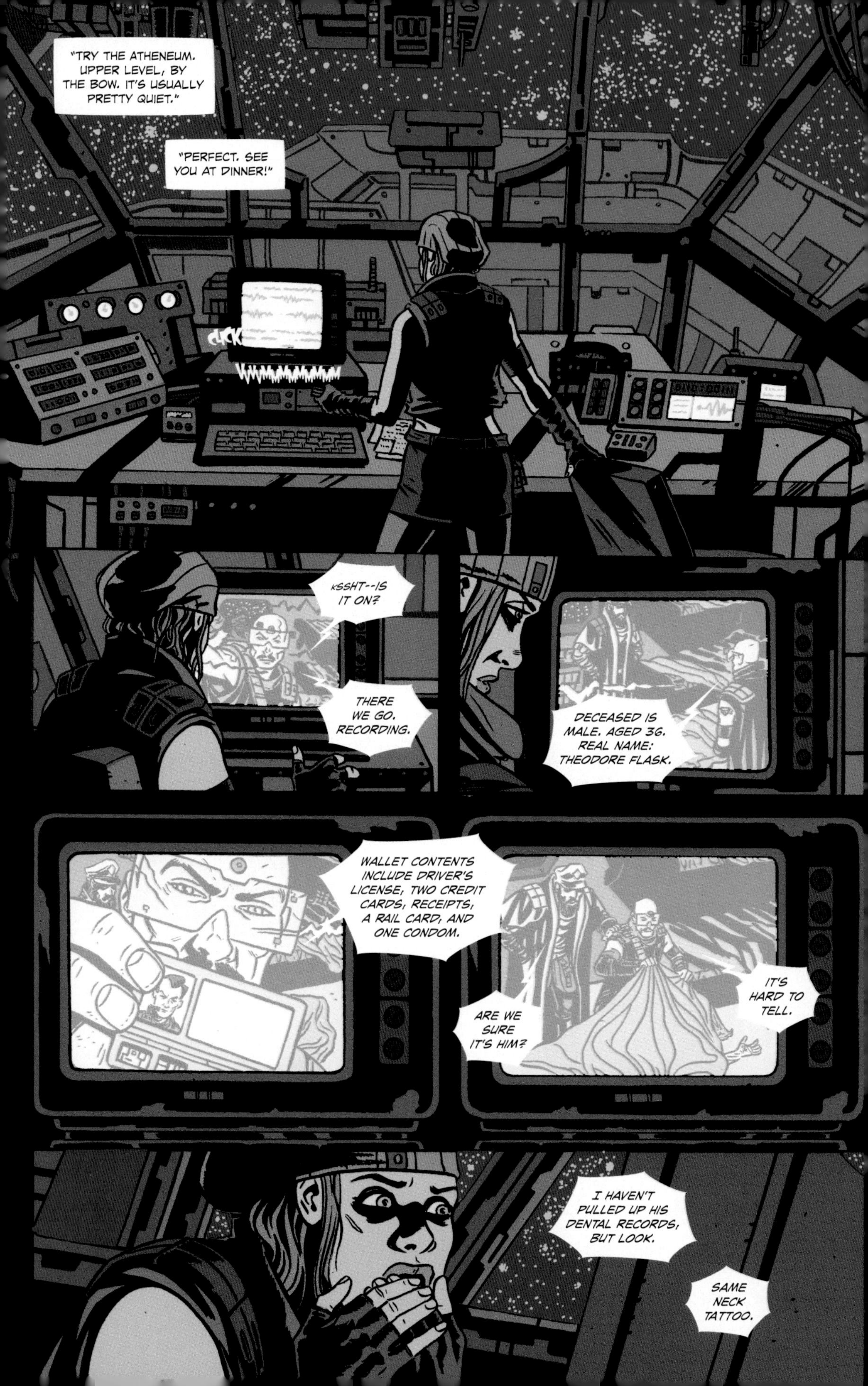
"TRY THE ATHENEUM. UPPER LEVEL, BY THE BOW. IT'S USUALLY PRETTY QUIET."
"PERFECT. SEE YOU AT DINNER!"
CLICK
WVVMMMMMMM
kSSHT--IS IT ON?
THERE WE GO. RECORDING.
DECEASED IS MALE. AGED 36. REAL NAME: THEODORE FLASK.
WALLET CONTENTS INCLUDE DRIVER'S LICENSE, TWO CREDIT CARDS, RECEIPTS, A RAIL CARD, AND ONE CONDOM.
ARE WE SURE IT'S HIM?
IT'S HARD TO TELL.
I HAVEN'T PULLED UP HIS DENTAL RECORDS, BUT LOOK.
SAME NECK TATTOO.

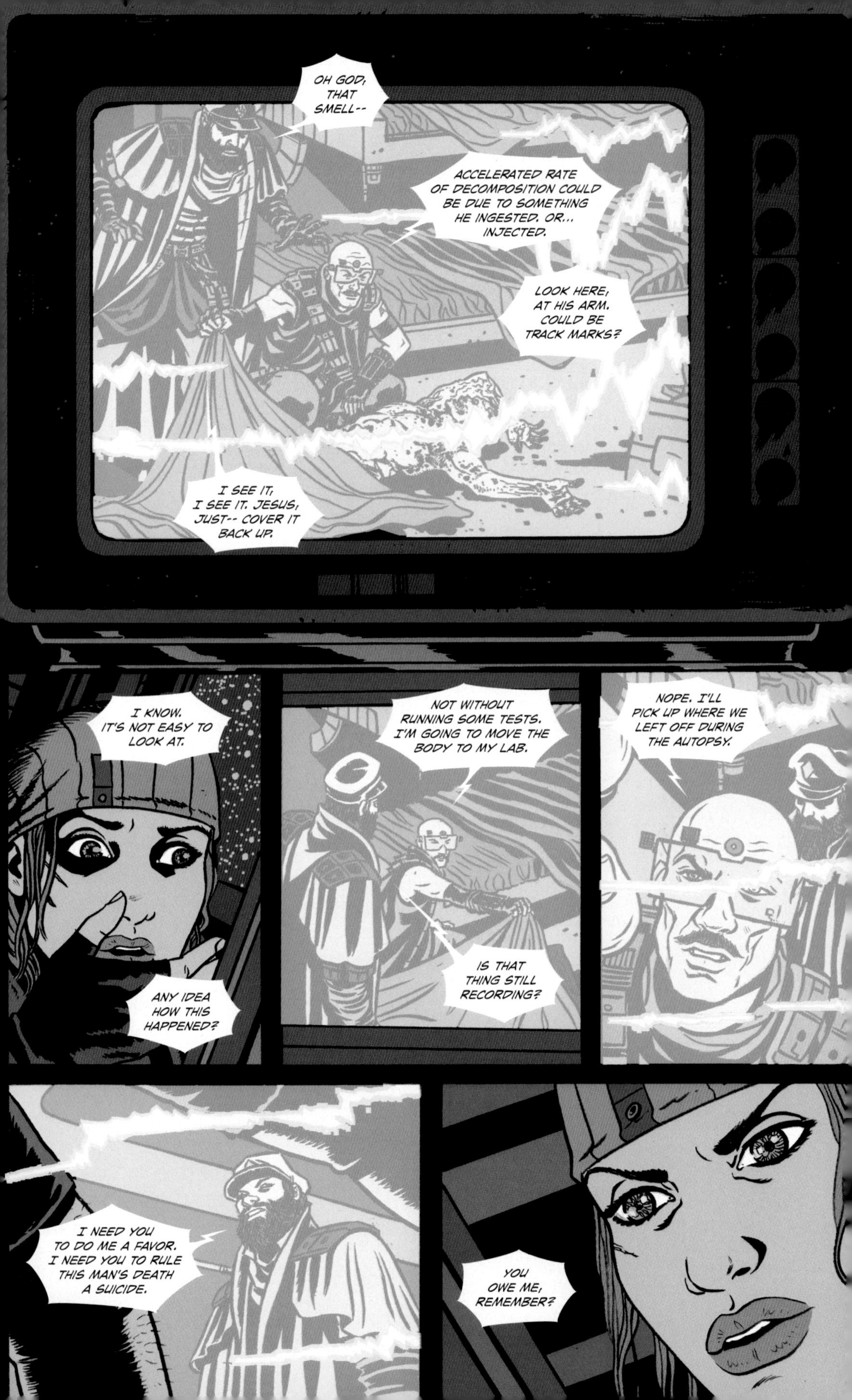
OH GOD, THAT SMELL--
ACCELERATED RATE OF DECOMPOSITION COULD BE DUE TO SOMETHING HE INGESTED. OR... INJECTED.
LOOK HERE; AT HIS ARM. COULD BE TRACK MARKS?
I SEE IT, I SEE IT. JESUS; JUST-- COVER IT BACK UP.
I KNOW. IT'S NOT EASY TO LOOK AT.
ANY IDEA HOW THIS HAPPENED?
NOT WITHOUT RUNNING SOME TESTS. I'M GOING TO MOVE THE BODY TO MY LAB.
IS THAT THING STILL RECORDING?
NOPE. I'LL PICK UP WHERE WE LEFT OFF DURING THE AUTOPSY.
I NEED YOU TO DO ME A FAVOR. I NEED YOU TO RULE THIS MAN'S DEATH A SUICIDE.
YOU OWE ME, REMEMBER?

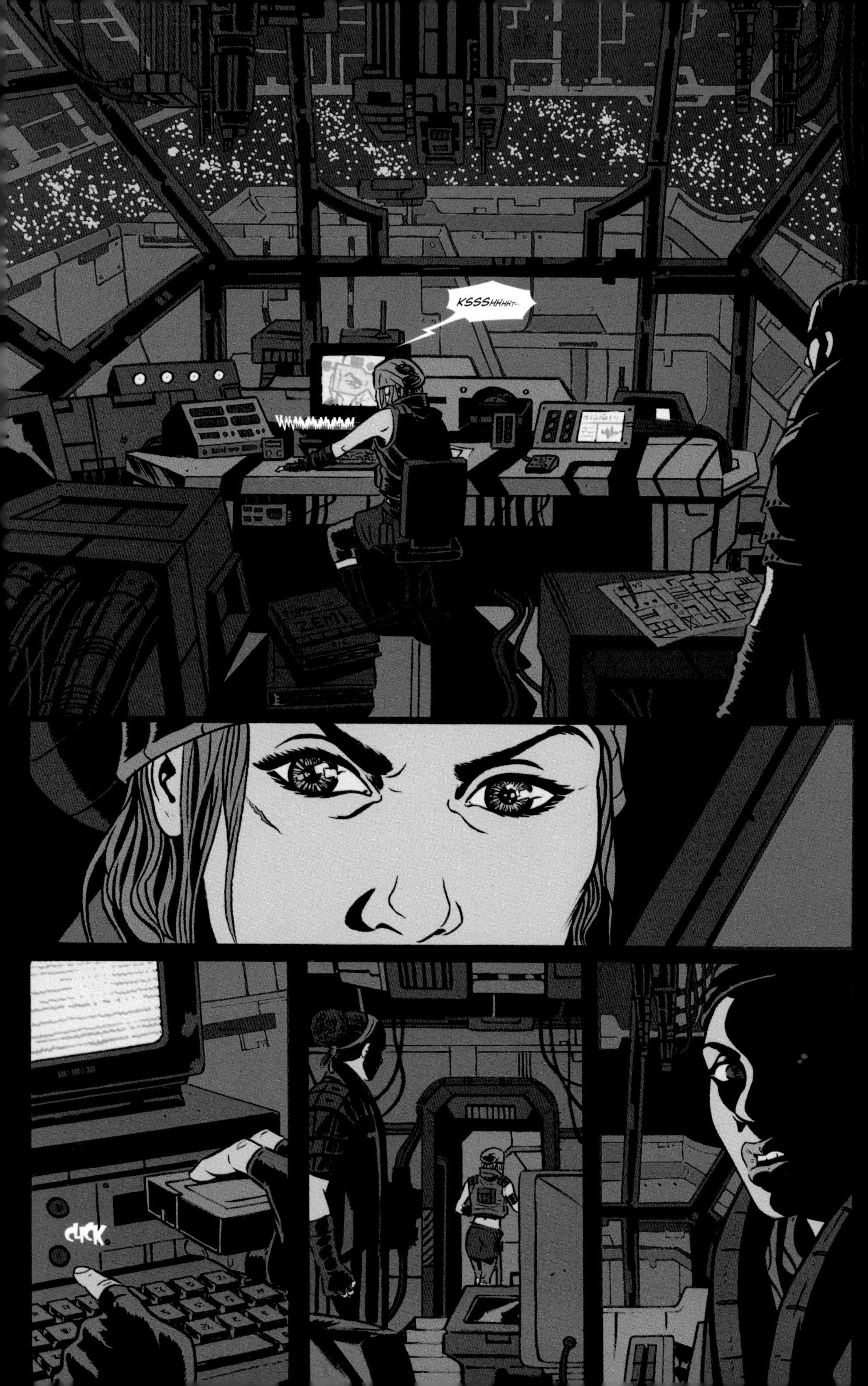
KSSSHHHHT--
CLICK

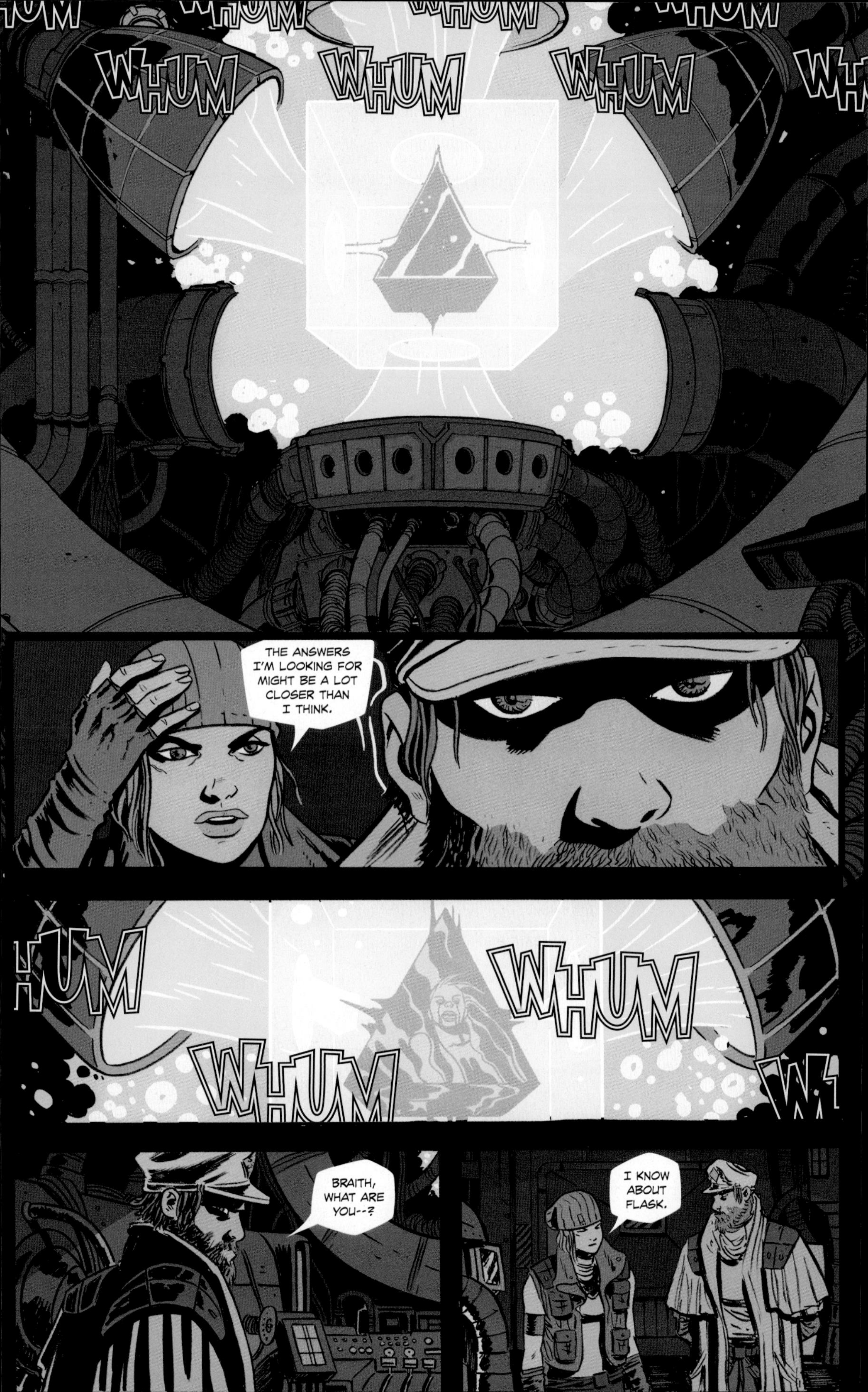

WHUM WHUM WHUM WHUM
WHUM WHUM WHUM
THE ANSWERS I'M LOOKING FOR MIGHT BE A LOT CLOSER THAN I THINK.
WHUM
WHUM
BRAITH, WHAT ARE YOU--?
I KNOW ABOUT FLASK.

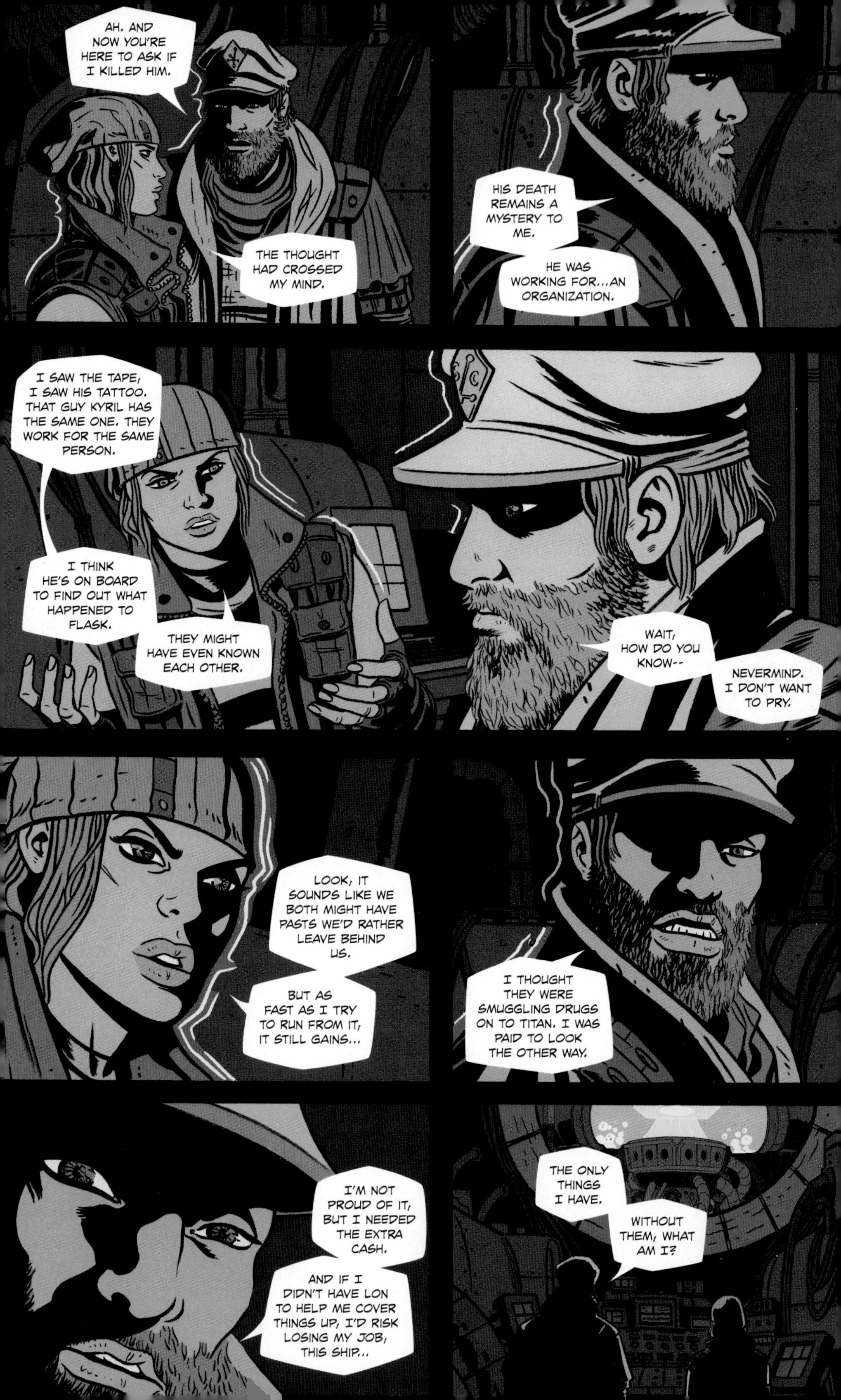
AH. AND NOW YOU'RE HERE TO ASK IF I KILLED HIM.
THE THOUGHT HAD CROSSED MY MIND.
HIS DEATH REMAINS A MYSTERY TO ME.
HE WAS WORKING FOR...AN ORGANIZATION.
I SAW THE TAPE, I SAW HIS TATTOO. THAT GUY KYRIL HAS THE SAME ONE. THEY WORK FOR THE SAME PERSON.
I THINK HE'S ON BOARD TO FIND OUT WHAT HAPPENED TO FLASK.
THEY MIGHT HAVE EVEN KNOWN EACH OTHER.
WAIT, HOW DO YOU KNOW--
NEVERMIND. I DON'T WANT TO PRY.
LOOK, IT SOUNDS LIKE WE BOTH MIGHT HAVE PASTS WE'D RATHER LEAVE BEHIND US.
BUT AS FAST AS I TRY TO RUN FROM IT, IT STILL GAINS...
I THOUGHT THEY WERE SMUGGLING DRUGS ON TO TITAN. I WAS PAID TO LOOK THE OTHER WAY.
I'M NOT PROUD OF IT, BUT I NEEDED THE EXTRA CASH.
AND IF I DIDN'T HAVE LON TO HELP ME COVER THINGS UP, I'D RISK LOSING MY JOB, THIS SHIP...
THE ONLY THINGS I HAVE.
WITHOUT THEM, WHAT AM I?

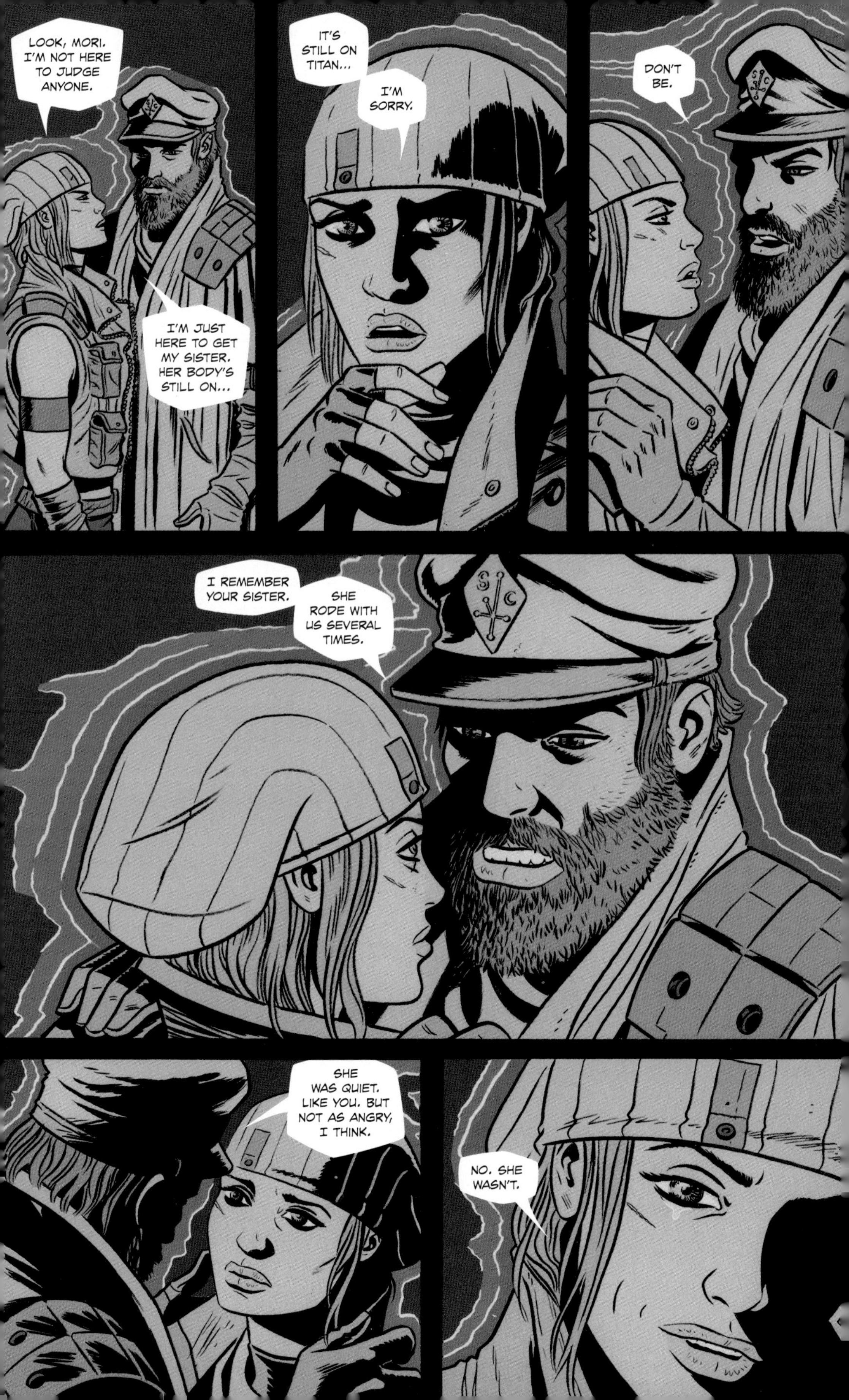
LOOK, MORI. I'M NOT HERE TO JUDGE ANYONE.
I'M JUST HERE TO GET MY SISTER. HER BODY'S STILL ON...
IT'S STILL ON TITAN...
I'M SORRY.
DON'T BE.
I REMEMBER YOUR SISTER.
SHE RODE WITH US SEVERAL TIMES.
SHE WAS QUIET. LIKE YOU. BUT NOT AS ANGRY, I THINK.
NO. SHE WASN'T.

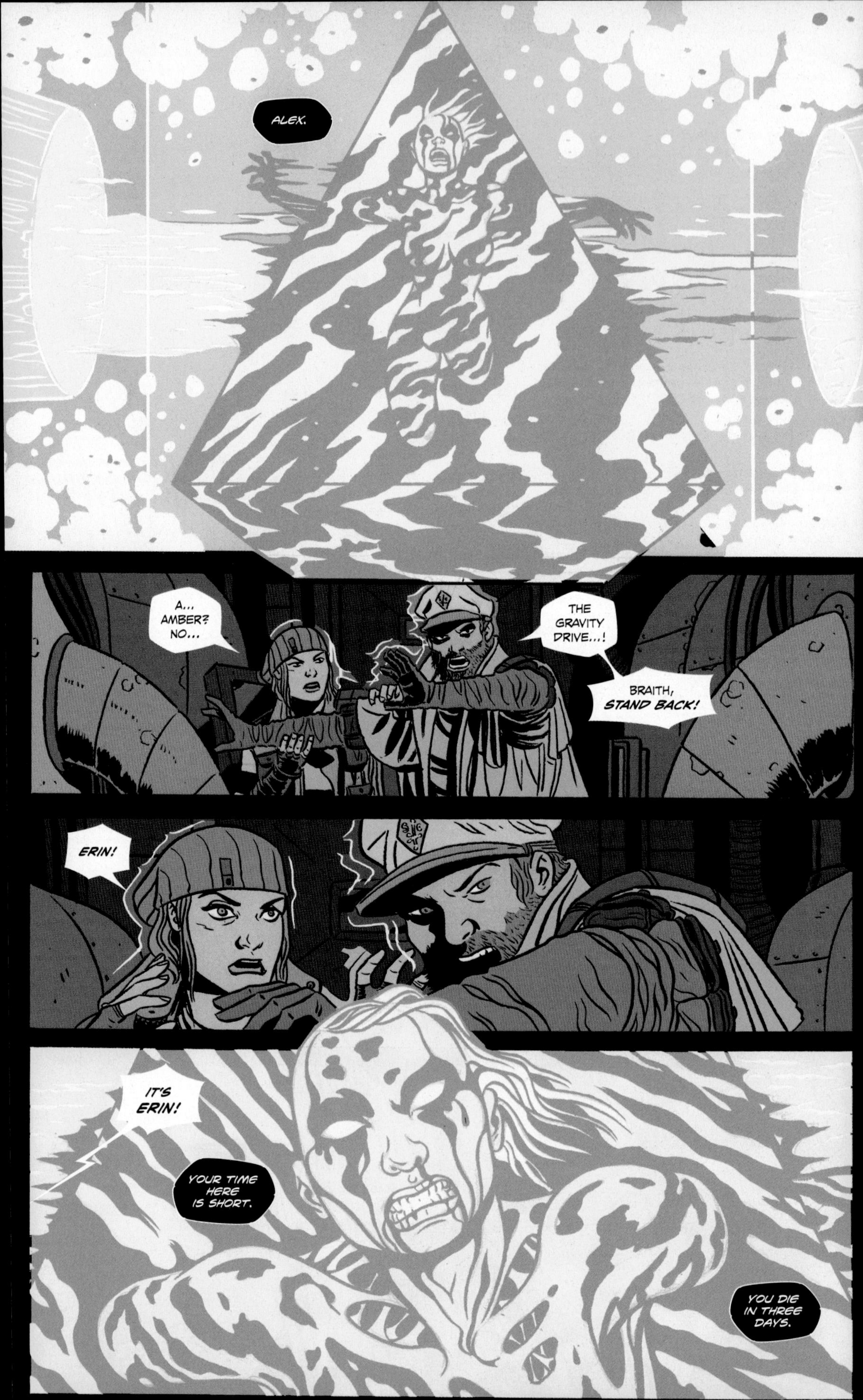
ALEX.
A... AMBER? NO...
THE GRAVITY DRIVE...!
BRAITH, STAND BACK!
ERIN!
IT'S ERIN!
YOUR TIME HERE IS SHORT.
YOU DIE IN THREE DAYS.

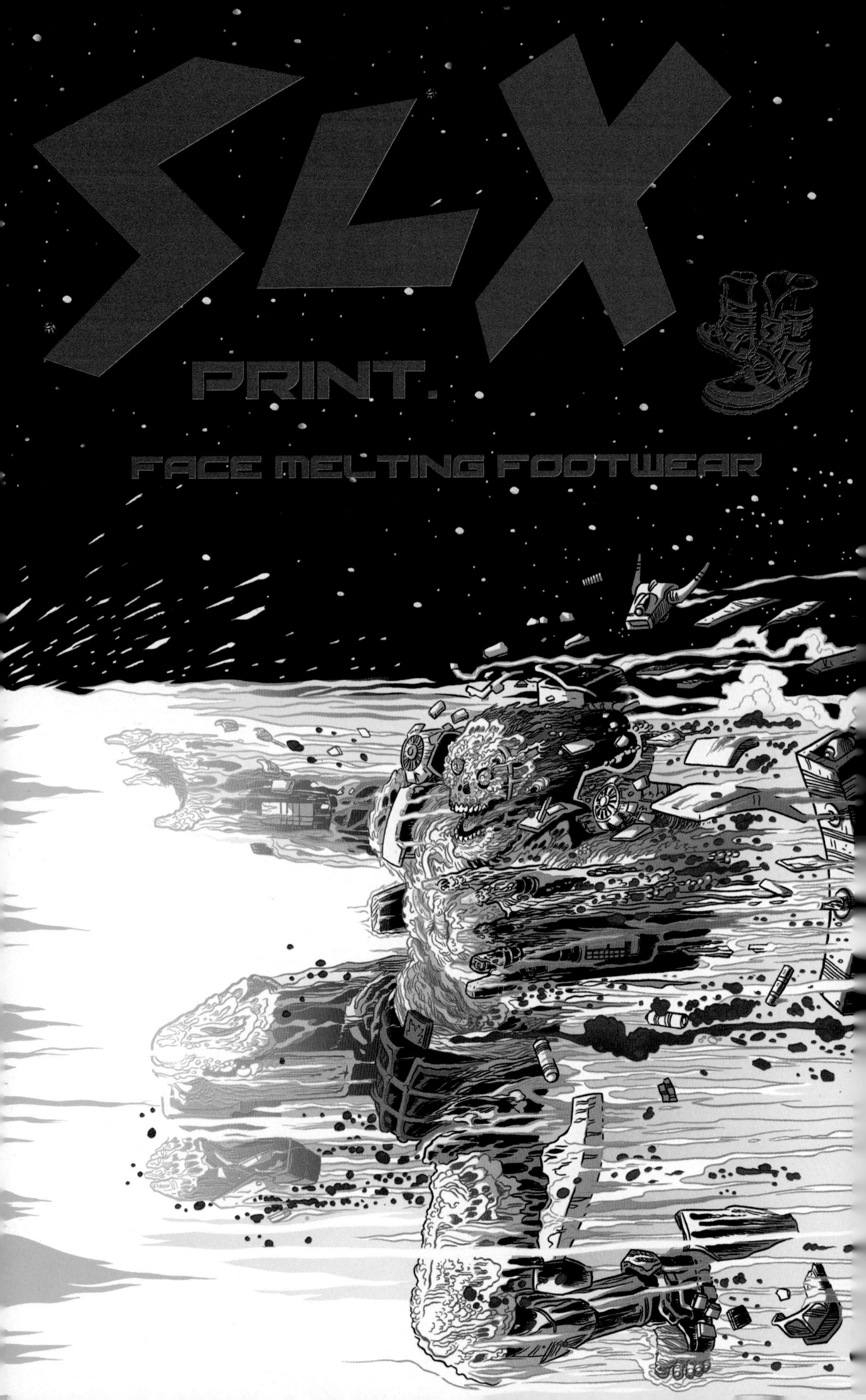
SLX
PRINT.
FACE MELTING FOOTWEAR

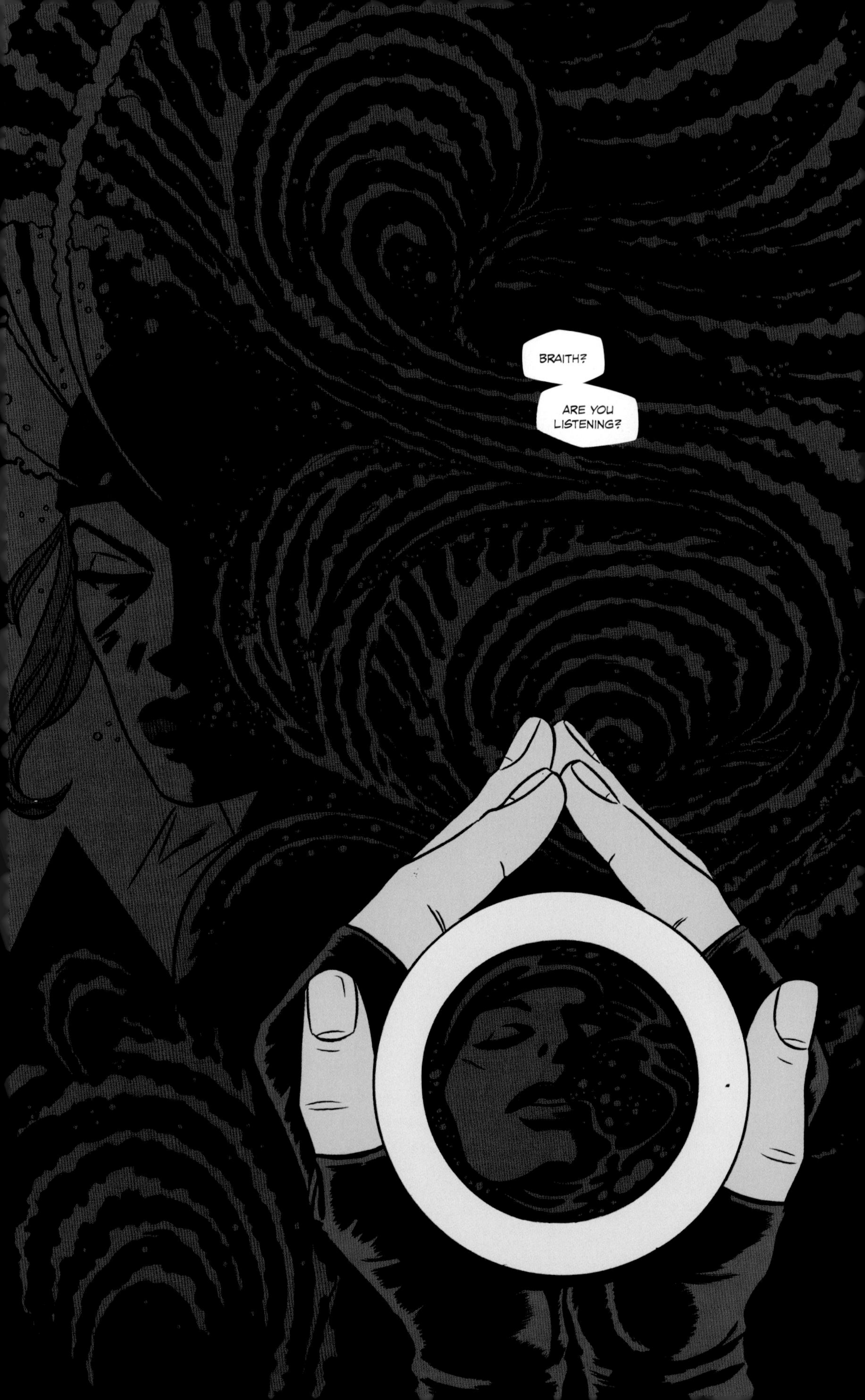
BRAITH?
ARE YOU LISTENING?

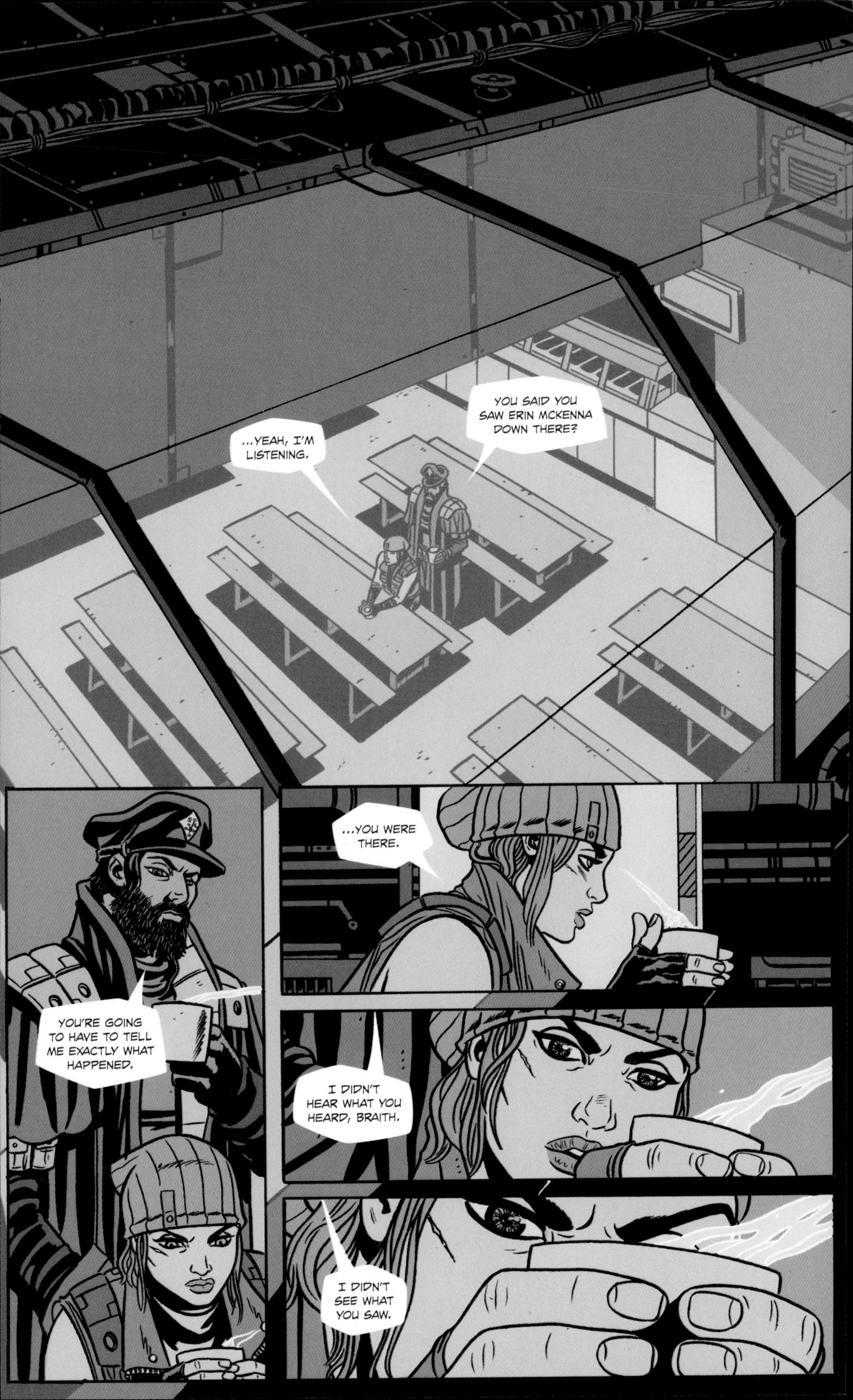
...YEAH, I'M LISTENING.
YOU SAID YOU SAW ERIN MCKENNA DOWN THERE?
YOU'RE GOING TO HAVE TO TELL ME EXACTLY WHAT HAPPENED.
...YOU WERE THERE.
I DIDN'T HEAR WHAT YOU HEARD, BRAITH.
I DIDN'T SEE WHAT YOU SAW.

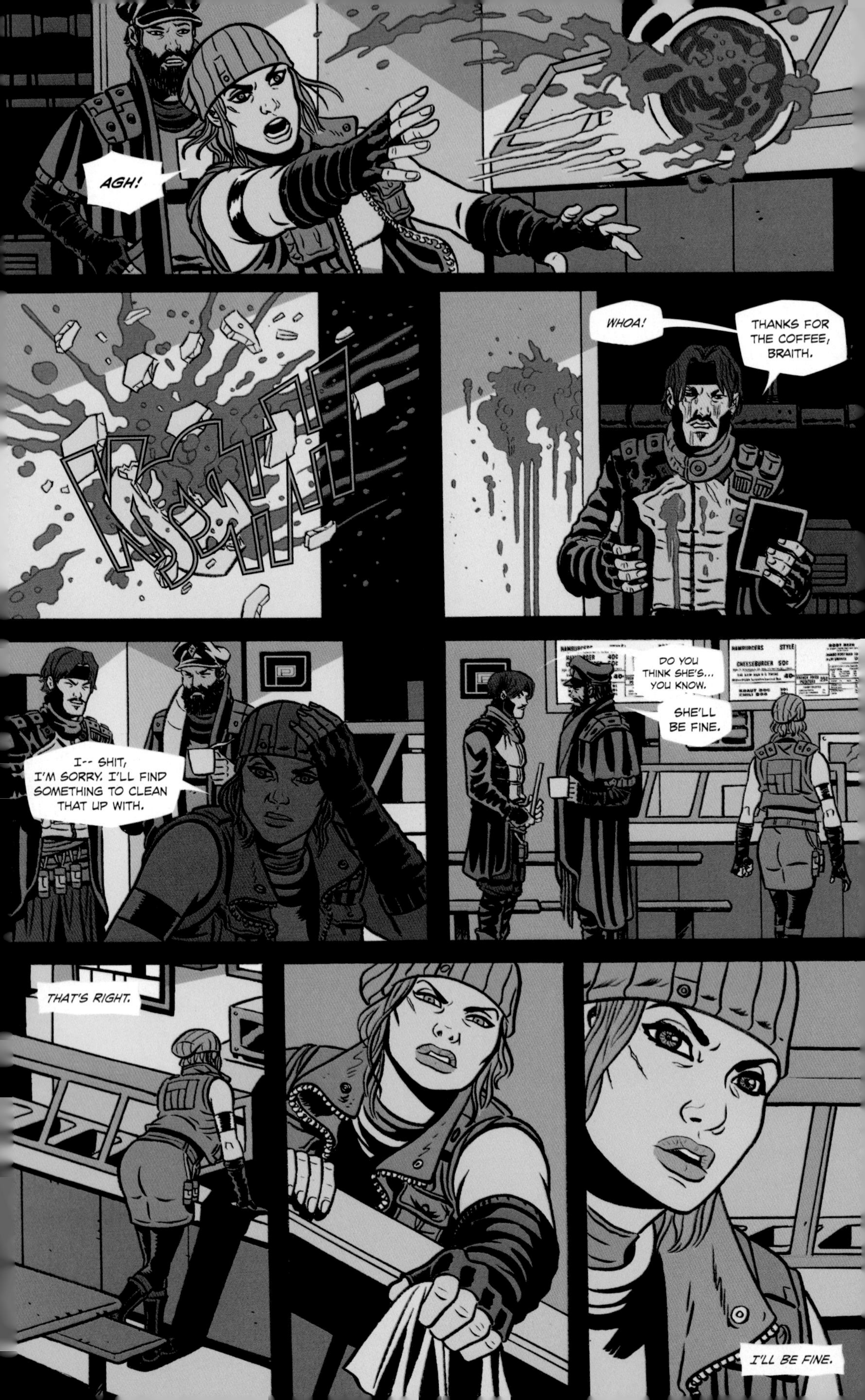

AGH!
KRSSH!
WHOA!
THANKS FOR THE COFFEE, BRAITH.
I-- SHIT, I'M SORRY. I'LL FIND SOMETHING TO CLEAN THAT UP WITH.
DO YOU THINK SHE'S... YOU KNOW.
SHE'LL BE FINE.
THAT'S RIGHT.
I'LL BE FINE.

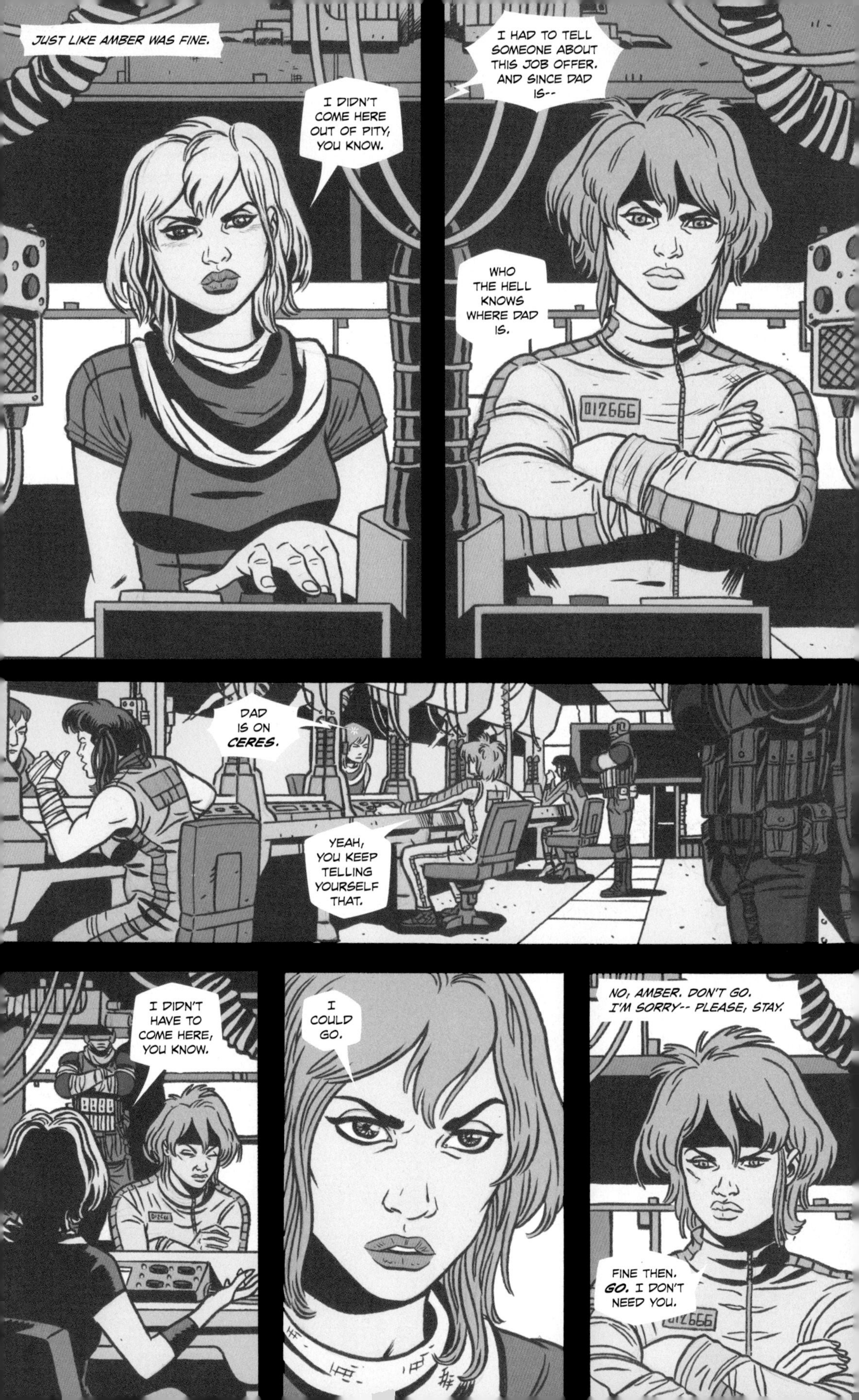
JUST LIKE AMBER WAS FINE.
I DIDN'T COME HERE OUT OF PITY, YOU KNOW.
I HAD TO TELL SOMEONE ABOUT THIS JOB OFFER. AND SINCE DAD IS--
WHO THE HELL KNOWS WHERE DAD IS.
012666
DAD IS ON *CERES*.
YEAH, YOU KEEP TELLING YOURSELF THAT.
I DIDN'T HAVE TO COME HERE, YOU KNOW.
I COULD GO.
NO, AMBER. DON'T GO. I'M SORRY-- PLEASE, STAY.
FINE THEN. ***GO.*** I DON'T NEED YOU.
012666

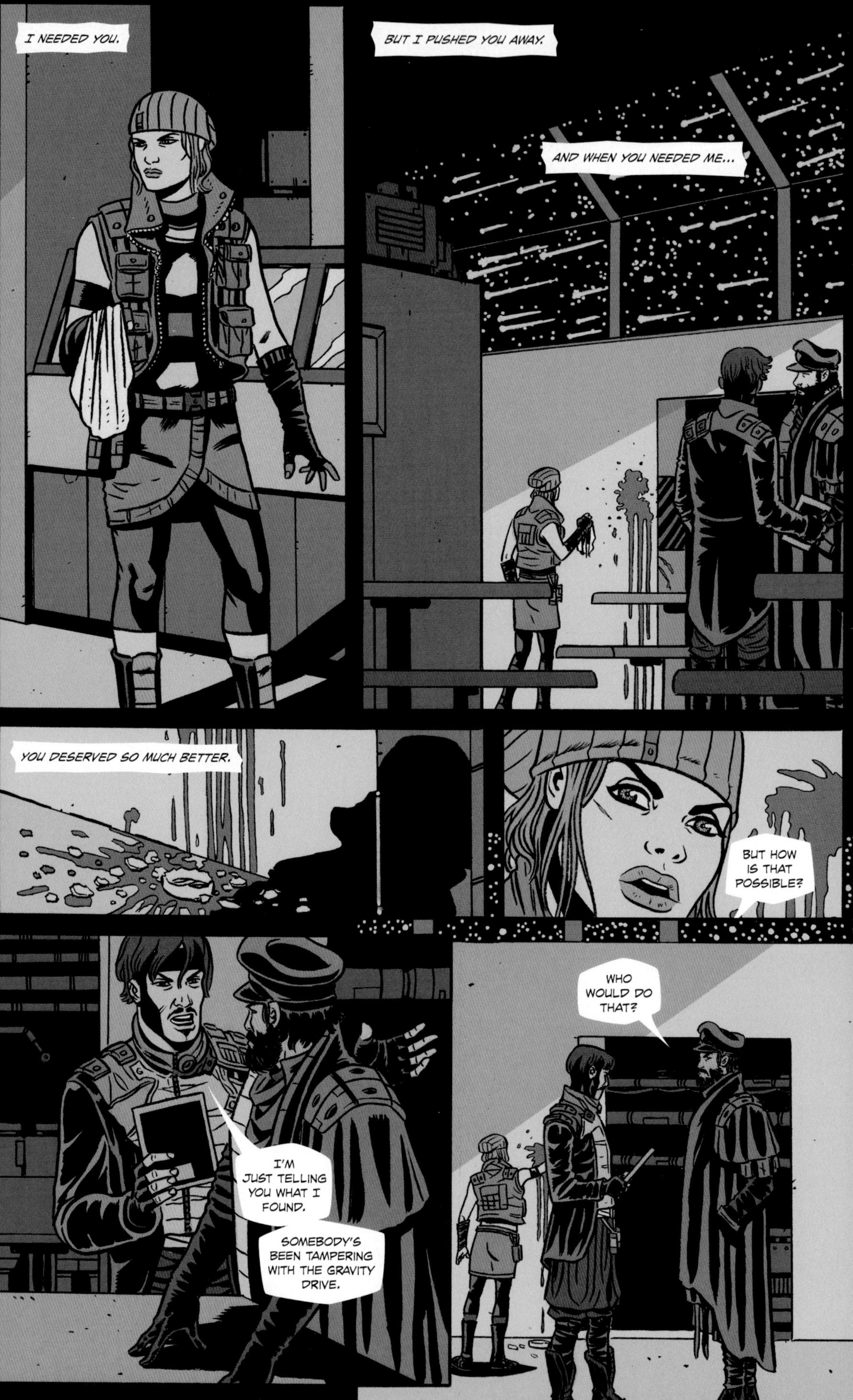
I NEEDED YOU.
BUT I PUSHED YOU AWAY.
AND WHEN YOU NEEDED ME...
YOU DESERVED SO MUCH BETTER.
BUT HOW IS THAT POSSIBLE?
I'M JUST TELLING YOU WHAT I FOUND.
SOMEBODY'S BEEN TAMPERING WITH THE GRAVITY DRIVE.
WHO WOULD DO THAT?

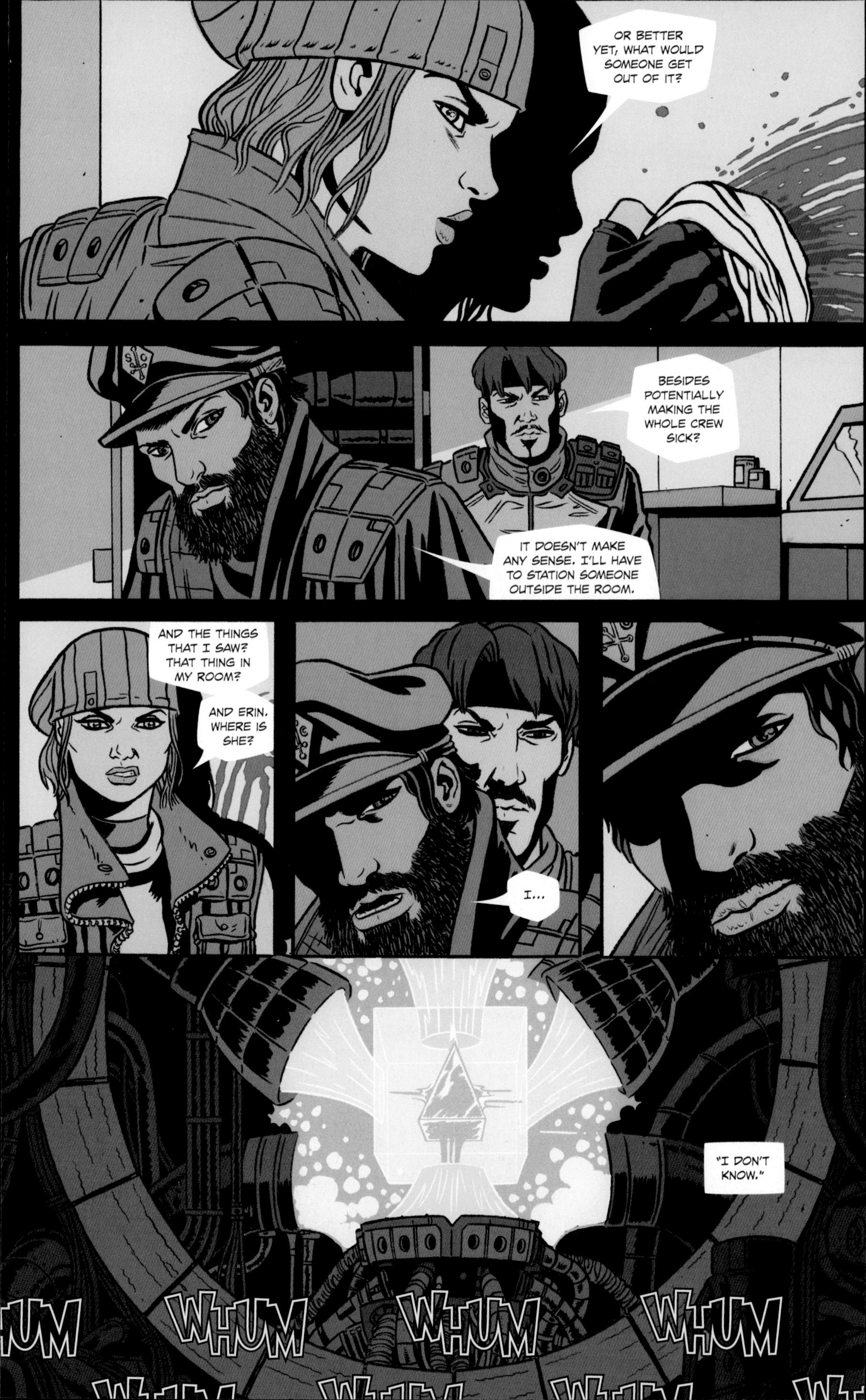
OR BETTER YET, WHAT WOULD SOMEONE GET OUT OF IT?
BESIDES POTENTIALLY MAKING THE WHOLE CREW SICK?
IT DOESN'T MAKE ANY SENSE. I'LL HAVE TO STATION SOMEONE OUTSIDE THE ROOM.
AND THE THINGS THAT I SAW? THAT THING IN MY ROOM?
AND ERIN. WHERE IS SHE?
I...
"I DON'T KNOW."
WHUM
WHUM
WHUM
WHUM

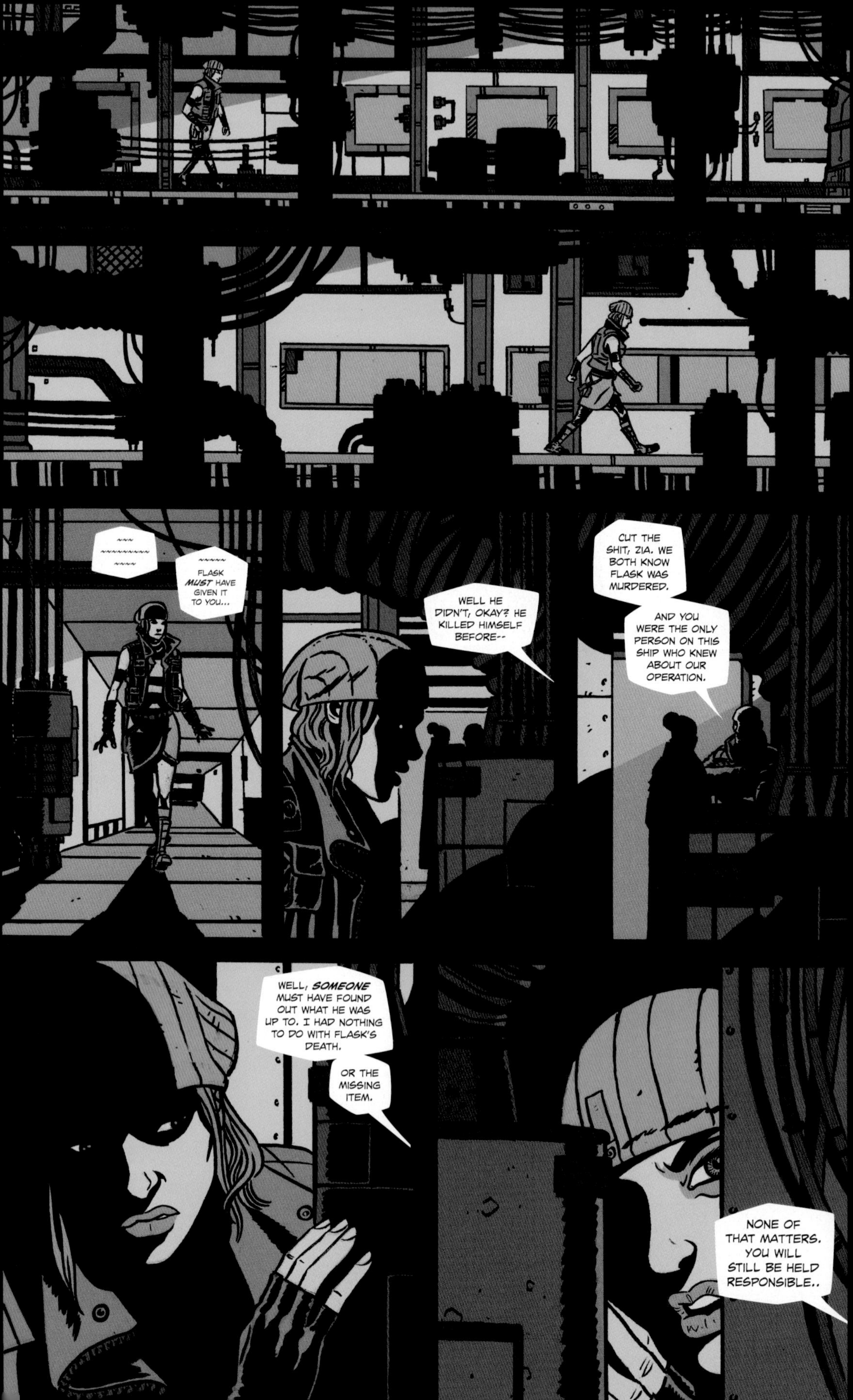
~~~
~~~~~~~~~
~~~~
~~~~~
FLASK *MUST* HAVE GIVEN IT TO YOU...
WELL HE DIDN'T, OKAY? HE KILLED HIMSELF BEFORE--
CUT THE SHIT, ZIA. WE BOTH KNOW FLASK WAS MURDERED.
AND YOU WERE THE ONLY PERSON ON THIS SHIP WHO KNEW ABOUT OUR OPERATION.
WELL, *SOMEONE* MUST HAVE FOUND OUT WHAT HE WAS UP TO. I HAD NOTHING TO DO WITH FLASK'S DEATH.
OR THE MISSING ITEM.
NONE OF THAT MATTERS. YOU WILL STILL BE HELD RESPONSIBLE..

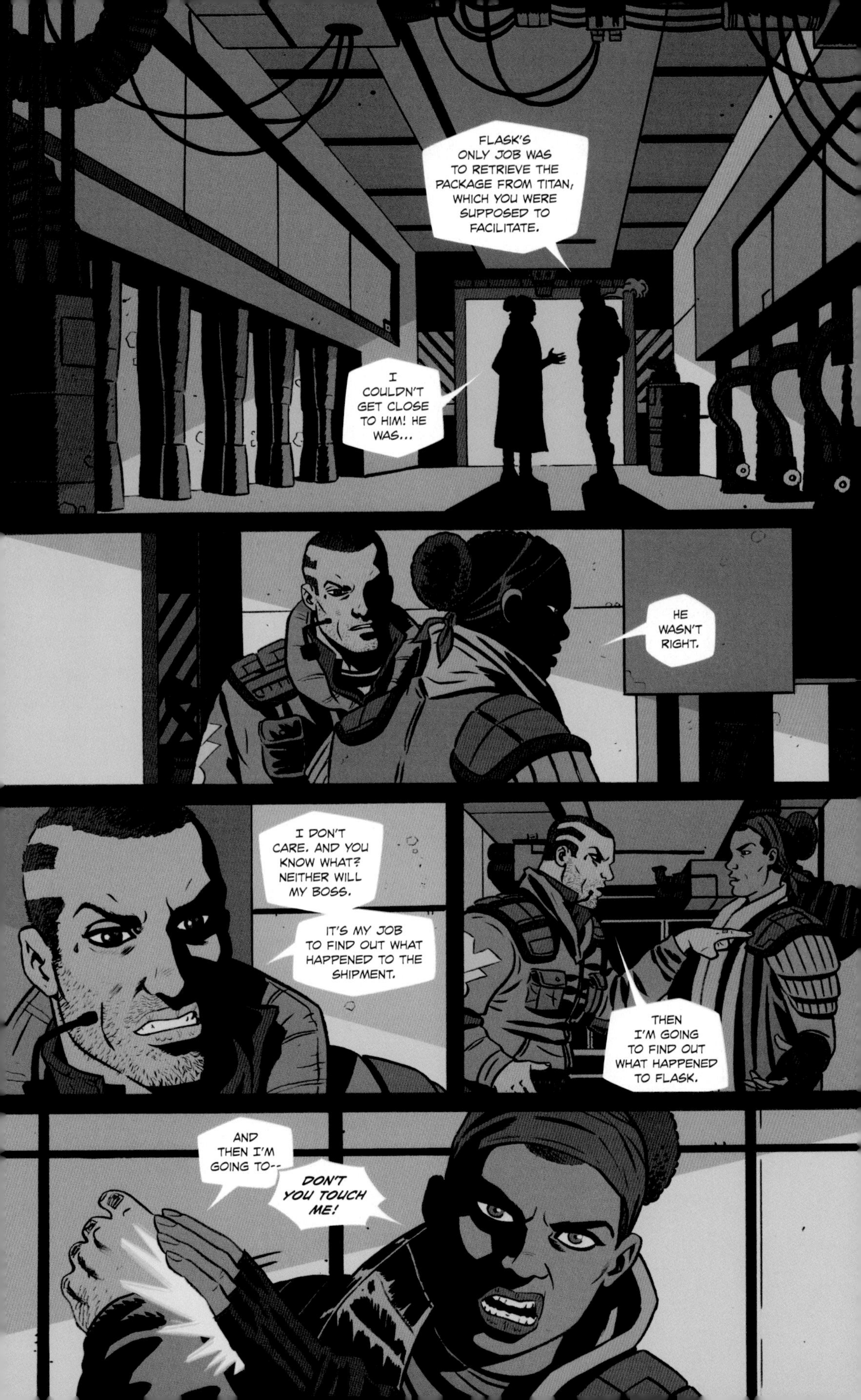
FLASK'S ONLY JOB WAS TO RETRIEVE THE PACKAGE FROM TITAN, WHICH YOU WERE SUPPOSED TO FACILITATE.
I COULDN'T GET CLOSE TO HIM! HE WAS...
HE WASN'T RIGHT.
I DON'T CARE. AND YOU KNOW WHAT? NEITHER WILL MY BOSS.
IT'S MY JOB TO FIND OUT WHAT HAPPENED TO THE SHIPMENT.
THEN I'M GOING TO FIND OUT WHAT HAPPENED TO FLASK.
AND THEN I'M GOING TO--
DON'T YOU TOUCH ME!

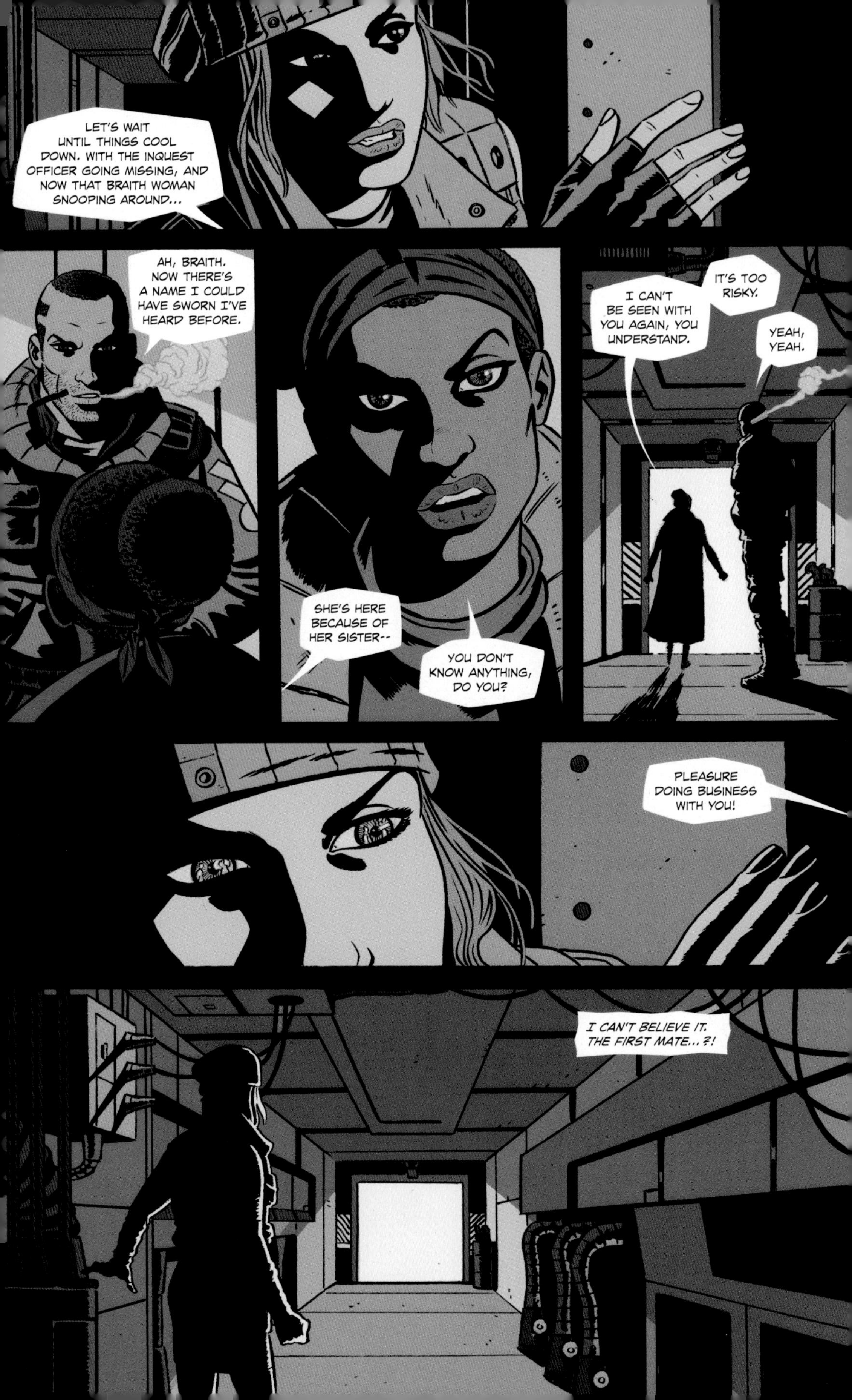
LET'S WAIT UNTIL THINGS COOL DOWN. WITH THE INQUEST OFFICER GOING MISSING, AND NOW THAT BRAITH WOMAN SNOOPING AROUND...
AH, BRAITH. NOW THERE'S A NAME I COULD HAVE SWORN I'VE HEARD BEFORE.
SHE'S HERE BECAUSE OF HER SISTER--
YOU DON'T KNOW ANYTHING, DO YOU?
I CAN'T BE SEEN WITH YOU AGAIN, YOU UNDERSTAND.
IT'S TOO RISKY.
YEAH, YEAH.
PLEASURE DOING BUSINESS WITH YOU!
I CAN'T BELIEVE IT. THE FIRST MATE...?!

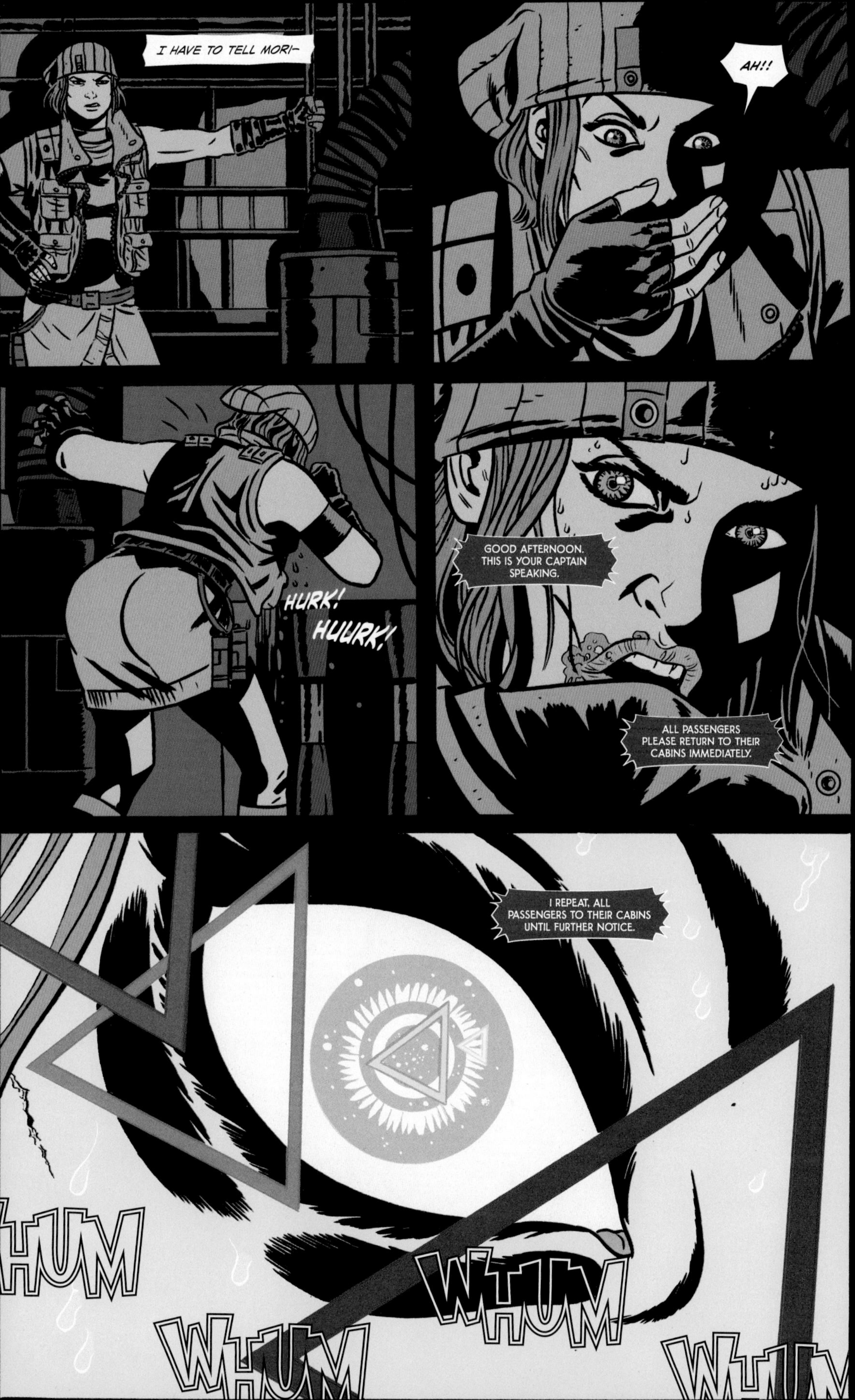
I HAVE TO TELL MORI—
AH!!
HURK!
HUURK!
GOOD AFTERNOON. THIS IS YOUR CAPTAIN SPEAKING.
ALL PASSENGERS PLEASE RETURN TO THEIR CABINS IMMEDIATELY.
I REPEAT, ALL PASSENGERS TO THEIR CABINS UNTIL FURTHER NOTICE.
WHUM
WHUM
WHUM
WHUM

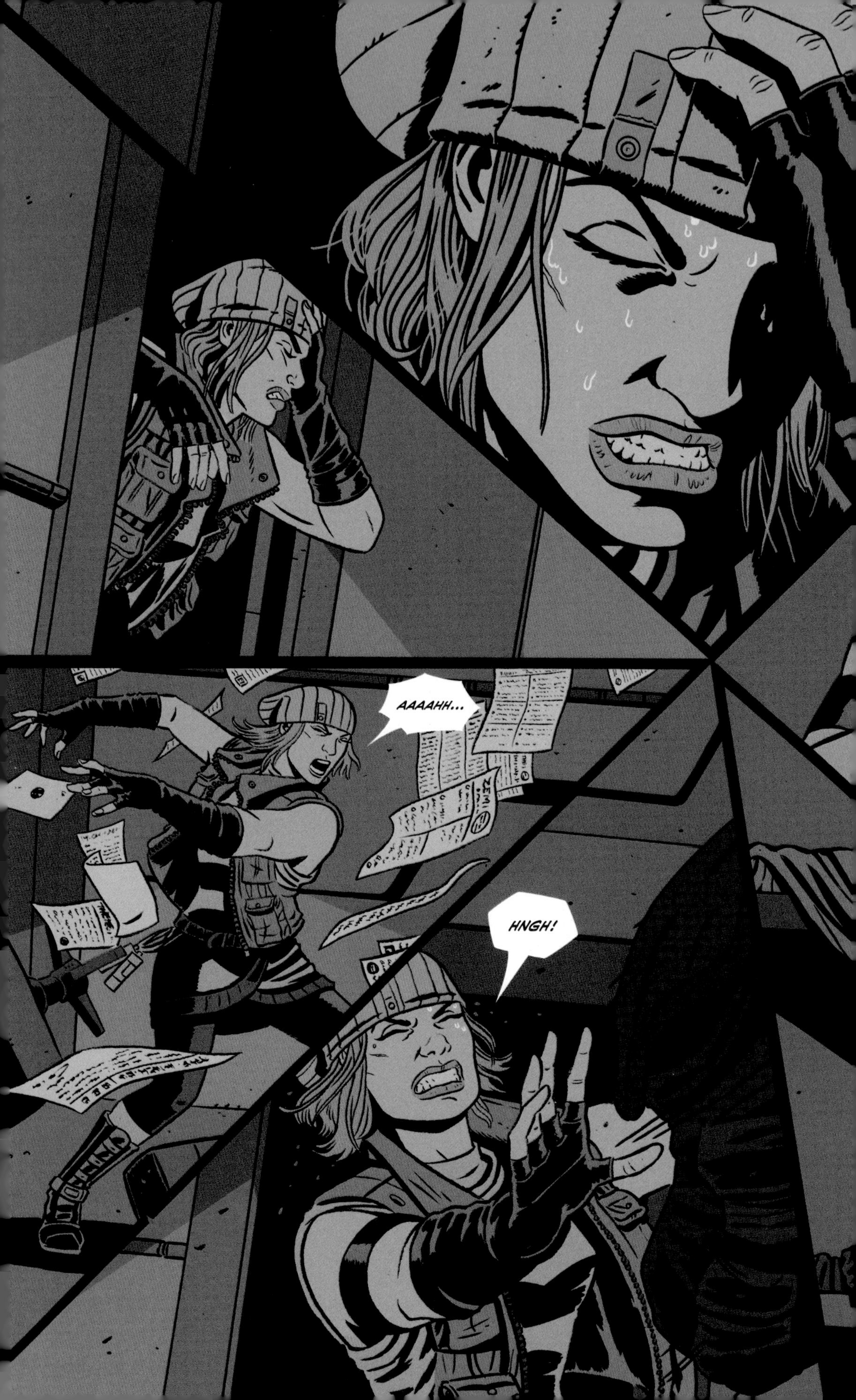
AAAAHH...
HNGH!

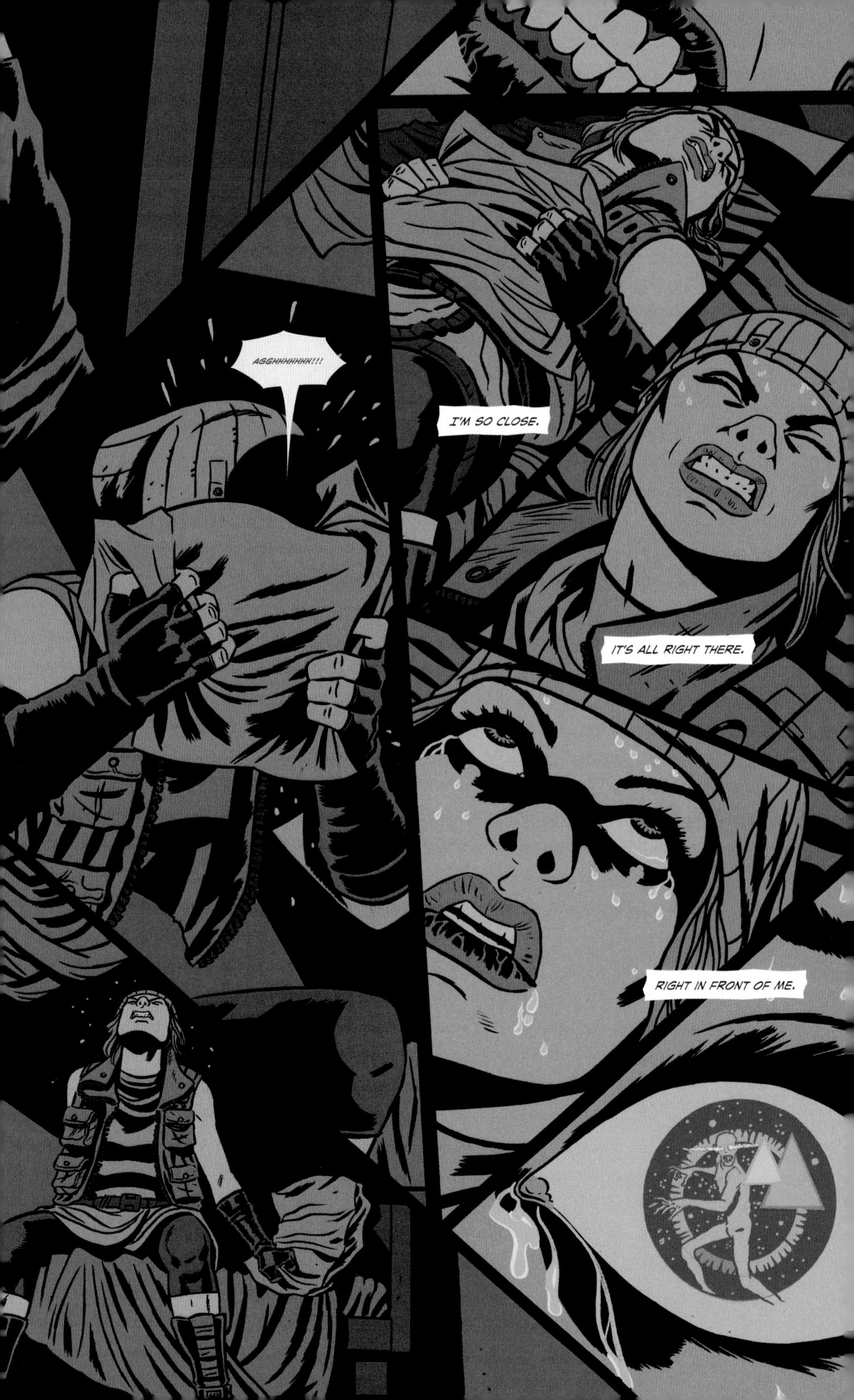
AGGHHHHHHH!!!
I'M SO CLOSE.
IT'S ALL RIGHT THERE.
RIGHT IN FRONT OF ME.

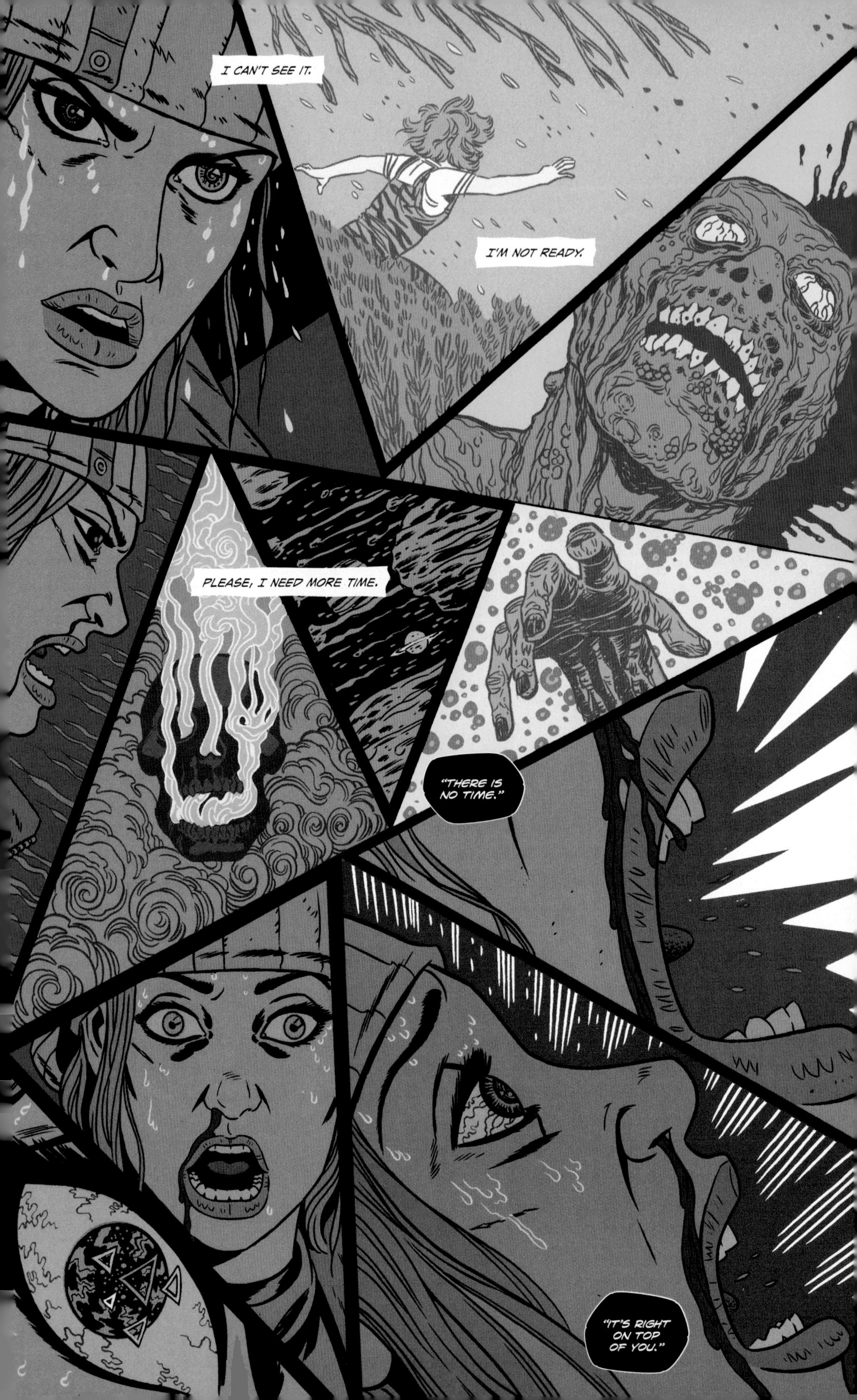
I CAN'T SEE IT.
I'M NOT READY.
PLEASE, I NEED MORE TIME.
"THERE IS NO TIME."
"IT'S RIGHT ON TOP OF YOU."

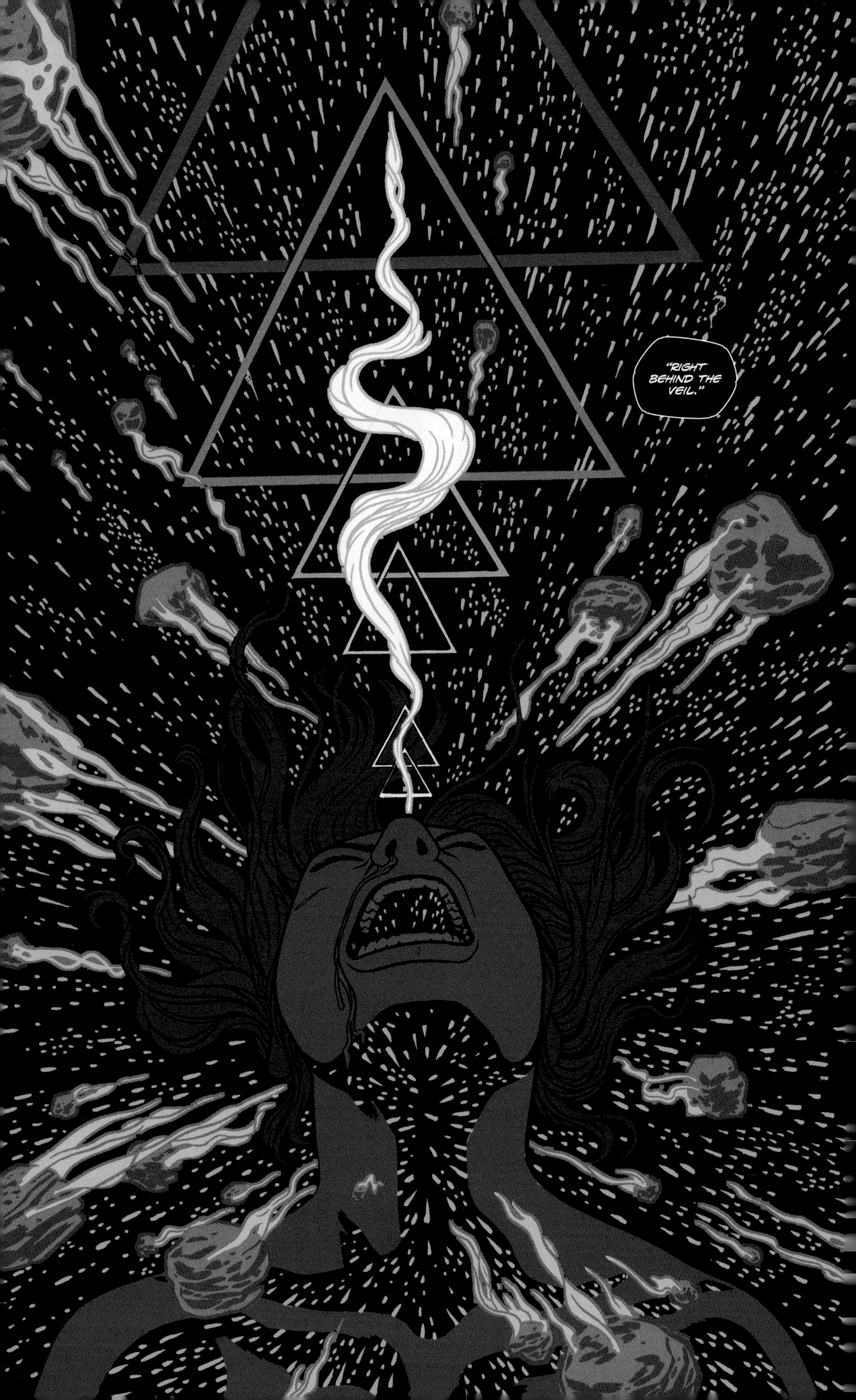
"RIGHT BEHIND THE VEIL."

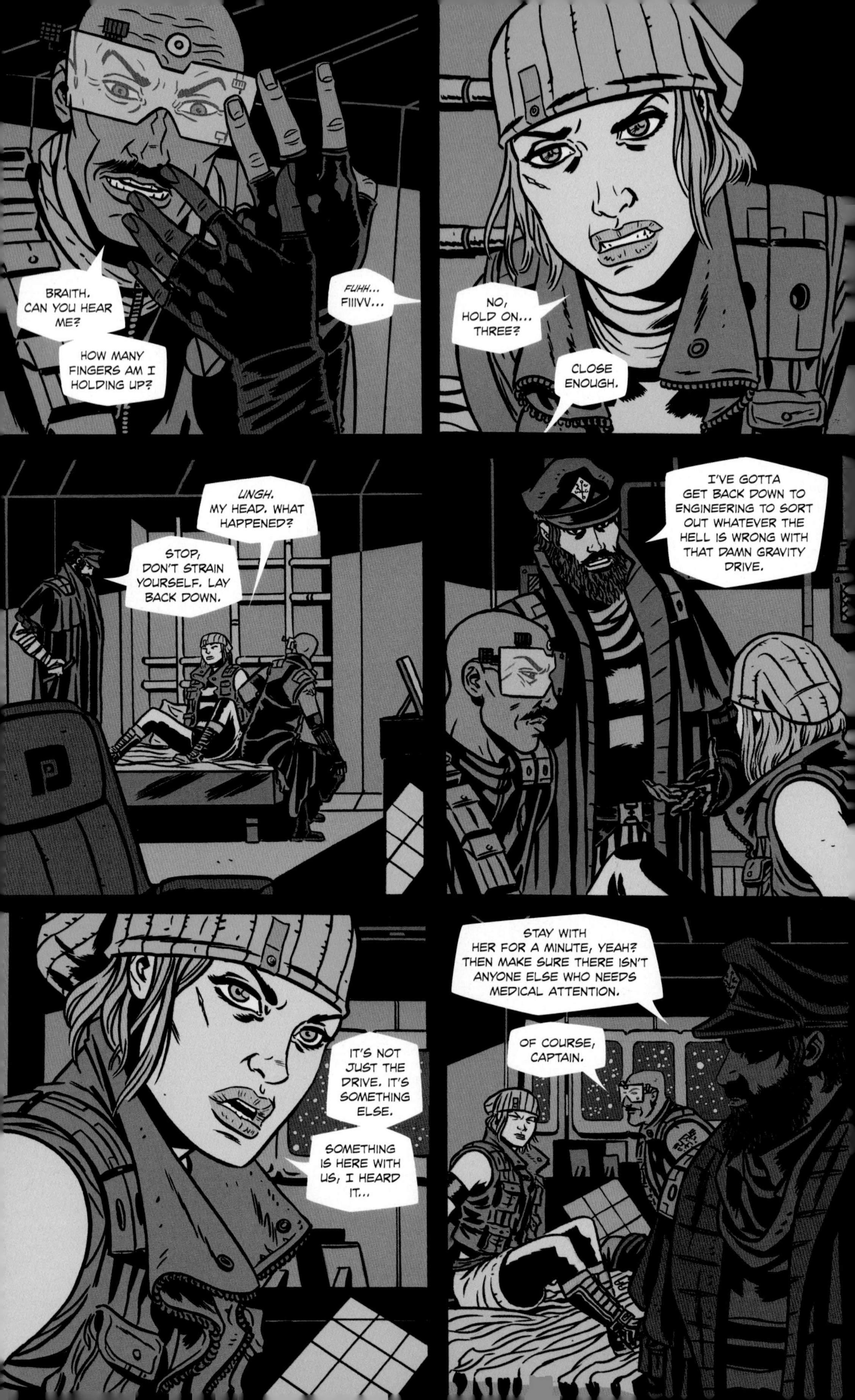
BRAITH. CAN YOU HEAR ME?
HOW MANY FINGERS AM I HOLDING UP?
FUHH... FIIIVV...
NO, HOLD ON... THREE?
CLOSE ENOUGH.
UNGH. MY HEAD. WHAT HAPPENED?
STOP, DON'T STRAIN YOURSELF. LAY BACK DOWN.
I'VE GOTTA GET BACK DOWN TO ENGINEERING TO SORT OUT WHATEVER THE HELL IS WRONG WITH THAT DAMN GRAVITY DRIVE.
IT'S NOT JUST THE DRIVE. IT'S SOMETHING ELSE.
SOMETHING IS HERE WITH US, I HEARD IT...
STAY WITH HER FOR A MINUTE, YEAH? THEN MAKE SURE THERE ISN'T ANYONE ELSE WHO NEEDS MEDICAL ATTENTION.
OF COURSE, CAPTAIN.

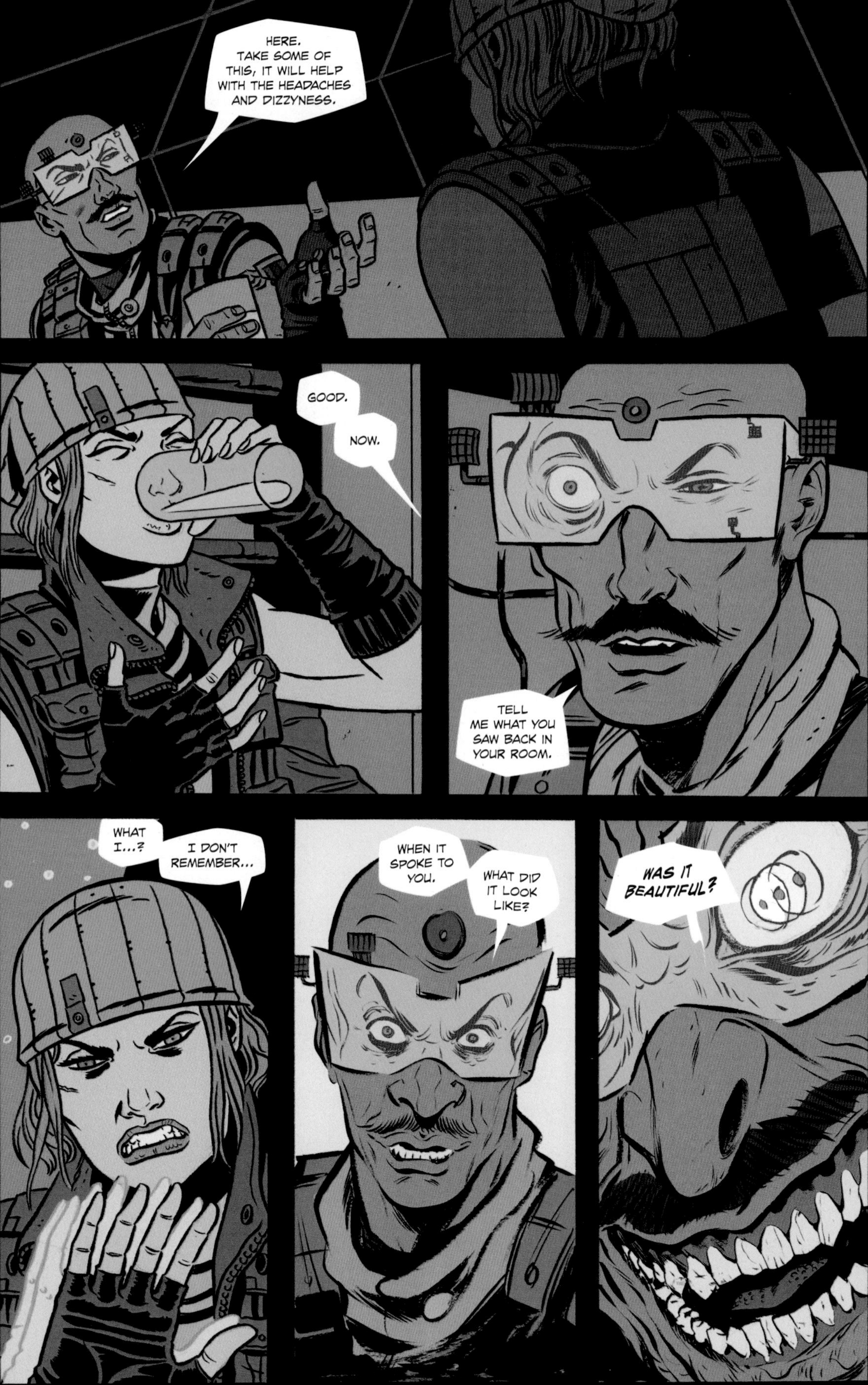
HERE.
TAKE SOME OF THIS, IT WILL HELP WITH THE HEADACHES AND DIZZYNESS.
GOOD.
NOW.
TELL ME WHAT YOU SAW BACK IN YOUR ROOM.
WHAT I...?
I DON'T REMEMBER...
WHEN IT SPOKE TO YOU.
WHAT DID IT LOOK LIKE?
WAS IT BEAUTIFUL?

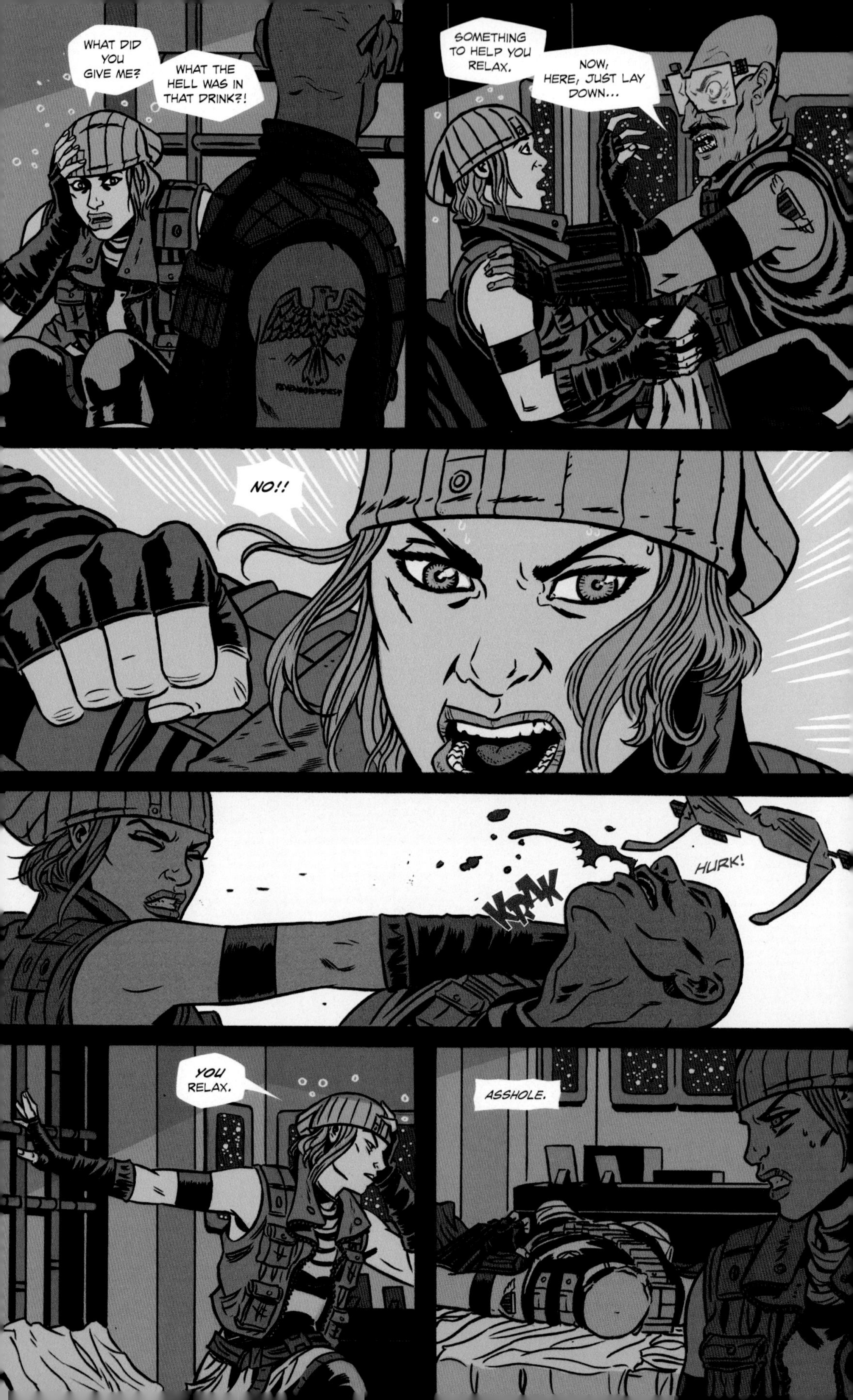
WHAT DID YOU GIVE ME?
WHAT THE HELL WAS IN THAT DRINK?!
SOMETHING TO HELP YOU RELAX.
NOW, HERE, JUST LAY DOWN...
NO!!
KRAK
HURK!
YOU RELAX.
ASSHOLE.

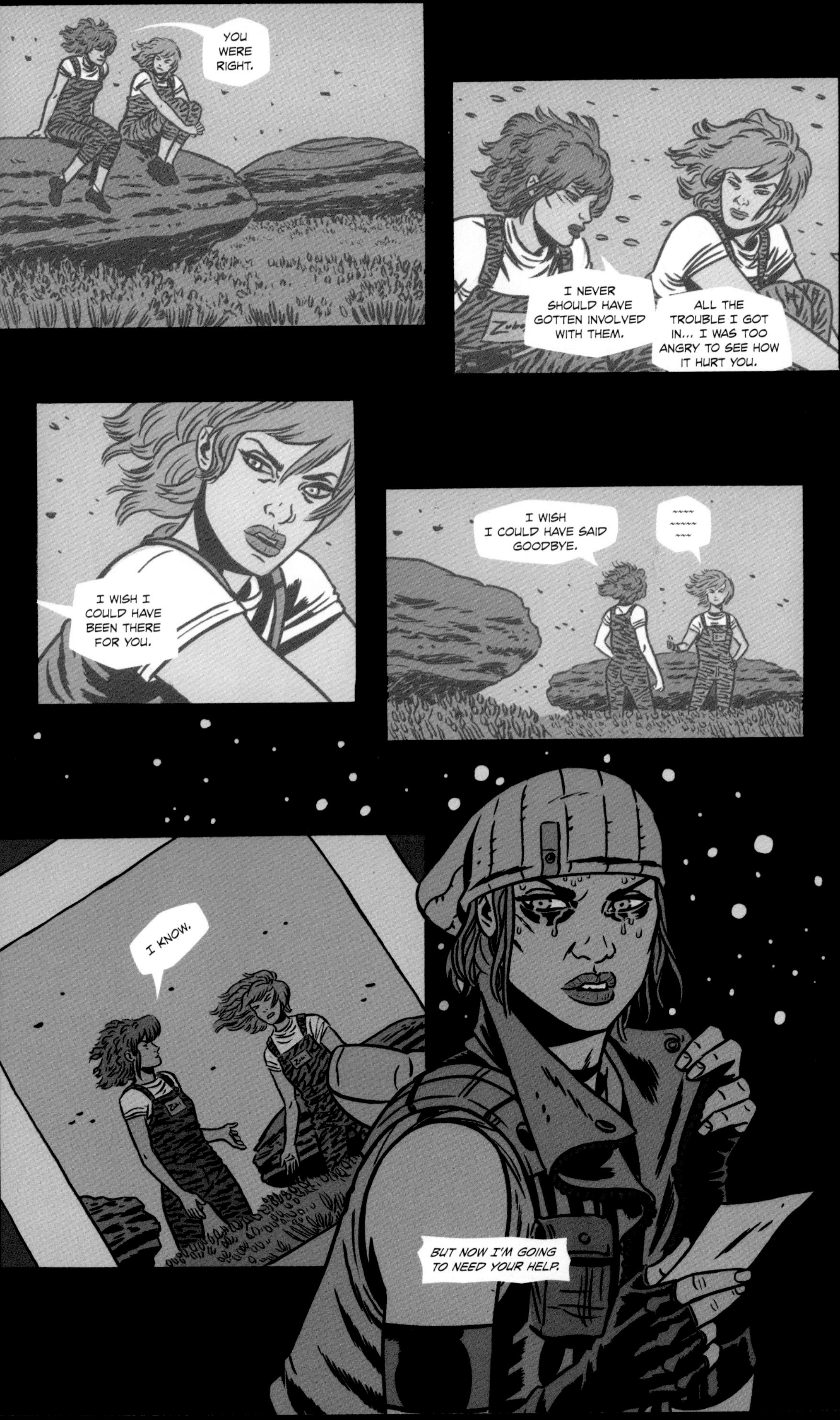
YOU WERE RIGHT.
I NEVER SHOULD HAVE GOTTEN INVOLVED WITH THEM.
ALL THE TROUBLE I GOT IN... I WAS TOO ANGRY TO SEE HOW IT HURT YOU.
I WISH I COULD HAVE BEEN THERE FOR YOU.
I WISH I COULD HAVE SAID GOODBYE.
~~~~ ~~~~~ ~~~
I KNOW.
BUT NOW I'M GOING TO NEED YOUR HELP.
~~~~

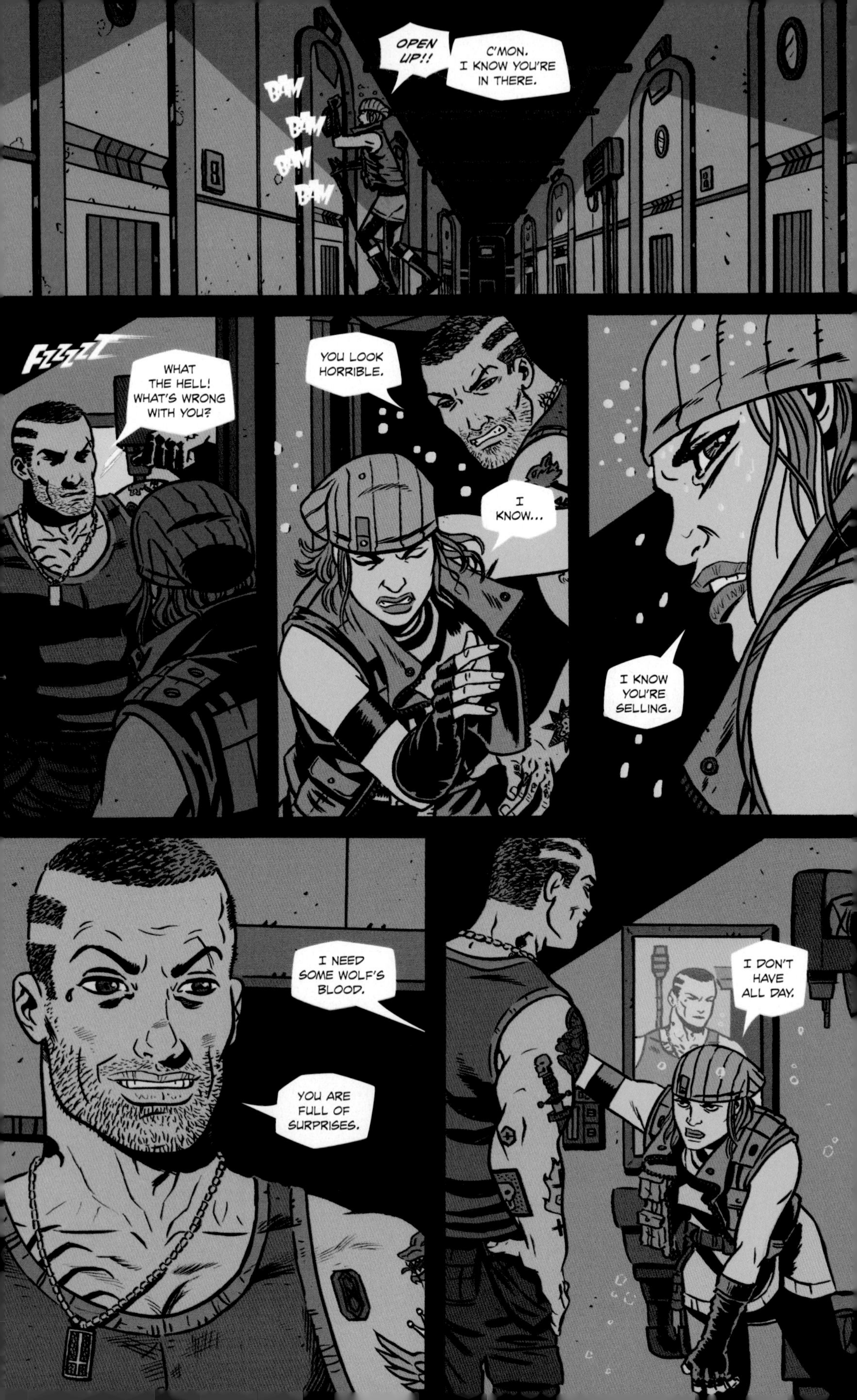
BAM
BAM
BAM
BAM
OPEN UP!!
C'MON. I KNOW YOU'RE IN THERE.
FZZZZT
WHAT THE HELL! WHAT'S WRONG WITH YOU?
YOU LOOK HORRIBLE.
I KNOW...
I KNOW YOU'RE SELLING.
I NEED SOME WOLF'S BLOOD.
YOU ARE FULL OF SURPRISES.
I DON'T HAVE ALL DAY.

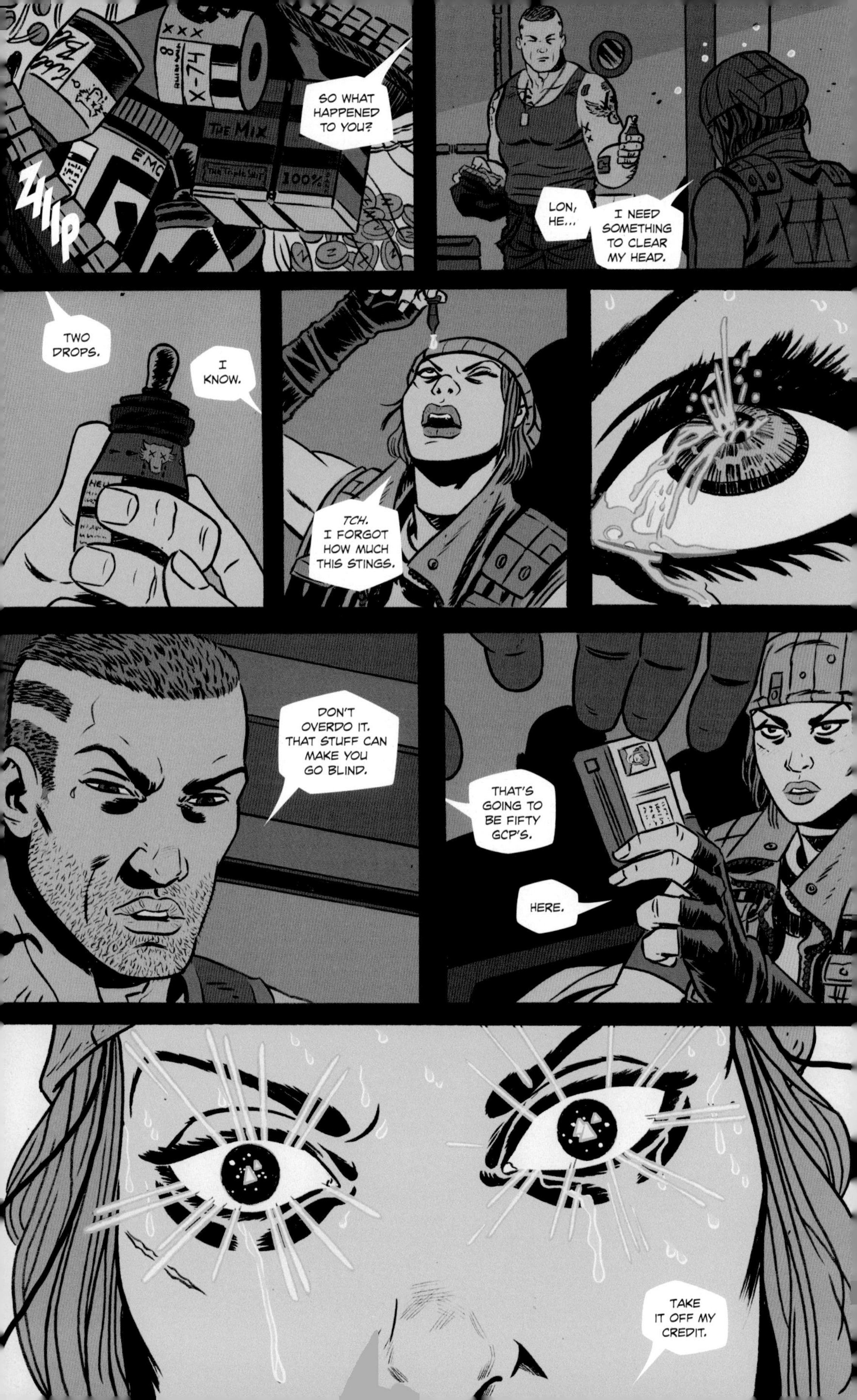
SO WHAT HAPPENED TO YOU?
ZHIIP
X-74
THE MIX
100%
EMC
LON, HE...
I NEED SOMETHING TO CLEAR MY HEAD.
TWO DROPS.
I KNOW.
TCH. I FORGOT HOW MUCH THIS STINGS.
DON'T OVERDO IT. THAT STUFF CAN MAKE YOU GO BLIND.
THAT'S GOING TO BE FIFTY GCP'S.
HERE.
TAKE IT OFF MY CREDIT.

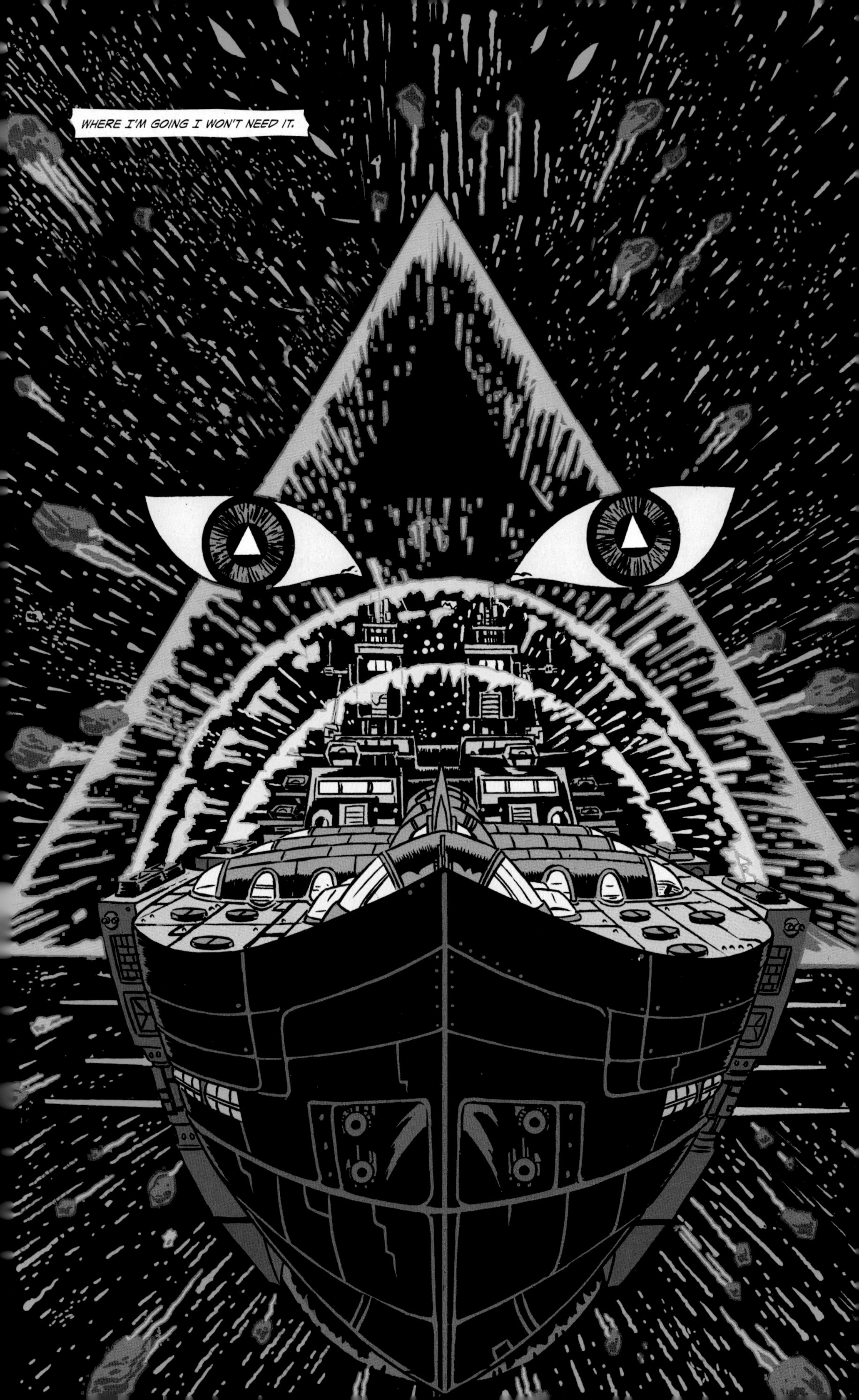
WHERE I'M GOING I WON'T NEED IT.

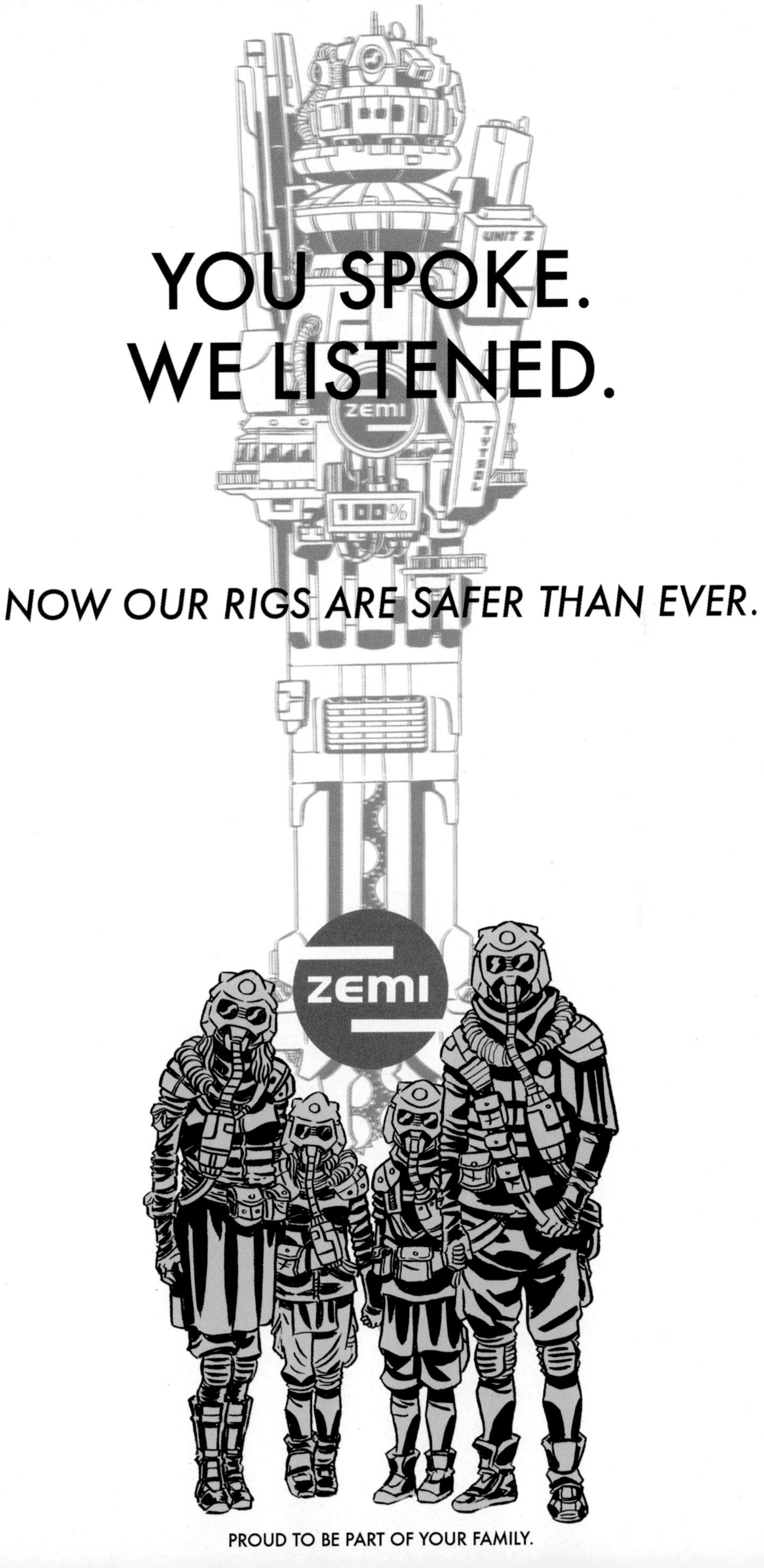

YOU SPOKE.
WE LISTENED.
NOW OUR RIGS ARE SAFER THAN EVER.
UNIT Z
ZEMI
TYTSOL
100%
ZEMI
PROUD TO BE PART OF YOUR FAMILY.

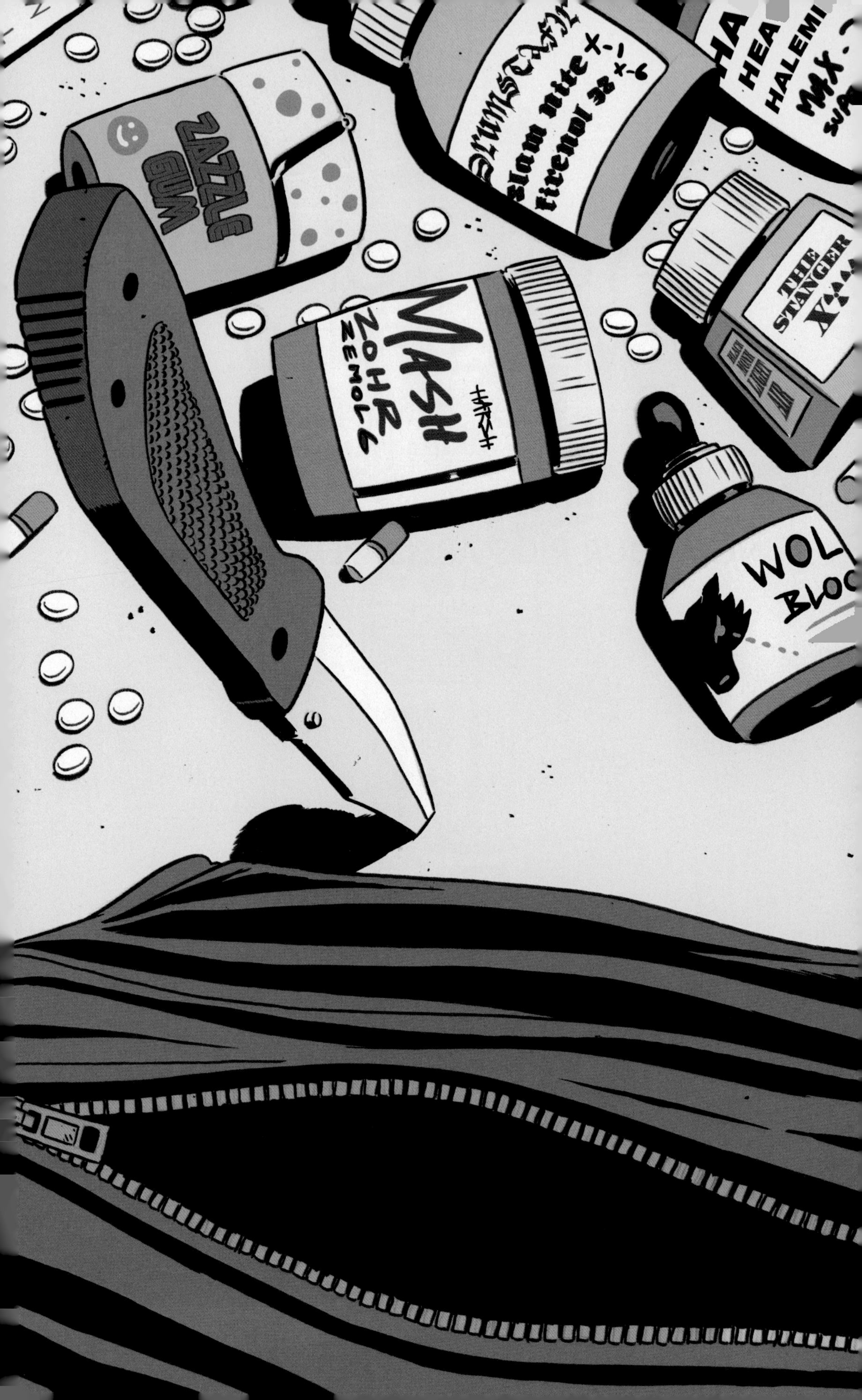
ZAZZLE GUM
MASH
slam nite
THE STANGER

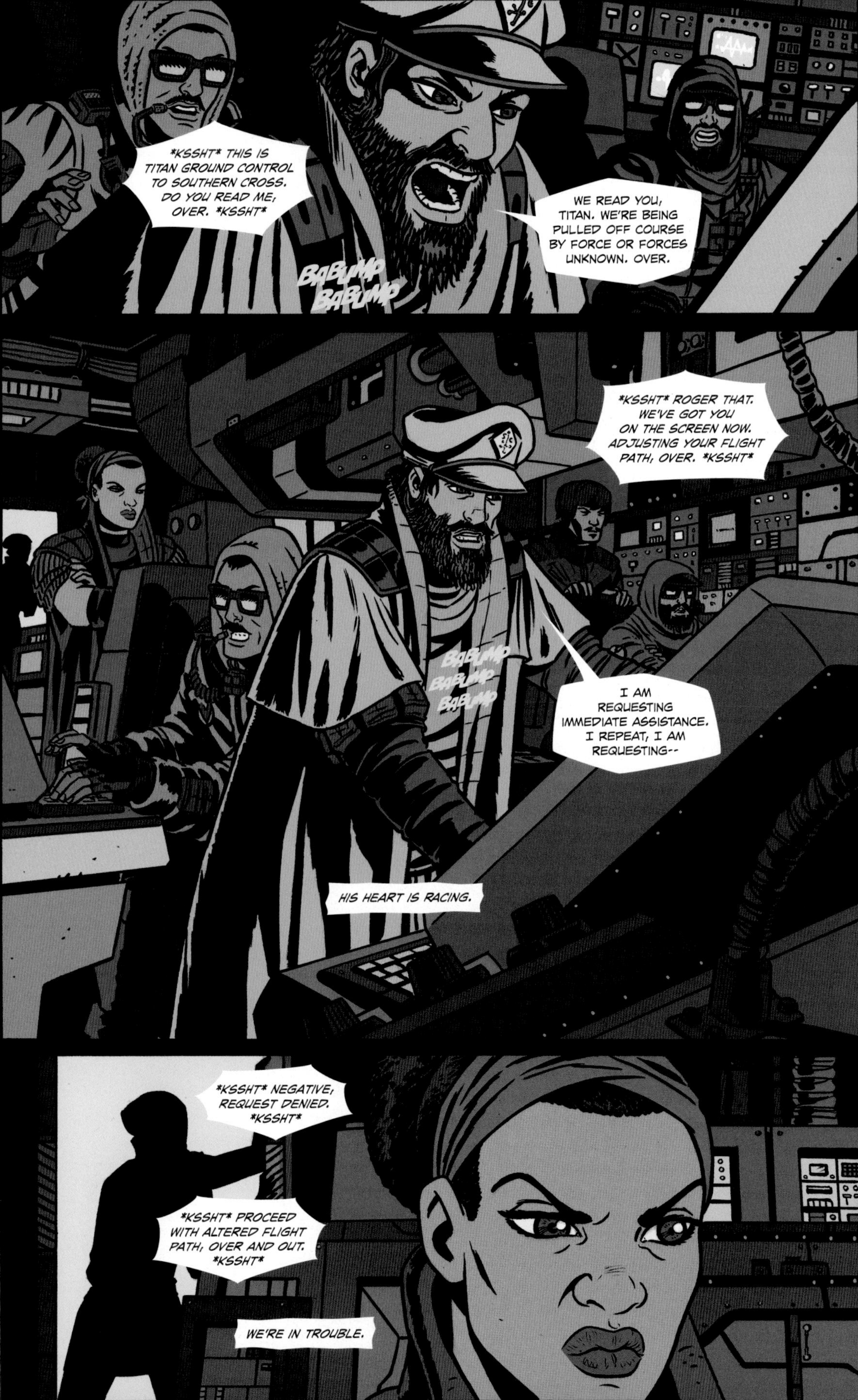
KSSHT THIS IS TITAN GROUND CONTROL TO SOUTHERN CROSS. DO YOU READ ME, OVER. *KSSHT*
WE READ YOU, TITAN. WE'RE BEING PULLED OFF COURSE BY FORCE OR FORCES UNKNOWN. OVER.
BABUMP BABUMP
KSSHT ROGER THAT. WE'VE GOT YOU ON THE SCREEN NOW. ADJUSTING YOUR FLIGHT PATH, OVER. *KSSHT*
BABUMP BABUMP BABUMP
I AM REQUESTING IMMEDIATE ASSISTANCE. I REPEAT, I AM REQUESTING--
HIS HEART IS RACING.
KSSHT NEGATIVE, REQUEST DENIED. *KSSHT*
KSSHT PROCEED WITH ALTERED FLIGHT PATH, OVER AND OUT. *KSSHT*
WE'RE IN TROUBLE.

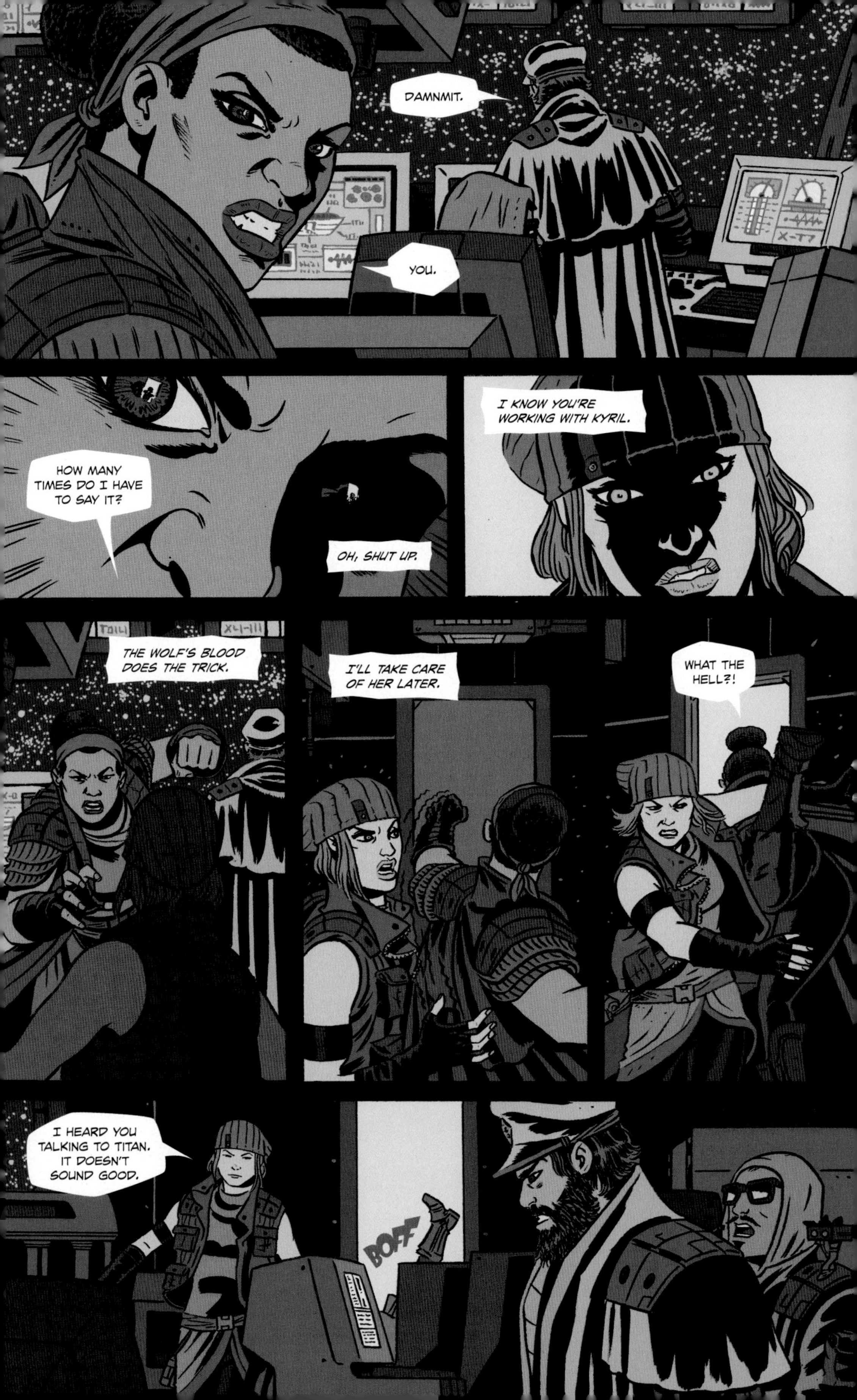
DAMNMIT.
YOU.
HOW MANY TIMES DO I HAVE TO SAY IT?
OH, SHUT UP.
I KNOW YOU'RE WORKING WITH KYRIL.
THE WOLF'S BLOOD DOES THE TRICK.
I'LL TAKE CARE OF HER LATER.
WHAT THE HELL?!
I HEARD YOU TALKING TO TITAN. IT DOESN'T SOUND GOOD.
BOFF

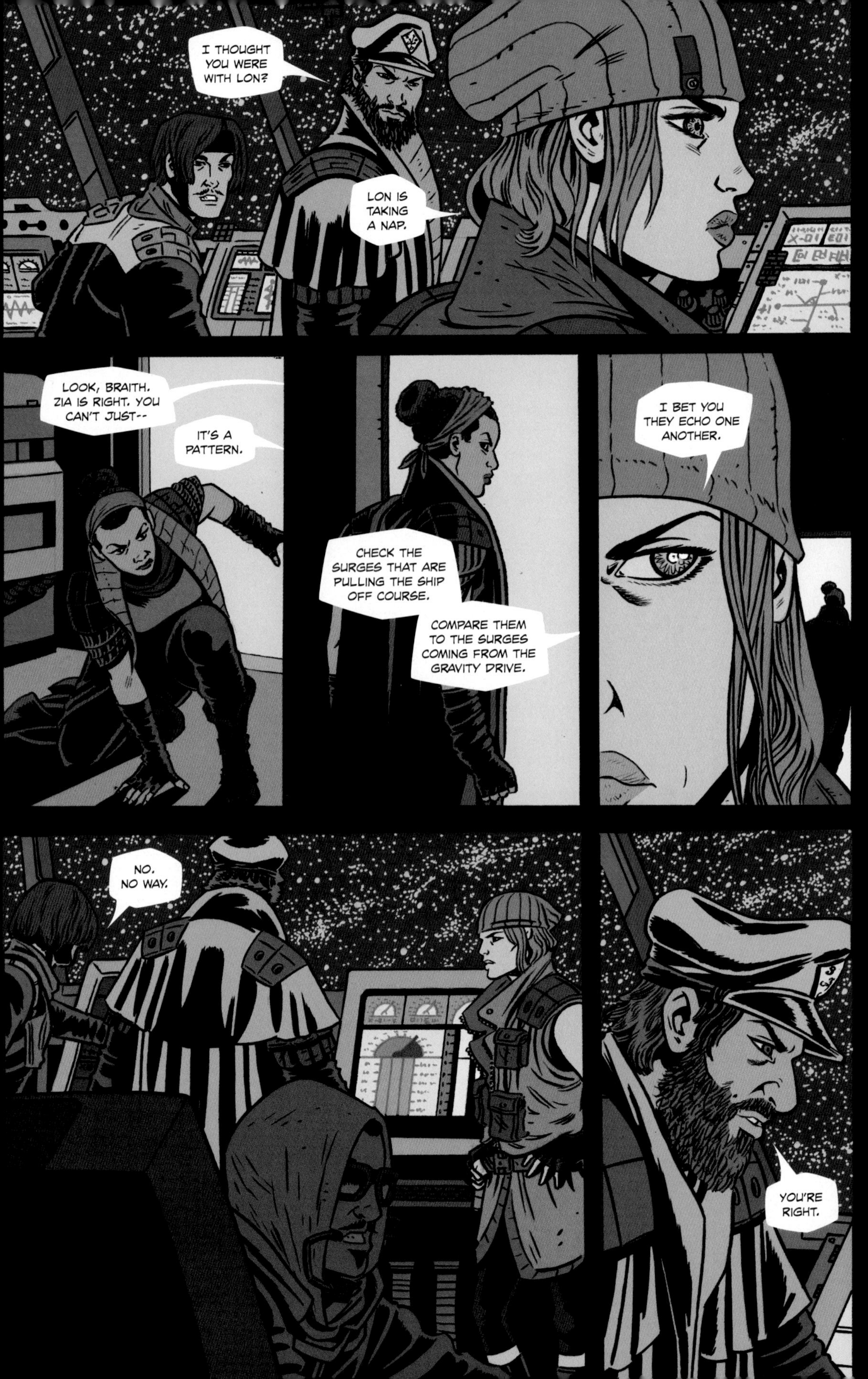
I THOUGHT YOU WERE WITH LON?
LON IS TAKING A NAP.
LOOK, BRAITH. ZIA IS RIGHT. YOU CAN'T JUST--
IT'S A PATTERN.
CHECK THE SURGES THAT ARE PULLING THE SHIP OFF COURSE.
COMPARE THEM TO THE SURGES COMING FROM THE GRAVITY DRIVE.
I BET YOU THEY ECHO ONE ANOTHER.
NO. NO WAY.
YOU'RE RIGHT.

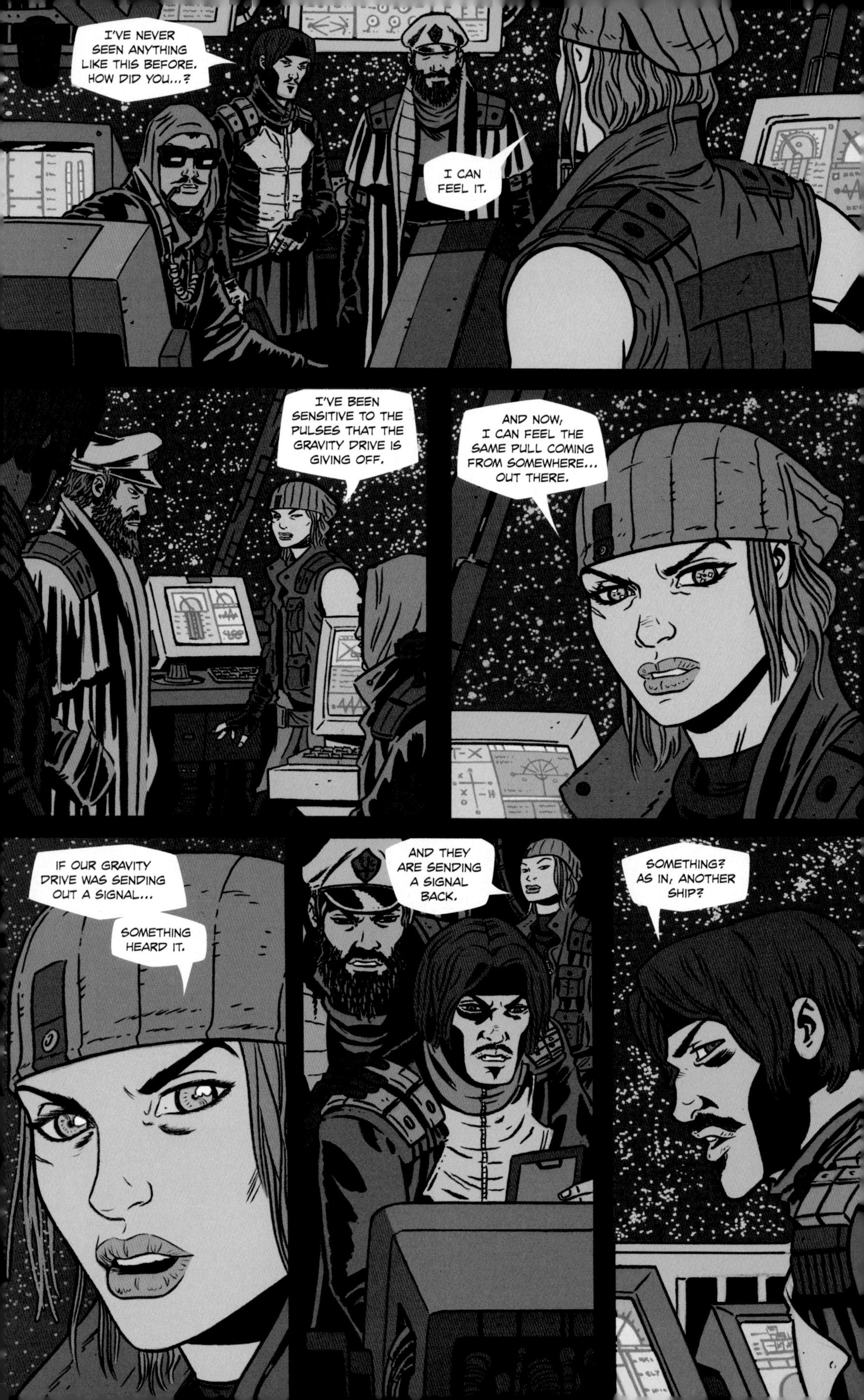
I'VE NEVER SEEN ANYTHING LIKE THIS BEFORE. HOW DID YOU...?
I CAN FEEL IT.
I'VE BEEN SENSITIVE TO THE PULSES THAT THE GRAVITY DRIVE IS GIVING OFF.
AND NOW, I CAN FEEL THE SAME PULL COMING FROM SOMEWHERE... OUT THERE.
IF OUR GRAVITY DRIVE WAS SENDING OUT A SIGNAL...
SOMETHING HEARD IT.
AND THEY ARE SENDING A SIGNAL BACK.
SOMETHING? AS IN, ANOTHER SHIP?

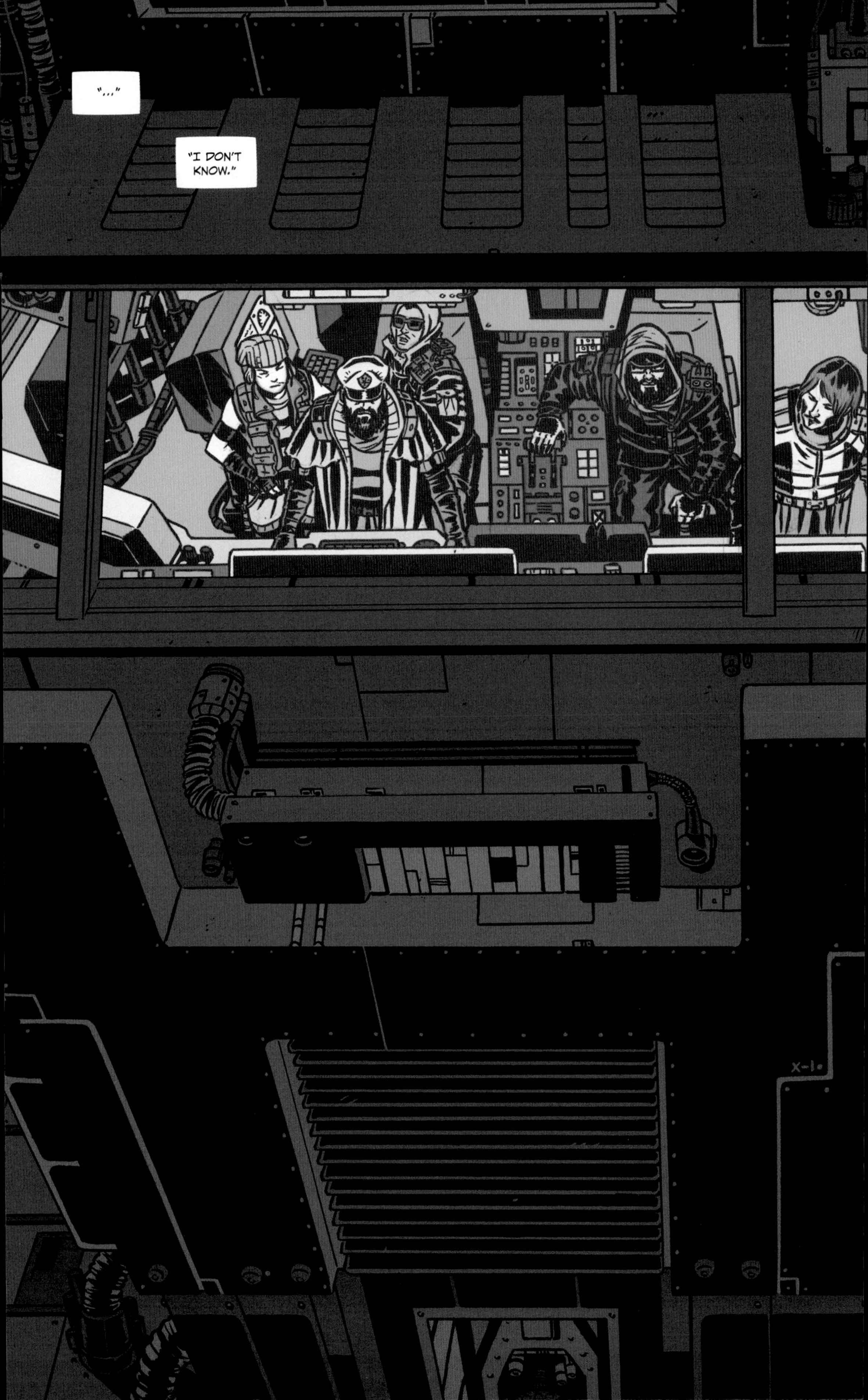
"..."
"I DON'T KNOW."
X-1

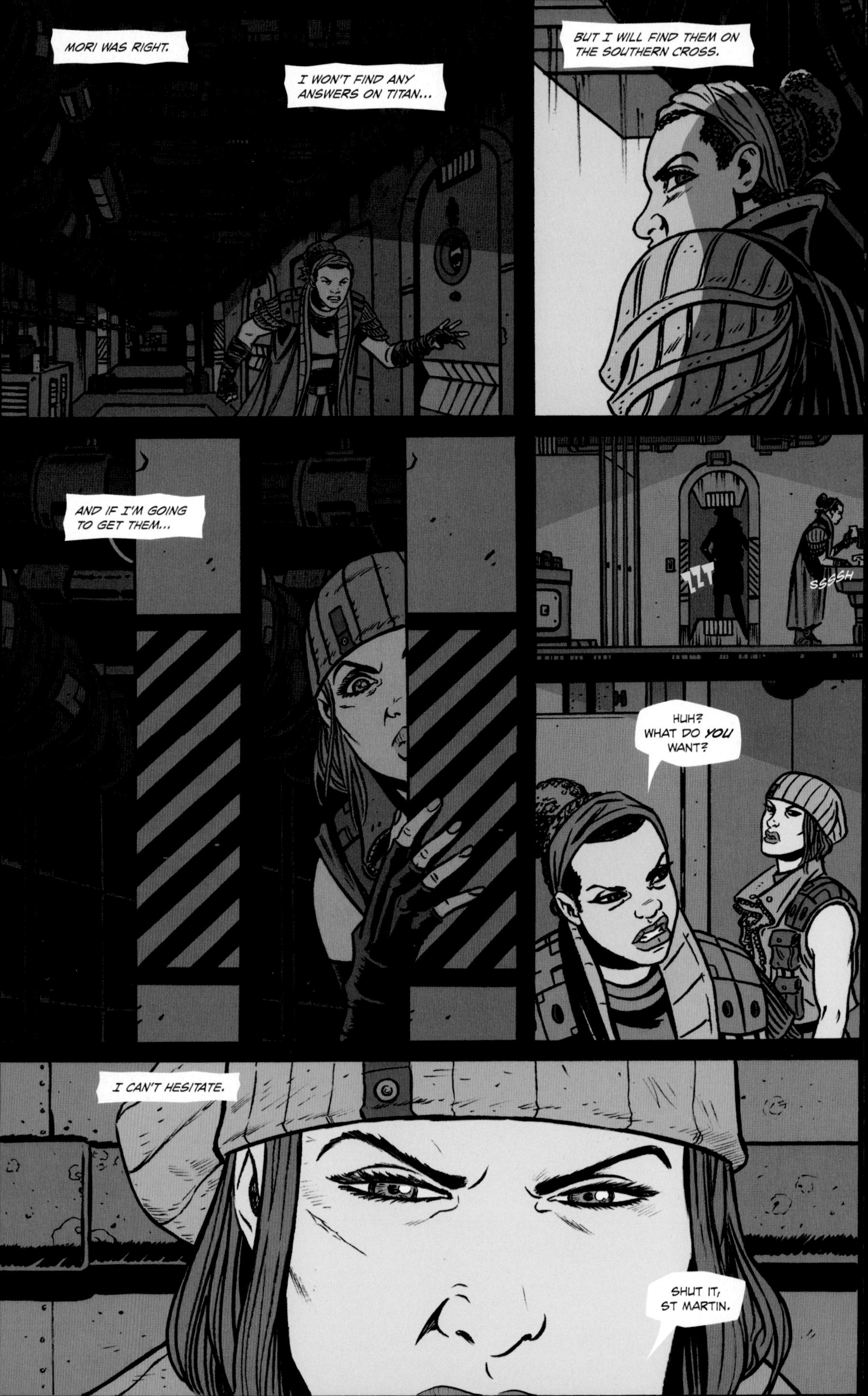
MORI WAS RIGHT.
I WON'T FIND ANY ANSWERS ON TITAN...
BUT I WILL FIND THEM ON THE SOUTHERN CROSS.
AND IF I'M GOING TO GET THEM...
ZZT
SSSSH
HUH? WHAT DO *YOU* WANT?
I CAN'T HESITATE.
SHUT IT, ST MARTIN.

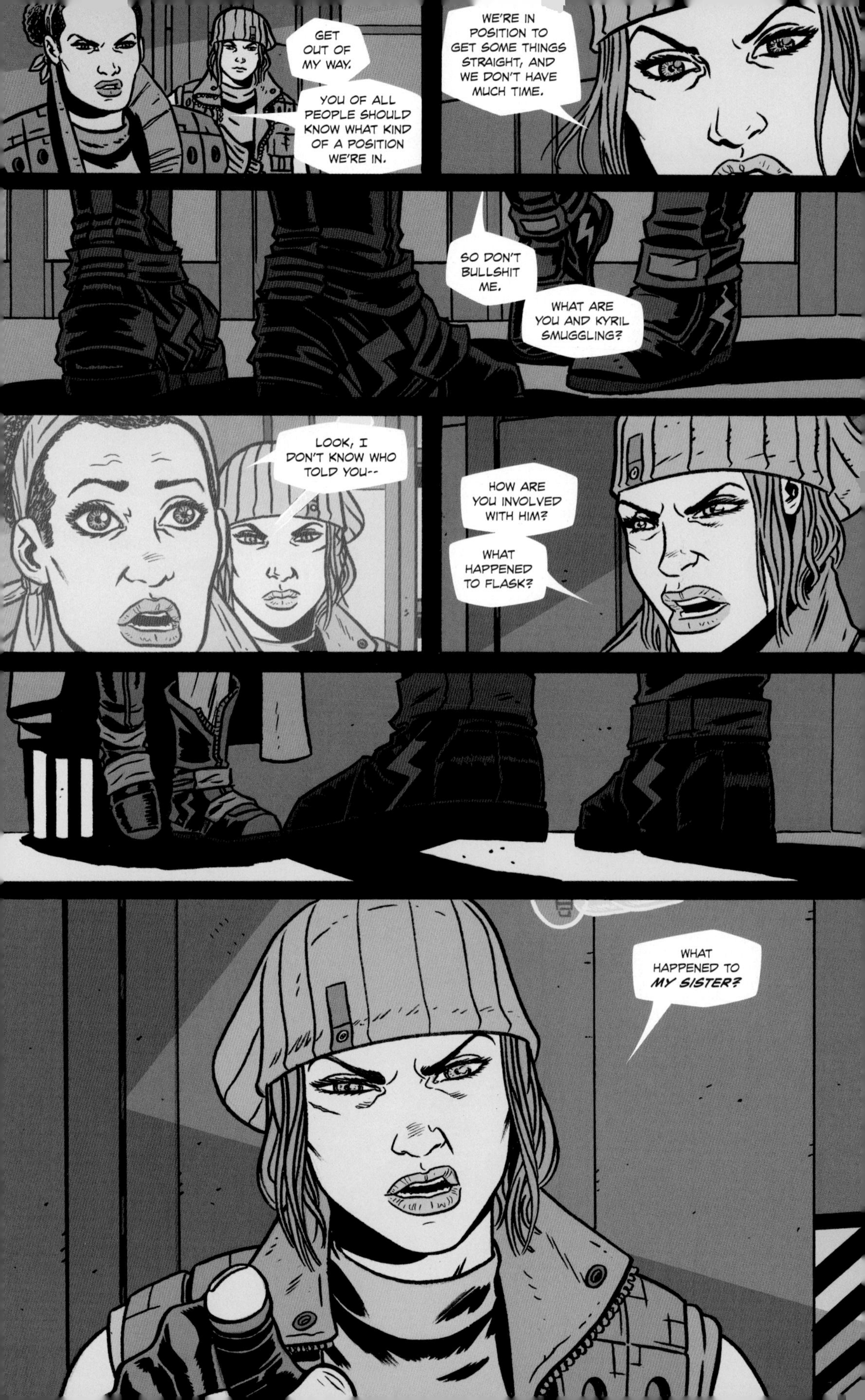
GET OUT OF MY WAY.
YOU OF ALL PEOPLE SHOULD KNOW WHAT KIND OF A POSITION WE'RE IN.
WE'RE IN POSITION TO GET SOME THINGS STRAIGHT, AND WE DON'T HAVE MUCH TIME.
SO DON'T BULLSHIT ME.
WHAT ARE YOU AND KYRIL SMUGGLING?
LOOK, I DON'T KNOW WHO TOLD YOU--
HOW ARE YOU INVOLVED WITH HIM?
WHAT HAPPENED TO FLASK?
WHAT HAPPENED TO *MY SISTER?*

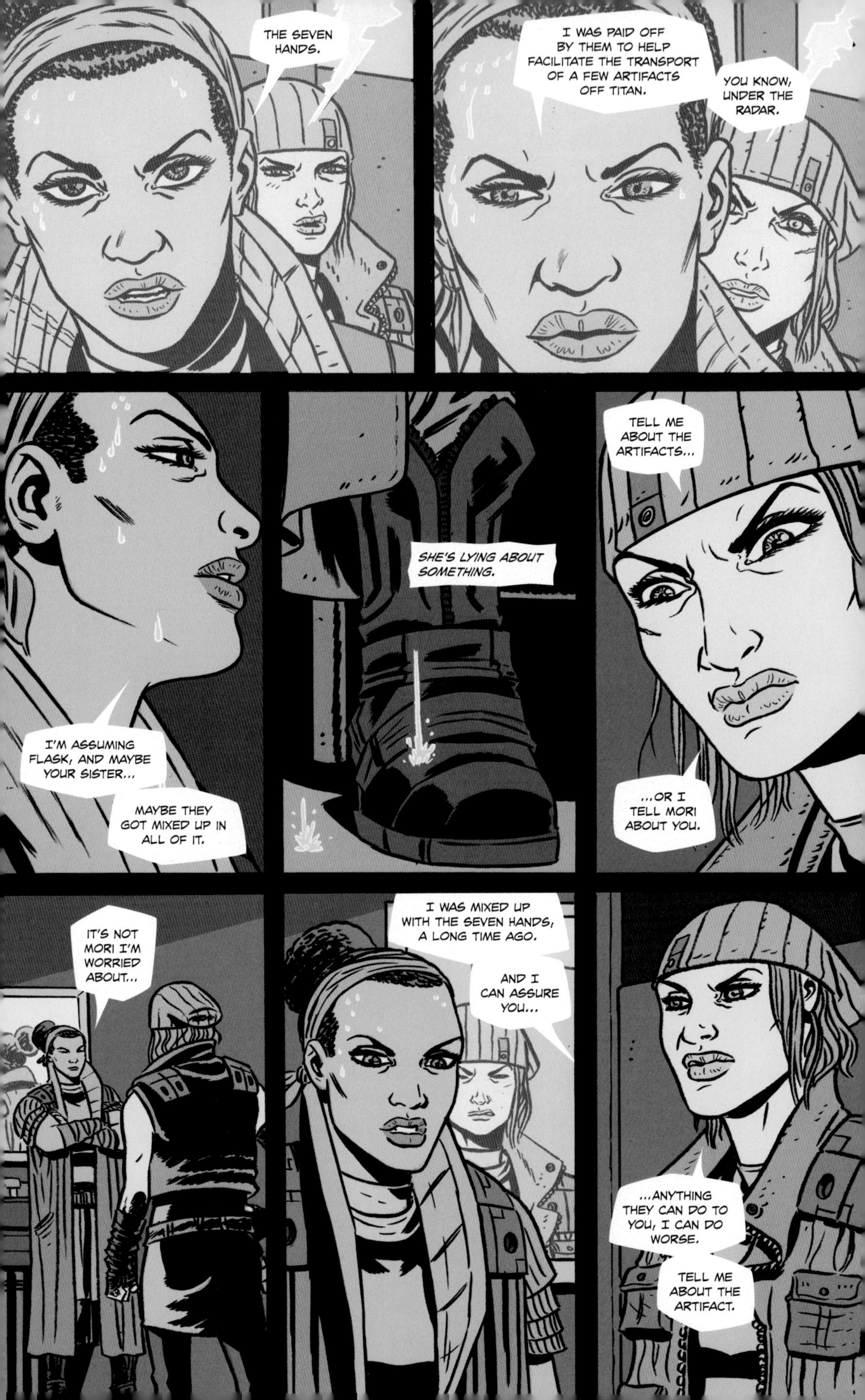
THE SEVEN HANDS.
I WAS PAID OFF BY THEM TO HELP FACILITATE THE TRANSPORT OF A FEW ARTIFACTS OFF TITAN.
YOU KNOW, UNDER THE RADAR.
I'M ASSUMING FLASK, AND MAYBE YOUR SISTER...
MAYBE THEY GOT MIXED UP IN ALL OF IT.
SHE'S LYING ABOUT SOMETHING.
TELL ME ABOUT THE ARTIFACTS...
...OR I TELL MORI ABOUT YOU.
IT'S NOT MORI I'M WORRIED ABOUT...
I WAS MIXED UP WITH THE SEVEN HANDS, A LONG TIME AGO.
AND I CAN ASSURE YOU...
...ANYTHING THEY CAN DO TO YOU, I CAN DO WORSE.
TELL ME ABOUT THE ARTIFACT.

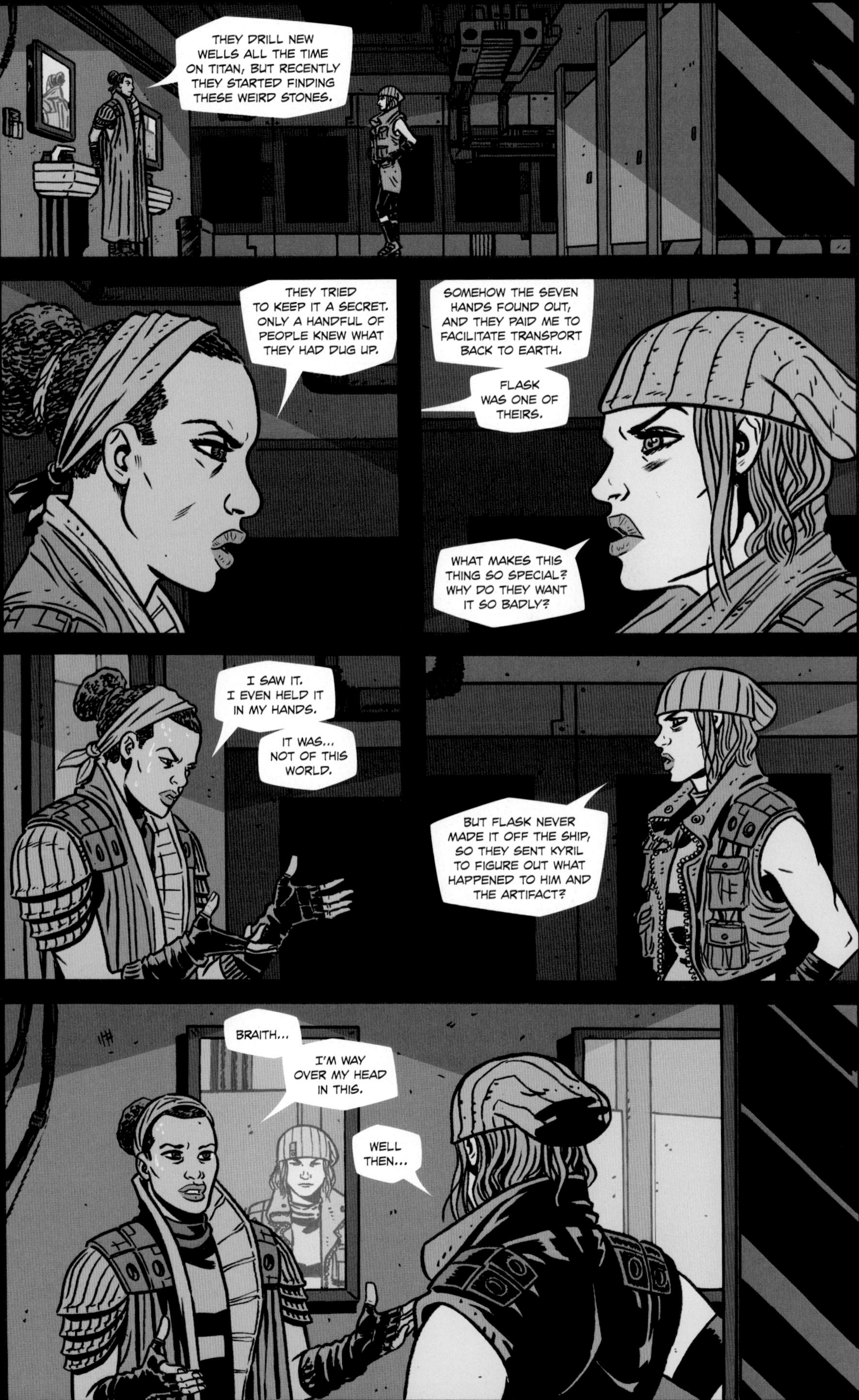
THEY DRILL NEW WELLS ALL THE TIME ON TITAN, BUT RECENTLY THEY STARTED FINDING THESE WEIRD STONES.
THEY TRIED TO KEEP IT A SECRET. ONLY A HANDFUL OF PEOPLE KNEW WHAT THEY HAD DUG UP.
SOMEHOW THE SEVEN HANDS FOUND OUT, AND THEY PAID ME TO FACILITATE TRANSPORT BACK TO EARTH.
FLASK WAS ONE OF THEIRS.
WHAT MAKES THIS THING SO SPECIAL? WHY DO THEY WANT IT SO BADLY?
I SAW IT. I EVEN HELD IT IN MY HANDS.
IT WAS... NOT OF THIS WORLD.
BUT FLASK NEVER MADE IT OFF THE SHIP, SO THEY SENT KYRIL TO FIGURE OUT WHAT HAPPENED TO HIM AND THE ARTIFACT?
BRAITH...
I'M WAY OVER MY HEAD IN THIS.
WELL THEN...

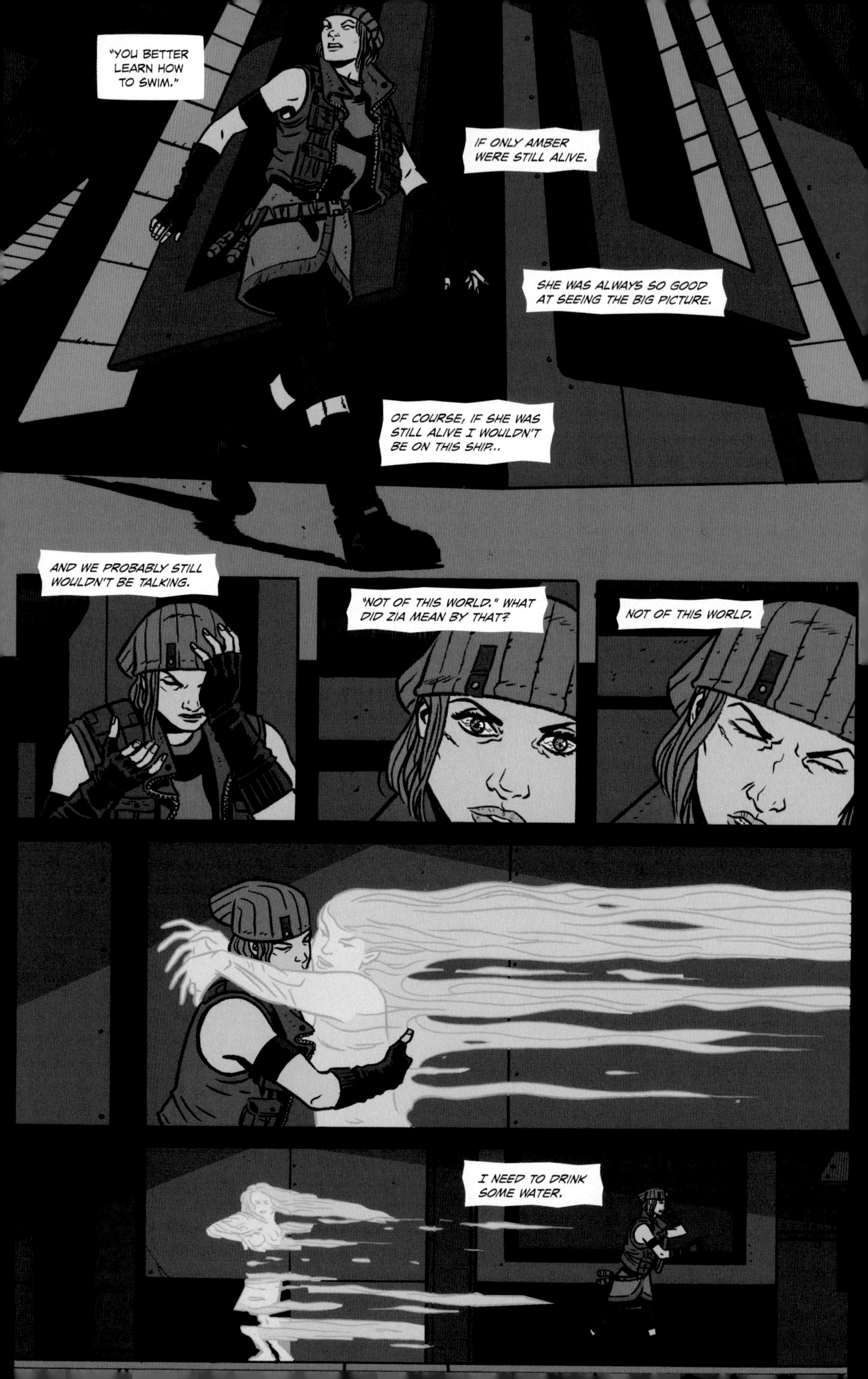
"YOU BETTER LEARN HOW TO SWIM."
IF ONLY AMBER WERE STILL ALIVE.
SHE WAS ALWAYS SO GOOD AT SEEING THE BIG PICTURE.
OF COURSE, IF SHE WAS STILL ALIVE I WOULDN'T BE ON THIS SHIP...
AND WE PROBABLY STILL WOULDN'T BE TALKING.
"NOT OF THIS WORLD." WHAT DID ZIA MEAN BY THAT?
NOT OF THIS WORLD.
I NEED TO DRINK SOME WATER.

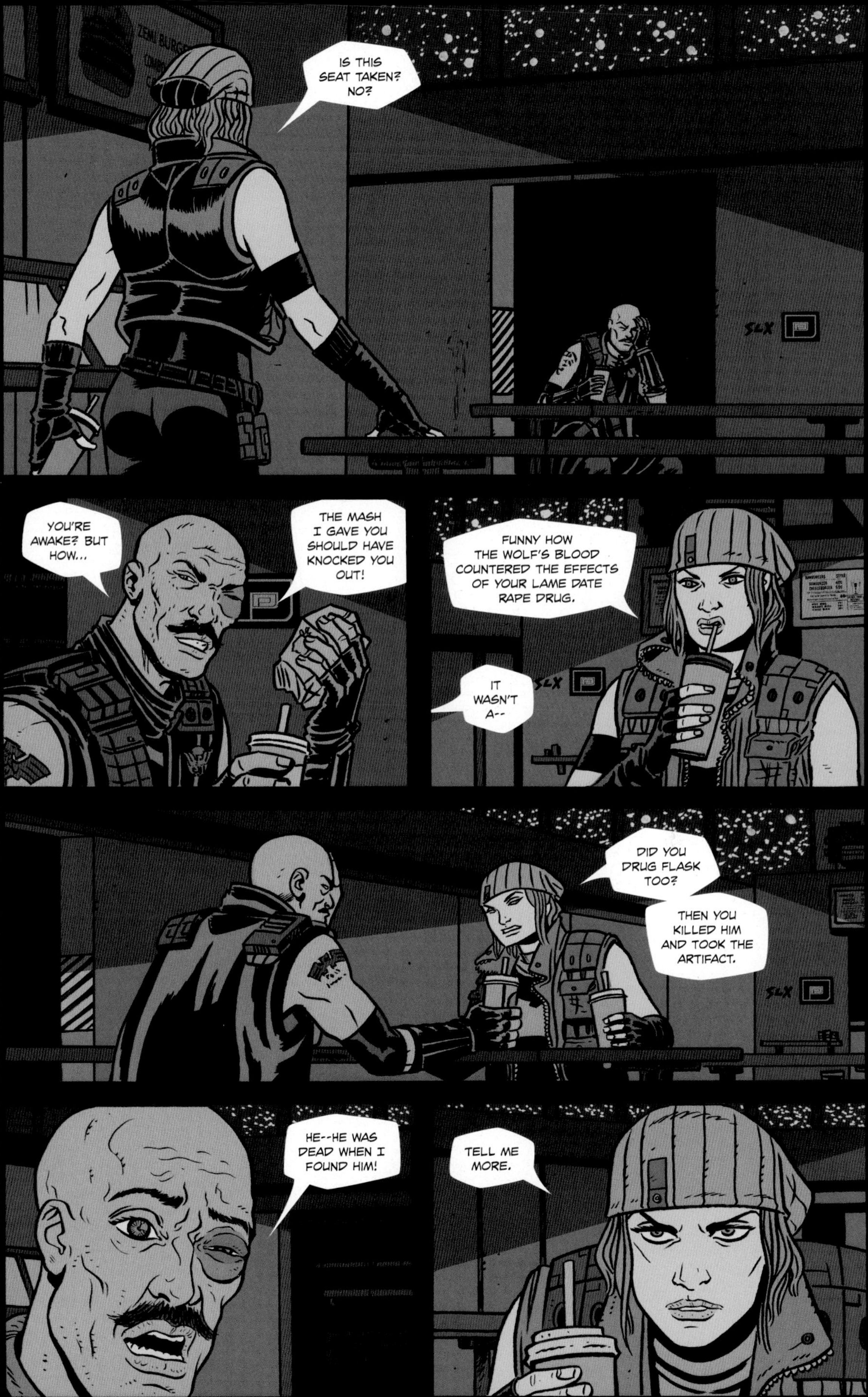
IS THIS SEAT TAKEN? NO?
YOU'RE AWAKE? BUT HOW...
THE MASH I GAVE YOU SHOULD HAVE KNOCKED YOU OUT!
FUNNY HOW THE WOLF'S BLOOD COUNTERED THE EFFECTS OF YOUR LAME DATE RAPE DRUG.
IT WASN'T A--
DID YOU DRUG FLASK TOO?
THEN YOU KILLED HIM AND TOOK THE ARTIFACT.
HE--HE WAS DEAD WHEN I FOUND HIM!
TELL ME MORE.

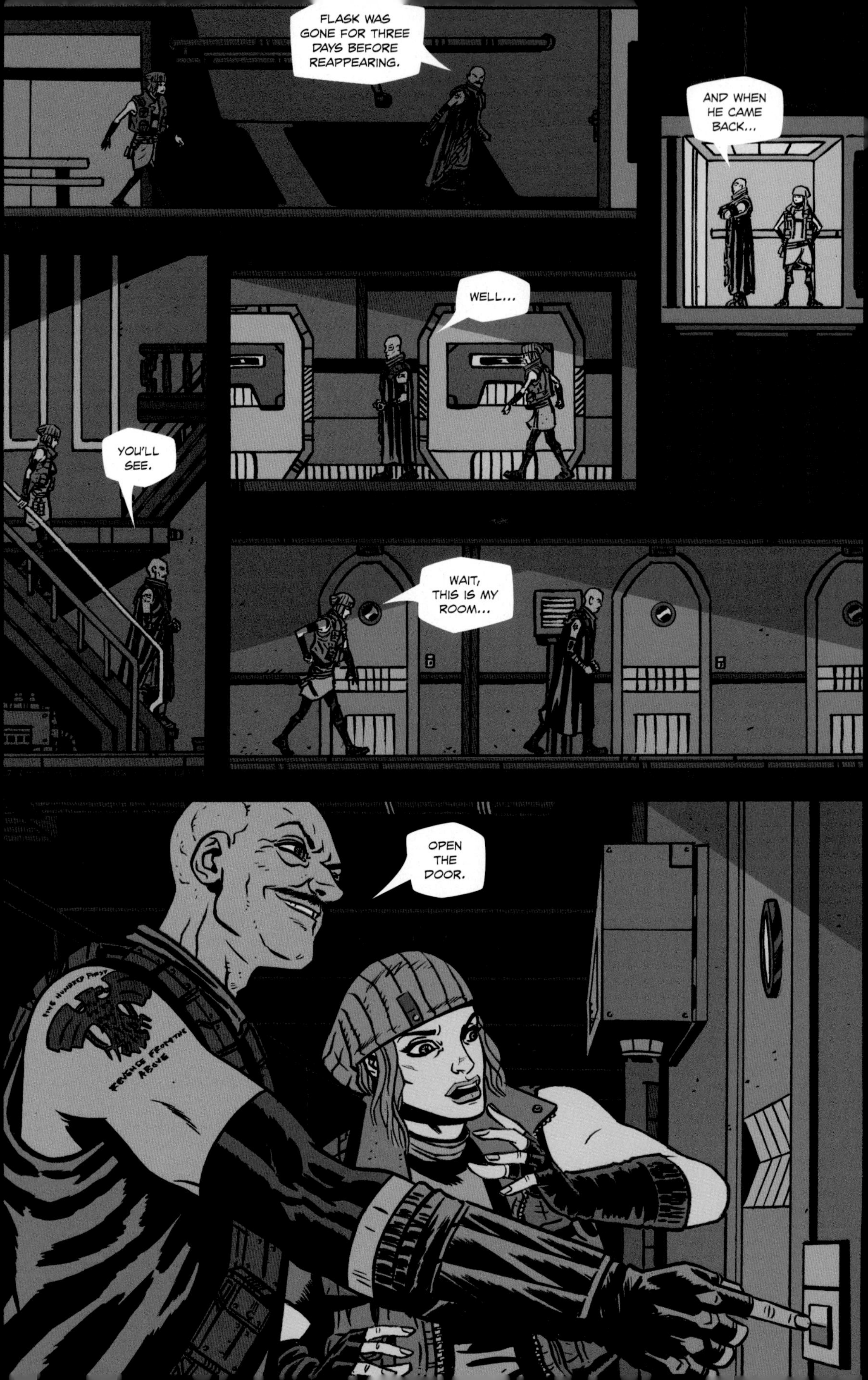
FLASK WAS GONE FOR THREE DAYS BEFORE REAPPEARING.
AND WHEN HE CAME BACK...
WELL...
YOU'LL SEE.
WAIT, THIS IS MY ROOM...
OPEN THE DOOR.
FIVE HUNDRED FIRST
REVENGE FROM THE ABOVE

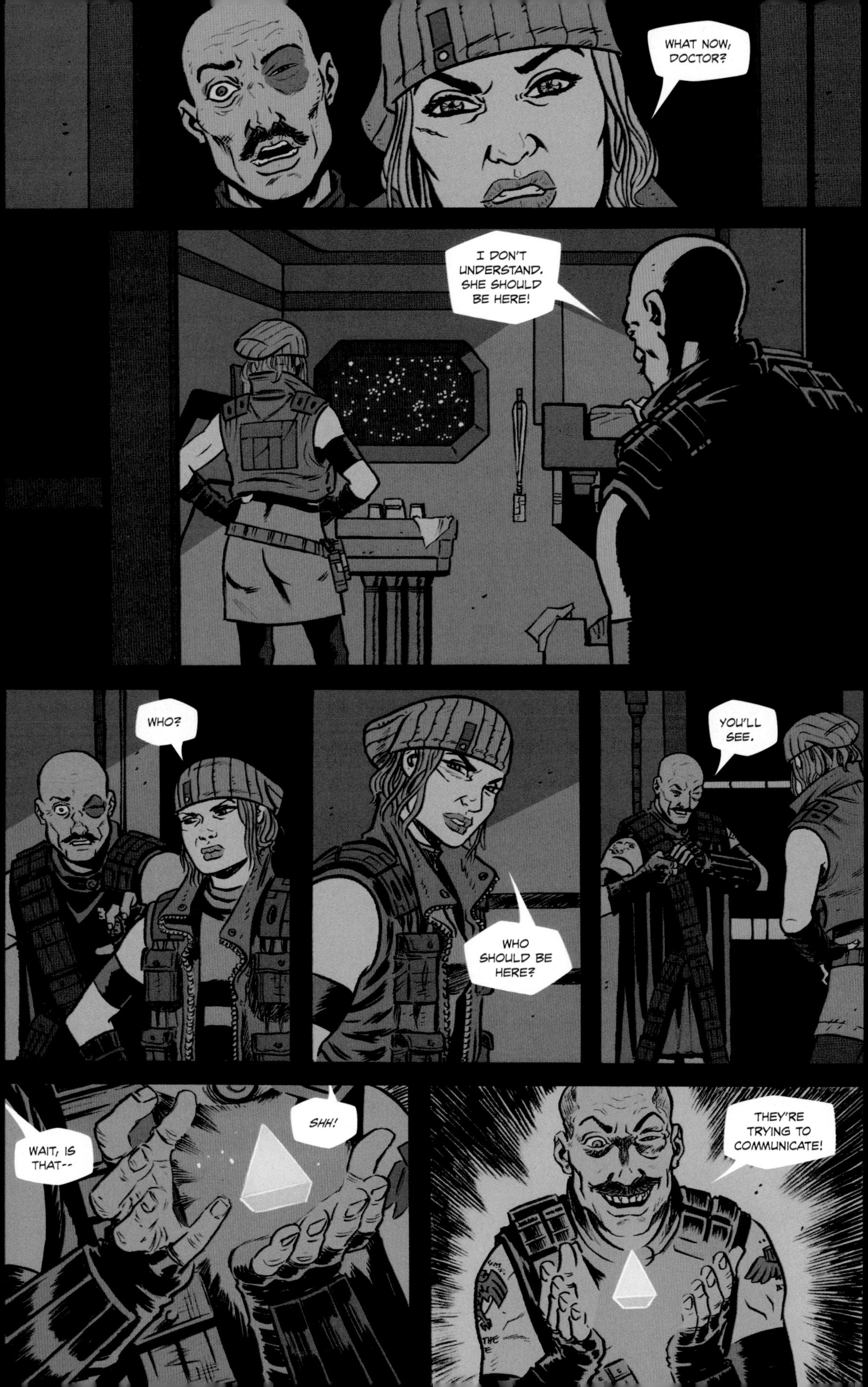
WHAT NOW, DOCTOR?
I DON'T UNDERSTAND. SHE SHOULD BE HERE!
WHO?
WHO SHOULD BE HERE?
YOU'LL SEE.
WAIT, IS THAT--
SHH!
THEY'RE TRYING TO COMMUNICATE!

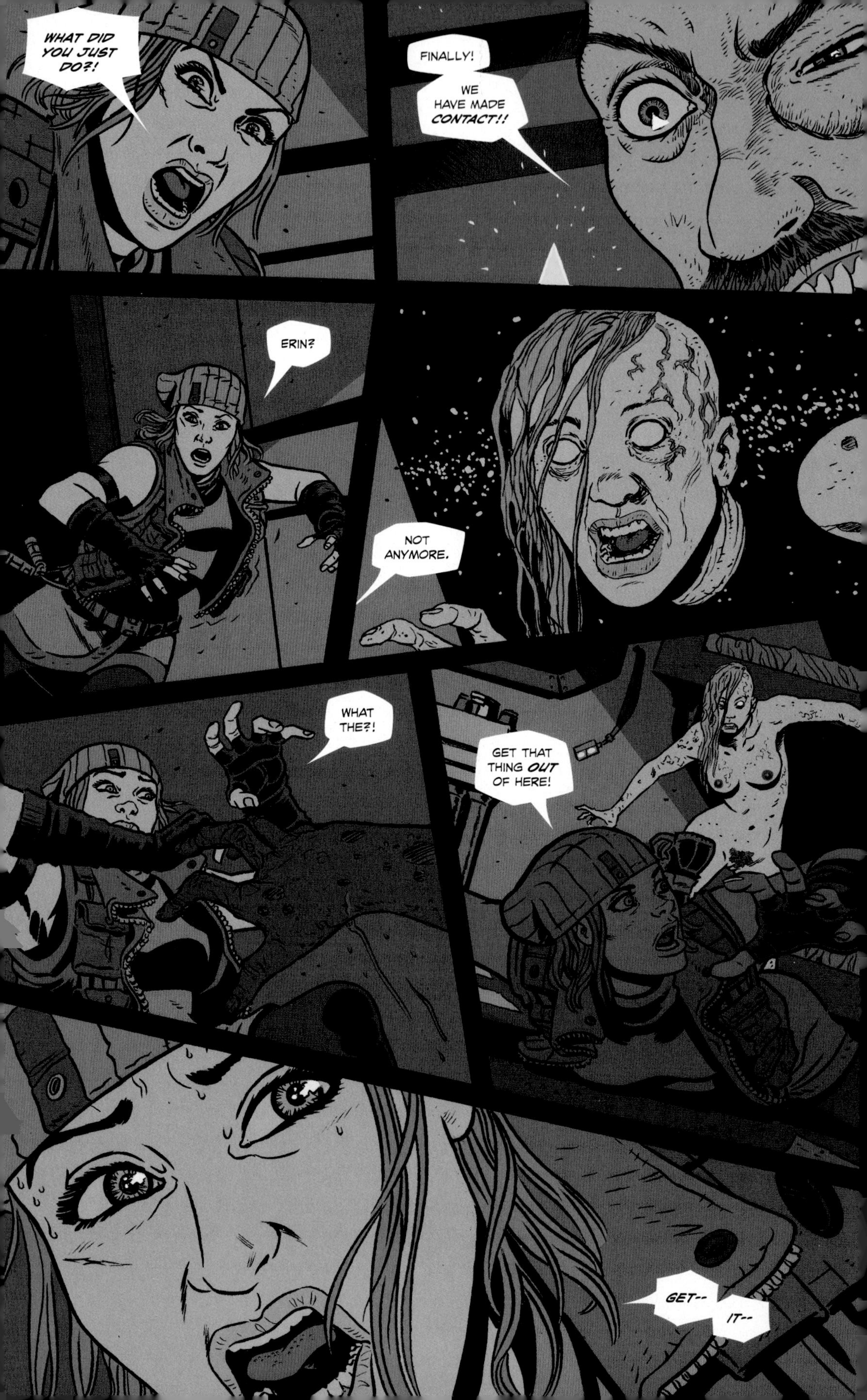
WHAT DID YOU JUST DO?!
FINALLY!
WE HAVE MADE CONTACT!!
ERIN?
NOT ANYMORE.
WHAT THE?!
GET THAT THING OUT OF HERE!
GET--
IT--

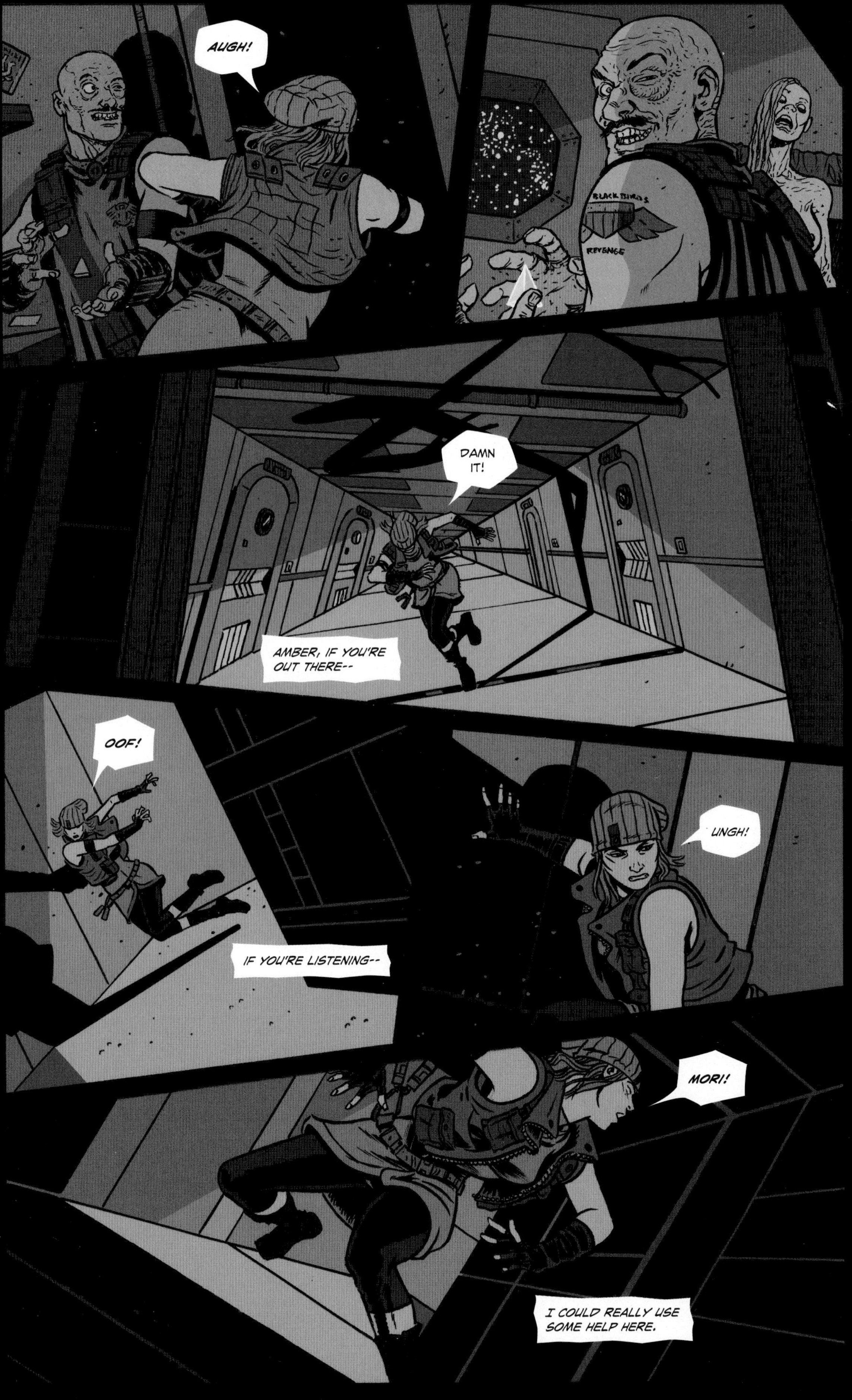

AUGH!
DAMN IT!
AMBER, IF YOU'RE OUT THERE--
OOF!
UNGH!
IF YOU'RE LISTENING--
MORI!
I COULD REALLY USE SOME HELP HERE.

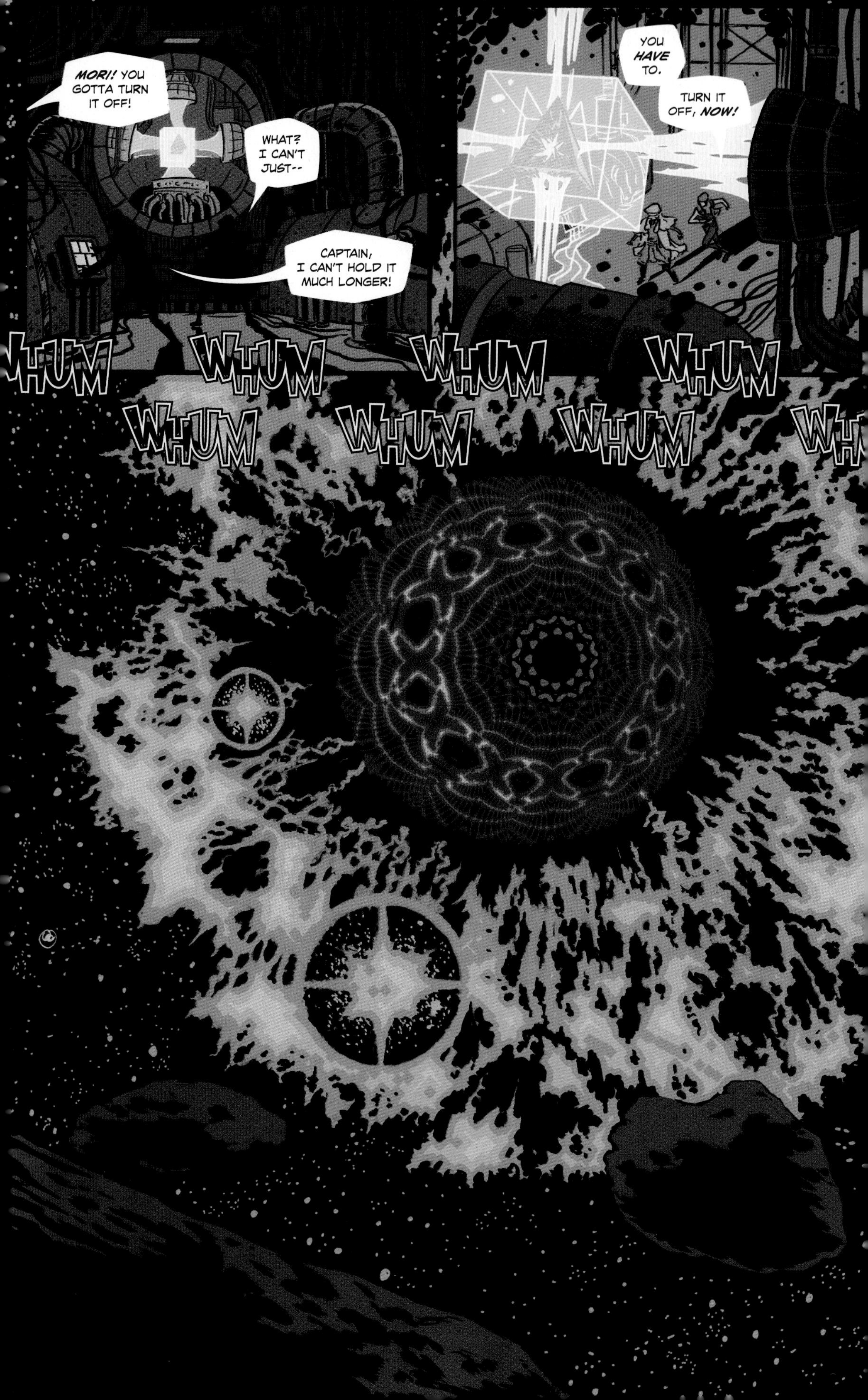
MORI! YOU GOTTA TURN IT OFF!
WHAT? I CAN'T JUST--
CAPTAIN, I CAN'T HOLD IT MUCH LONGER!
YOU HAVE TO.
TURN IT OFF, NOW!
WHUM
WHUM
WHUM
WHUM
WHUM
WHUM
WHUM

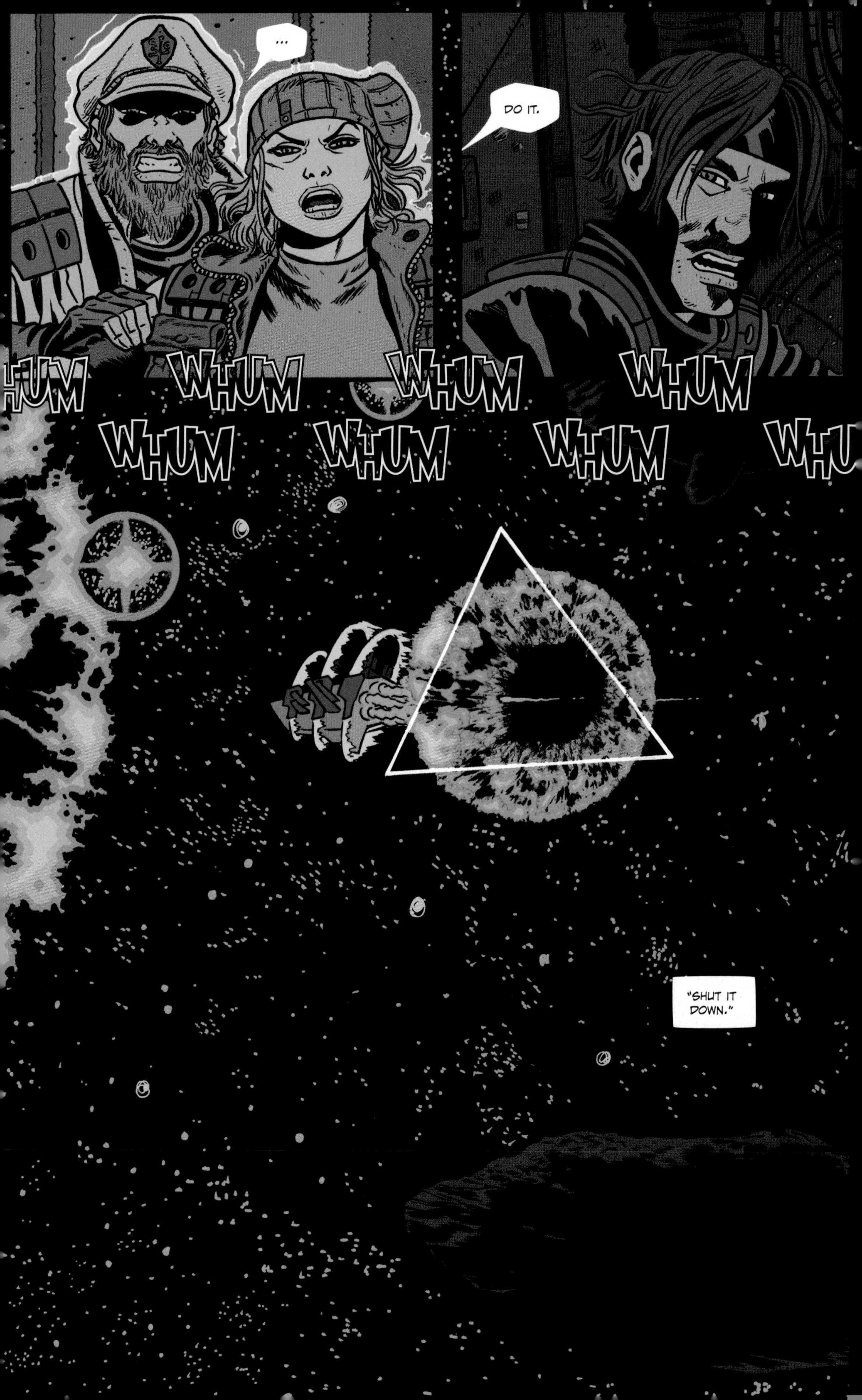
...
DO IT.
WHUM WHUM WHUM WHUM
WHUM WHUM WHUM
"SHUT IT DOWN."

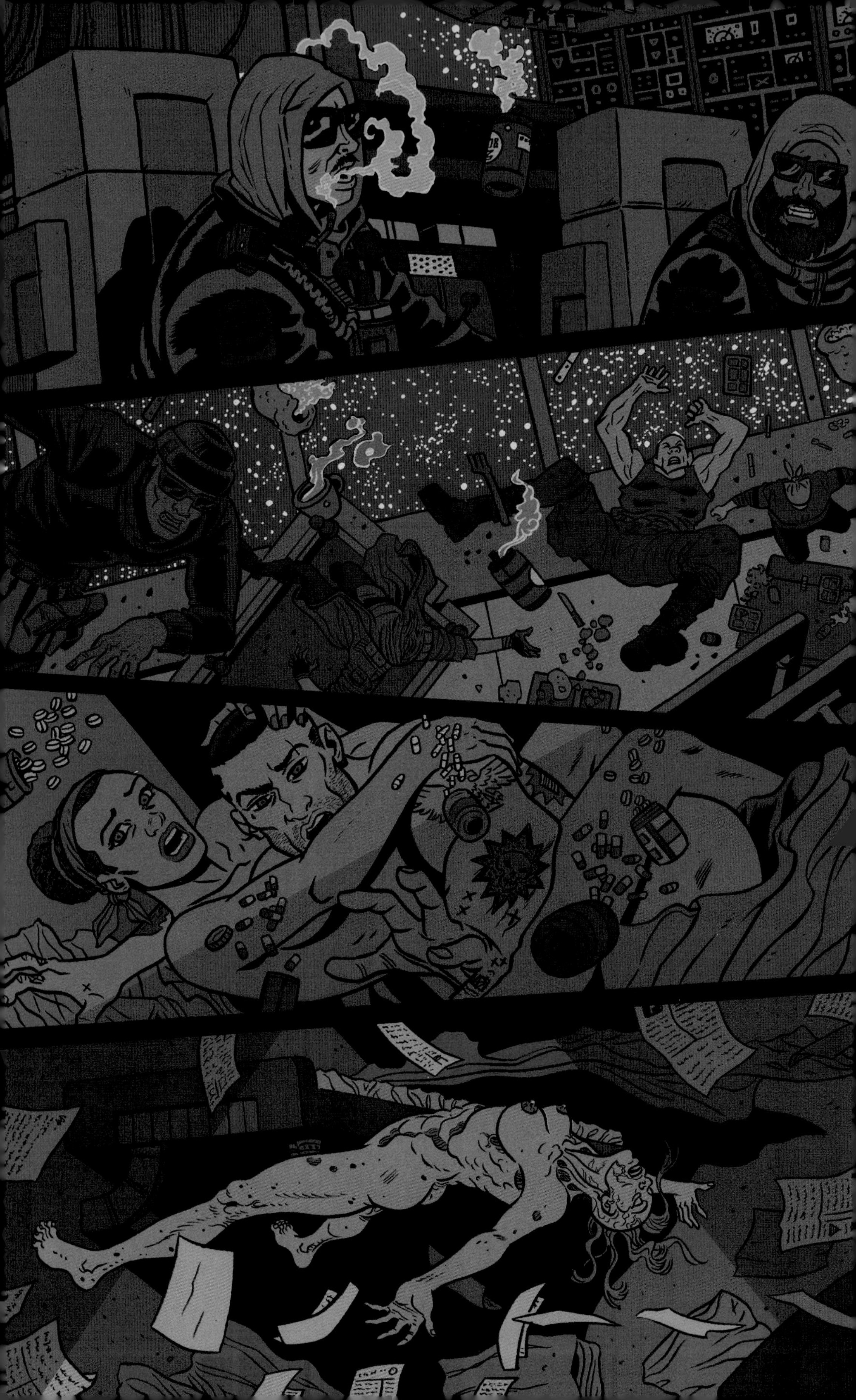

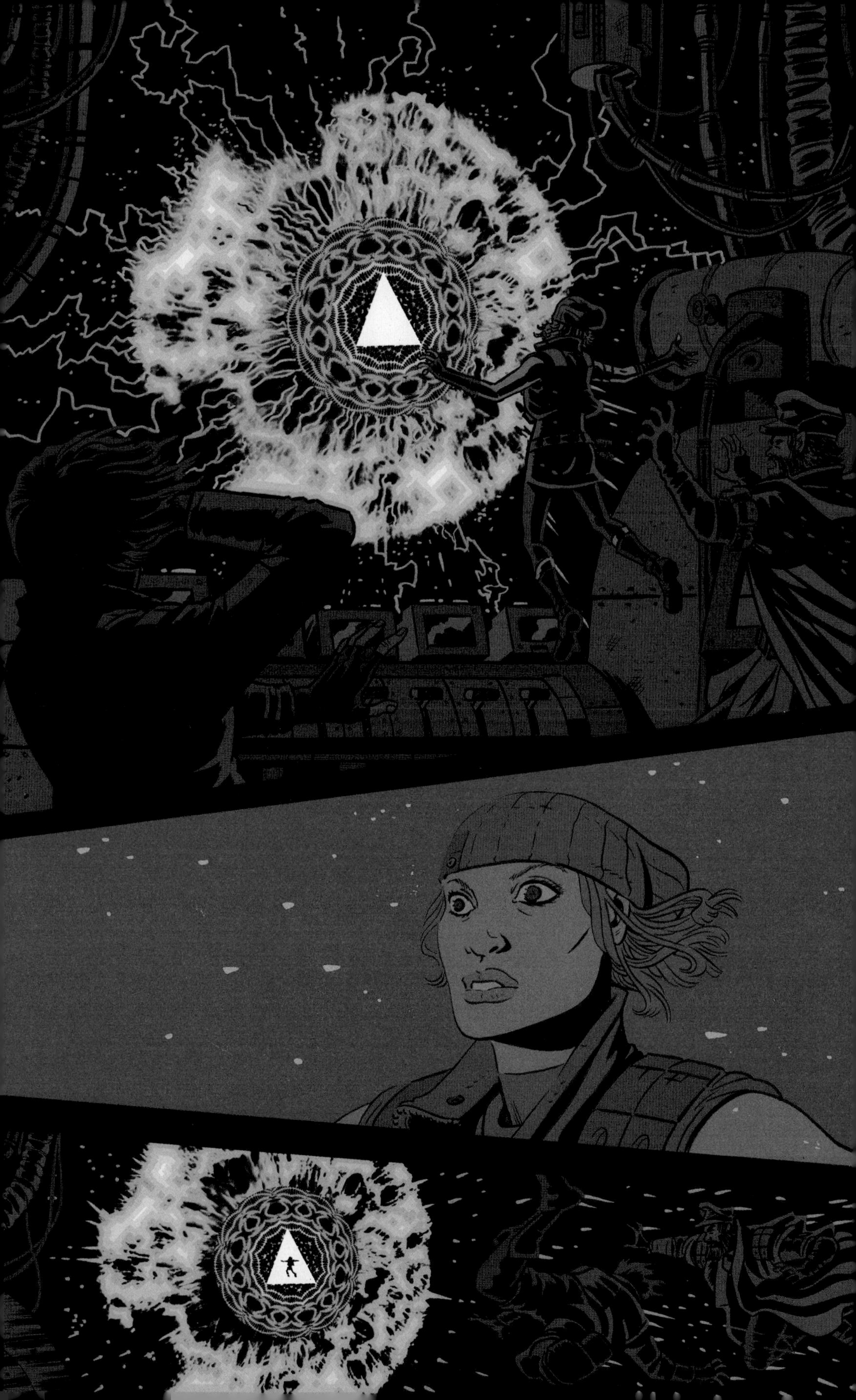

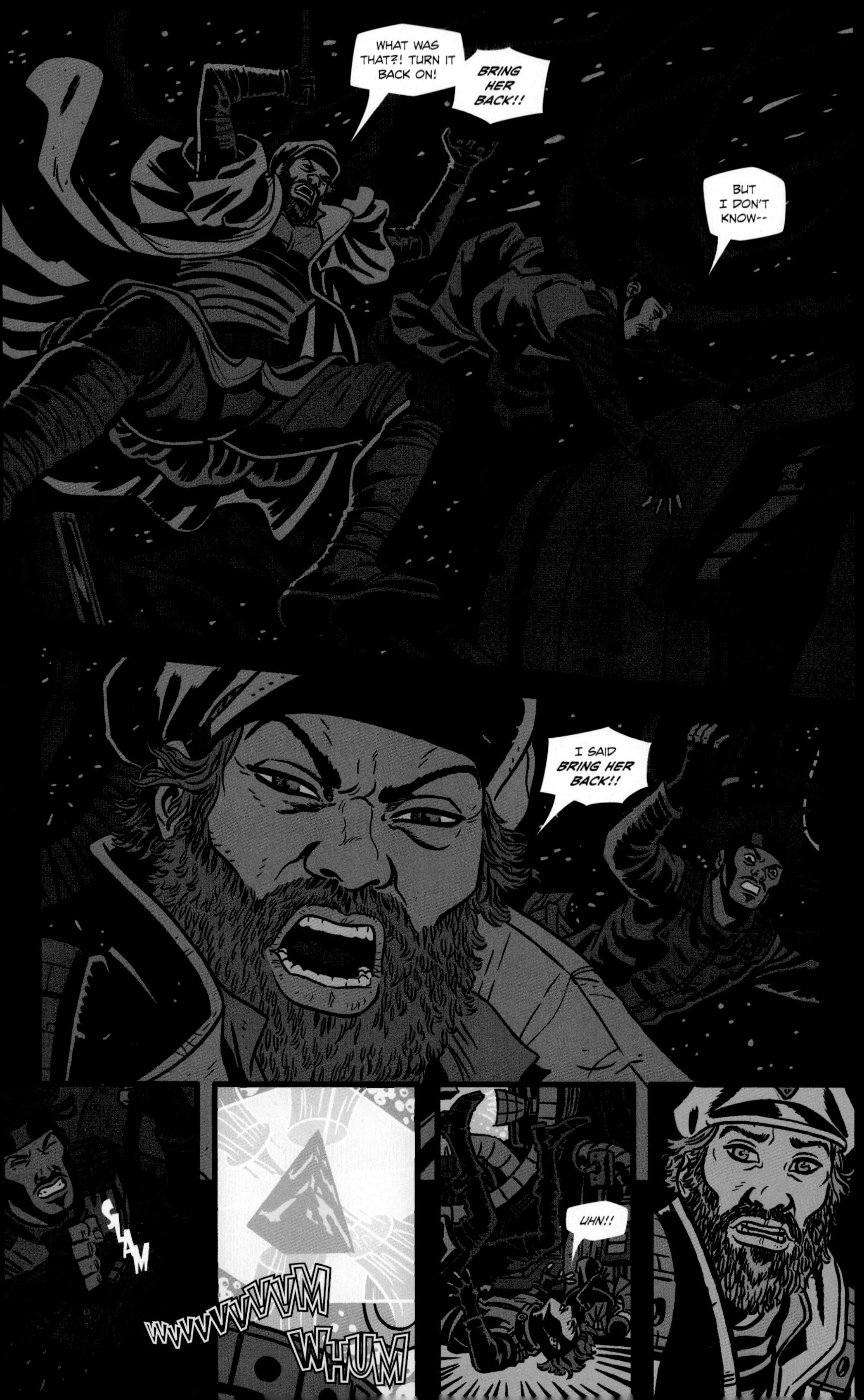
WHAT WAS THAT?! TURN IT BACK ON!
BRING HER BACK!!
BUT I DON'T KNOW--
I SAID BRING HER BACK!!
SLAM
WVVVVVVVM
WHUM
UHN!!

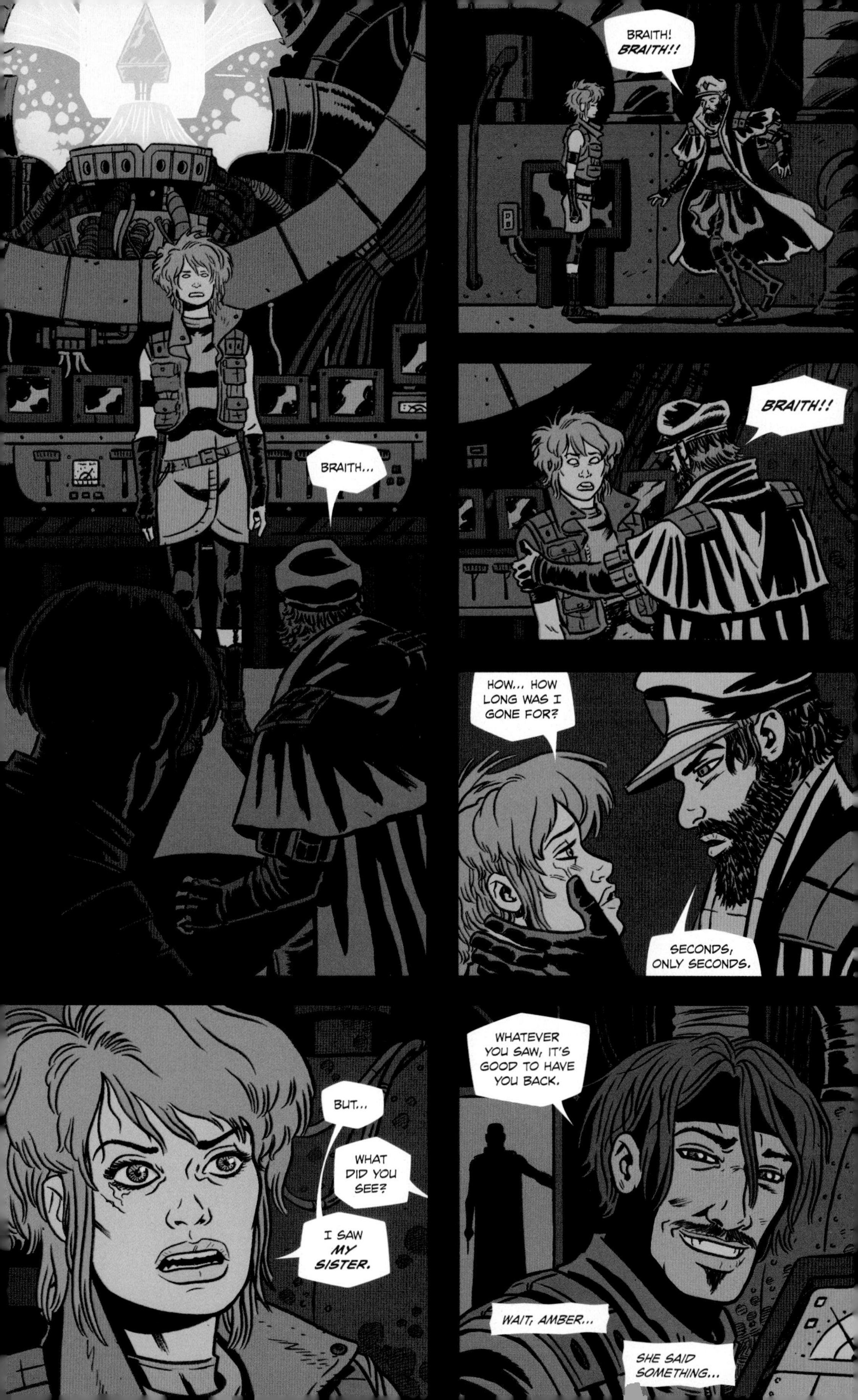
BRAITH...
BRAITH!
BRAITH!!
BRAITH!!
HOW... HOW LONG WAS I GONE FOR?
SECONDS, ONLY SECONDS.
BUT...
WHAT DID YOU SEE?
I SAW *MY SISTER.*
WHATEVER YOU SAW, IT'S GOOD TO HAVE YOU BACK.
WAIT, AMBER...
SHE SAID SOMETHING...

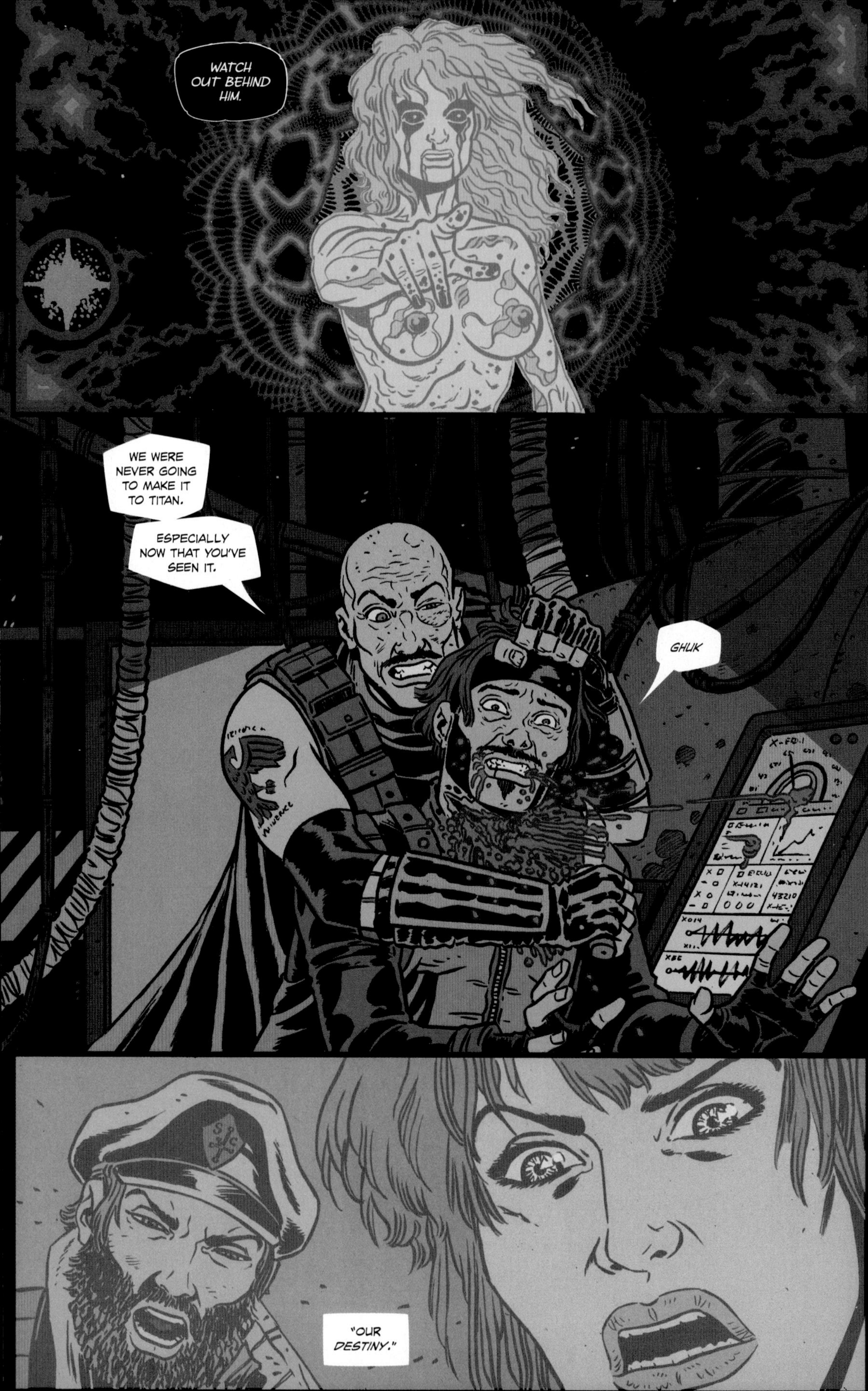
WATCH OUT BEHIND HIM.
WE WERE NEVER GOING TO MAKE IT TO TITAN.
ESPECIALLY NOW THAT YOU'VE SEEN IT.
GHUK
"OUR DESTINY."

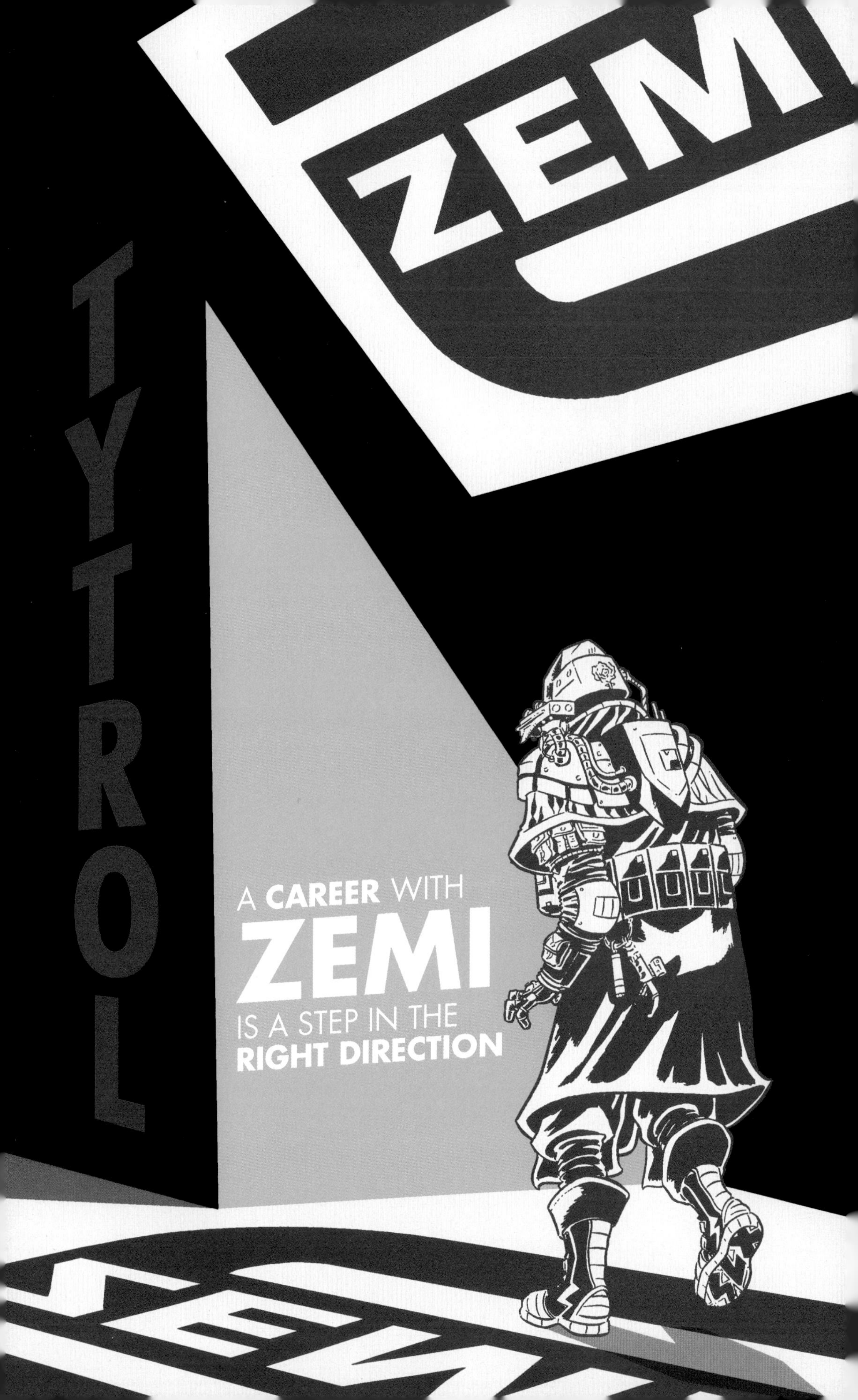

ZEM
TYTROL
A CAREER WITH
ZEMI
IS A STEP IN THE
RIGHT DIRECTION

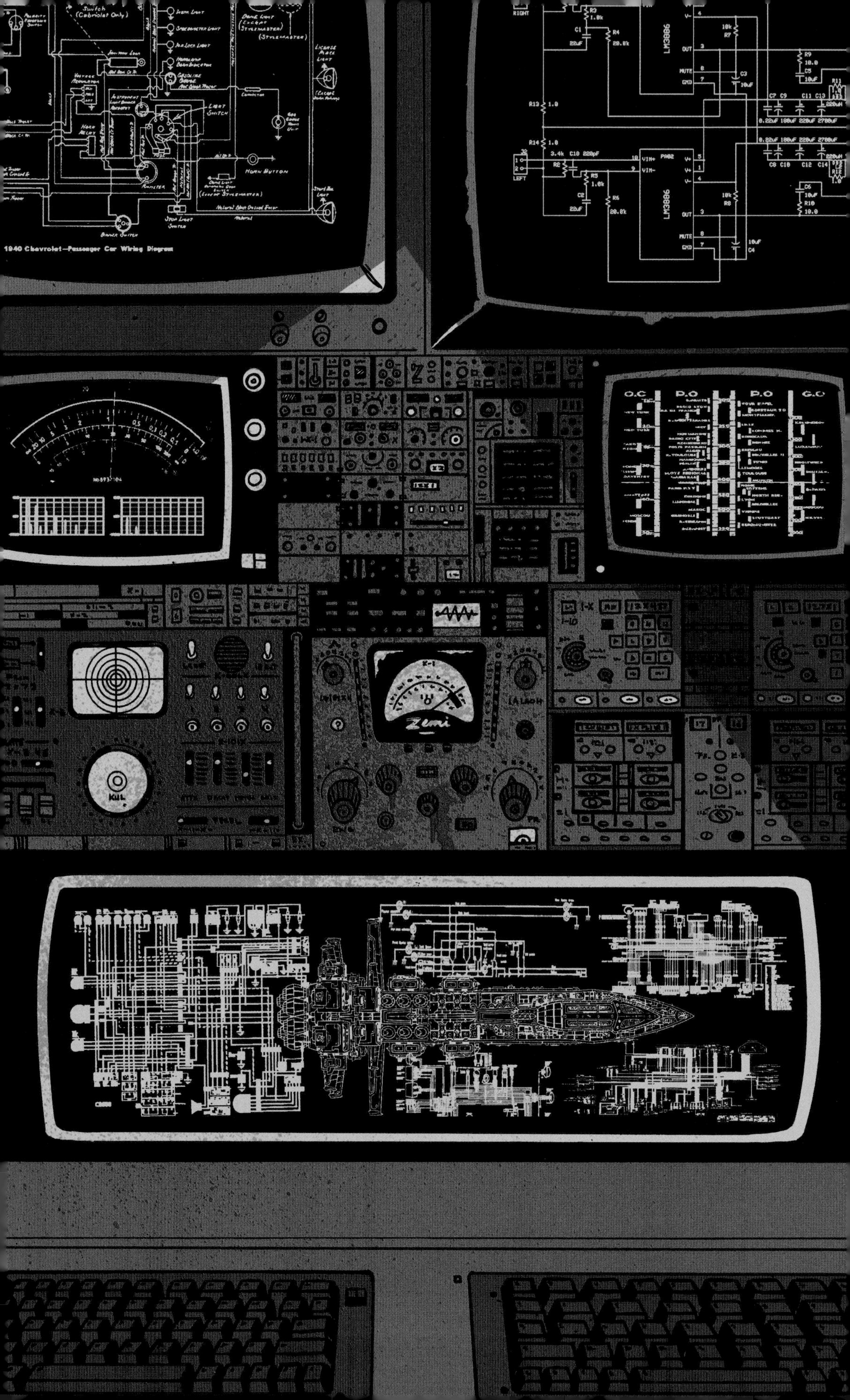
1940 Chevrolet—Passenger Car Wiring Diagram
Switch (Cabriolet Only)
Horn Button
LM3886
RIGHT
LEFT
O.C
P.O
P.O
G.O
Zemi

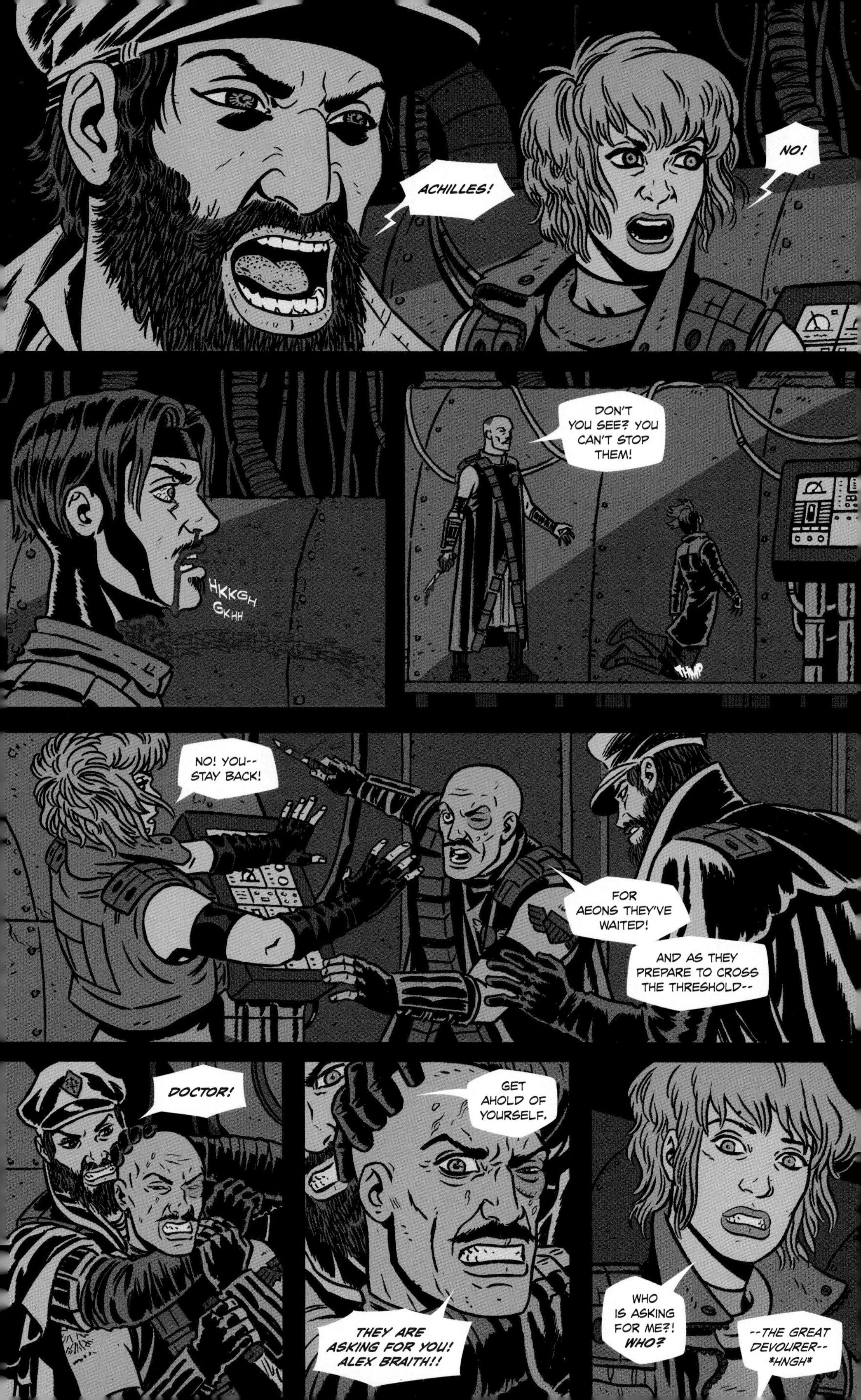
ACHILLES!
NO!
HKKGH GKHH
DON'T YOU SEE? YOU CAN'T STOP THEM!
THMP
NO! YOU-- STAY BACK!
FOR AEONS THEY'VE WAITED!
AND AS THEY PREPARE TO CROSS THE THRESHOLD--
DOCTOR!
GET AHOLD OF YOURSELF.
THEY ARE ASKING FOR YOU! ALEX BRAITH!!
WHO IS ASKING FOR ME?! WHO?
--THE GREAT DEVOURER-- *HNGH*

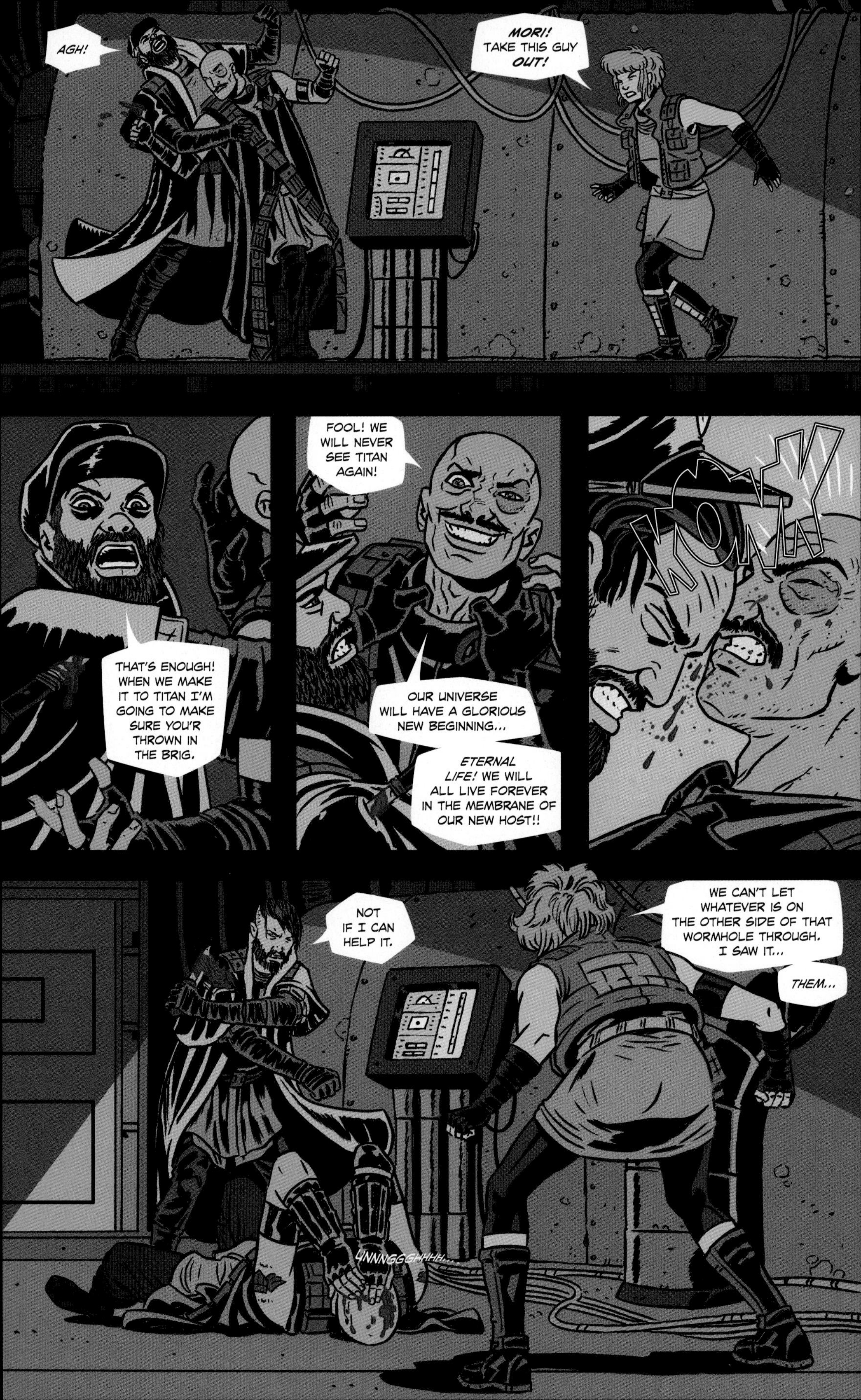

AGH!
MORI! TAKE THIS GUY OUT!
THAT'S ENOUGH! WHEN WE MAKE IT TO TITAN I'M GOING TO MAKE SURE YOU'R THROWN IN THE BRIG.
FOOL! WE WILL NEVER SEE TITAN AGAIN!
OUR UNIVERSE WILL HAVE A GLORIOUS NEW BEGINNING...
ETERNAL LIFE! WE WILL ALL LIVE FOREVER IN THE MEMBRANE OF OUR NEW HOST!!
WONK
NOT IF I CAN HELP IT.
WE CAN'T LET WHATEVER IS ON THE OTHER SIDE OF THAT WORMHOLE THROUGH. I SAW IT...
THEM...
UNNNGGGHHHH...

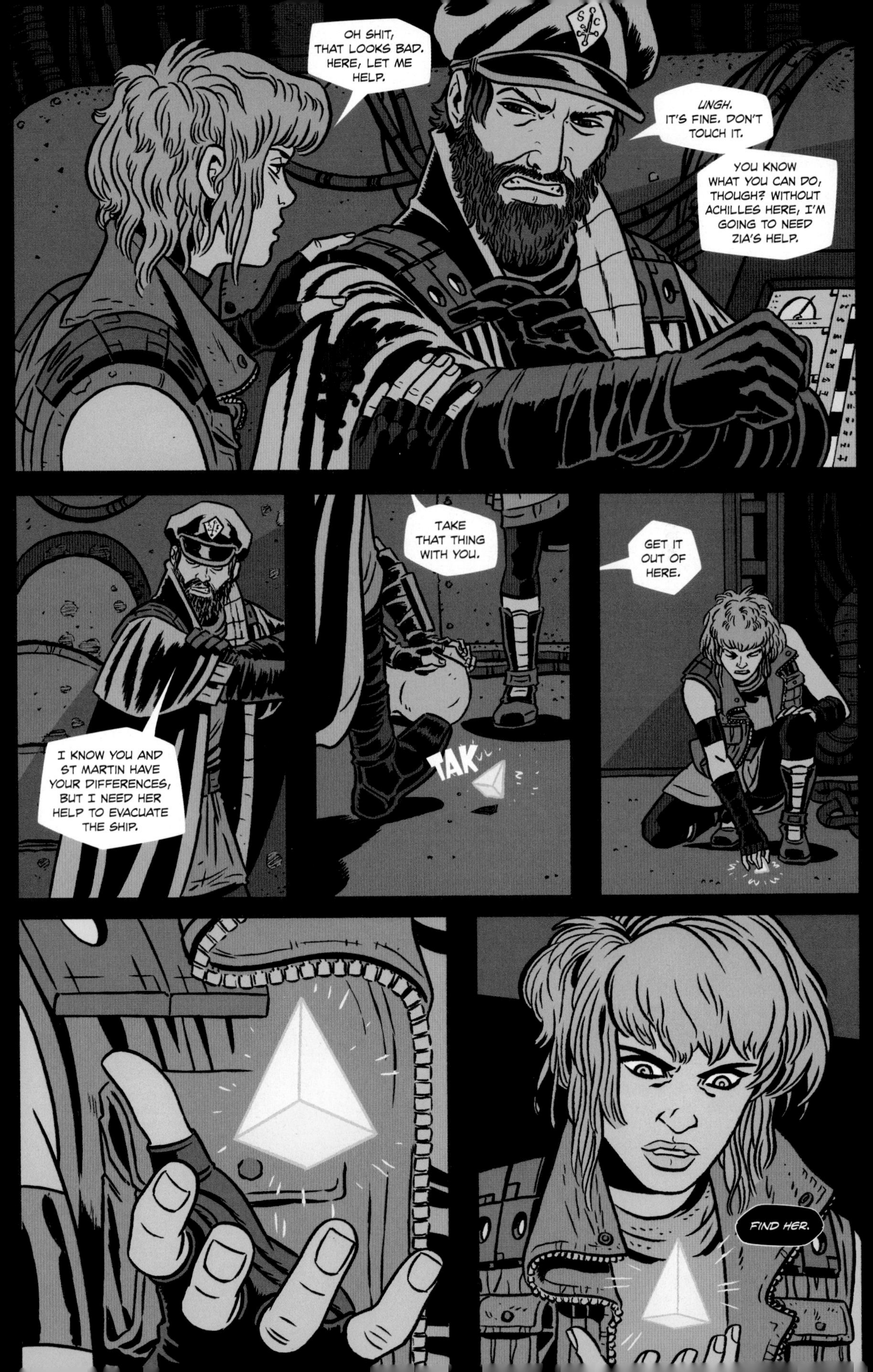
OH SHIT, THAT LOOKS BAD. HERE, LET ME HELP.
UNGH. IT'S FINE. DON'T TOUCH IT.
YOU KNOW WHAT YOU CAN DO, THOUGH? WITHOUT ACHILLES HERE, I'M GOING TO NEED ZIA'S HELP.
I KNOW YOU AND ST MARTIN HAVE YOUR DIFFERENCES, BUT I NEED HER HELP TO EVACUATE THE SHIP.
TAKE THAT THING WITH YOU.
TAK
GET IT OUT OF HERE.
FIND HER.

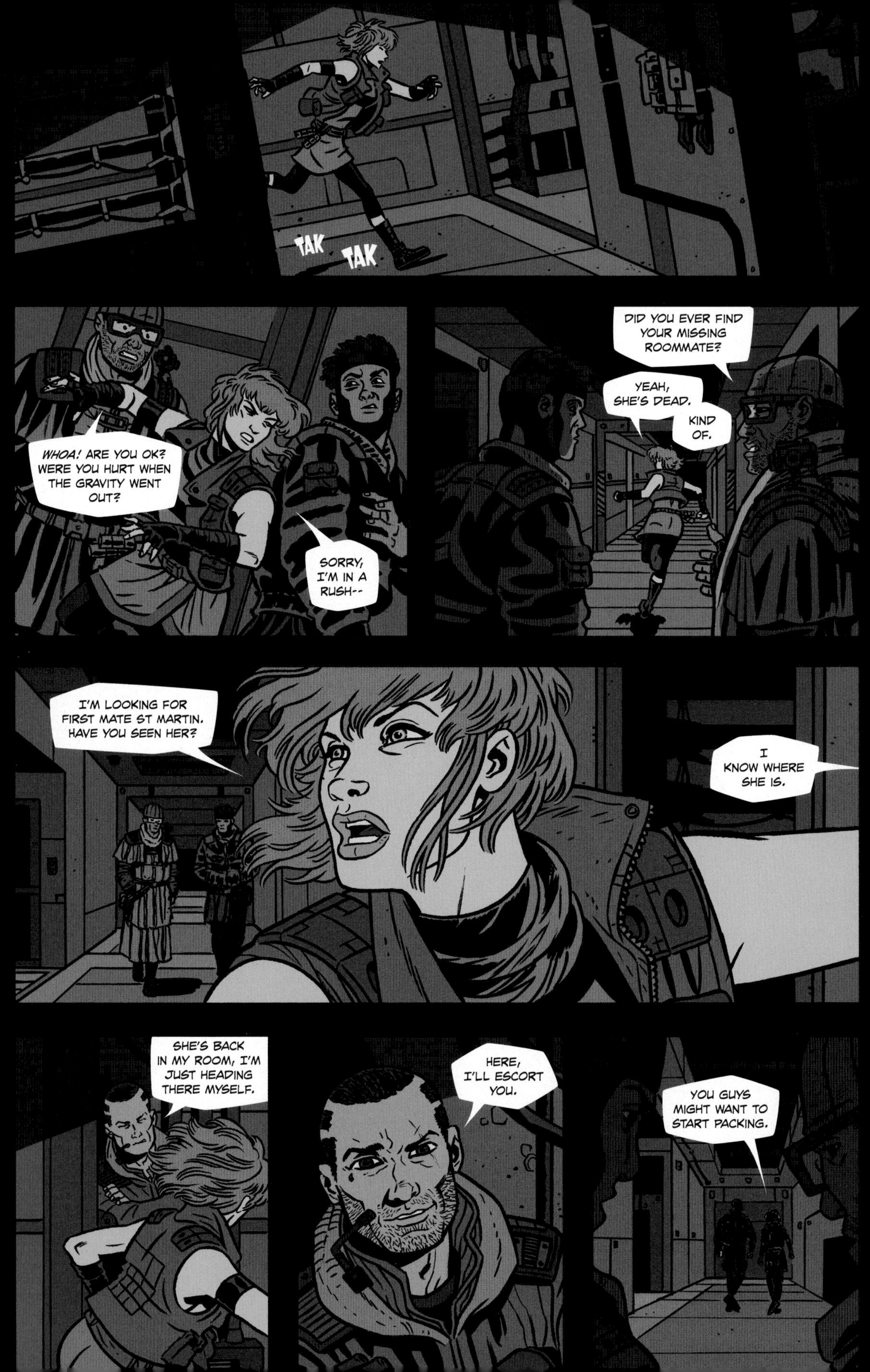
TAK
TAK
WHOA! ARE YOU OK? WERE YOU HURT WHEN THE GRAVITY WENT OUT?
SORRY, I'M IN A RUSH--
DID YOU EVER FIND YOUR MISSING ROOMMATE?
YEAH, SHE'S DEAD.
KIND OF.
I'M LOOKING FOR FIRST MATE ST MARTIN. HAVE YOU SEEN HER?
I KNOW WHERE SHE IS.
SHE'S BACK IN MY ROOM, I'M JUST HEADING THERE MYSELF.
HERE, I'LL ESCORT YOU.
YOU GUYS MIGHT WANT TO START PACKING.

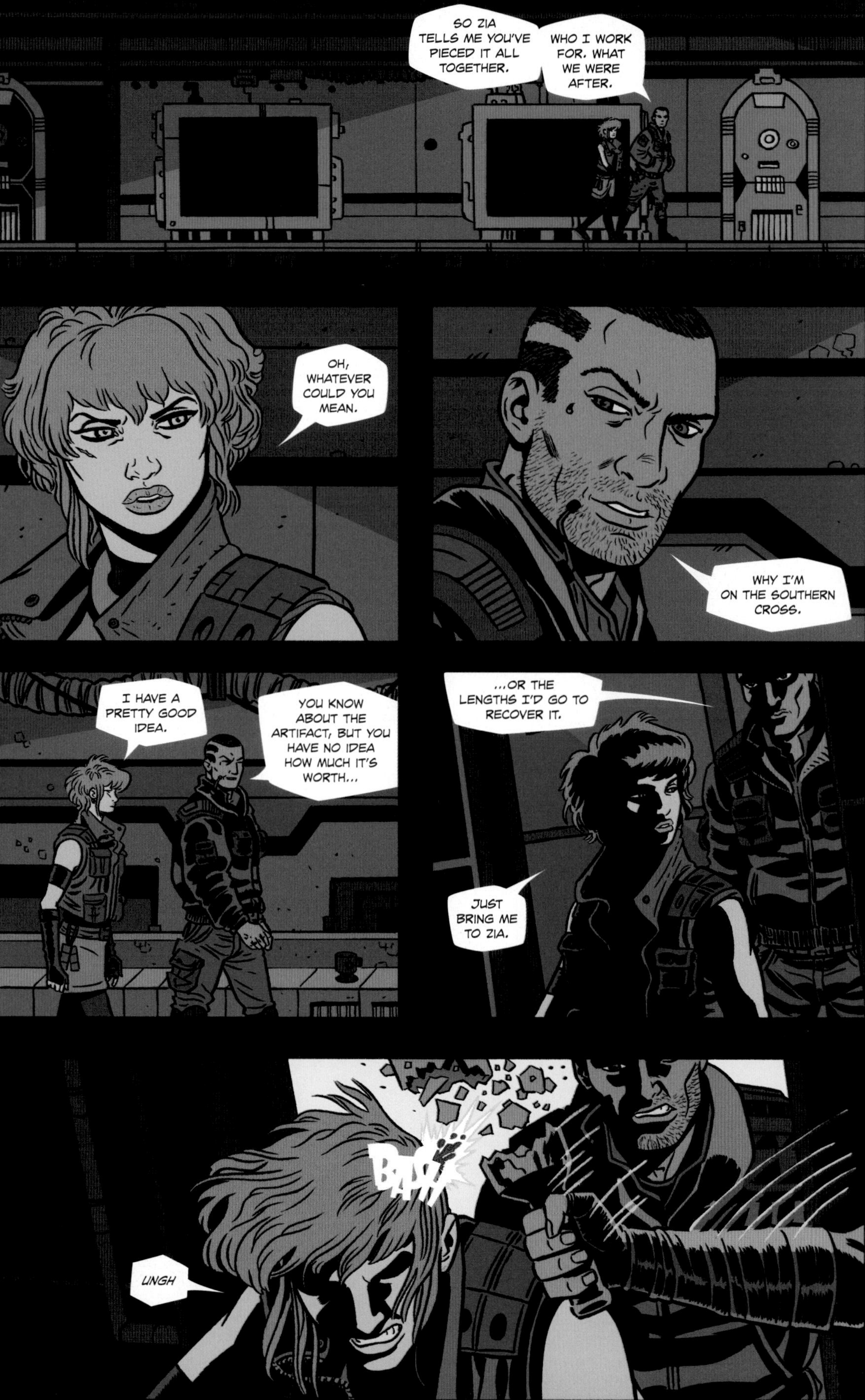
SO ZIA TELLS ME YOU'VE PIECED IT ALL TOGETHER.
WHO I WORK FOR. WHAT WE WERE AFTER.
OH, WHATEVER COULD YOU MEAN.
WHY I'M ON THE SOUTHERN CROSS.
I HAVE A PRETTY GOOD IDEA.
YOU KNOW ABOUT THE ARTIFACT, BUT YOU HAVE NO IDEA HOW MUCH IT'S WORTH...
...OR THE LENGTHS I'D GO TO RECOVER IT.
JUST BRING ME TO ZIA.
BASH
UNGH

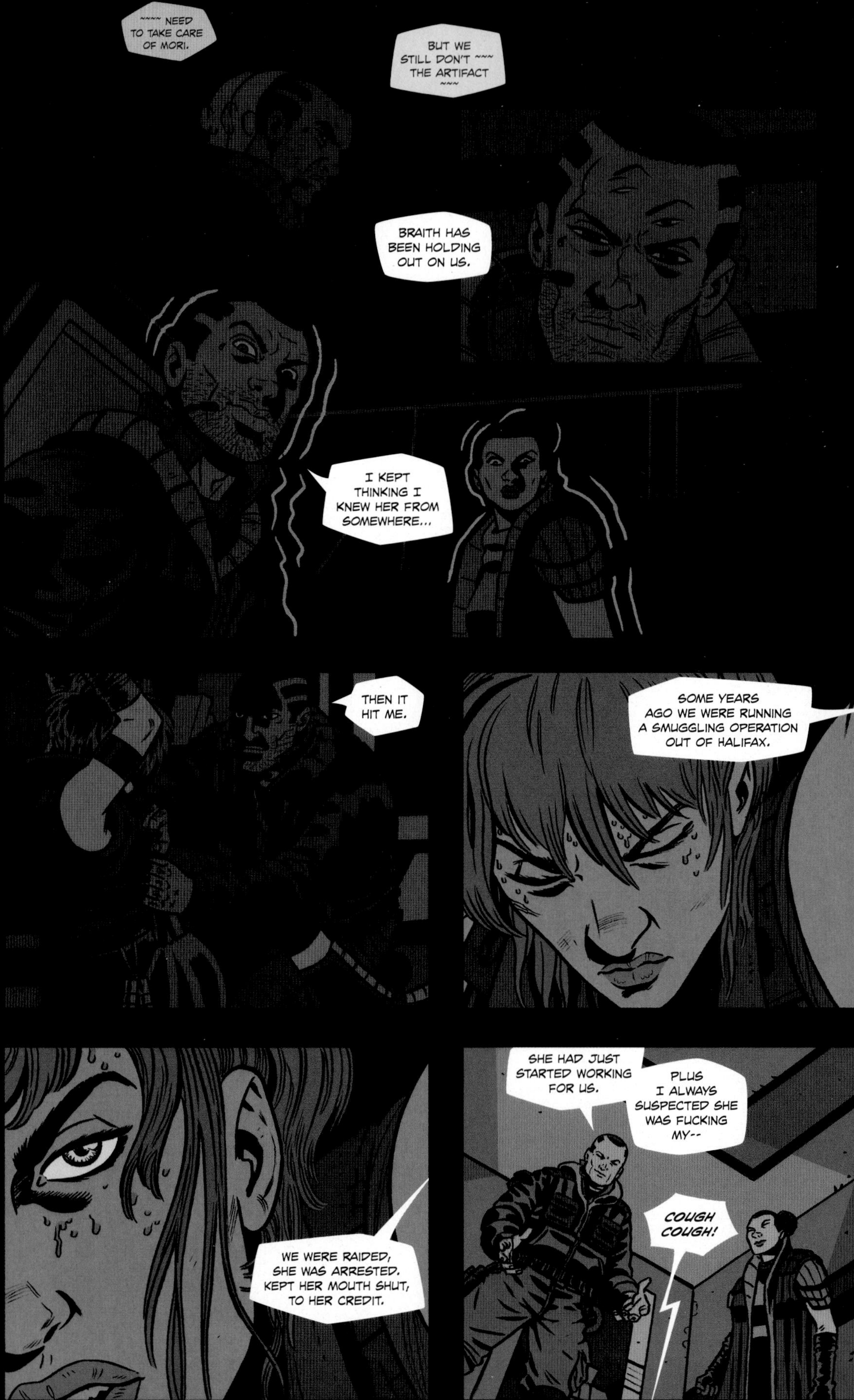
NEED TO TAKE CARE OF MORI.
BUT WE STILL DON'T ~~~ THE ARTIFACT ~~~
BRAITH HAS BEEN HOLDING OUT ON US.
I KEPT THINKING I KNEW HER FROM SOMEWHERE...
THEN IT HIT ME.
SOME YEARS AGO WE WERE RUNNING A SMUGGLING OPERATION OUT OF HALIFAX.
WE WERE RAIDED, SHE WAS ARRESTED. KEPT HER MOUTH SHUT, TO HER CREDIT.
SHE HAD JUST STARTED WORKING FOR US.
PLUS I ALWAYS SUSPECTED SHE WAS FUCKING MY--
COUGH COUGH!

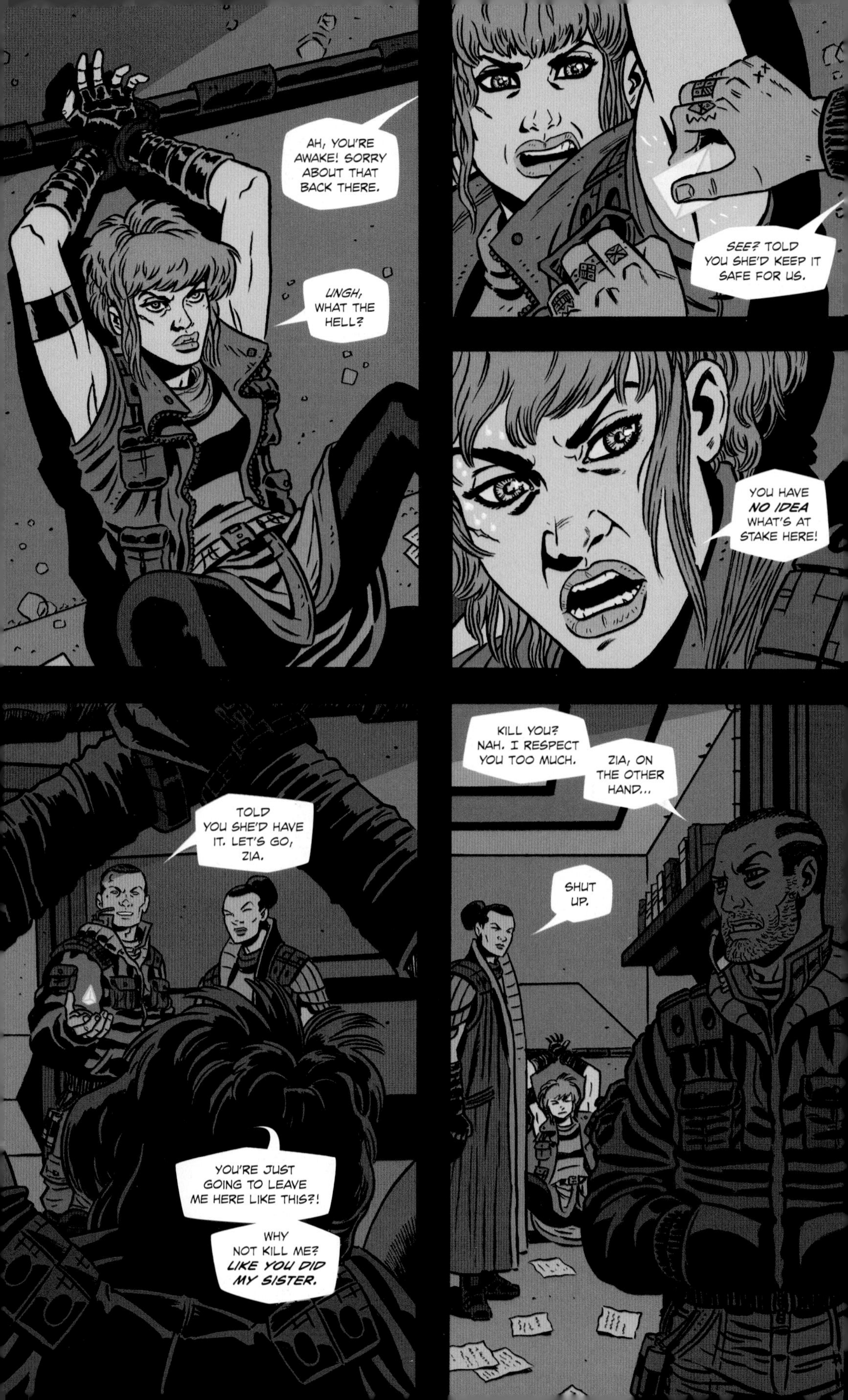
AH, YOU'RE AWAKE! SORRY ABOUT THAT BACK THERE.
UNGH, WHAT THE HELL?
SEE? TOLD YOU SHE'D KEEP IT SAFE FOR US.
YOU HAVE NO IDEA WHAT'S AT STAKE HERE!
TOLD YOU SHE'D HAVE IT. LET'S GO, ZIA.
YOU'RE JUST GOING TO LEAVE ME HERE LIKE THIS?!
WHY NOT KILL ME? LIKE YOU DID MY SISTER.
KILL YOU? NAH. I RESPECT YOU TOO MUCH.
ZIA, ON THE OTHER HAND...
SHUT UP.

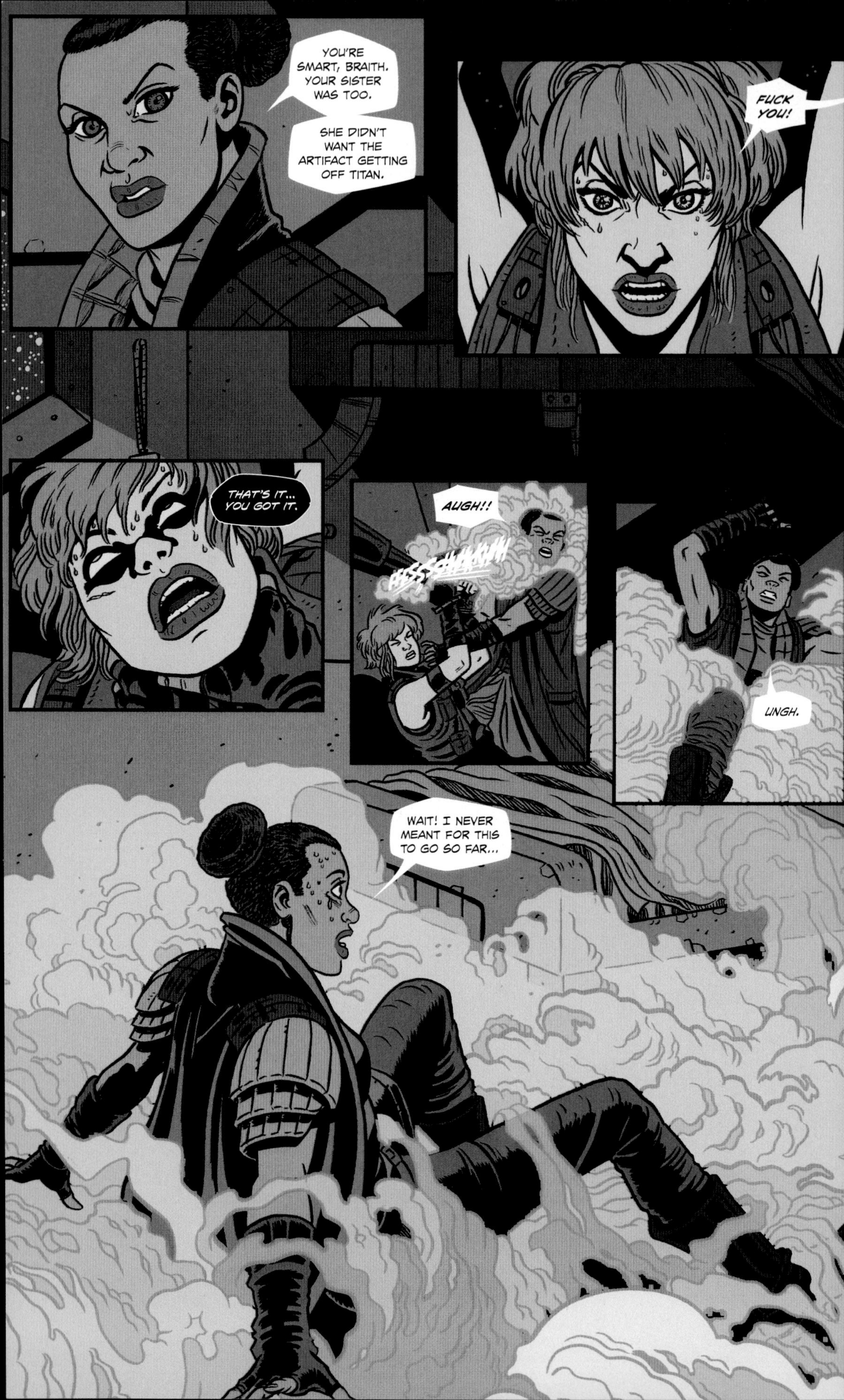
YOU'RE SMART, BRAITH. YOUR SISTER WAS TOO.
SHE DIDN'T WANT THE ARTIFACT GETTING OFF TITAN.
FUCK YOU!
THAT'S IT... YOU GOT IT.
AUGH!!
UNGH.
WAIT! I NEVER MEANT FOR THIS TO GO SO FAR...

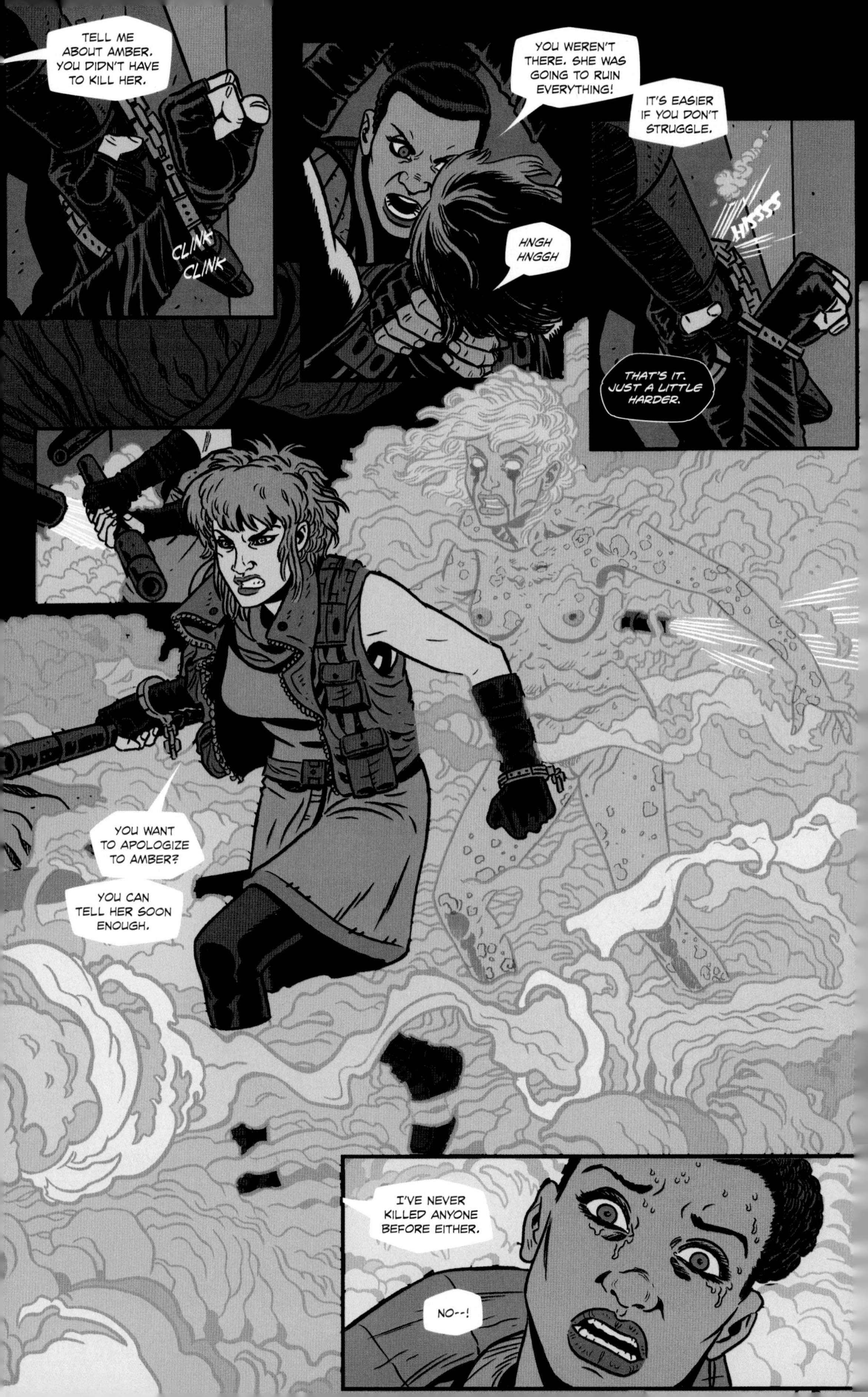
TELL ME ABOUT AMBER. YOU DIDN'T HAVE TO KILL HER.
CLINK CLINK
YOU WEREN'T THERE. SHE WAS GOING TO RUIN EVERYTHING!
HNGH HNGGH
IT'S EASIER IF YOU DON'T STRUGGLE.
HISSSS
THAT'S IT. JUST A LITTLE HARDER.
YOU WANT TO APOLOGIZE TO AMBER?
YOU CAN TELL HER SOON ENOUGH.
I'VE NEVER KILLED ANYONE BEFORE EITHER.
NO--!

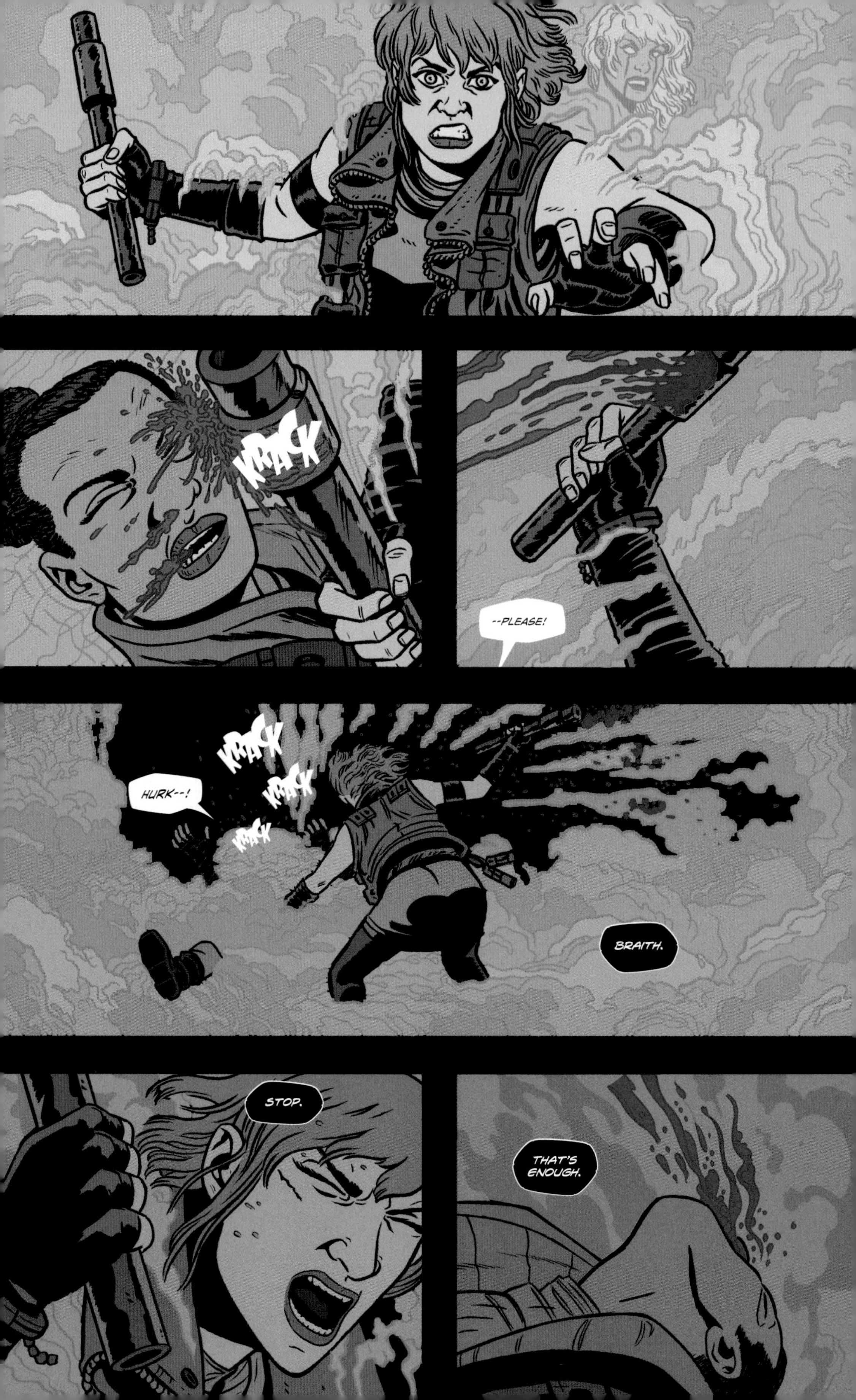
KRACK
--PLEASE!
KRACK
HURK--!
KRACK
KRACK
BRAITH.
STOP.
THAT'S
ENOUGH.

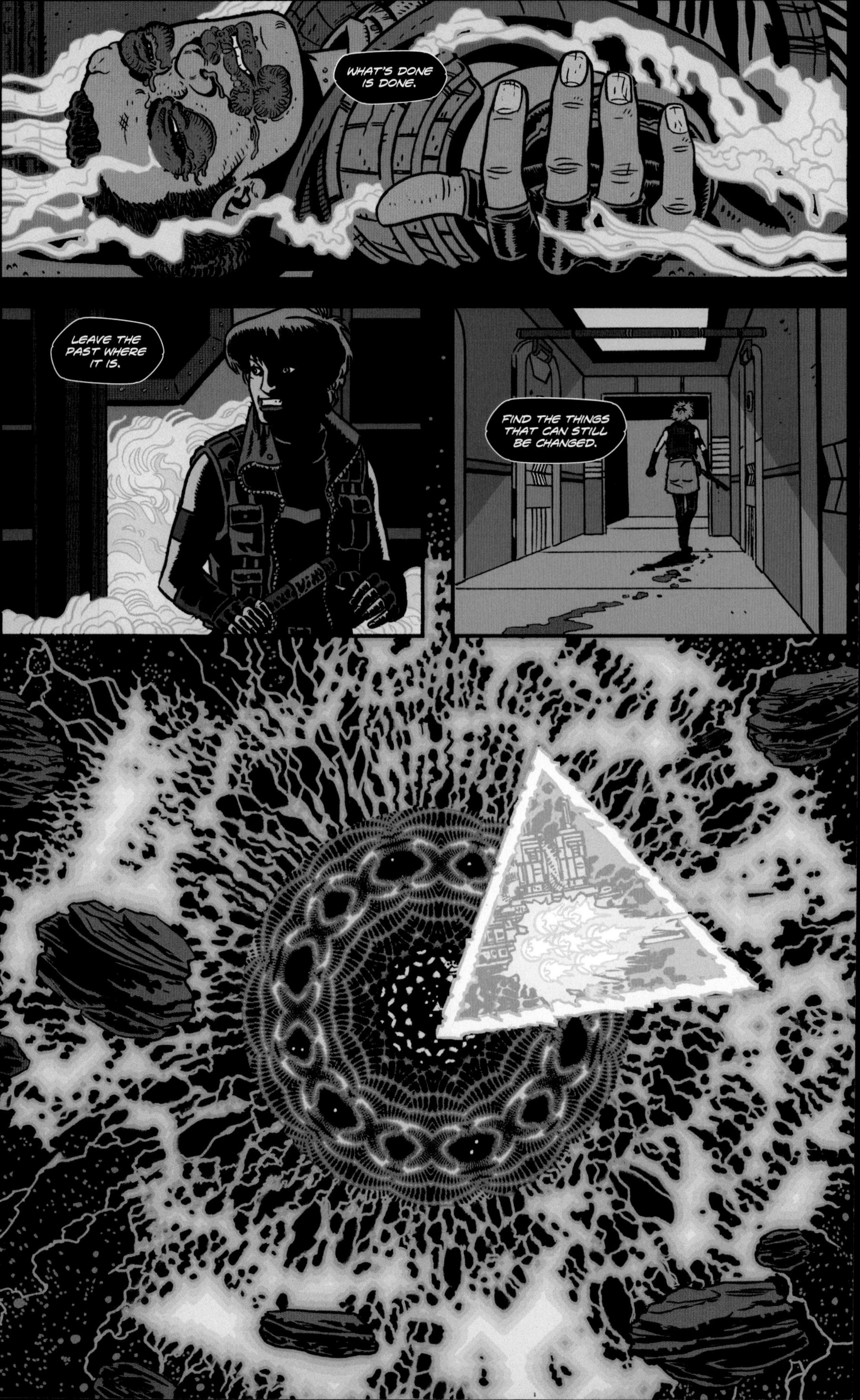
WHAT'S DONE IS DONE.
LEAVE THE PAST WHERE IT IS.
FIND THE THINGS THAT CAN STILL BE CHANGED.

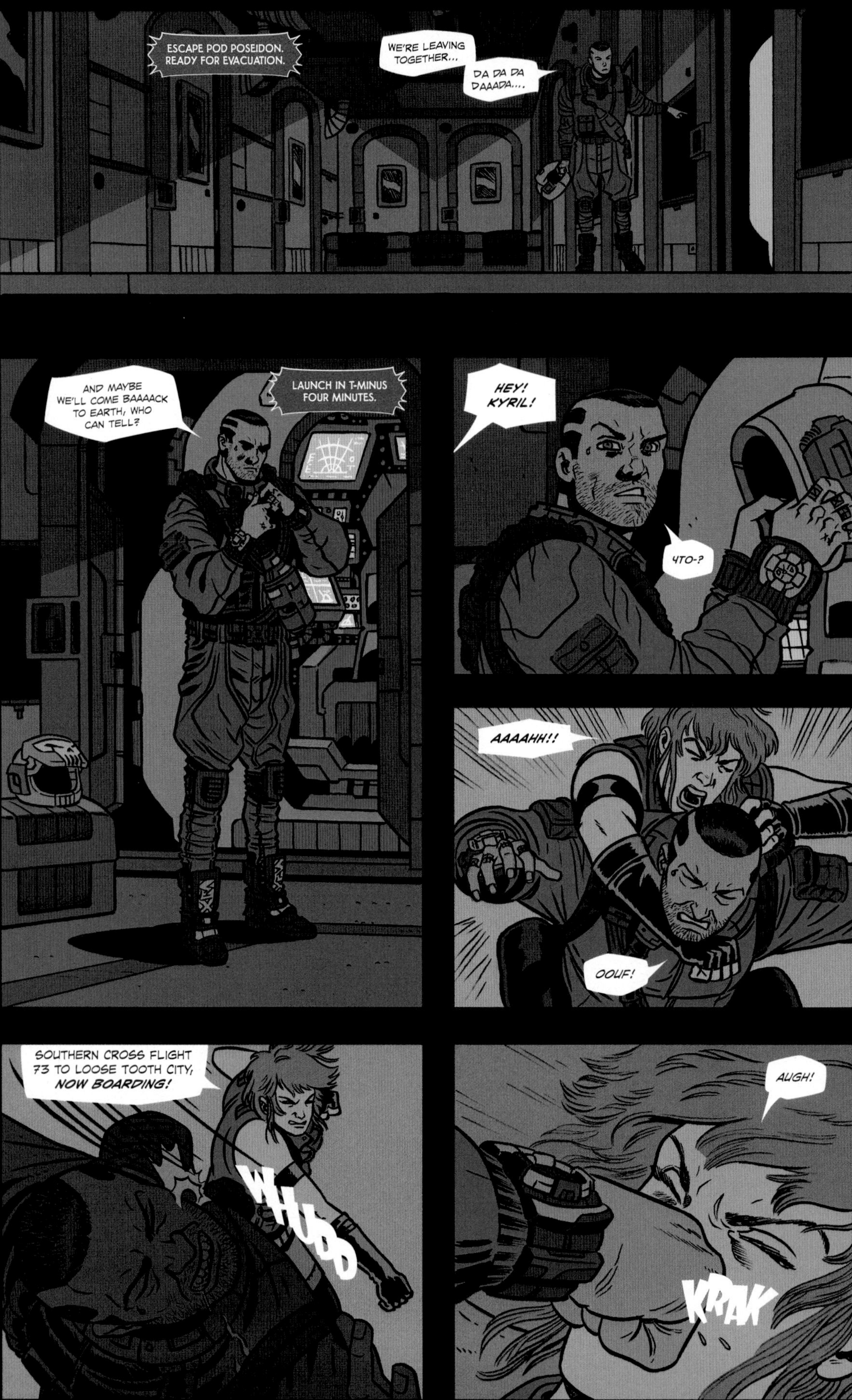
ESCAPE POD POSEIDON. READY FOR EVACUATION.
WE'RE LEAVING TOGETHER...
DA DA DA DAAADA....
AND MAYBE WE'LL COME BAAAACK TO EARTH, WHO CAN TELL?
LAUNCH IN T-MINUS FOUR MINUTES.
HEY! KYRIL!
ЧТО-?
AAAAHH!!
OOUF!
SOUTHERN CROSS FLIGHT 73 TO LOOSE TOOTH CITY, NOW BOARDING!
WHUDD
AUGH!
KRAK

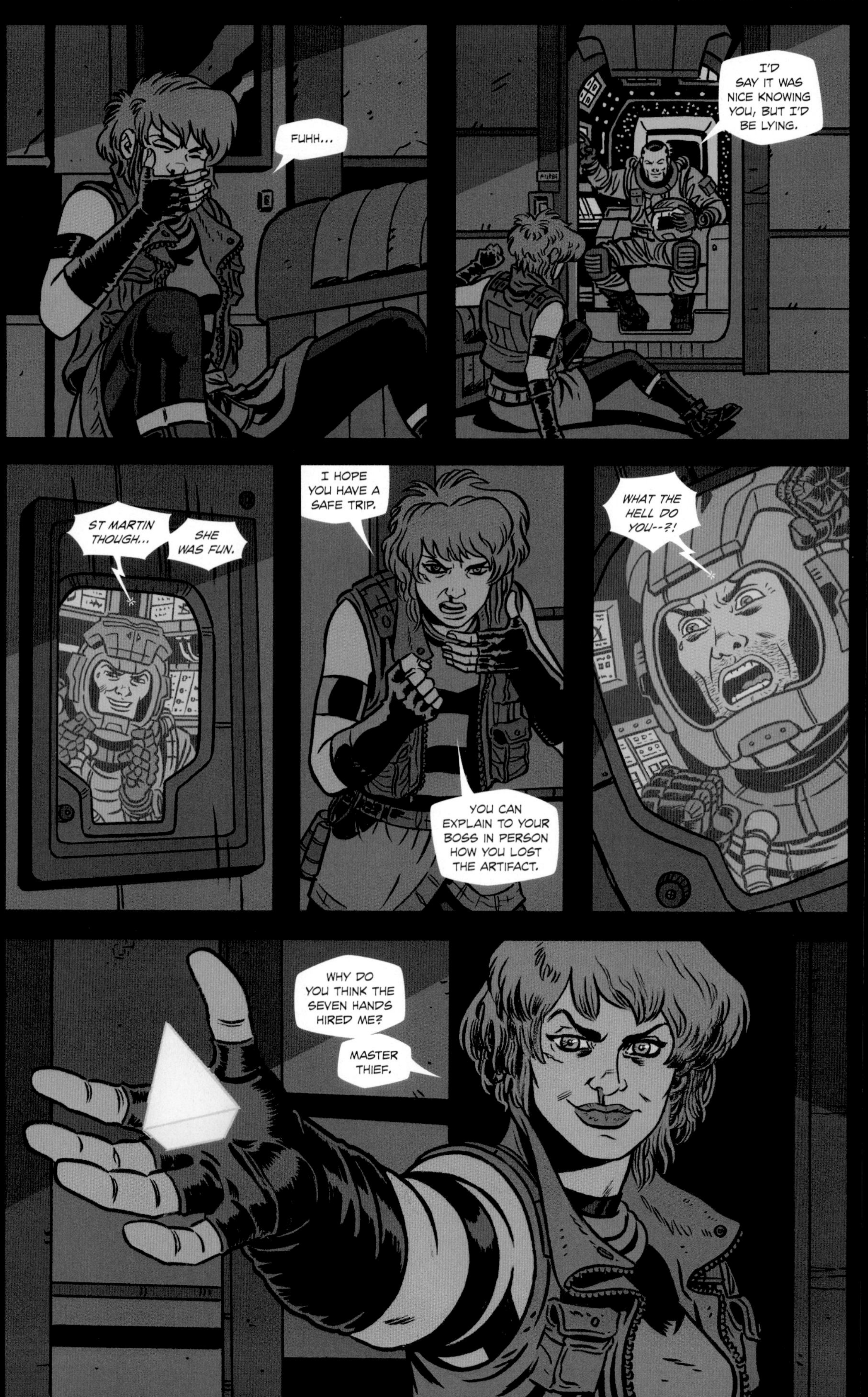
FUHH...
I'D SAY IT WAS NICE KNOWING YOU, BUT I'D BE LYING.
ST MARTIN THOUGH...
SHE WAS FUN.
I HOPE YOU HAVE A SAFE TRIP.
YOU CAN EXPLAIN TO YOUR BOSS IN PERSON HOW YOU LOST THE ARTIFACT.
WHAT THE HELL DO YOU--?!
WHY DO YOU THINK THE SEVEN HANDS HIRED ME?
MASTER THIEF.

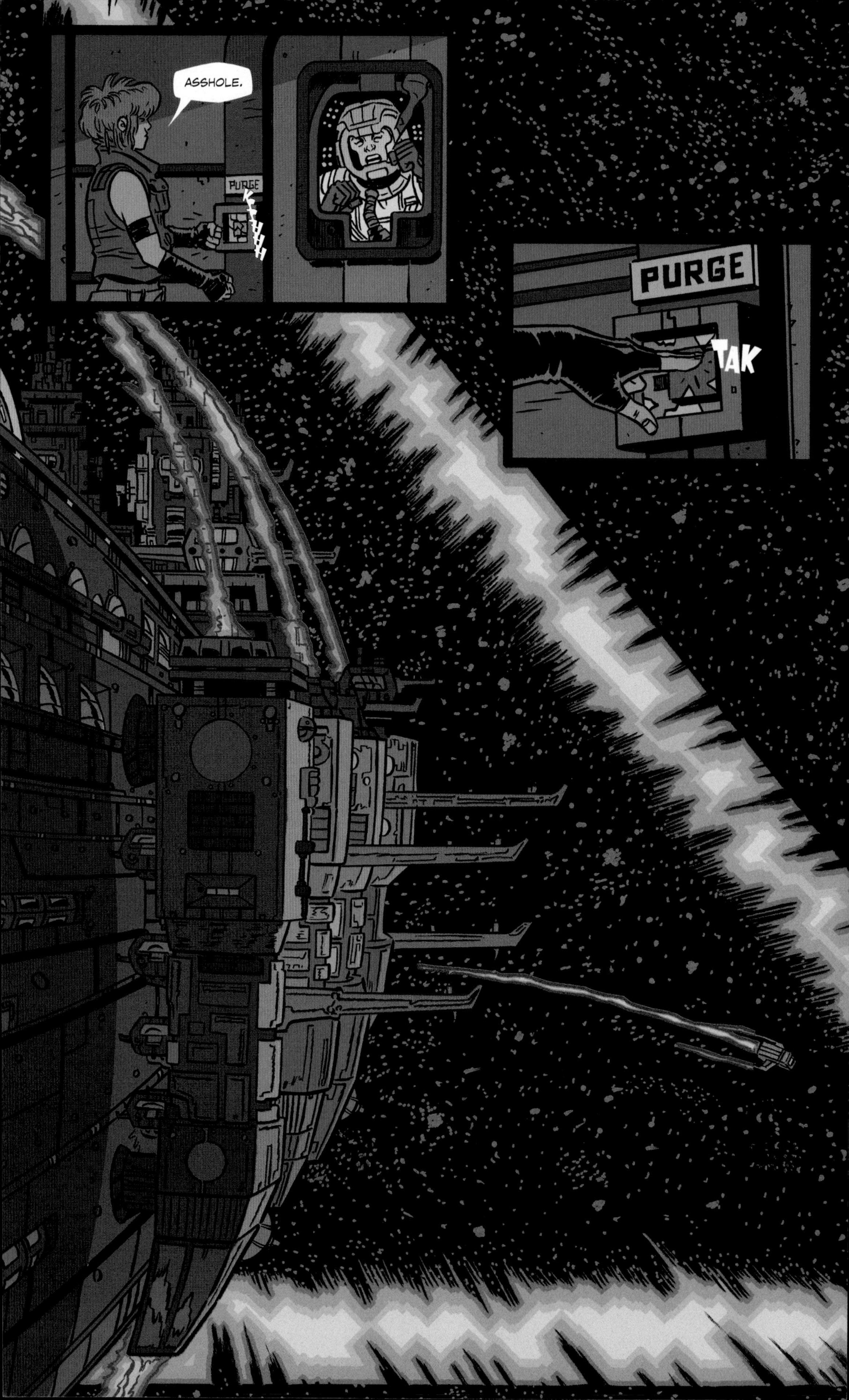
ASSHOLE.
PURGE
PURGE
TAK

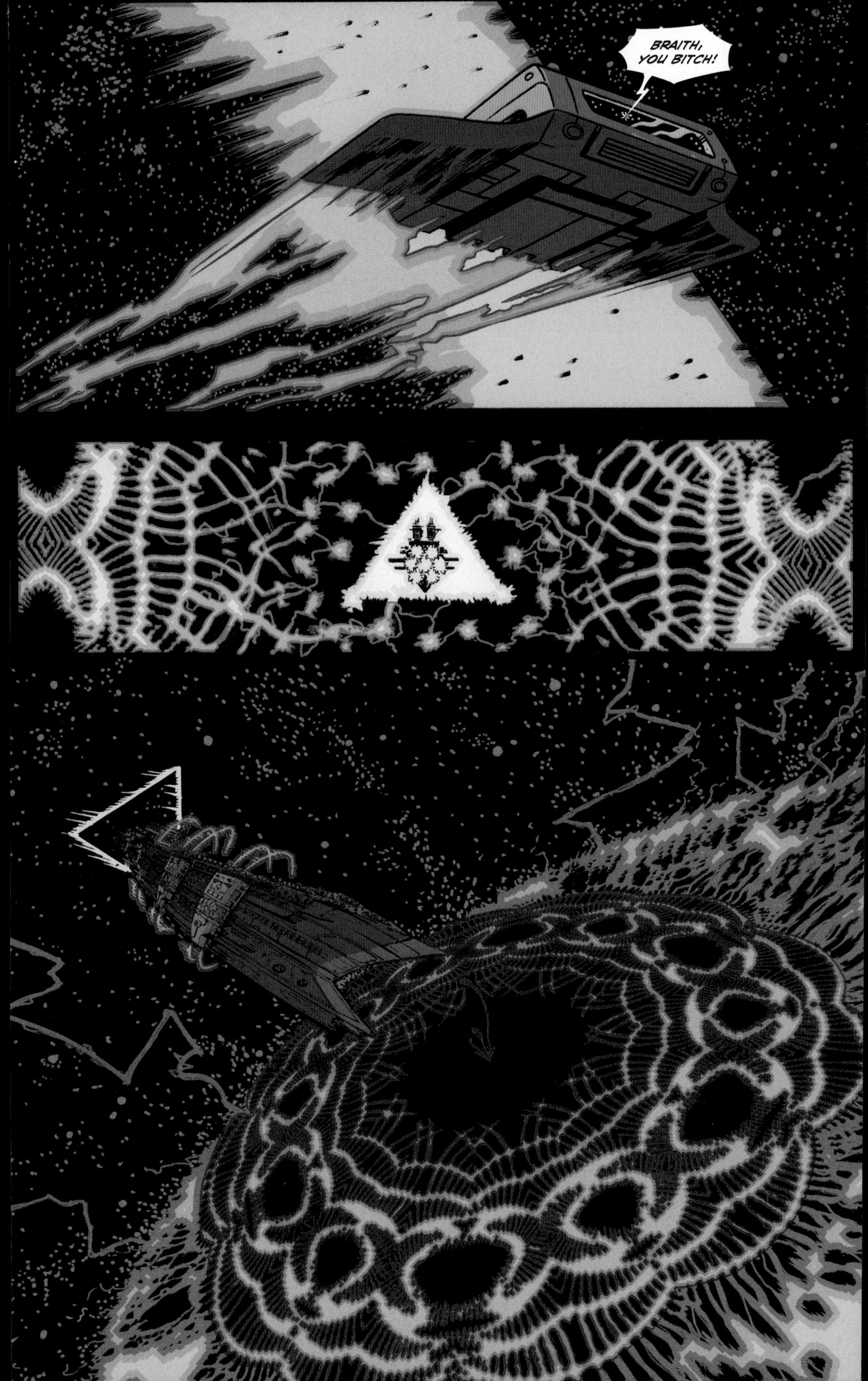
BRAITH, YOU BITCH!

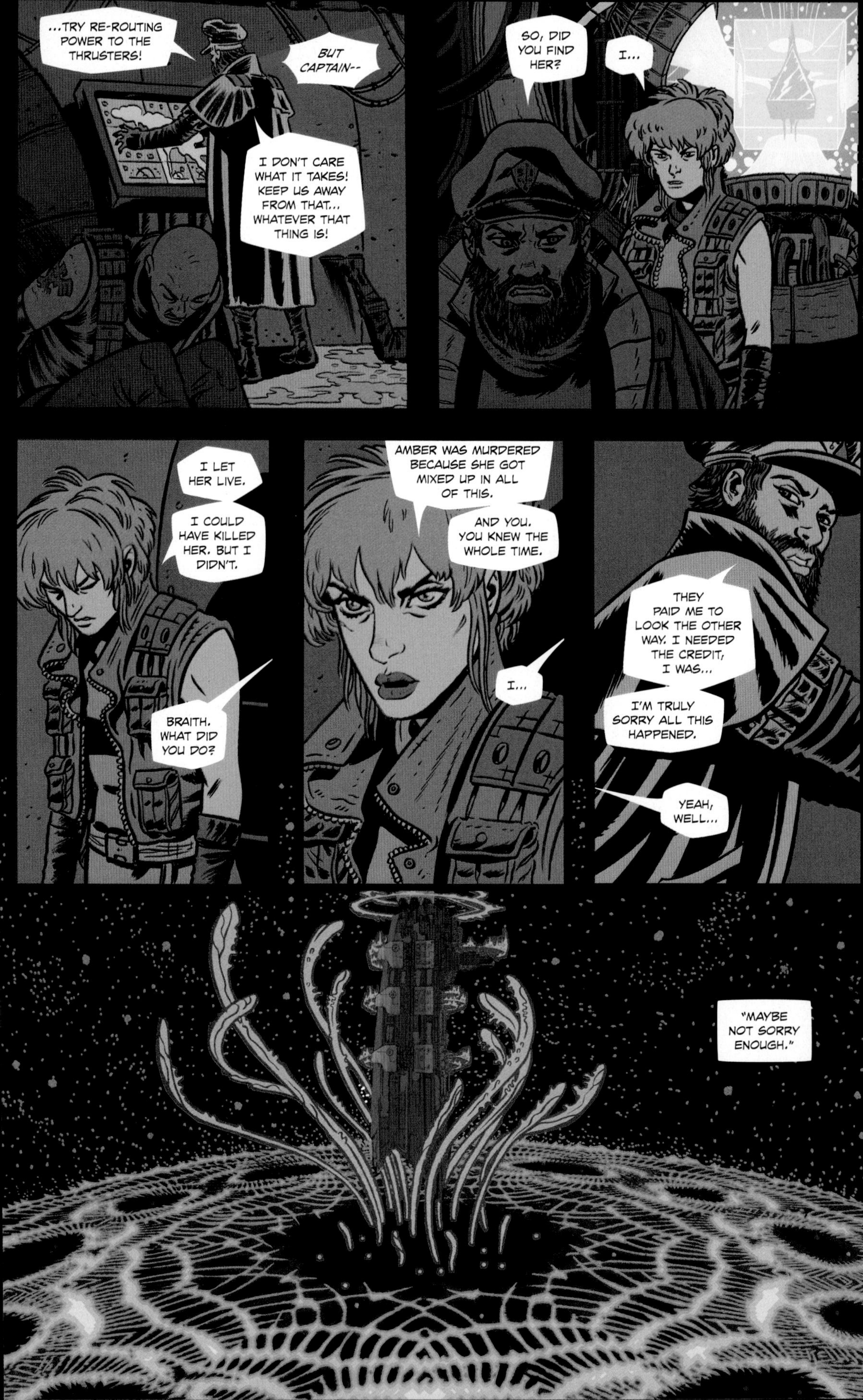
...TRY RE-ROUTING POWER TO THE THRUSTERS!
BUT CAPTAIN--
I DON'T CARE WHAT IT TAKES! KEEP US AWAY FROM THAT... WHATEVER THAT THING IS!
SO, DID YOU FIND HER?
I...
I LET HER LIVE.
I COULD HAVE KILLED HER. BUT I DIDN'T.
BRAITH. WHAT DID YOU DO?
AMBER WAS MURDERED BECAUSE SHE GOT MIXED UP IN ALL OF THIS.
AND YOU. YOU KNEW THE WHOLE TIME.
I...
THEY PAID ME TO LOOK THE OTHER WAY. I NEEDED THE CREDIT, I WAS...
I'M TRULY SORRY ALL THIS HAPPENED.
YEAH, WELL...
"MAYBE NOT SORRY ENOUGH."

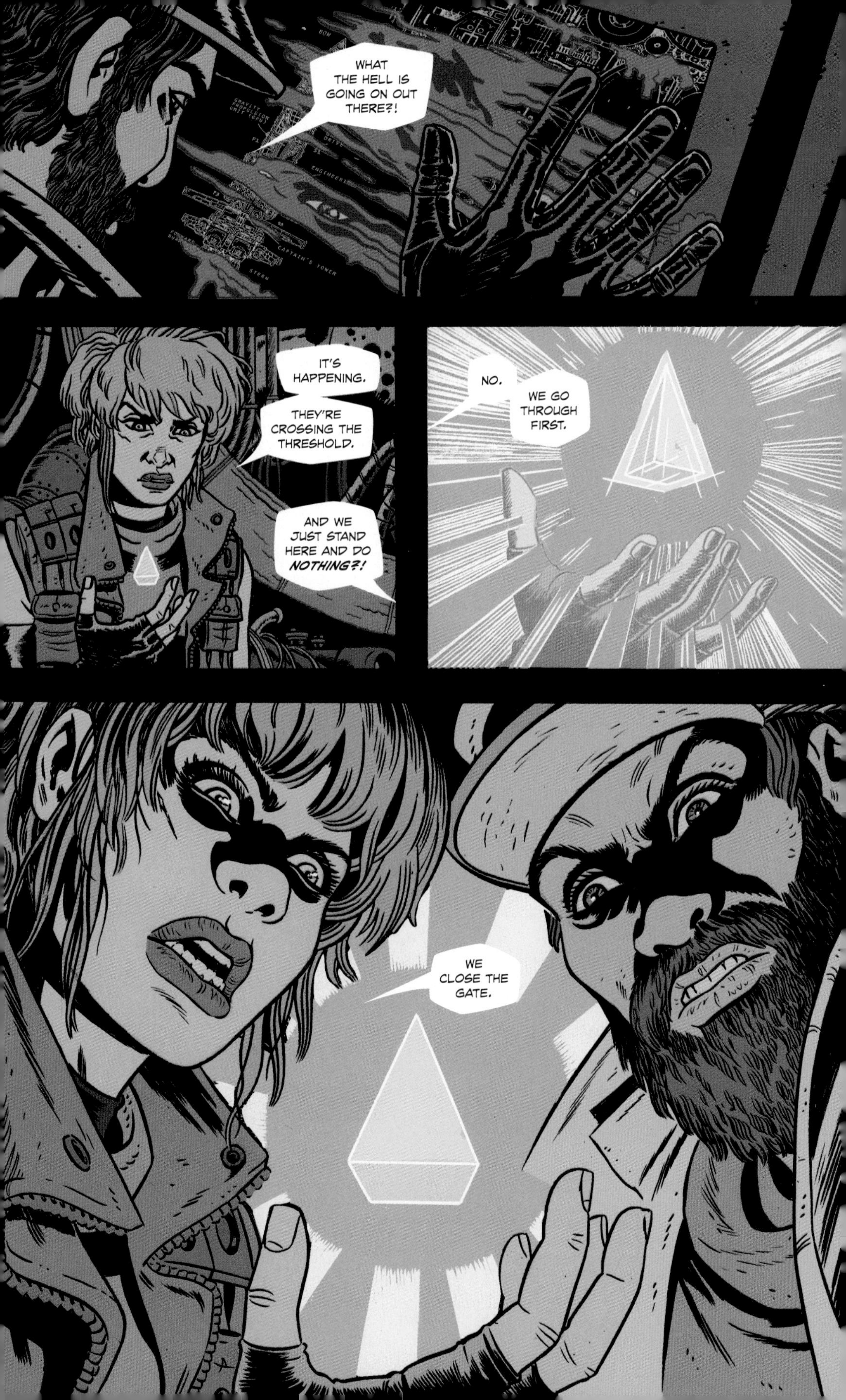
WHAT THE HELL IS GOING ON OUT THERE?!
IT'S HAPPENING.
THEY'RE CROSSING THE THRESHOLD.
AND WE JUST STAND HERE AND DO *NOTHING?!*
NO.
WE GO THROUGH FIRST.
WE CLOSE THE GATE.

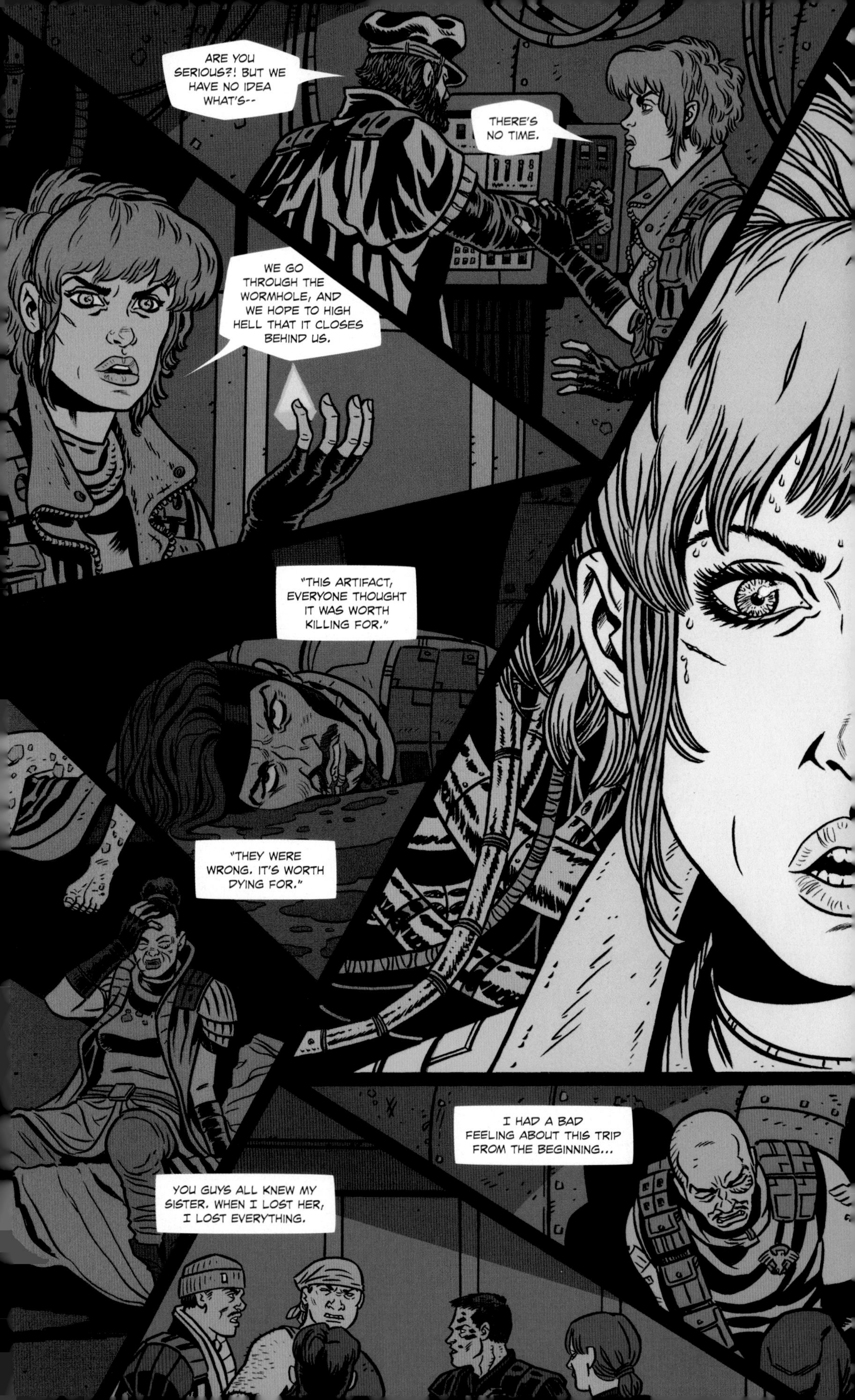
ARE YOU SERIOUS?! BUT WE HAVE NO IDEA WHAT'S--
THERE'S NO TIME.
WE GO THROUGH THE WORMHOLE, AND WE HOPE TO HIGH HELL THAT IT CLOSES BEHIND US.
"THIS ARTIFACT, EVERYONE THOUGHT IT WAS WORTH KILLING FOR."
"THEY WERE WRONG. IT'S WORTH DYING FOR."
I HAD A BAD FEELING ABOUT THIS TRIP FROM THE BEGINNING...
YOU GUYS ALL KNEW MY SISTER. WHEN I LOST HER, I LOST EVERYTHING.

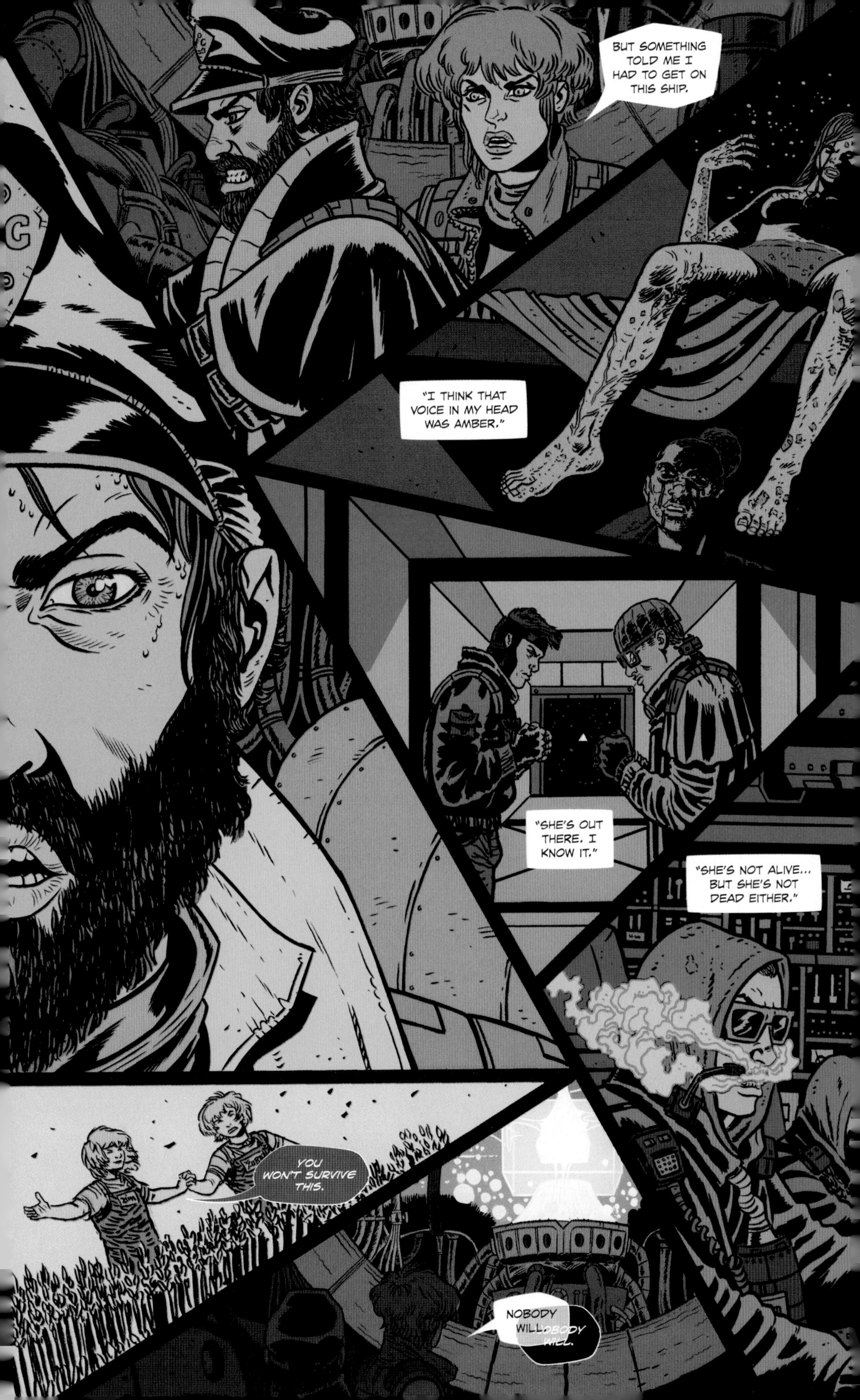
BUT SOMETHING TOLD ME I HAD TO GET ON THIS SHIP.
"I THINK THAT VOICE IN MY HEAD WAS AMBER."
"SHE'S OUT THERE. I KNOW IT."
"SHE'S NOT ALIVE... BUT SHE'S NOT DEAD EITHER."
YOU WON'T SURVIVE THIS.
NOBODY WILL.
NOBODY WILL.

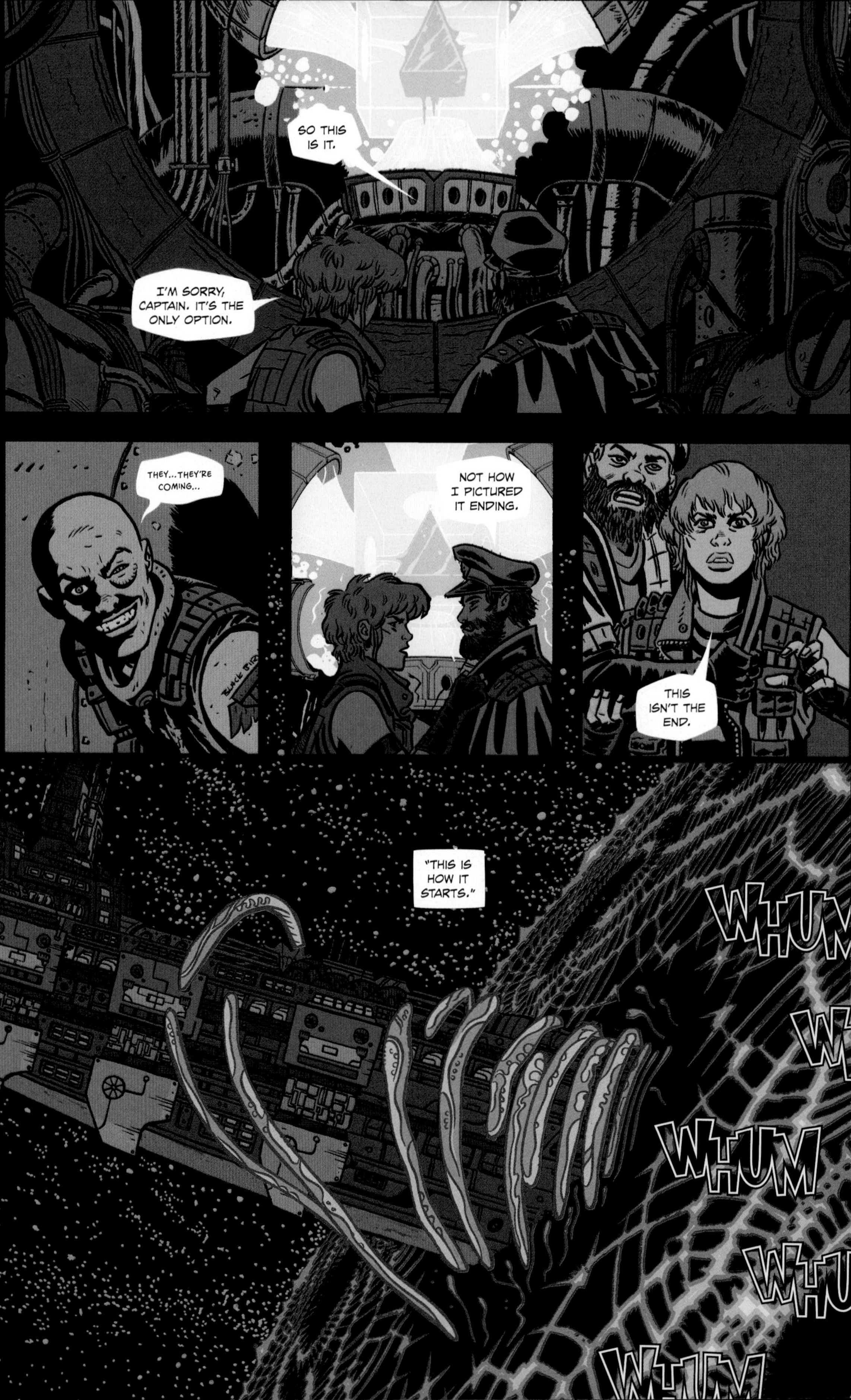
SO THIS IS IT.
I'M SORRY, CAPTAIN. IT'S THE ONLY OPTION.
THEY... THEY'RE COMING...
NOT HOW I PICTURED IT ENDING.
THIS ISN'T THE END.
"THIS IS HOW IT STARTS."
WHUM

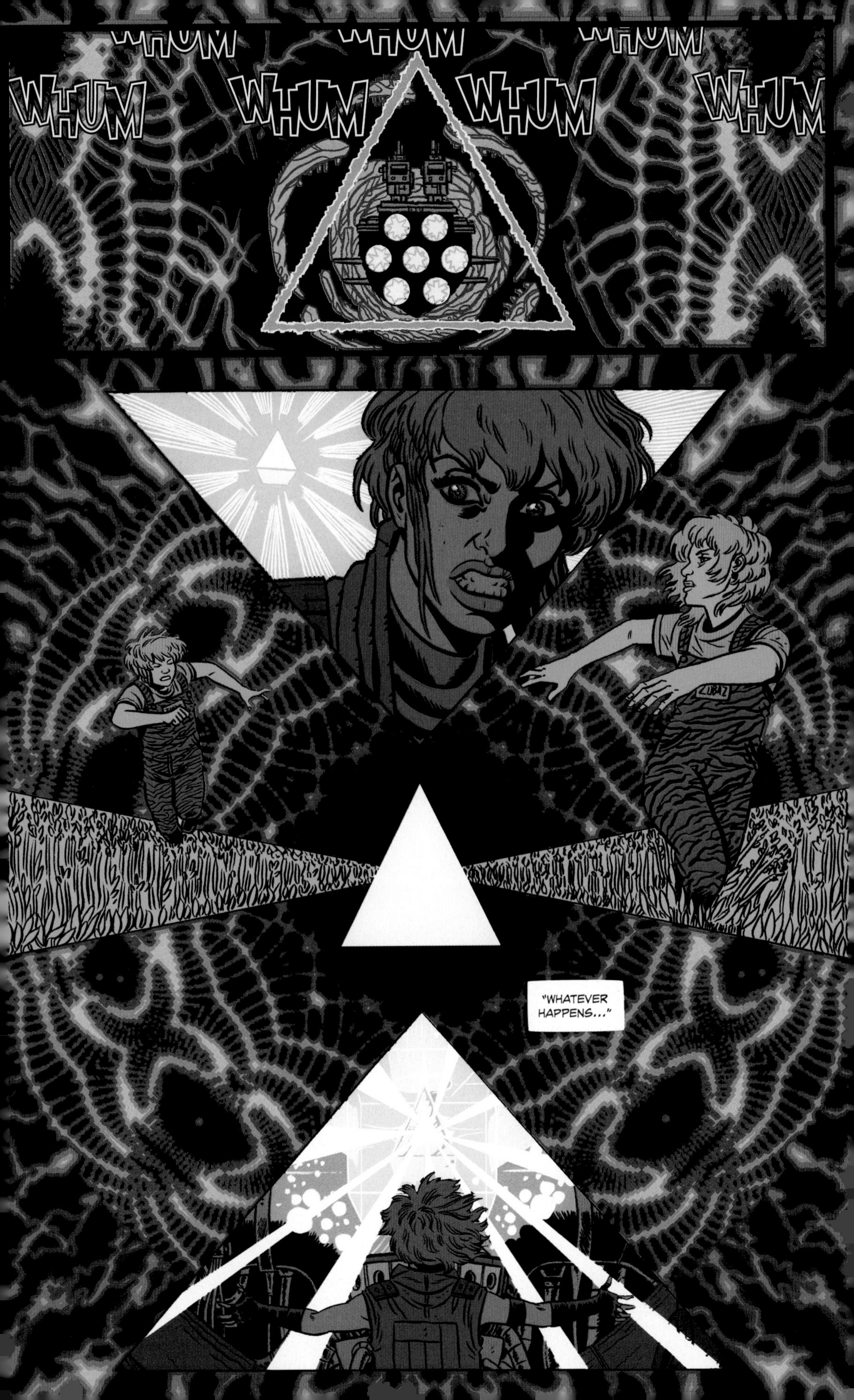
WHUM WHUM WHUM WHUM
"WHATEVER HAPPENS..."

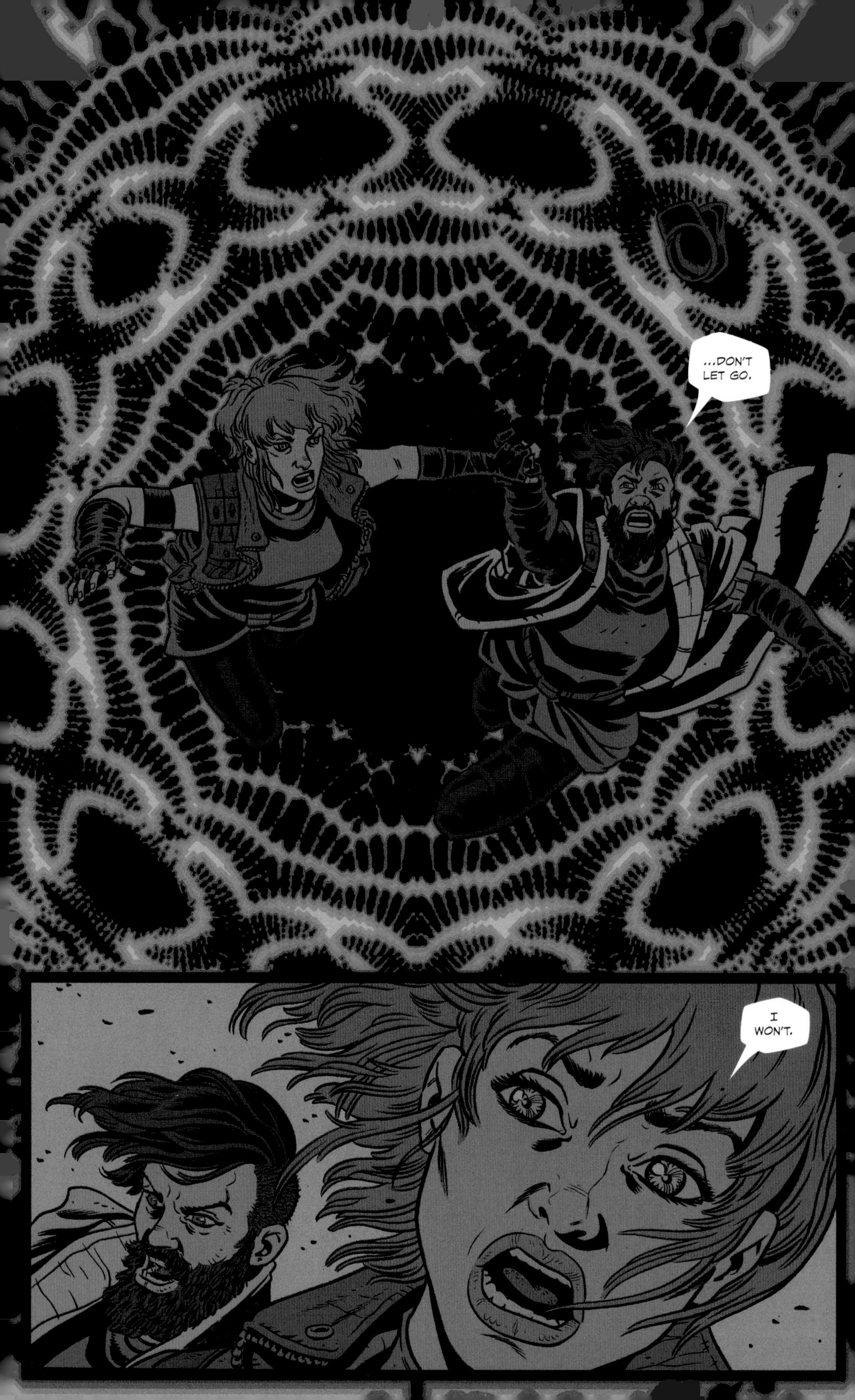
...DON'T LET GO.
I WON'T.

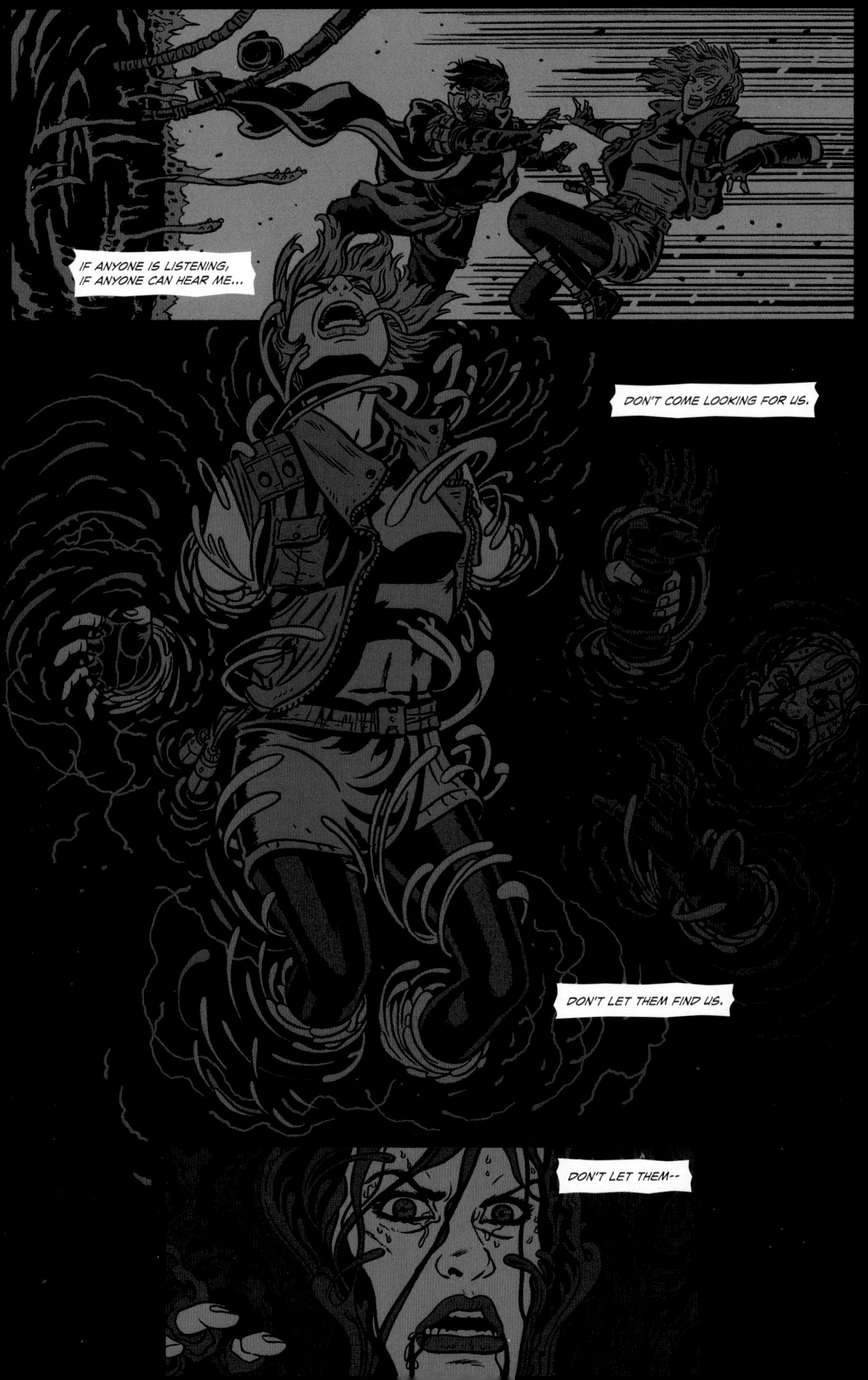
IF ANYONE IS LISTENING,
IF ANYONE CAN HEAR ME...
DON'T COME LOOKING FOR US.
DON'T LET THEM FIND US.
DON'T LET THEM--

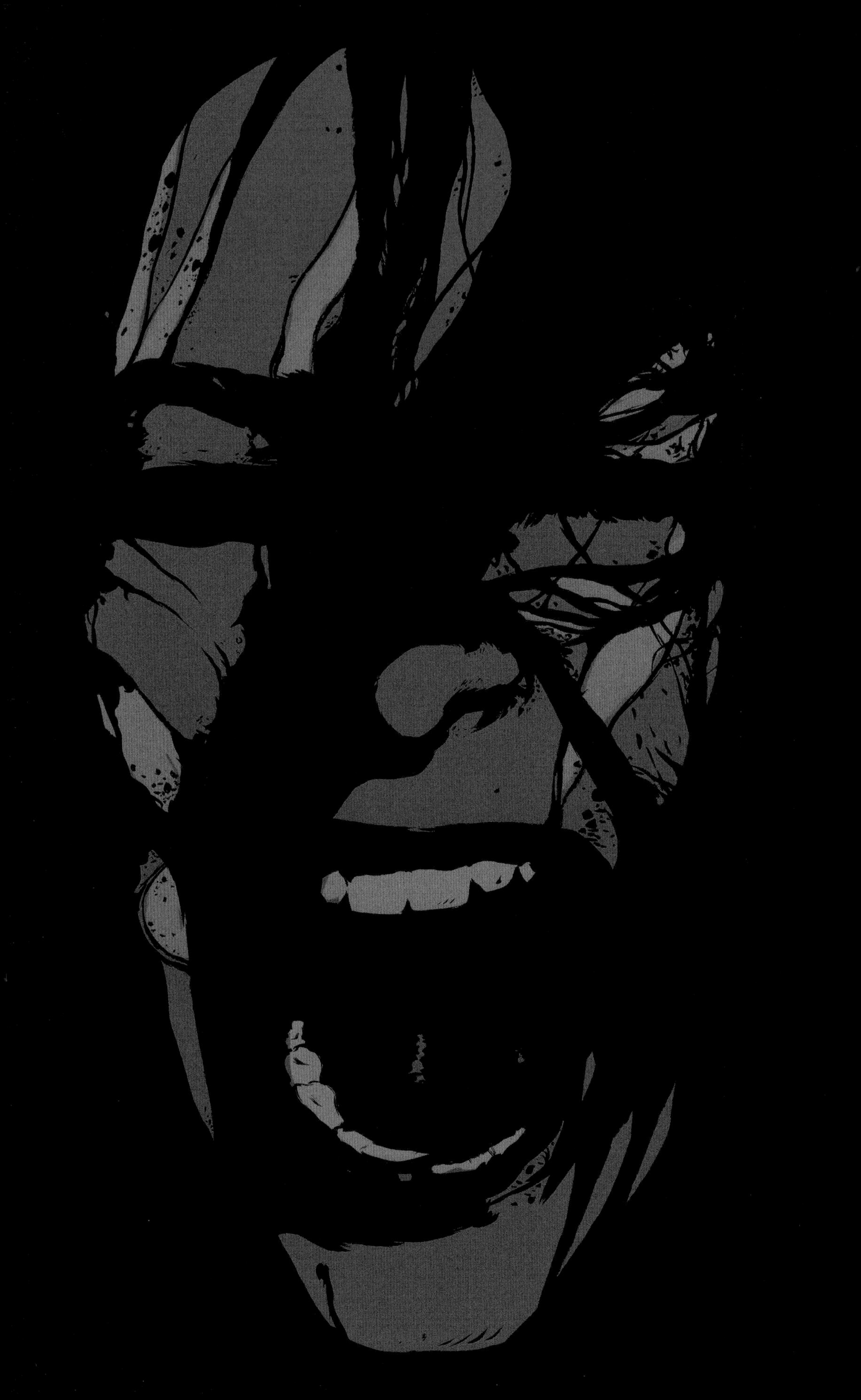

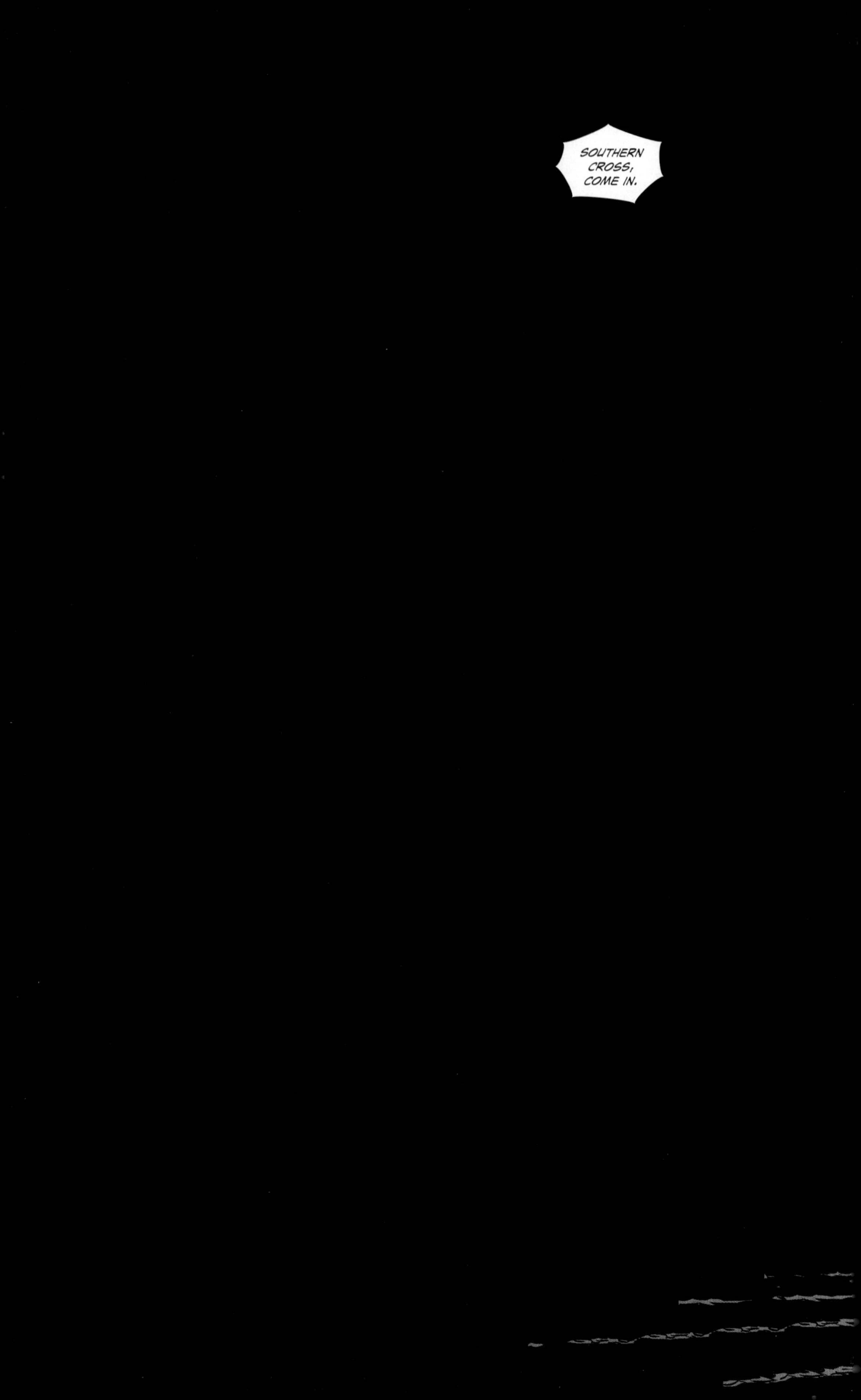
SOUTHERN CROSS, COME IN.

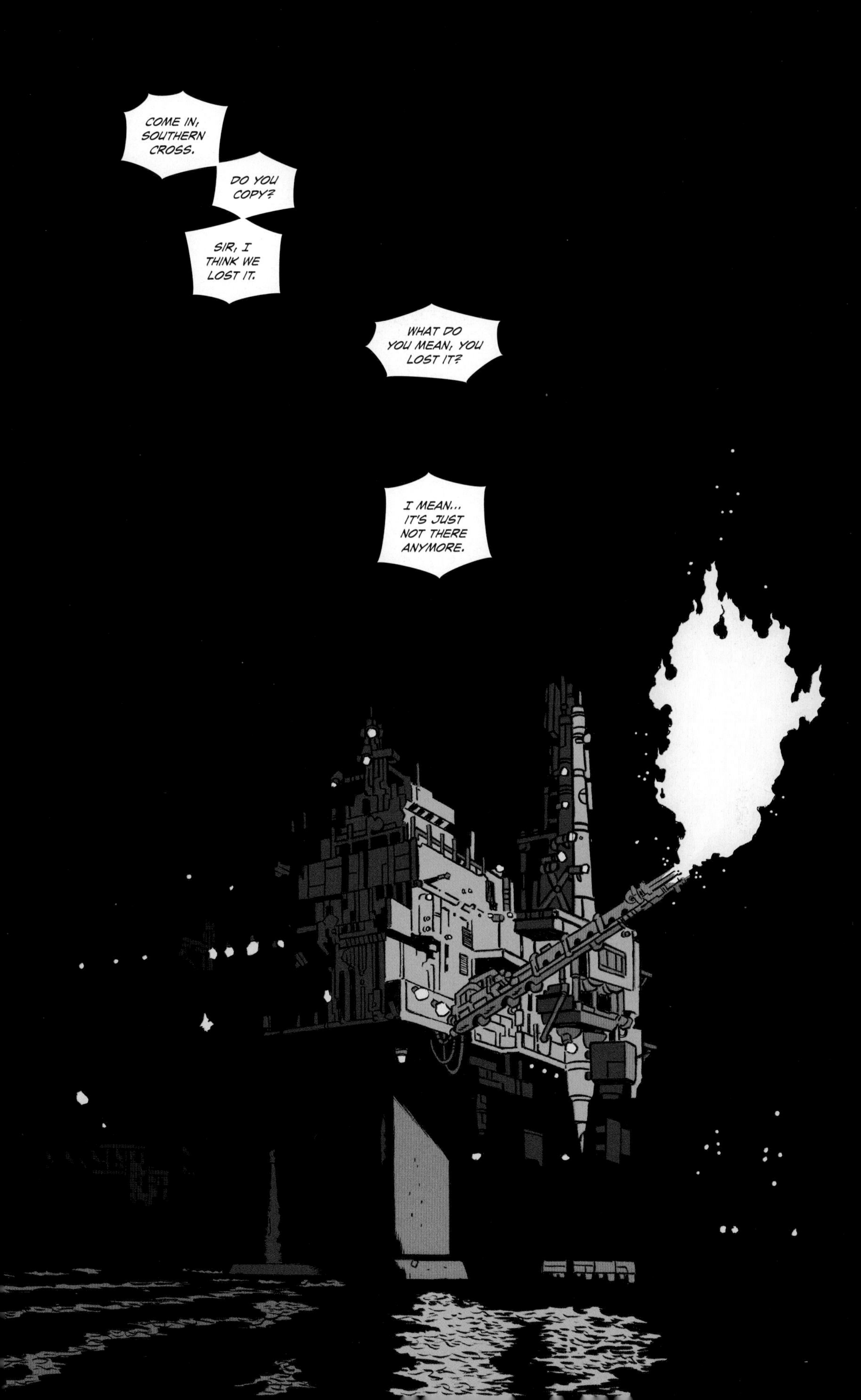
COME IN, SOUTHERN CROSS.
DO YOU COPY?
SIR, I THINK WE LOST IT.
WHAT DO YOU MEAN, YOU LOST IT?
I MEAN... IT'S JUST NOT THERE ANYMORE.

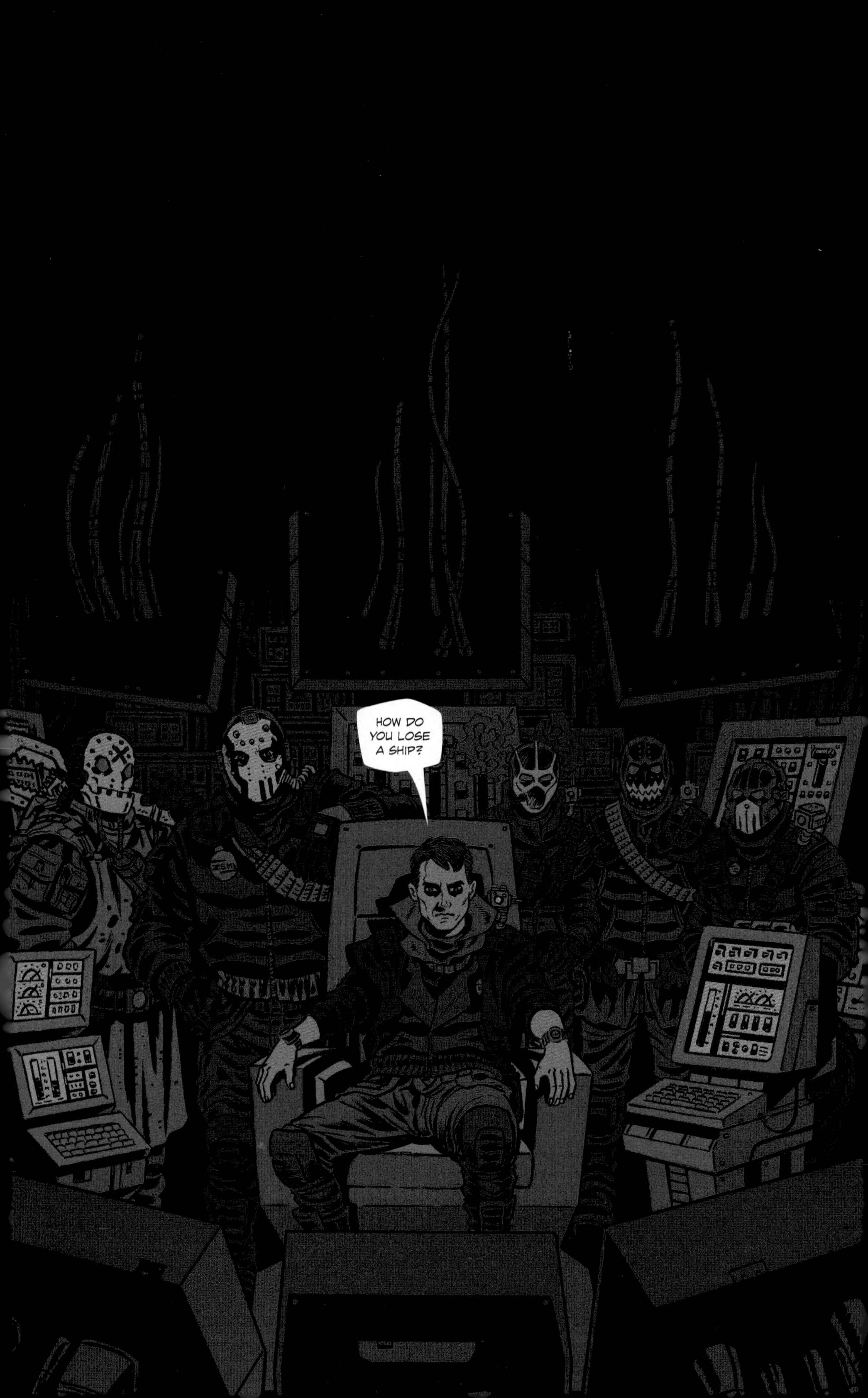
HOW DO YOU LOSE A SHIP?

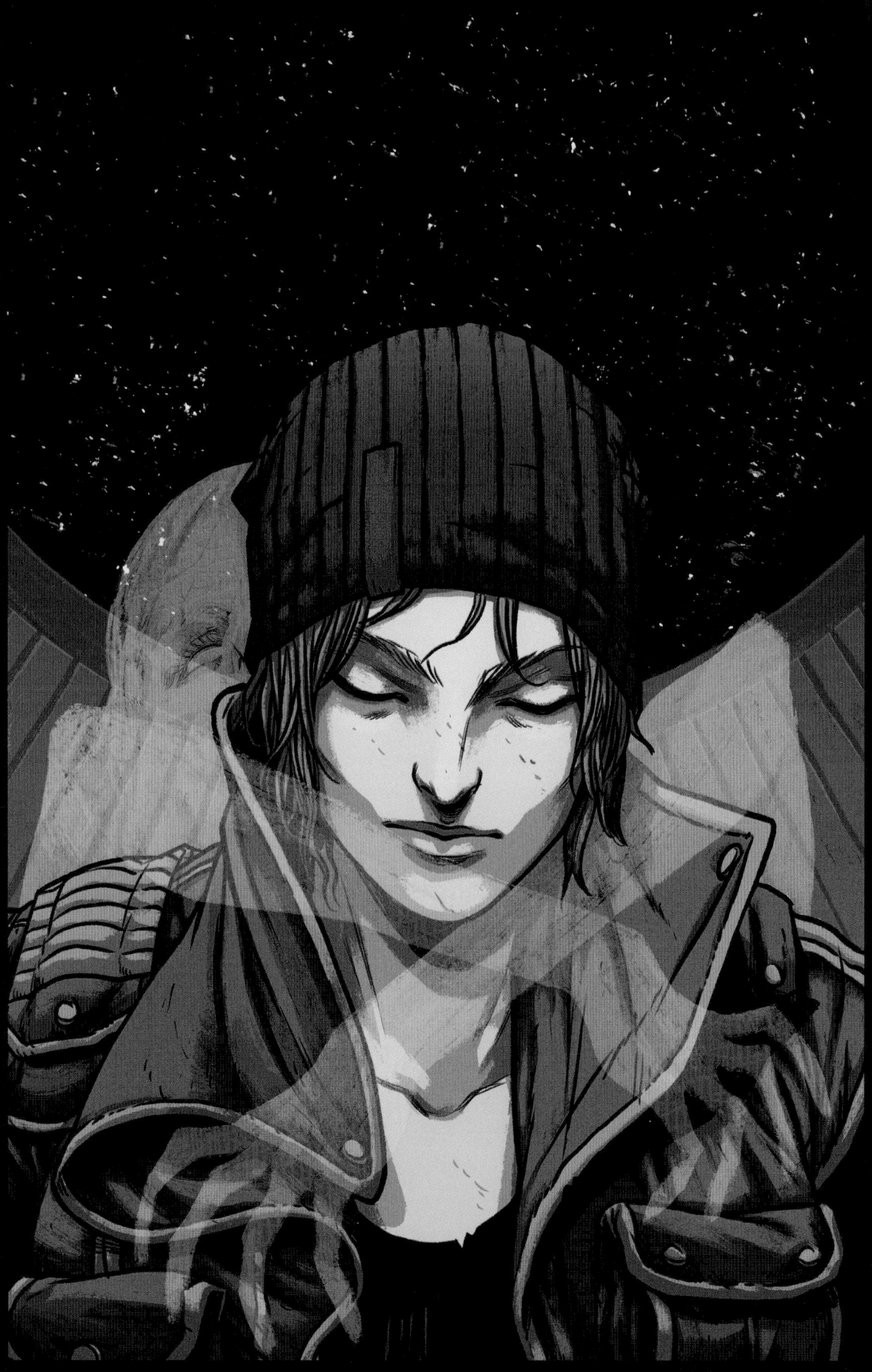

ISSUE 01 COVER | BECKY CLOONAN

ISSUE 02 COVER | BECKY CLOONAN

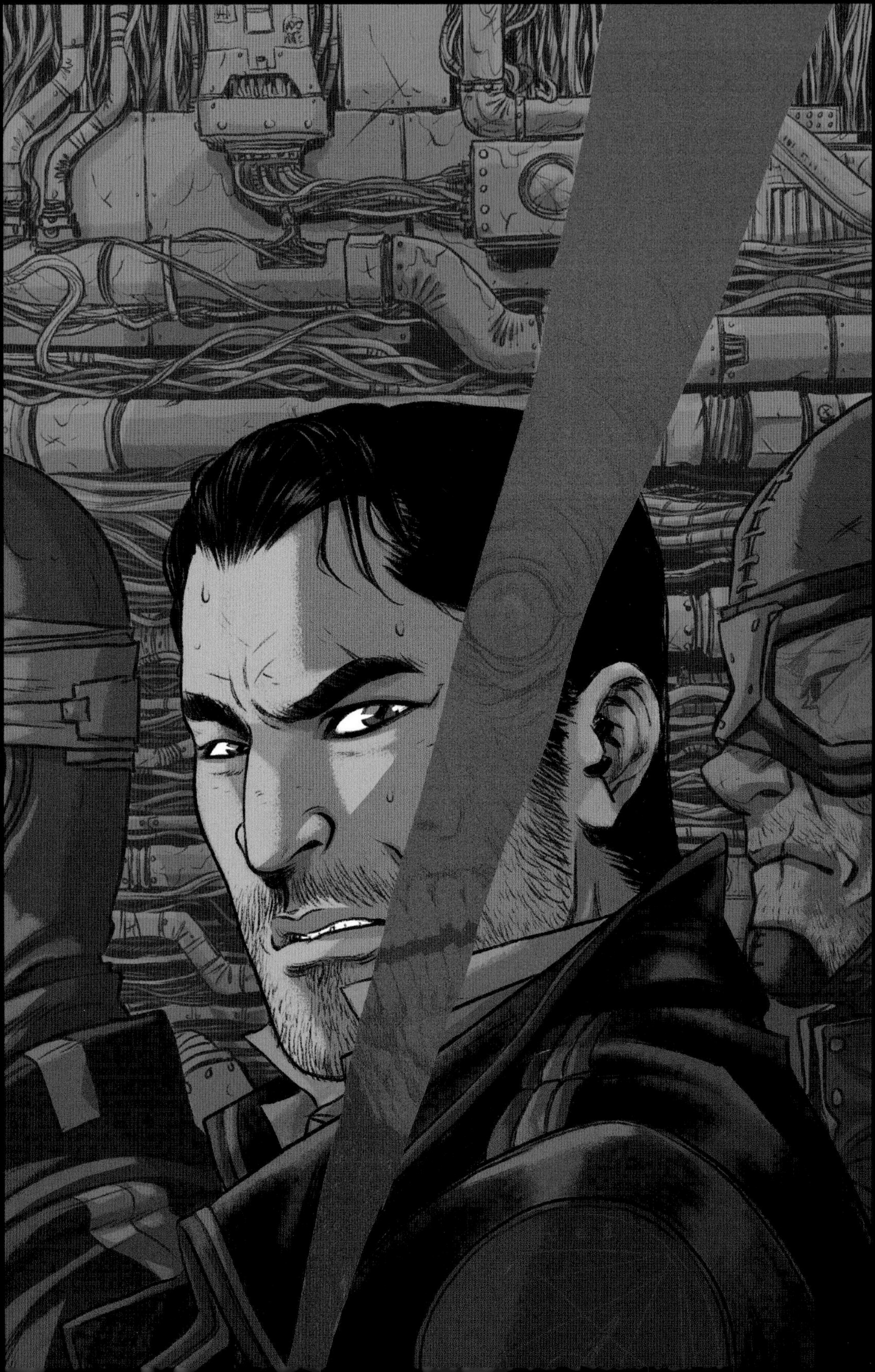

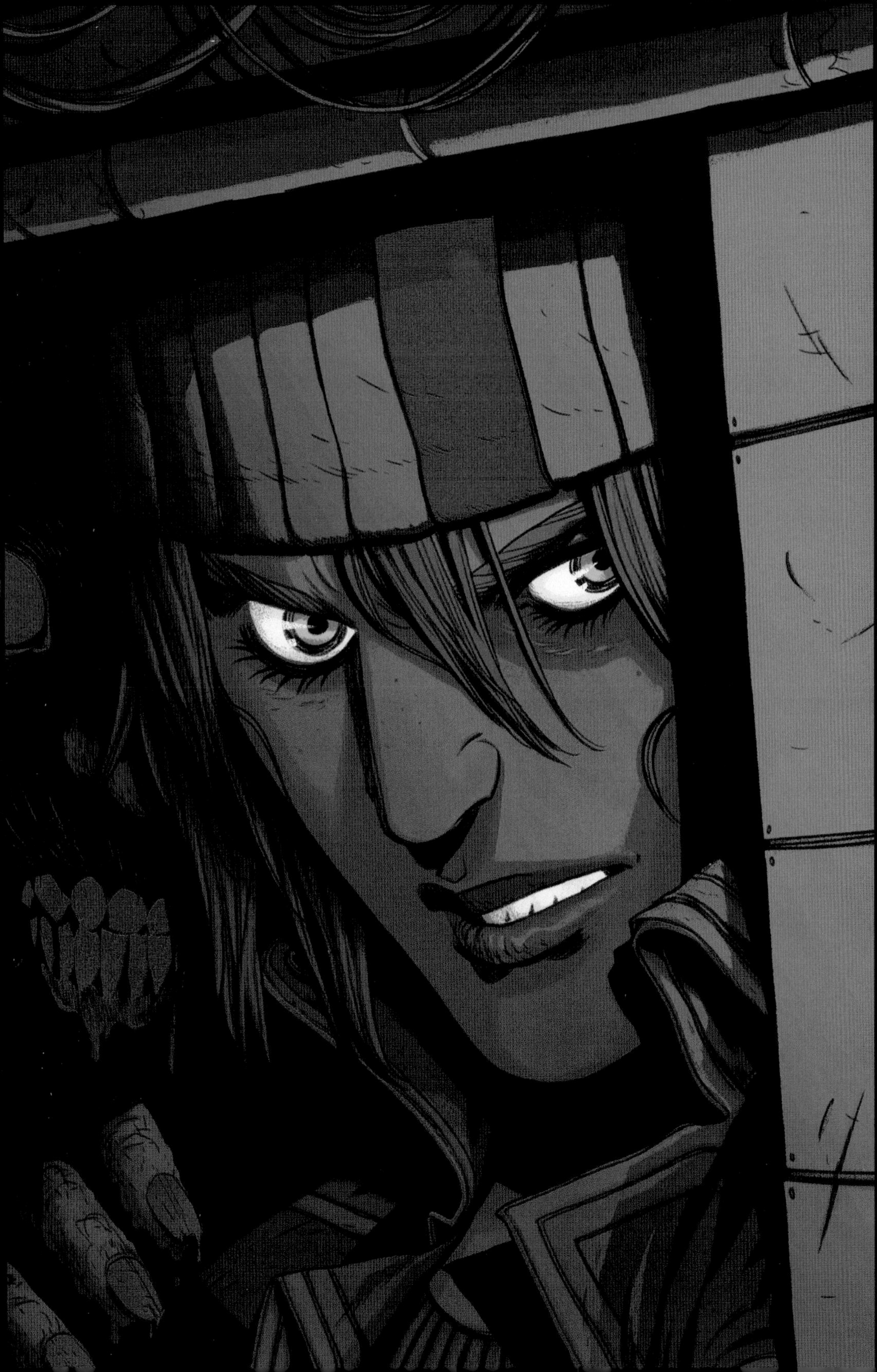

ISSUE 04 COVER | BECKY CLOONAN

ISSUE 05 COVER | BECKY CLOONAN

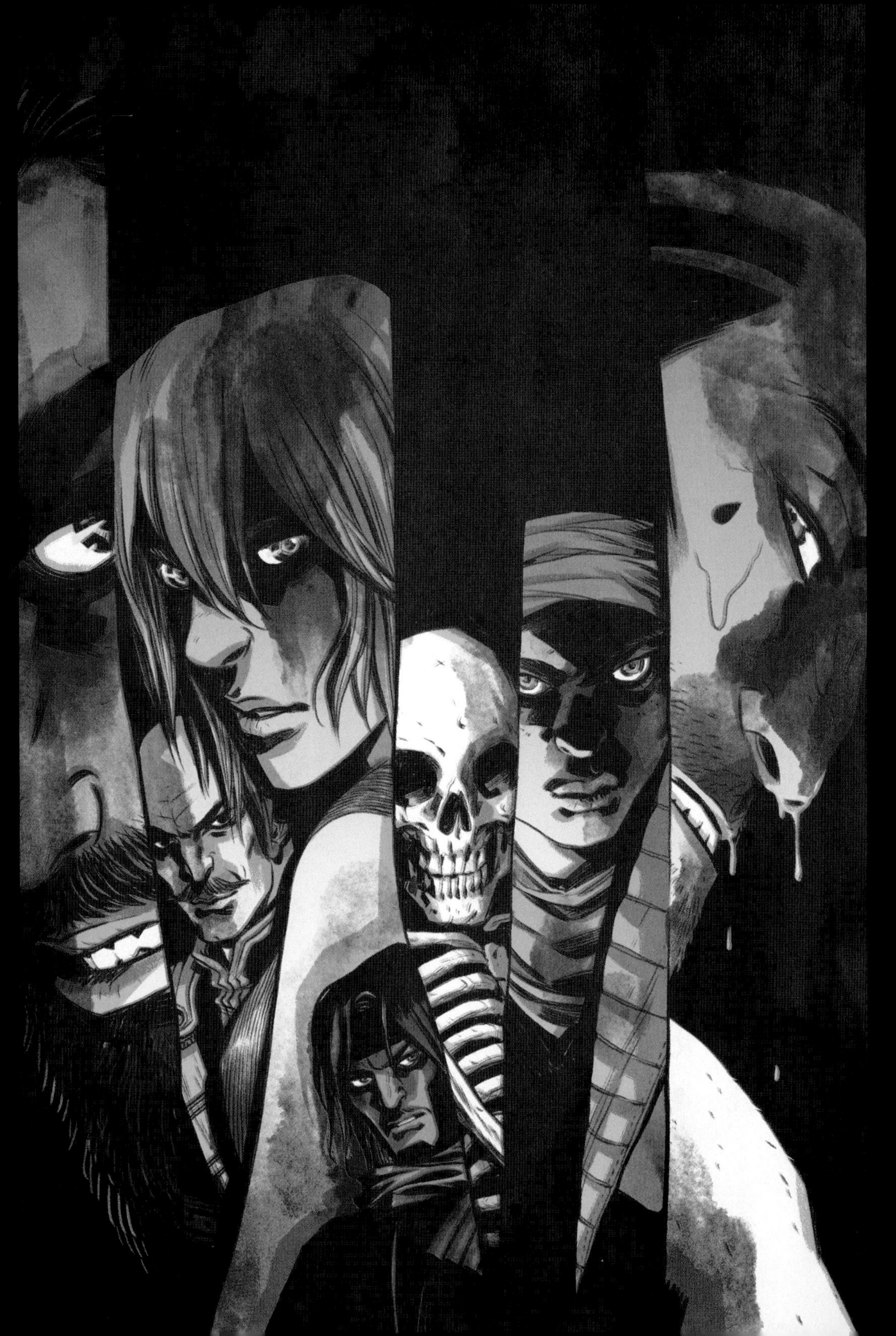

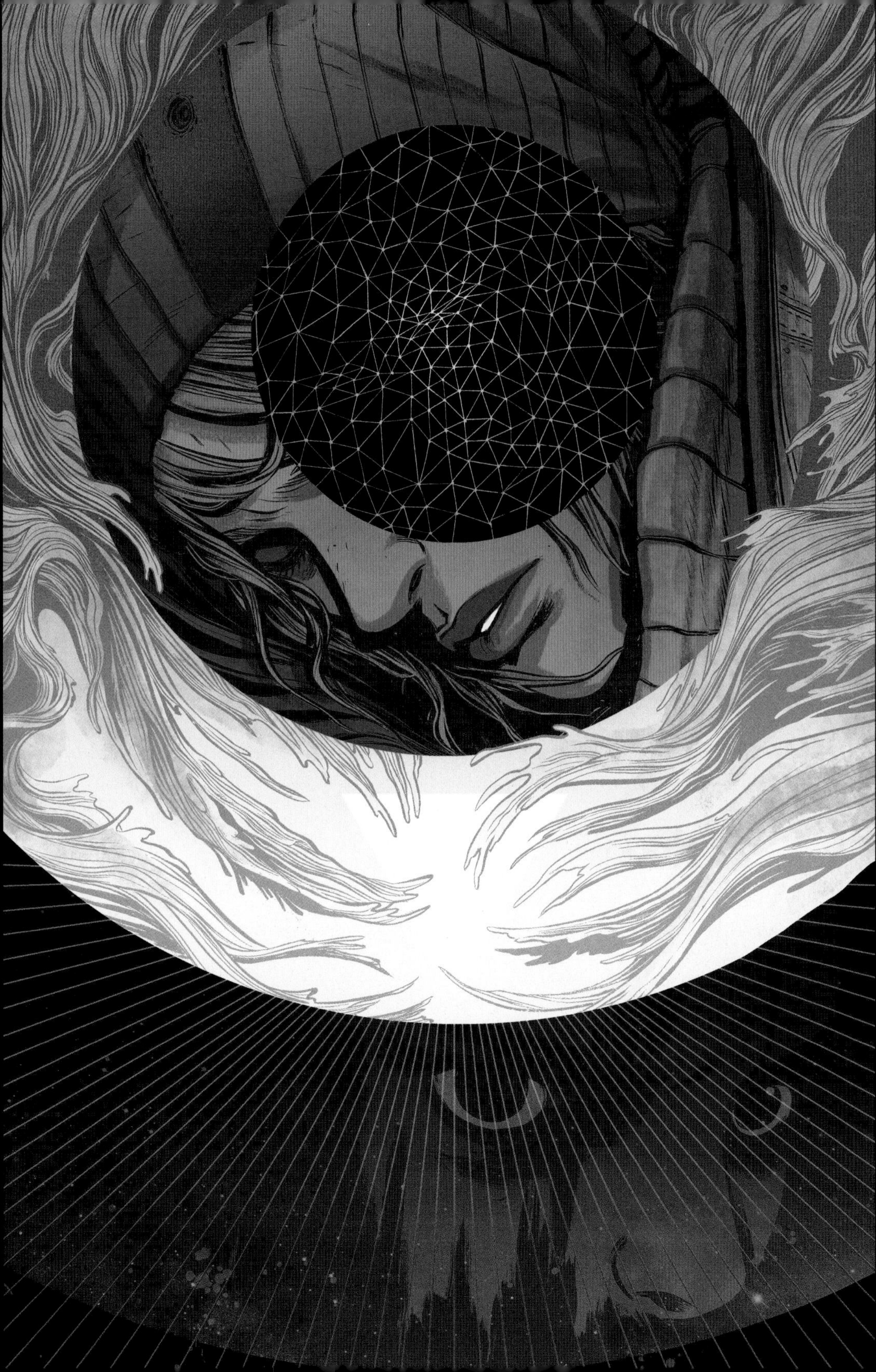

ISSUE 06 COVER | BECKY CLOONAN

THE BIG BANG EXCLUSIVE ISSUE 01 VARIANT COVER | MATT TAYLOR

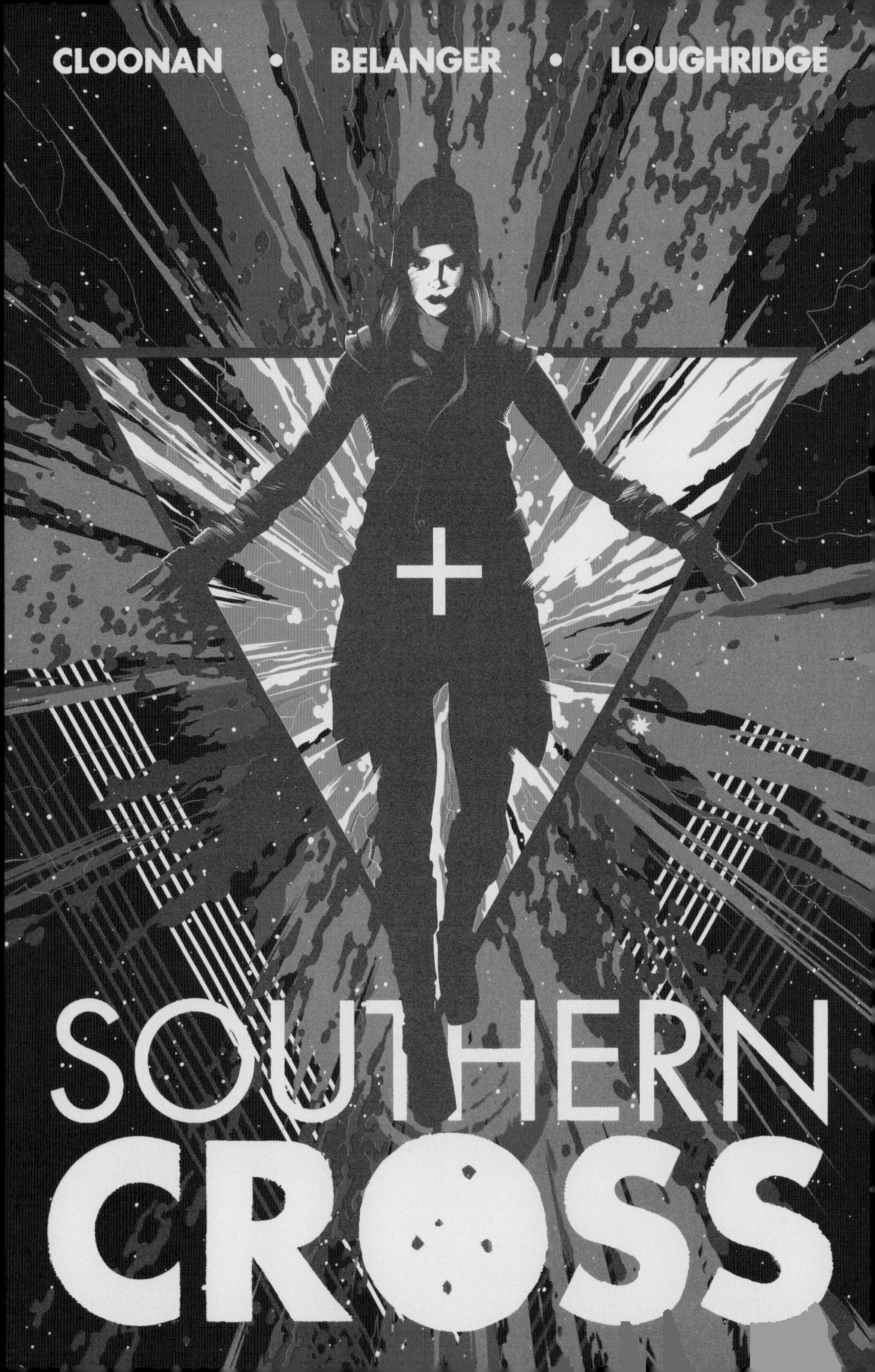
CLOONAN • BELANGER • LOUGHRIDGE
SOUTHERN
CROSS

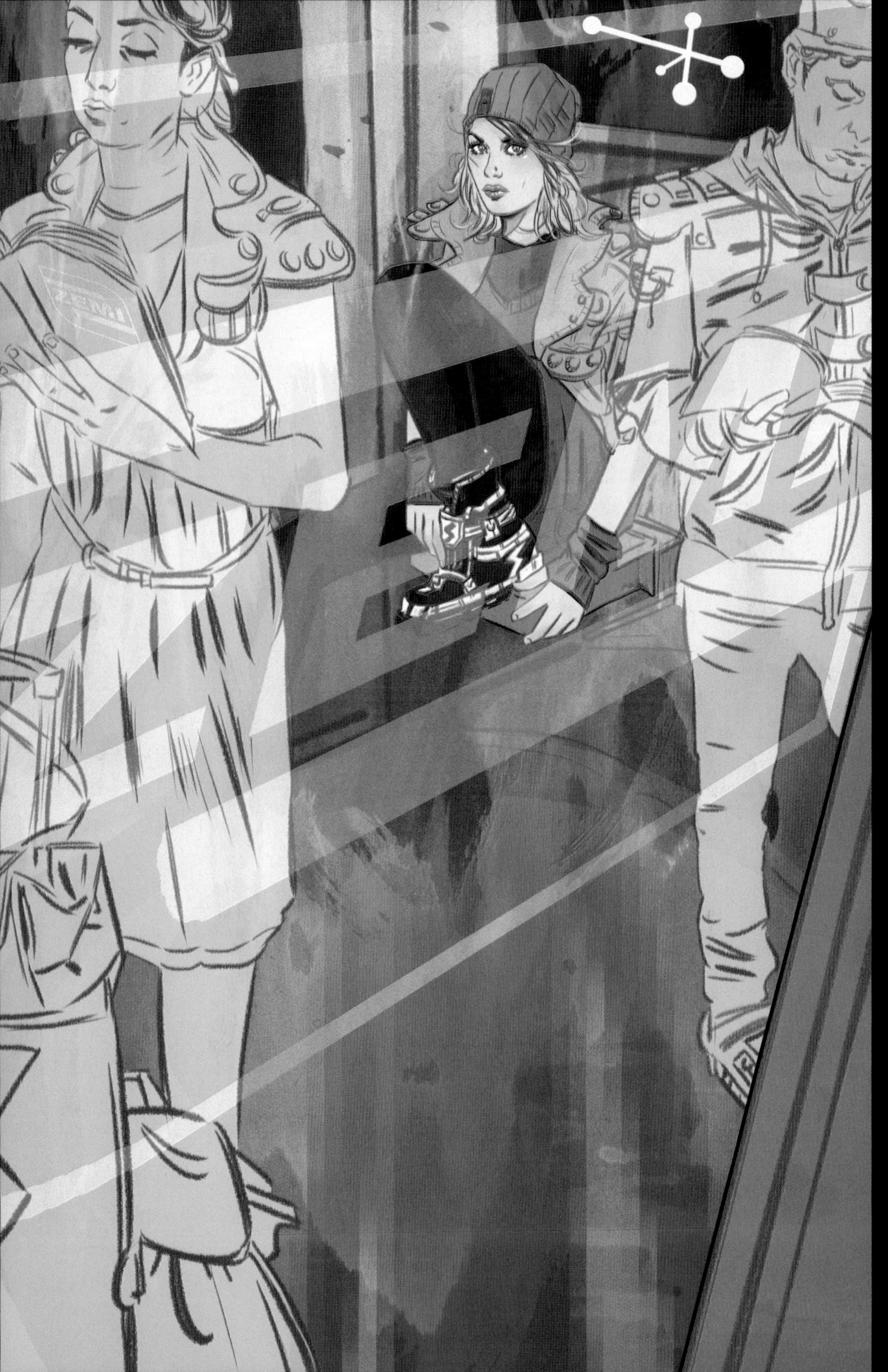

ISSUE 01 GHOST VARIANT COVER | TULA LOTAY

FAN EXPO EXCLUSIVE ISSUE 01 VARIANT COVER | BEN MARRA

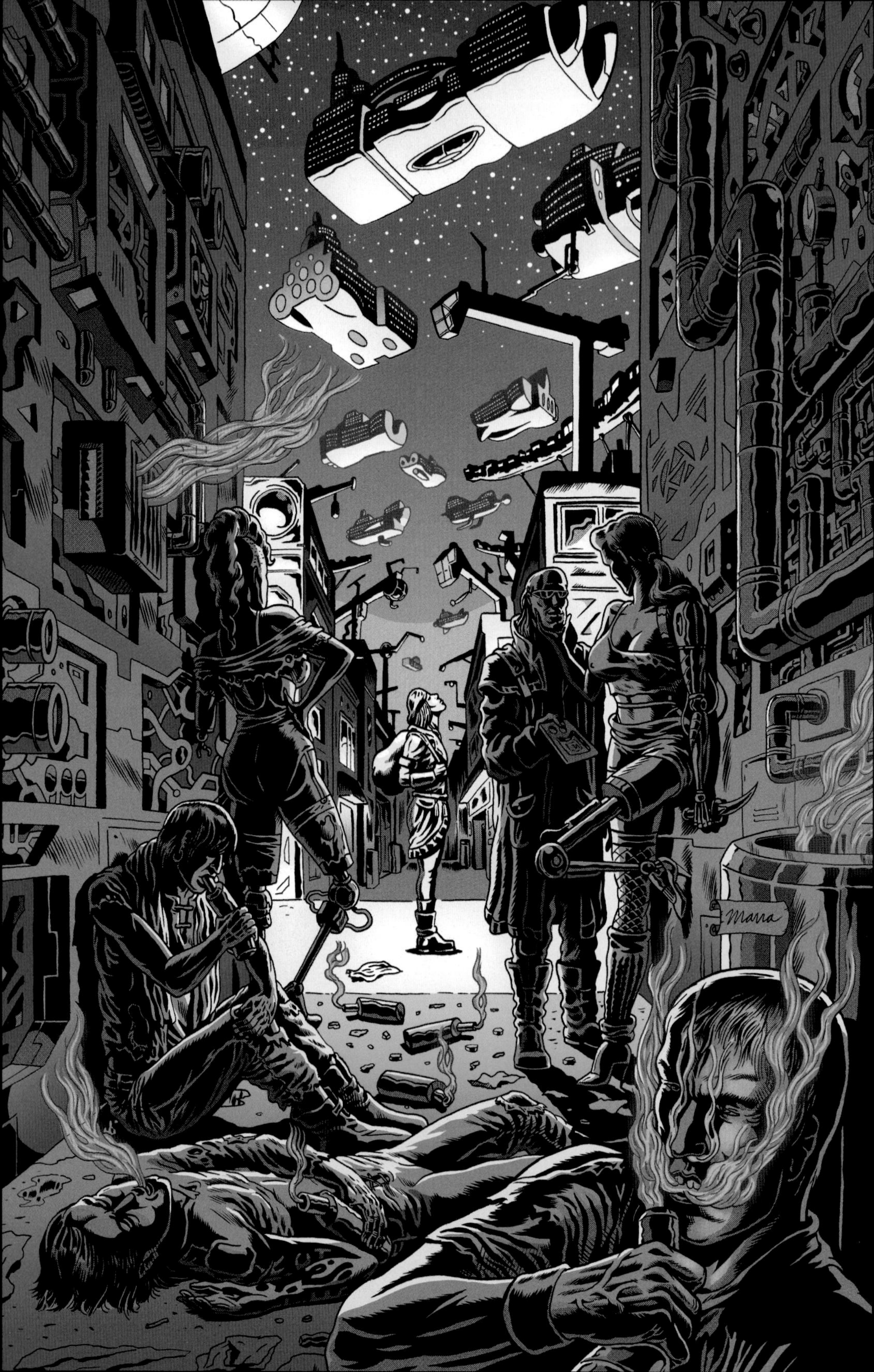
Marra

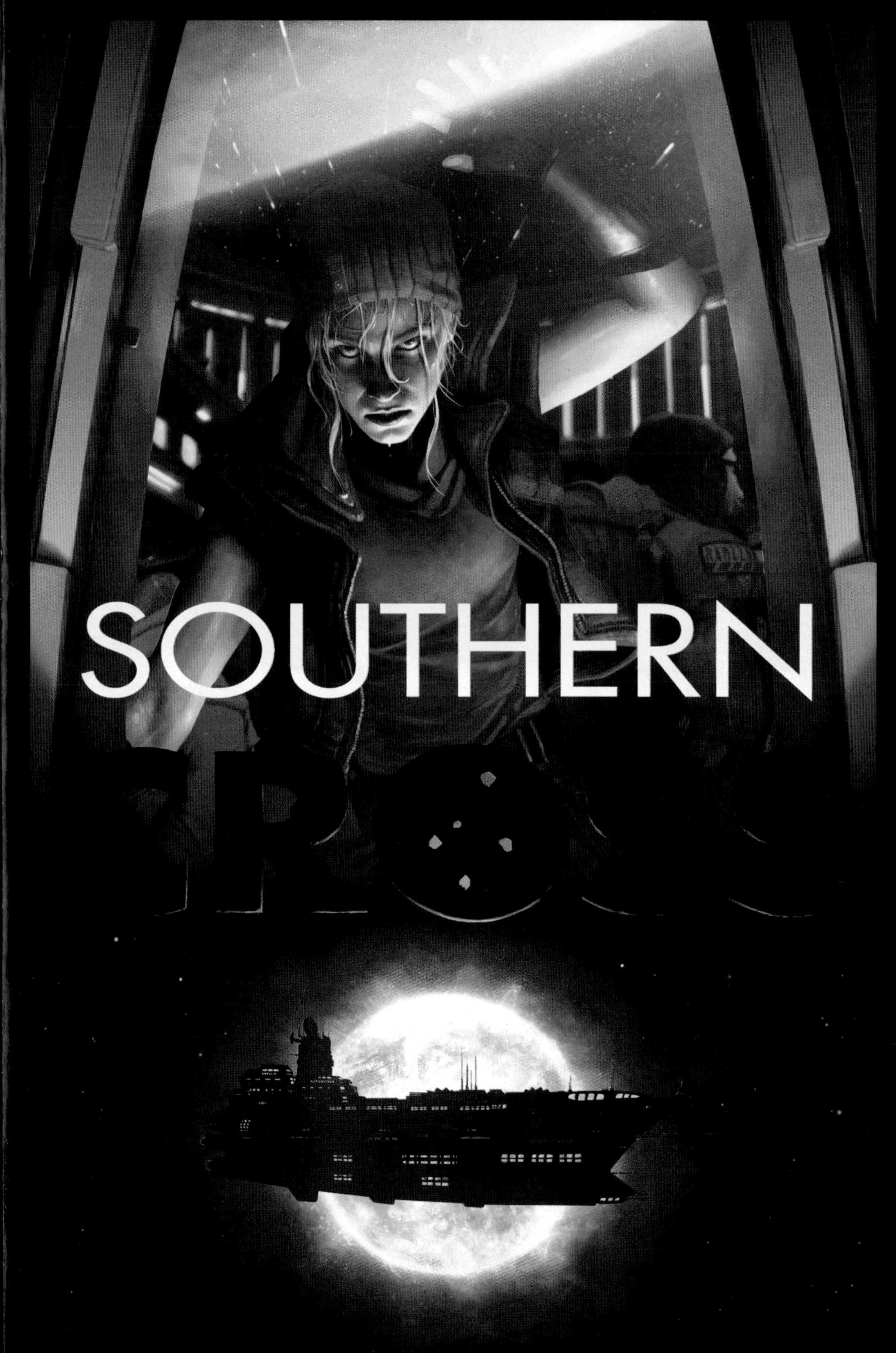
SOUTHERN

SOUTHERN CROSS PIN-UP | RAHZZAH MURDOCK

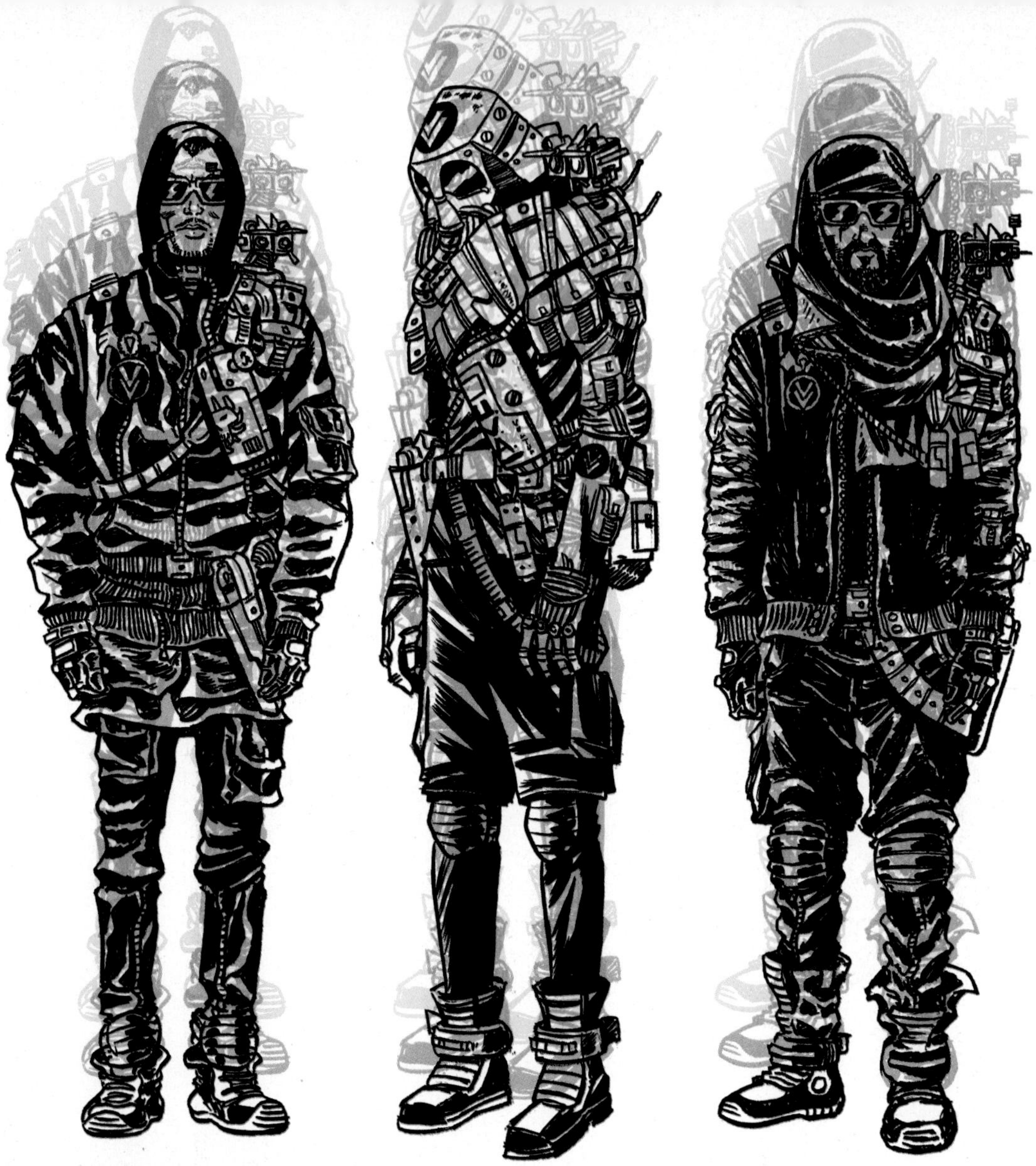

PILOTS OF THE SOUTHERN CROSS

BECKY CLOONAN
Becky Cloonan is a writer/illustrator/necromancer who (at the time of writing) recently gave up her nomadic lifestyle for a home in Austin, Texas. Her first book was published in 2002; since then her profile and workload have steadily risen to include comics for Dark Horse, Marvel, Image, DC and Vertigo, and a slew of self-published Eisner winning books. A woman of mystery and reputation, whose reputation is only exceeded by her mystery.

LEE LOUGHRIDGE
Lee Loughridge is an artist best known for his work as a colorist on the Batman Adventures titles. Loughridge was nominated for the International Horror Guild Award for best illustrated narrative in 2001 for his work on the comic edition of *The House on the Borderland*. He was also nominated for a Hugo Award for his work on *Fables, War and Pieces*. He resides in Southern California where the sun has given him skin like a turkey and the libido of said turkey.

ANDY BELANGER
Hailing from the frozen hellscape of Montreal, Andy Bélanger spends his nights illustrating for comics, video games and TV. Each night in the waning hours of darkness, he seeks out demonic forces in order to join their hellish crusade. Bélanger has worked for DC Comics, Wildstorm, Image, Devil's Due, and Boom!. He also illustrated the 4 volume adventure *Kill Shakespeare* for IDW, and self-published an unholy bible titled *Black Church*. He works at Studio Lounak with his canine companion Prince and a creeper cat named Harley.

SERGE LaPOINTE
It can be said without a doubt that Serge LaPointe is the best inker, colourist, and letterer in Verdun. In his spare time, he acts as art director, project manager, and designer for the Montreal-based Studio Lounak, which he co-founded in 2010 with Fabrice Forestier and Gautier Langevin. French Canadian born and raised, he resides in Verdun with the love of his life, two Lego maniacs and a fish.